THE BIG GIRLS

By Nancy Holmes

THE DREAM BOATS

THE BIG GIRLS

Nancy Holmes

DOUBLEDAY & COMPANY, INC.

GARDEN CITY, NEW YORK

1982

All of the characters in this book are ficti-
tious, and any resemblance to actual persons,
living or dead, is purely coincidental.

ISBN 0-385-17293-1
Library of Congress Catalog Card Number 81–43290

Copyright © 1982 by Creative Publishing, Inc.
ALL RIGHTS RESERVED
PRINTED IN THE UNITED STATES OF AMERICA
FIRST EDITION

For my little girls . . .
Emily
Nancy
and Sydney

THE BIG GIRLS

THE MED

June 1954

The great white yacht lay sleeping in her berth in the harbor of Monte Carlo. Two night watchmen, due to be relieved at 4 A.M., went about their silent duties. Until then, the captain slept, too. The water slap-slapped gently against the sides of the two-hundred-foot yacht in the warm darkness of pre-dawn; the only other sound was the purring susurrus of the generators.

George Sherril, owner of *Ehukai III*, slept soundly in his cabin. He had come aboard late the afternoon before and gone over with his captain the final plans for the long cruise out to Istanbul. Everything was in order, of course. In George Sherril's carefully planned life, hardly anything was ever out of order. His five guests, also sleeping, had every reason to

anticipate a perfect voyage. *Ehukai III* would slip out of the
harbor by dawn, bound for Corsica and then Capri.

There were three women aboard, two of them sleeping
alone. Delphine Munro was tucked into the four-poster bed of
the white cabin, the absolute favorite of the ladies invited to
cruise on *Ehukai III*. The lucite posts of the bed and the large
porthole windows were draped with pleated white chiffon,
hardly yachtlike, but then George Sherril was not known as a
practical man. The white rugs in Delphine's cabin had embroidered borders of pale pink and coral and yellow hibiscus
blooms, George's bow to his native Hawaii. Delphine and
George had known each other since she was born and although, at twenty-two, she was only fifteen years younger
than her host, he was her mentor as well as her best friend.

In the cabin next to Delphine, Princess Alia was half sleeping, waiting to hear the noise of the engines starting. Alia had
come on board with Kenneth Bennett the afternoon before
and Kenneth had arranged it so that she could stay quietly in
her cabin until after they cleared the port the next day. Alia
was exhausted after a month's stay in Paris, and the only person she knew on the yacht was Kenneth. She would meet the
others tomorrow; tonight she had begged off. Once the group
had gone ashore to dine, Alia persuaded the captain to show
her every inch of *Ehukai III*. She had never been on a yacht
before and the captain took pride in taking her around. What
did the name mean, *Ehukai III*? To Alia, it sounded somewhat like her native Turkish, but the captain explained that it
was the Hawaiian word for sea spray, and that all of Mr.
Sherril's home and business enterprises were named Ehukai,
one way or another. Soon she would meet her host, George
Sherril, and Delphine Munro, and the newly wedded Lord
and Lady Kilmuir. Now, in her half sleep, she heard the engines start. Alia leaped out of bed and rushed to the closet.
The captain had said she could come up on the bridge and
watch as they left the harbor. They were moving! She was in
a new world with new people, except for Kenneth. She was
on her way home to Istanbul and Baraket, and her wedding.

When Jeremy Andrew Charles Brooke, Lord Kilmuir, heard the sound of the engines starting, he stirred slightly and reached for Camilla. He opened one eye to see if she was sleeping. She was lying on her side facing him, snoozing like a kitten. Jeremy opened his other eye sleepily and raised his head, looking into her face. She is going to be a star, he thought. Even in her sleep she looks like a star. Silken blond curls framed her face, which, in repose, was even more fascinating than when she wore her bright, vivacious daytime look. She was a handful, and that was why Jeremy had been drawn to her in the first place. His father had raised hell about his marrying her, no title, no money, but as far as Jeremy was concerned he'd noticed that the old boy was quite drawn to her himself now. Jeremy reached over and stroked her small warm breasts. She moved closer to him, muttering something indistinguishable in her sleep. He gathered her into his arms in the big bed. Thank God George Sherril was an American who knew how to do things. All the English yachts that Jeremy had been on had single beds or bunks. This was a bit of all right.

"What is it, darling?" Camilla asked, as he stroked the line of her back and hips. Christ, she was warm.

"It's me, making love to you."

"At this hour?" she said, nevertheless responding to him.

"What else are yachts and honeymoons in June for, Camilla Kilmuir? I ask you."

"You may call me Lady Kilmuir," Camilla said, folding herself about him.

Several hours later, *Ehukai III* had cleared the port of Monaco and was cruising steadily at eighteen knots. The day was coolish and sunny, perfect weather, and the Mediterranean was the largest single sapphire that ever had existed. The Kilmuirs were still in their cabin, while Delphine was sunning herself beside the swimming pool, which was kept only half filled to avoid slosh while they cruised. Delphine was impatient to meet the alluring and mysterious Princess Alia. What a marvelous time we are going to have, she thought, looking out from under the brim of her hat at George and Kenneth, who were sipping coffee in the sunny upper-deck café, the heartbeat of *Ehukai III*. Breakfast, luncheons and sometimes informal buffet suppers were served in the café, George's favorite part of his own yacht. Films were shown there, and a nightcap was always available. The Kilmuirs should be along soon now, since it was getting on toward lunchtime. Where was the fascinating Princess Alia? Kenneth was the only one of them who knew her, the rest of them were dying to meet her. Delphine and Camilla already knew each other from a weekend with George on Long Island a few months before. Delphine sat bolt upright. Had it really been only a few months before? Her whole life had changed so completely since she'd left home in Honolulu six months ago. It was all another world.

HONOLULU

January 1954

Delphine Munro came running out across the lawn from the lanai when she heard the helicopter clattering above. Her brother, Jay, piloting the chopper, looked down on her as she ran out to greet him, her scarlet dress brighter than the flame trees. She looks like a red hibiscus, he thought, and I am going to miss her.

Jay hovered over Queen's Surf, drinking in its beauty for a moment before putting the helicopter down on the east lawn. Queen's Surf had been home to him since the day he was born and he was used to it, but it was truly spectacular from the air. The big main house was low and white with a series of small bungalows connected to it by roofed breezeways, all of them clustered luxuriously together at the foot of Diamond

Head. Emerald lawns surrounded the house on three sides; the fourth side was the beach and the surf for which the house was named. Long hedges of night-blooming cereus edged a series of separate gardens, and the wild red of the flame trees dramatized the serene green-and-white order that prevailed. On the sea side—*makai* was the Hawaiian word for it—coconut palms clacked busily in the trade winds. Guests arriving at Queen's Surf entered from the main road just past Waikiki, through gates made of ancient surfboards that were lashed together, three to a side. It was a quiet, stunning entrance, giving no clue to the grandeur of the place. Unless seen from the air, Jay thought. Typical of my family, we've kept our classically low profile regardless of our unlimited fortune. It's my father's innate sense of privacy, bequeathed to his children.

Delphine was right there when he set the helicopter down, ducking under the still-spinning rotor blades and pulling at the door latch.

"Hurry up, for heaven's sake!" she said, tugging at him. Her tawny skin was almost the same shade as the amber-colored hair that tumbled free on her shoulders, and her green-flecked hazel eyes were full of warmth and mischief. "Dad and Winona are waiting for us to have a farewell glass of champagne, and I need you to get me through this good-bye scene. Do you know, I've never had to say good-bye before? Do you believe that I am really going out of the nest, that it's almost plane time?" She linked her arms tightly around his waist and, for all her chatter and bravado, he knew she dreaded the imminent parting. Jay was three years older than Delphine, but brother and sister were so identical in looks that they were mistaken often for twins. They had both inherited their sandy-gold coloring from their father, and both were overly tall and slender. Rather than moving, they seemed to lope with tremendous grace.

"I can't believe you are really leaving us, no," Jay said, hugging her. "And with only George to protect you. Since George owns and knows more about New York than he does of Hawaii, I am not going to worry about you."

"Listen, it's exciting to be going east. How many times have we been out to the Philippines and Japan? We always seem to face west and go west for our travels. If I live in New York for a year, I'm going to go to Europe at least once. I've never been to Paris, never seen London. Jay, let's go see Paris in April. You can't stay here forever and I want to go traveling with you."

"Chestnuts in blossom, all that?"

"Yes! Promise?"

"I promise."

George Sherril had been like a member of the Munro family, albeit an immensely independent one, since his parents had been killed in 1934 when George was only eighteen. The Sherril fortune was endless, even larger than the Munros'. Banking interests and land holdings in the Hawaiian Islands and California, as well as in New York, had assured him, even before his parents' deaths, of an income that ran well over two million dollars a year. What sealed the deep bond between George and the Munros was the fact that, six months after the death of his parents, he became aware that his father's dear friend and executor of the estate, Fred Marston, was cheating him blind. When he was quite sure that large funds were funneling out of Sherril and into Marston accounts, he'd gone to Bob Munro.

"Why, that rotten son of a bitch," Bob Munro had said. "The thing I don't understand is why he took you for a fool. You're young but you're a Sherril, and I can't believe Marston would be this stupid."

In a short time, they had exposed Marston's duplicity. When the noose tightened, Marston had come begging to George, pleading innocence. George was embarrassed for the man, who was his godfather as well as his father's friend, but it was a hard lesson learned young.

"If you can find a way to get all the money back into the

right accounts, Bob Munro and I will see if we can keep you out of jail. That's all. You know and I know what you did. Now get out."

For a while after that, George took an avid interest in his estate and, by the time he was twenty-one, he and Bob Munro had set up Sherril trusts that were impeccable. George could go to the far ends of the earth if he chose to, and he did choose to. In the next few years of traveling, he discovered that he had a sharp and curious business mind and a Midas touch.

"George, you went off on a pleasure lark to Tahiti, and you've come back with a seawater conversion plan that is going to make another fortune. For both of us." Bob Munro was impressed.

"Good," George said. "You take care of the money; I'll be the rover."

He kept Ehukai, his Black Point estate and the house that he'd been born in, open and staffed all year, but gradually he spent more time in New York. He bought a Long Island farmhouse and restored it, naming it Ehukai Farm, continuing to use the Hawaiian word that he loved.

Now Delphine was coming to live in New York at George Sherril's instigation. "I have an idea that Delphine should be allowed to stretch her mind," he had written to Winona and Bob. "She is too bright to die on the vine in the islands, no matter how much we all love it there. Jay has his helicopter business now, and Delphine needs contrast and stimulation. Let her come to New York. I'll take care of her, and there are plenty of suitable and attractive places for her to live. I even have a possible job in mind for her that has to do with the jades. 'Sow a character, reap a destiny,' someone said, and I need to have at least one Munro near me."

As Delphine and Jay walked across the lawn, George's suggestion had become reality.

"Thank God we can go to the airport in the helicopter," Delphine said. Jay had bought it the year before when he had been discharged from the Marines after finishing a tour of duty in Korea. It was the first private helicopter in the islands, and he had gradually developed a small transport service both in Honolulu and on the big island of Hawaii. The helicopter had changed Jay's and Delphine's lives. He had promptly taught her to fly it, a fact known and approved of by Bob Munro but kept from Winona, who refused to set foot in it.

"Oh, I wish we could go to Puuwaawaa once more." Delphine said. "I'll miss it most of all." Puuwaawaa was the quarter-of-a-million-acre Munro ranch on the big island of Hawaii. Together she and Jay had explored all of it in the chopper, tracing the old lava flows from past Mauna Kea eruptions, gigantic tentacles of volcanic rubble that laced the land, inundated more than half its acreage. They spent days and nights with the cowboys in their blue-and-white-checked palaka shirts, wearing straw cowboy hats banded with leis made of tiny wild orchids and the miniature pansies and roses that grew only on Hawaii. They searched out hidden waterfalls and found beaches no one saw and no road reached. The chopper helped them find lost cattle for the ranch boss, and they spent many nights singing the old, old Hawaiian songs with men who had worked on the ranch for the family since before both of them had been born.

Winona and Bob Munro were waiting on the lanai. Winona was small and bright and dark, the exact opposite to her tall, slender children. The only family similarity was in their voices, where a trace of Winona's Boston ancestry could be heard. Winona's family were *kaamaainas*—old-timers, in Hawaiian—who had come out as missionaries many years before. "They came out to do good and did well" was the envious expression heard often in the islands.

"Your brother is going to miss you even more than we will, my darling," Winona Munro said.

"No he won't," Delphine replied in the lilting voice inherited from Winona, tones that were both patrician and gay.

"Jay will come and see me; you two will stay here and revel in all this gorgeous squalor." She sank down on the hikiai, that comfortable Hawaiian combination of bed and couch piled high with cushions, that graced every lanai in Hawaii. Her scarlet dress stood out against the flamboyant green-and-white leaf-printed linen covers. She was deliberately turning her back to the sea. Already the golden light of late afternoon was throwing long shadows on the lawn, and the Munro family ritual was to watch the sunset together every evening, the closest time they spent together. As eager and excited as she was, as much as she wanted to go, Delphine had always been passionately fond of her life in the islands and of her family. They sipped their drinks slowly and avoided the subject of parting, but Jay sensed her mood. In a little while, he looked at his watch and stood up.

"Time to go," he said. "It will take us a few minutes to get off."

"Darling," Winona said as they strolled slowly out to the helicopter, "call me as soon as you reach New York. George will meet you, and it's not all that long until Christmas."

"Mother, this is only January!" Delphine said, unaware that she had lapsed back into the word unused since early childhood. Jay and Delphine had always called their mother by her first name; there was only one Winona.

One of the Filipino boys had loaded her luggage. She hugged and kissed her parents and got in, watching as they moved back toward the lanai so the chopper takeoff wouldn't blow them to bits. As they lifted off, she blew kisses at them, tears in her eyes.

"You saw the box?" Jay asked.

"Of course," Delphine replied, reaching for the slender bamboo box on top of her luggage on the rear seat. She put it on her lap and, when she opened it, the three fragrant leis gave forth a delicious whiff of spice and jasmine. The fat yellow carnations, pungently beautiful, were from Jay. Six strands of pikaki, like carved ivory blossoms, were from her father, and the delicate, almost unearthly white ginger in fragile butterfly layers were Winona's. Now the tears streamed down her face.

"Jay, you know what we have to do."

"Dummy," Jay said, reaching for her hand. "Who grew you up? Who threw leis overboard with you from the *Lurline* or the *Mariposa* when we went back to the mainland to school? Stop crying. You're going to be one of the first to throw them out of a helicopter."

"Oh, how I wish those lovely white ships were still sailing. Remember boat day, how we used to sail, buried from knees to nose under all the leis, the music playing and everyone we knew and a lot we didn't coming down to see us off?"

"I remember. Pulling away from the Aloha Tower, confetti streamers everywhere and the band bawling out 'Beyond the Reef,' making all of us cry. Then when we'd get past Diamond Head, you and I would sneak off together and throw a lei over so we'd surely return. The legend will hold, Del; these will come back to shore from the helicopter. Besides, we're almost at Ehukai. You can take a last look at it and tell George how everything looks."

George Sherril's seaside palace, the first Ehukai, lay beneath them. The carved white splendor of the house—low and surrounded with Japanese gardens—seemed miles away from the long point of land that nudged its way into the Pacific. No one in Hawaii had ever needed a swimming pool on the sea, but George did and, as usual, he was right. The point had once had a series of small volcanic rock pools that he had enlarged into one, shaped as much by nature as by Sherril taste. It was fed by the sea in every shade from palest aquamarine to deep cobalt, and the sea spray—*ehukai*—crashed gently against the cliffs, blowing a cooling shower across the pool on the hottest golden days.

Jay reached over and opened the window on Delphine's side, hovering twenty feet above the Pacific.

"Go on, Del, let them go."

Delphine kissed the three leis and dropped them out, one by one. As Jay lifted the helicopter and turned in the direction of the airport, she strained to see beneath her. Tears clouding her eyes, she finally found the tiny circle of yellow, bright in the turquoise water, and saw the two faint outlines of white nearby, all drifting gently toward the shore.

HOLLYWOOD
February 1954

"Hello, Red."

The voice came from behind her. Camilla Stuart turned around and found the big cowboy who had been watching her at lunchtime in the commissary. She knew he had a small role in the film, and he was obviously perfectly cast. He had on some aged soft leather chaps with a fringed leather jacket. His cotton shirt was not new, nor was the classic cotton scarf tied into a knot around his neck.

"I beg your pardon," Cam said, off guard, falling right back into the British accent she was trying so hard to kill for her few lines in the film.

"They call me Red, too, ma'am," he said, taking off the Stetson and making a sweeping bow to her. He was quite attractive, big and strong and friendly looking, with sandy red hair. He was teasing her.

"Nobody calls me Red," she snapped, turning back to watch the proceedings on the set. When men became too forward with her too quickly, she gave them short shrift. Men like that were rarely of any importance and they could do nothing for you. A man with manners would find a way to be introduced properly, and she wasn't interested in bit-part actors. She only wanted to be noticed by the director or producer of the film and, God knows, neither of them had paid any attention to her so far.

"I beg *your* pardon, ma'am. My name is Russ Marshall," he said to her back. "When people who don't know me call me Tex, I turn my back on them, too. I didn't mean to be smartass, but no one ever introduces anyone on a movie set. I know your name is Camilla Stuart and that you're English. I saw you in the commissary for the tenth time today and I wanted to get to you before the film is finished. That's all."

"Are you a Texan?" she asked, turning to look at him. His tone was nice, and she had been rude. Outside of Hollywood, California, the only other place in America that she was curious about was Texas.

"I'm from Plainview, ma'am." What is this "ma'am" business? she thought. "Ma'am" is for the royals. "That's up in the north of Texas, the part we call the Panhandle. It's hotter than the hinges of hell there in the summer and colder than Siberia in the winter, so I beat it out here to California whenever I can and get a job at any studio that's shooting a western. I'm not really an actor; I just have the right duds."

"Are you a cowboy?"

"In a manner of speaking. At home I work cattle with my daddy at roundup time. We ship cattle twice a year. But what I really want to do is write. Maybe one of these days they'll give me a job in the story department. They pick my brains enough around here for what goes on in Texas, on the ranches or in the bars. Next year, I'll move on from acting and get paid for all the real stuff I tell them about."

Cam's mind clicked. There was something appealing about him. If he rode in roundups and shipped cattle, maybe Daddy had a ranch. A big one. Maybe he was one of those Texas millionaires.

"Oh, I would like to see Texas someday. I've read about it at home in England, but I can't imagine what it's really like, any more than I could have visualized California before I came here."

The assistant director called for all extras on set for the last shot of the day.

"Listen," Russ said, "I don't like to move so fast, but this is my last day here. We go on location tomorrow out in the desert near Indio for a week or ten days to finish up all this cowboy-and-Indian stuff. May I take you to dinner tonight?"

"If you like," Cam said, smiling at him for the first time. She had no dates, and she hadn't met anyone except the publicity man on the film since she had arrived. They certainly were a funny bunch. When she'd become the Prettiest Girl in England, they'd made such a fuss over her and promised her the moon if she would only sign a two-year contract and go to Hollywood immediately. Even though her first part was a small one, they assured her it would lead to larger ones. Now that she was here, she'd been left alone, isolated, unnoticed, except for one ghastly trip to the beauty department. There, in what seemed like a conspiracy, they had done everything possible to change the looks that had won her a contract. The most dramatic change was her hair, which was now amber red instead of its natural silken blond. It actually suits me rather well, she thought. Or maybe it doesn't, her thoughts continued. I haven't had any attention from anyone but the publicity man, and he was a slimy character who had done nothing for her.

Russ smiled at her, a happy look in his eyes.

"Great," he said. "I'll pick you up at seven-thirty and we'll go somewhere nice for dinner. Where do you live?"

"Chateau Marmont," she said, "Suite six-oh-four. I'll be ready."

Camilla had brought some pretty dresses with her from London but she hadn't even bothered to unpack. They were too dressy to wear to the studio, and no one had bothered to ask her to go out to dinner or anywhere else until now. She rummaged through the two suitcases in her big storage closet until she found them and dragged them out for inspection. Yes, the lavender silk one would be the best. The color suited her and it had a sweater trimmed with silk bowknots, something to throw over her shoulders against the cool of California evenings. She called downstairs for the housekeeper to bring her the iron. Dear old Chateau Marmont had no such niceties as valet service, but they were very homey and they did try to please her. The Chateau was classic Hollywood-French architecture, an apartment hotel complete with fake turrets and a slanting roof that towered over the peeling whitewashed exterior. The rambling building was built into a steep hill at a bend in Sunset Boulevard, and it dominated all the tacky souvenir shops and bad chain restaurants below. It had a seedy sort of elegance, a little bit like some country hotels in England. There was a swimming pool and at the back there was a raggy, unkempt garden, overflowing with contrasting California flora and fauna. Shaggy palms and shiny-leafed avocado trees blended with tall, waving poinsettias, while yellow California daisies and purple petunias ran wild. Cam had chosen to live in the Chateau rather than the more polished Beverly Hills Hotel since the room allowance from the studio meant she could have a suite here for the price of a room at the Beverly Hills. She also had a terrace overlooking Sunset Boulevard and the skyline of Los Angeles, and even though the green-and-white-striped awning was torn in several places and the terrace furniture somewhat broken down, she had some space to move around in, not confined to one room.

As she ironed the lavender silk dress, she felt a small spark of excitement. A date! You'd think she was a leper, the way she had been isolated. She'd sat by herself night after night, looking at the lights that carpeted Los Angeles and wondering if she would ever meet anyone interesting in California. Mr. Russ Marshall wasn't devastating by a long shot, but he seemed acceptable enough and it would be fun to go out with a man again. Even Jeremy, poor Jeremy, home in England, calling her all the time, would seem charming to her now. Jeremy was the dullest man she'd ever met, title or no, and with no sex appeal, but at least he paid attention to her.

She put on white strip sandals and fished through the suitcase again for a small white handbag she wanted. When she was ready, she took an appraising glance at herself in the long mirror on the closet door. Not bad. Cam wasn't tall, but she was perfectly proportioned and voluptuous without an ounce of fat on her. Her new look was terrific with her hair the color of burnished amber. Thank God it was not too harsh for her English-rose complexion. She looked fresh and shiny, and her bright, bright green eyes looked even more vivid now.

As she was putting on a pair of white loop earrings the phone rang. "Tell Mr. Marshall I'll be right down," she said. She walked down the two flights of steps to the lobby. Russ was at the foot of the stairs, watching with obvious approval as she came down the last flight.

"You looked pretty enough in those western clothes on the set but you look sensational now," he said. "I was going to take you to a dark, expensive hamburger joint out in the valley, but now I'm going to take you to a place full of light and show you off to everyone."

Cam laughed. "Nice," she said. He was nice.

The top was down on the white convertible Cadillac in the driveway.

"Do you mind?" he asked. "It's warm tonight and the drive to the beach is pretty. I'll put it up if you like." He had on a blue-and-brown tweed sports jacket with tan gabardine slacks and his white cotton sport shirt was open at the neck. He was attractive, not in a patrician sense, but in a sort of expensive middle-class way. There were Texas plates on the Cadillac, so it was obviously his own car.

"No, I love being able to have the top down. In England the weather is so filthy most of the time that this is a luxury to me. And I've never been to the beach."

"You haven't? Where have you been?" he asked, as they drove out Sunset Boulevard. How long have you been here?"

"Oh, I've been here for over two weeks, and I've been home in the Chateau Marmont by myself every night. I don't mind because I don't know my way around, but it is nice to get out."

"How do you happen to be here anyway?" Russ asked. "English girls aren't exactly a dime a dozen in Hollywood."

"I got a lot of publicity in England because Norman Parkinson, a very famous photographer there, photographed me. When the pictures came out in British *Vogue*, some dumbbell called me up and asked me if I wanted to go to Hollywood. The money they offered was super, and can you imagine anyone who wouldn't want to come to Hollywood?"

"No. But *are* you an actress or do you want to be one?"

"No . . . I'm not, actually, and I don't think I want to be one if this sort of nonsense that we go through every day is how films are made. God, it's boring."

"What do you want to do?"

"I want to be somebody. I was brought up in country England, and I want to see the whole world. I think I'd go anywhere I was invited as long as I'd never been there before. I want to know everyone."

Russ laughed. She meant what she was saying.

"So do I. We'll start our romance at a restaurant on a moonlit California beach and we'll take it from there."

"Be careful of that word romance," Cam admonished him. "I'm not sure I can cope with a Texan. I don't speak the language."

"Yes you do," Russ said. "I can tell."

The Pacific Ocean stops Sunset Boulevard dead in its tracks

at Santa Monica. Russ turned right and they drove ten miles north to Holiday House, a small hotel built dramatically on a cliff that jutted out over the sea. Even though Russ had not made a reservation, the captain greeted him by name and took them immediately to one of the best tables by the window.

It was dusk and the sun was a huge flaming ball of deep orange. It seemed almost as big as the sky, and Cam was fascinated to see it go from round to half round in seconds and to finally watch as the last tip sank dramatically into the sea, leaving a flaming sky behind.

"It's spectacular, really spectacular," she said. "I've never seen anything like this. What a fabulous place." She was at ease with him and found it relaxing to be her natural English self again. Most Americans made her nervous, but not Russ. Just my luck, she thought, what with his leaving tomorrow. Back into your cage at the Chateau.

LÂDIK, TURKEY
April 1937

The old yellow dog lying asleep on the greasy dirt floor of the garage where Tarek was working on his truck gave the first warning of what was about to happen. The old dog's head came up quickly, stiff-necked, and he looked dazedly around with a sleepy, yet wary, look. Suddenly he got to his feet with a swift movement, swifter than any movement Tarek had seen him make in years. He started to yowl softly, a painful noise from deep in his throat; then he ran toward Tarek, crashing against his legs. He was barking now, yelping in some awful sort of pain. Tarek thought he was dying; he was an old boy and obviously he was going through his death agony. Just then Tarek felt something like an imbalance—not even a shudder—of the ground beneath him and he knew it was an earthquake. It wasn't the first time he had felt it—tremors like this were frequent in the Black Sea region of Turkey—but something about this one was different. The bare light bulb on the long cord in the dark garage began to swing almost imperceptibly back and forth, back and forth, and it seemed to be jiggling up and down at the same time. Tarek had seen that happen before, too, but the yellow dog seemed to have gone totally mad, racing around in circles, yowling and banging himself into the side walls of the garage. Tarek felt a dizziness come over him, but it was a dizziness from his feet, not his head.

It was almost noontime. The women and children of the village would be back from their morning chores, waiting for their husbands to come home for lunch. Tarek thought of Dacha and the baby, but even before the thought became tangible there was a fearful tremor that cracked open one wall of the garage, splitting it in two and sending everything on the ground or the walls flying into the air. It was then that the rumbling began, and Tarek knew that he had never felt anything like this before. No more than two minutes had gone by since the dog had first raised his head. Tarek felt panic hit him as if a rock had been hurled into his stomach and he ran out into the street, sweating all over and yelling at himself in sheer terror. He ran first in the direction of his house, vaguely hearing the sounds of chaos around him. Already the noises were awful, screams of fear, but worse was the feeling that the earth was turning upside down, dumping every known thing—shops, trees, houses, huts, streams, carts, animals, fruit stands and the few trucks and cars that existed in the village —into a new universe which had also gone mad—up, down, sideways, in every direction at the same time. The world was coming to an end. This was not a simple earthquake that rattled the dishes and shook the houses and frightened everyone half to death. This was the end.

Tarek changed his course and ran for the outside edge of

the village. He instinctively knew better than to try to make it
through the narrow streets where, by now, everything would
have fallen and no one would be able to pass. He could cut
back in from the hillside and work his way down to his house.
Running as fast as his legs would take him, he heard the
crack of doom. Right before his eyes, the earth split open and
he felt himself with nothing beneath his feet, in midair and
then falling, falling out or up or down into some abyss of
nothingness. The last thing he saw as he was flung through
the air was a wide gap that opened as wide as the river that
bordered the village, and earth, trees, rocks—everything was
falling into the deep fissure.

When he came to, he was lying on the side of a road that
was a road no more and it was no longer on flat ground. It
had become the side of a forty-foot-deep gorge filled with the
rocks and trees and loose earth that had tumbled with him
helter-skelter into the deep new ravine, almost burying him.
As consciousness returned, he heard the faint sounds of disaster around him, shouts and screaming that seemed to come
from far away, and the lesser cries of young children and babies filled the air. Baby. The baby and Dacha. Tarek's head
cleared and he pulled himself to his feet as best he could,
sliding precariously on the loose earth. He scrambled up
the side of the ravine, pulling at uprooted bushes and fallen
trees to help himself, and headed in the direction where he
thought his house had been. He was stumbling rather than
running, but suddenly he stopped in his tracks. Ahead, a vast
cloud of dust and smoke was rising hundreds of feet in the
air. The village that had been there was no more; all that was
left was a gigantic pile of rubble, the remains of what had
once been his town. Tarek knew now that Dacha and the
baby must be dead, buried somewhere in all the rock and
debris. He clambered over it all, striving to make out where
his house might have been. Some walls still stood and some
few retaining beams stuck out like matchsticks in the dust-
filled air. The sun shone brightly above and the sky was blue,

but the village was destroyed. Through the yellowish pall Tarek saw the fragments of a wall and doorway that looked somehow familiar, and he clawed his way toward it. He knew that there were bodies; he had seen dead bodies and he had heard the cries of those trapped and dying in the residue of the earthquake. But he cared nothing about them. His instinct was leading him to where his wife and child should be, had once been, where his home had been, where he had lived. He fought the rubble, trying to reach the other side of the still-standing wall to get to the remainder of the familiar doorway, and he finally managed to reach it, crawling on his hands and knees.

On the other side, he found Dacha's body. Her head was crushed, blood streaming everywhere, and her limp body told him that she was dead. The baby was beneath her, half buried under her skirts. Tarek screamed and tore at Dacha's body, pulling the baby roughly from under her. The baby had been half smothered, but now she opened her eyes and started to cry—a pathetic, whimpering noise—and reached out for Tarek. Tarek folded her in his arms, awkwardly patting her poor little body and cooing to her. She was covered with blood and dust. He put her down gently on a sandy mound beside him, hoping she wouldn't feel that he was leaving her and start to cry again. He pulled off his shirt, the only thing he had to wipe her off with. Searching frantically around, he scratched in the rubble until he found a pipe that was leaking water. He could still hear a few cries, those of the poor souls who had been his neighbors and friends, but he ignored everything but the baby. He tore a sleeve off his shirt and wet it, then tenderly wiped the baby's little face and body clean. She beamed at him, gurgling happily.

There was a terrible silence now; he could hear nothing, no sound at all. He picked up the baby and made his way through the debris, slowly this time. There was no reason to hurry. He had no idea where he was going, where there was to go, but he had to get out of it. They would go as far away from the death of his town as they could. They would never come back. There was nothing to come back to.

Tarek made his way to Trebizond, where the townspeople were as kind to him as they could be. The same thing could happen to them any day. He left the baby with an old couple who could take care of her, and he found a job driving a truck. When the chance came for him to work in Istanbul, he went there and, with a stroke of good fortune, became chauffeur to a rich man. He sent money for the baby's care but he didn't go back to Trebizond. He had learned that he and the baby were two of only a handful who had survived the earthquake, but it was better not to think about that. Dacha was dead and the child was fine.

The circumstances of his job brought him back to Trebizond several years later. When he saw the baby, she had grown into a little girl and he realized instantly that she was going to be very beautiful. He had a premonition about her, a feeling that he tried to brush aside, but it was insistent. There was something different about her. She was a quiet child. The old couple had treated her well but she had been kept in a remote, isolated environment which probably accounted for her quietness. Now they were very old and Tarek searched around for another place for her, as he couldn't keep her himself. Her next home was with a noisy family who lived and worked in the bazaar. The change only made the child draw back even more into herself.

When she was about ten, she asked Tarek if he knew anything about her or her family. He told her about the earthquake, but he did not tell her that he was her father. If his premonition about her was correct, she would need a protector. Her beauty would take her to the world. From now on, he would see to it that she received some training in the things necessary for a poor, beautiful girl to know. She didn't need a common man for a father. He would guide her and help her as best he could. Alia could become a princess someday.

NEW YORK
February 1954

Three weeks after her arrival in New York, Delphine had moved into an apartment high above Central Park and was hard at work at a job that she was more than qualified to handle. George introduced her to Rodney Galliher, an expert in jades. From the time she was a child, Delphine had known about and loved jades. Her parents had collected them for years, amassing one of the finest collections in the world, and Bob Munro had breathed life into every piece for Delphine. Rodney Galliher not only knew of the Munro collection, he also needed someone like Delphine to help him mount two or three small exhibitions a year in Washington, Boston and St. Louis, and in New York. She could lecture on them as well. She was a godsend to Rodney, as George Sherril was a godsend to Delphine Munro. Everything that was happening to her was his doing. Queen's Surf seemed a million miles away, but it was there; it would always be there, a safe haven, her beloved home.

"George, stop whatever you are doing right this minute and come over here," she said into the phone, looking out of the glass wall of windows at the view of Central Park fifteen stories beneath her. "The ivory cabinet has just arrived and been put in place. It's the most exquisite thing I have ever seen. Hurry up, it's starting to snow. Wait until you see the cabinet in this light. And you must be the first to see it. I'll take you to lunch before we drive down to Ehukai, but do come on. I'm opening some good white wine and some cassis and making us a delicious kir."

"Right, darling girl," George said. "Give me half an hour. Keep the kir cool."

George Sherril enjoyed being generous with those he loved. He was pleased with Delphine, with her success, and with himself for having taken her under his wing. She was a beauty, there was no doubt about that. Her coloring, the way she dressed, the way she walked and that quality in her voice that was so special—all added up to an overall beauty that particularly appealed to George. There was a subtlety, an unshouting elegance about her, that was especially attractive in one so young. Amazing, too, was how quickly she had taken on a New York coloring. George had always been sure she would turn out well, ever since he had seen her growing up in Honolulu. After all, one had only to look at her mother to see the potential: breeding showed in the bones.

Half an hour later, he presented himself at her door. Delphine dragged him into the center of the big living room. The walls were white-beige, the floors were covered with oatmeal wool carpeting, and the silvery blinds at the windows were pulled high to let in the light. It was snowing hard already and the beige and white of indoors was flowing, folding itself into the gray and white of the winter landscape outside.

"Look at that cabinet," she commanded.

"By God, you're right. So was I. It's splendid there."

"An ivory cabinet is a pretty spectacular present. Do you give all your girls this sort of treasure?"

"Only close friends of the family," George said, pleased with Delphine's surroundings. She had chosen celadon-green linen for the couches and chairs, a perfect background color for some of her own fine jades. The cabinet was almost ten feet high, intricately carved, and was a piece of furniture that seemed both massive and delicate. It stood on the long wall of the living room between the fireplace and window, just the right sort of exotica to set the mood of the apartment.

"All in all, darling girl, you have achieved a rather romantic apartment. Probably just in time. . . . Any lovers yet?"

"Not yet, but I expect you'll take care of that, too," she said. "Right now all it takes to make me happy in New York is a view of the most gorgeous park in the most exciting city in the world plus the sure knowledge that some poor bereft maharajah is still searching for his treasure, not having a clue that you have whipped off with it. And a man I can never thank for all he has done for me." Her green-flecked hazel eyes searched out his.

"Now, nothing serious. It was meant for you. Even that maharajah would have given it to you. Get your coat, we'll have a quick bite at 'Twenty-one.' We may have some trouble getting out to Ehukai in this weather."

LONG ISLAND

March 1954

Ehukai Farm was the second of George Sherril's homes and a continuation of his love for the Hawaiian word. It had been a fruit-and-vegetable farm, forty verdant acres of Long Island soil near Manhasset, until George bought it and poured money into making it the perfect country place less than an hour from the city. George had restored the original farmhouse with affection, discovering little by little how meticulously it had been built well over a century ago. He respected the way its original builder had done things, the care he had taken, and George brought the farm back to far better than its original condition. He loved it.

Intimacy was the keynote at Ehukai Farm, and no news traveled from there to either the gossip columns or the financial pages. George's third wife, Dorothy, had made the mistake of feeding Suzy, New York's top gossip columnist, a few small details which Suzy, being a close friend, knew better than to print without clearing first with him. George resented this stupid invasion of his privacy, and that mistake of Dorothy's was one of the reasons for their divorce.

In Honolulu and California George had always been somewhat disoriented by the constant sameness, the absence of changing seasons. He kept the apple and peach orchards on the farm intact, and he watched the blowing of pink and white blossoms across the lawns and onto the flagstone terraces each spring with delight in his heart. It was a time he never missed.

The ground floor on the farm consisted of a huge, comfortable living room with slipcovers of printed English linen on all the couches and chairs, low lamps with buff-colored pleated linen shades. An English butler's tray table was used as the bar at the foot of the stairway, submerged beneath a myriad collection of bottles so guests could fix their own drinks at will. George's bedroom was a separate suite with dressing room, sauna and small sitting room, the entrance almost hidden off the living room. Throughout the house, old pegged-wood floors were polished to a shining smoothness. George had opened up the small rooms of the rambling farmhouse, turning two or three into one much larger one. Beautiful sporting prints ran throughout the downstairs. Upstairs, four guest bedrooms were furnished with Early American pieces, deceptively simple in their perfection. The walls were covered with a tiny figured wallpaper, and ruffled white organdy curtains hung from every window. The staff consisted of Fox, George Sherril's English butler for almost twenty years, and two Irish maids who were lorded over by both Fox and Marlene, George's Irish cook, who produced miraculous, simple food. Marlene was on a polite first-name basis with most houseguests, and God help them if she began calling them by their surnames.

The major additions that George had made at the farm

were a large pool and pool house at the bottom of the hill and an air-conditioned and heated tennis court with a trellised roof that slid open when the weather was mild. When both the pool and the tennis court were finished, George's Scottish gardener had begun foundation plantings of rhododendrons and azaleas, and had cultivated lush flower beds that bordered house, pool and tennis court.

In summer, the lawn was a small mountain of emerald green with the pristine white farmhouse sitting right on top of it. Now, in the snow, it was monochromatically serene and beautiful.

"George!" Delphine exclaimed as they drove gingerly through the drifts of snow that had begun to pile up in the driveway. "It's as beautiful as the first Ehukai. Is everything you own as perfect as this?"

"Wait until you see the yacht," George said smugly. "Come in, come in. Fox will give us some tea."

HOLLYWOOD

March 1954

Cam was sitting on the terrace, remembering what a good
time she'd had the night before, when the phone rang.

"Do you know where Indio is?"

"No," Cam said, glad to hear Russ's voice.

"Do you have to work tomorrow?"

"Yes," Cam said. "Till noon."

"Then you have the weekend off?"

"Yes, until Tuesday."

"If I have a car pick you up and bring you to one of the
prettiest places I know, would you come?"

She hesitated.

"It's a hotel called La Quinta, between Indio and Palm

Springs, where the movie stars play. I'm not on the call sheet for tomorrow, but they won't let any of us leave here. I could get a cottage for you. It's a nice place."

"Yes," she said. "I'd like to."

"Good," Russ said. "The car will pick you up at the Chateau at four. You'll be here by six-thirty. Your cottage is called Ocotillo. I'll be there waiting for you with a bottle of champagne."

"You knew I'd come?" Cam said. "You already have the car and the cottage?"

"Yes," Russ said. "I hoped you would come; let's put it that way. You're the one who said you wanted to see the whole world, and this is part of it. We're going to have a wonderful time." When Russ hung up the phone, he wondered where he had gotten the confidence to brazenly reserve a cottage at La Quinta and invite this knockout British girl to come for the weekend. Russ was an essentially shy man. If he'd been at home in Texas, he would never have had the nerve to ask a girl to spend the weekend with him, but, on the other hand, there wasn't anything like La Quinta around Plainview anyhow. And then there was the question of the old boy. Russ shook his head, thinking about his father. He was well into his eighties now, getting senile, and meaner than a snake ever since Russ's mother had died a dozen years ago. Russ loved and admired his father, respected him, although he seemed more like a grandfather to him. Old Mr. Marshall had been in his late fifties when Russ was born.

California was a lifesaver to Russ. His father had spent most of his life on their big, isolated Z Bar Ranch, loving the vast country, but from the time Russ was a kid he had wanted to go to the big city. Plainview was no big city. On a school trip, Russ discovered California. Now, he spent part of every year in the Los Angeles–Hollywood area and he planned eventually to make California his home. Not while his father was alive, but that wouldn't be for too many more years. He would always keep the ranch, and he got home every few weeks to make sure everything was all right. There was another disturbing factor there. Sally. Even though they were married less than a year, and had been divorced now for over six months, she was still a thorn in his side. She was a pretty little girl who had turned big eyes on Russ, depending on him to get her away from the shrewish mother and father who bullied her. Russ's father had raised holy hell when he and Sally had run off and gotten married, threatening and meaning to cut him off if he so much as set foot on Z Bar Ranch with her. Russ bought a house in town, a nice house, but Sally had from the beginning isolated herself in it, crying all day if Russ left her side and wallowing in self-pity. She was a brainless weakling. In ten hellish months, Russ never had a moment's happiness with father or wife, and admitted his failure quickly. He arranged for a divorce, settled the house and a fair amount of income on Sally and walked out the door. At first she was after him every minute, crying, threatening suicide or anything she could to get his attention. When he told his father about the divorce, he had gotten a long lecture about marrying beneath himself and then about being divorced. The Marshalls did not divorce. When the picture offer came, Russ beat it to California, looking forward to time on his own with no scenes or arguments. Or tears.

Camilla Stuart was nothing like the wispy Sally, nor was she tough or boring as a lot of the girls he'd met in California were. Camilla was nothing like any girl he had known. She was English, with that great British accent, and as far as Russ was concerned she was more sophisticated than any girl he'd met. She could stand on her own two feet nicely, and she was sexy. Besides, she gave him a new feeling of confidence. Russ had gone to some trouble to learn about good food and wines, and had made himself known in most of the best places in Southern California. Camilla admired his expertise. On top of that, Russ had a consuming interest in literature which Camilla shared. He had a feeling that she knew something about being in bed with a man too. It wouldn't take long to find out. Russ was looking forward to the weekend.

La Quinta was in the desert, a hundred miles or so east of Los Angeles and a favorite hideaway, as Russ had told her, for some of the biggest movie stars. The orange tile-roofed hotel and surrounding cottages were set in an emerald-green garden that was almost burdened down with a plethora of flowers. Cam's cottage was an oasis of privacy. True to his word, Russ was waiting when she arrived, a bottle of Dom Pérignon cooling in an ice bucket and a fire blazing in the fireplace. It was pitch-dark; the looming San Jacinto Peak, more than ten thousand feet of it, gave wild drama to the desert and also blocked out the sun by four o'clock on winter afternoons.

"Welcome," Russ said, kissing her on the forehead and tipping the bellboy ten dollars. "Tonight we're having Mexican food at Teresa's in Indio. But not until we do away with this champagne."

"Champagne Charlie, I should call you," Cam said, hanging her things away in the closet. "Thank God you're not a beer man."

"Oh, but I am, and you will be, too. It's the only thing to drink with Mexican food."

They sat in front of the fire, sipping the Dom Pérignon. Russ brought her up to date on the film. It was mostly stunt-man stuff now; if she liked, she could come on location with them on Monday.

"A holiday!" she said, a sense of well-being spreading through her. "And a chance to see something besides the pea-green walls of the Chateau."

"Yes," Russ said, leaning toward her. He took her in his arms and kissed her. Cam felt herself responding instantly. Why not? He hadn't grabbed her; he'd made his move easily, and if she had backed off he would have accepted her refusal. There was no pressure and she liked that. It was nice to meet a man who was as self-assured as she was, and there was no question in her mind about going to bed with him. She would or would not, depending on her mood. She wasn't all that attracted to him, but that strong quality of his appealed to her, and he was a man, not a boy. She'd never liked boys or old men. Jeremy was a boy and he always would be, with a schoolboy crush on her. Still, it was nice to have a rich, titled Englishman crazy about her even if he was immature and basically Australian. And, although it was probably British snobbism on her part, she hadn't expected sophistication from Russ or any American. It was nice that Russ knew how to do things, how to arrange things properly, and, obviously, had plenty of money. He had arranged the weekend perfectly.

When they came back from Teresa's Russ paused at the door to her cottage.

"Are you going to ask me to come in?"

"Of course."

"Are you going to send me away later, out into the desert, alone with that motley film crew?"

"Of course not," Cam said, her eyes glittering.

"We've caught fire," Camilla said, stalking nude around the room. Russ was lying in bed, the bedclothes pulled up around him. It was cold; what was she doing wandering around with no clothes on in the freezing desert morning?

"In this weather?" Russ said. "I'm freezing, what the hell are you talking about? Come back to bed."

"Sissy," she said. "This weather is considered warm and toasty in England. And I'm hot, hot from you. Do you make love to everyone like this? Where do you find the time?"

Russ laughed at her. They had not slept, not at all. Camilla was predatory in bed and as independent as a cat. When they had closed the cottage door the night before, she hadn't wasted a second. "Build up the fire," she ordered. "I'll be right back." And she was. She came back into the sitting room, wrapped in one of the blankets from the bed, dragging the rest of them with her. There was a fur rug; soft, silky fox pelts, in front of the fireplace.

"There," she announced, pointed a finger downward, flinging the blankets aside and dropping the one wrapped around her to the floor. "There's where we start."

Russ caught his breath when he first looked at her body and caught it again when he touched her. She was perfect. She was silkier and softer than the furs beneath them, which made him want to stroke her and pet her, let his desire build slowly and last forever. Camilla would have none of that sensuous luxury. She was the seductress, the leader, it was she who made the demands. Russ had never been in bed with a girl who behaved the way Camilla did. There was not one iota of self-consciousness to her, and she dug into him as if he were an eight-course meal, twining herself around him, running her hands down his back and under his arms, down his thighs, making him hard, making him reach for her to pin her down under him, but not letting him. She rushed him, attacking, sitting on top of him, the light from the fire blazing more color into her face and kindling the near-flame of her hair, prodding him to be quick and catch up with her. If that was how she was, and what she wanted, fine, even though Russ had never known anyone like her. Most of the other girls had expected him to lead, tried to please him. Not Camilla. She wanted him and he knew it, just as he was crazy for her, and that was that. She talked to him, too much, nothing romantic about what she said. "Give him to me now, goddammit," she said. "Not on your life," he muttered back at her, turning her over on her stomach and sitting on her for a change. "You've run things up until now, you'll get him when I want you to." A feeling of exultation ran through him nevertheless. Here was a someone who could match him, overmatch him even, whose attitude toward making love was counterpoint to his. He let her go, let her do what she wanted, and he lost track of where they were, in front of the fire, in bed, the hot shower later. Finally worn out, they still had not slept. He told her things he'd never discussed with a woman before, and she talked to him.

Even though Camilla was the perfect partner, Russ had no

intention of allowing her—or anyone else—into his life on a permanent basis. Luckily, she would be going back to England soon, before anything could get out of control. Lying down, Camilla was the most desirable girl he would ever have. Standing up, she might be too much of a handful. This was no time to think about it.

"Come here," he said, desire for her rampant again. "If we've caught fire, why am I so cold?"

TREBIZOND, TURKEY
October 1953

Alia was a lonely girl. She had no friends except Tarek and she knew nothing about herself. She came from nowhere, if that was possible, she had no mother, no father, no sisters or brothers. No family, beyond the old couple she lived with, and they left her completely to herself unless they wanted something. She waited on them hand and foot but they never spoke except to give her an order. Tarek came to see her; Tarek was the one person who had always been in her life.

When she was old enough to understand, and to question him, he told her how he had found her, alone and crying in the midst of the rubble of the terrible earthquake that had completely destroyed the small village. "It doesn't matter, Alia. Lâdik is gone. You and I were about the only ones left alive there, and we live in Trebizond now. Lâdik is gone. Think about the future." It undoubtedly had been the village of her birth. Tarek had taken her away from the dead village and brought her to Trebizond. He had found the old couple to take care of her until she was old enough to wait on them. Tarek was her only friend.

Alia was unaware of her beauty, but from the time she was about ten years old, men weren't. When they started to molest her in the market or on the streets, she told Tarek. Tarek had been watching her grow and knew it was time for a change. He sold her into the small harem of one of the men he drove for, and with the money he was paid for her he bought her some clothes. He explained that she would be safer living in the small harem of a decent man until she grew up a little more, then he would get her away from it.

There were seven women in the harem, all of them coarse and ugly and all of them jealous of Alia from the day she came into their midst. Alia kept to herself as much as she could and let them scrap and fight each other. She was aloof to everyone except Mahmed, the man who owned her. He was not a bad man and he was a virile lover. He taught Alia how to please a man. She was his pet. When he brought friends home with him, Alia knew if she was offered to one of the men that he was Mahmed's special friend because Alia was a special gift. She never talked with the others, not of Mahmed or his friends or the arts of love. They left her alone and went on hating her, she was so obviously the favorite.

Tarek saw her every week, and as she grew older he taught her to read. He would bring a book whenever he could, sometimes in English, and he helped her learn to speak English as well as to read it. Being a chauffeur, he explained to her, it was good for him to speak many languages, and English was the most useful. She must learn English too. Alia absorbed every word Tarek told her, and buried herself in the books that he brought.

Occasionally, he would take her out of the harem, usually when Mahmed was away in Istanbul. They would go to the

beach and he would buy her ice cream and tell her stories
about Istanbul. She had a lively imagination. Tarek also
taught her to dream.

"You won't be in the harem forever," he said. "Someday you
will go and live far away from here in a great house."

"I don't mind it," Alia said. Tarek had been the only person
who was good to her except Mahmed, who gave her nothing
but her food and a bed. She shouldn't complain about anything to Tarek.

"That's because you don't know the difference," Tarek admonished her. "One day I will take you to Istanbul, and you
will have silk dresses and jewels to wear every day."

Instead of pleasing others, her beauty was a source of
trouble. It puzzled Alia that the women hated her only because she was prettier than they were. Her skin was lighter
than that of any of the others, and she was taller, and her
bone structure was more delicate. Her dark hair was silkier
in texture. As she grew up, she began to resemble her mother
more and more. Tarek wept once, brief, bitter tears when
he saw Dacha's mark on Alia. Dacha . . . Tarek's poor dead
wife was Russian, born in the small town where she was
killed in the earthquake. Her Russian-born parents had
drifted to Turkey from the Caucasus; they had been killed
too, as almost everyone had but Tarek and Alia. Tarek saw
that Alia was going to become even more beautiful than
Dacha had been. Her days in the small Trebizond harem
were coming to an end. He must find a new place for her. A
place where she would be valued. He thought about her constantly, and one day, the path opened.

Alia was sitting reading when she heard Tarek's insistent
voice on the other side of the courtyard wall, almost hissing
at her in the warm evening air.

"Alia," he whispered. "Bring your prettiest caftan and come
with me. Quickly."

"How can I, Tarek? Mahmed has friends coming here tonight."

"Never mind. Come at once." Alia didn't hesitate. What Tarek wanted her to do, she did. How he would explain her absence to Mahmed would come later.

Tarek drove his rattling car swiftly on the rough roads to a house on the outskirts of Trebizond, a large white house that she had never seen before. When he spoke to the caretaker at the entrance gate, they were allowed to pass at once and Tarek opened the door to the house with a key he drew from his pocket.

"Is this your house, Tarek?" Alia asked, looking in wonder at all the space, the rich furnishings and the paintings on the walls.

"No," Tarek said. "If it were, you would be living here with me. It is the house of a friend of mine who is away. There is no one in the house, only the caretaker outside. I am going to leave you here now. You will find some food in the kitchen. Find the bath and use it, especially the mirror. Look well into the mirror and make yourself your most beautiful."

"Why, Tarek, why?"

"Later tonight, I will return and let a man in, by himself. I don't know what time, and I am not sure that he will come at all. But you wait out here in the courtyard until you hear me. This is a very important man. Do your best work with him, Alia; this man can give you the world."

When Tarek left, Alia explored every inch of the empty house. It was an eerie feeling, going through empty rooms in a house that belonged to someone else. She felt like a thief, even though she touched nothing. She marveled at the luxury all around her, and the bathroom was the most wonderful part of the house. There was running water, something Alia had never seen inside a house before. Tarek's friends must be very rich to have all this. She poured bucket after bucket of water over herself, washing her hair and rubbing her body with some scented oil that she had been hoarding. She put on her simple white cotton caftan.

When it began to get dark, she settled herself on a long,

wide outdoor couch in the courtyard, as Tarek had instructed her to, where she could see the door and hear Tarek when he returned. If he returned.

It was a long waiting time for her, hearing all the night sounds as she lay there with nothing else to do. She fell asleep several times, but even when she was asleep her ears were listening. Sometime before midnight she heard Tarek's car and she came wide awake, suddenly nervous about the man he was bringing. She had only known Mahmed and his friends and even though she knew she was well versed in pleasing a man, suppose this one didn't like her? If he was from Istanbul, he must have hundreds of beautiful girls much more beautiful than she was, in her sparse cotton caftan. Why would he want her? And what could she say to him? Maybe it would be better if she pretended to be asleep; then if he didn't like her he could leave. What would Tarek want her to do?

When she heard the door open, she was lying as still as if she were in a morgue, pretending to be asleep. It didn't matter who the man was; she was ready for him. Tarek had told her that this man could give her the world. She was ready for that, too.

HOLLYWOOD
March 1954

Russ called just before noon, an excited tone in his voice.

"Cam, I've got something arranged for you. I ran into a guy this morning who writes for the Los Angeles *Times*. His name is Jacobs, Jim Jacobs. We graduated from journalism school together in Texas. He writes features, and he's got a lot of space. I told him about you and he wants to do a story."

Cam laughed. "That little rotter of a publicity man has been promising me an article by Jim Jacobs for weeks. Now you've gotten it. Oh, it will be fun to tell the weasel!"

"I told him about the Prettiest Girl in England and he loves it. Throw on something nice, not too sexy, and let him have a look at your legs, but in a ladylike way. I'll pick you up in an hour. We'll go to the Polo Lounge. Okay?"

"Oh yes, marvelous. I'll be ready."

Cam put on one of the dresses she had brought with her from England, thin white silk with tiny green flowers printed on it. Russ showed his approval when he picked her up.

"Just right. I've made a reservation in the garden, and we're going to be ten minutes later than Jim is. I told Eddie, that headwaiter I've been overtipping for years, which table I wanted. You look perfect."

Jim Jacobs watched as Cam and Russ walked across the garden off the Polo Lounge at the Beverly Hills Hotel. She walked wonderfully and all eyes turned toward her as they took their seats. Oh yes, he thought, the contrast of this girl against the lushness and profusion of tangled flowers and the palms of Beverly Hills is fine. Barney will be here in an hour with his camera. He stood up when Russ introduced them.

"If you aren't the prettiest girl in England, then you certainly are one of the most beautiful girls in California," he said. Good story here; he felt it.

Cam won him over quickly. She combined her cool British accent with a nice warmth and an obvious but not blatant interest in him as a man. They fell into conversation easily, and Jim had his story formed in his mind before they finished lunch. She was infinitely quotable, unlike the average bubble-headed starlets that he frequently interviewed. Barney appeared at three with his camera and Cam posed, sitting alone on one of the white wrought-iron chairs, in an almost prim position.

"Jesus," Barney said, after shooting off two rolls of film. "You're sensational! Your body looks like a nice, refined iceberg, but your eyes and legs look like you could start a forest fire." Cam laughed. Russ watched the procedure with approval.

"Thanks, Jim. I didn't give you a bum steer, did I?" Russ knew the answer already.

"Look in the paper on Sunday. She's too good for everyday. You can call me and tell me how you like it."

The story ran front and center in the View section of the

Times on Sunday. The picture of Cam took up the top third
of the page. It sprang out, a compelling portrait of a girl who
combined immense sex appeal with an unmistakably ladylike
quality. Running across the page above the picture, the lead
line posed a question: "Why Is the Prettiest Girl in England
Rotting in the Factory of Hollywood?" Jim Jacobs had gone
all out. "Gorgeous girls have always been a dime a dozen in
Hollywood," he wrote. "Camilla Stuart is an example of what
the film moguls ignore. Here we have a new Vivien Leigh and
she can't even get arrested." He went on to say that part of
the system was to ignore the young future talents unless they
were sheltered by one of the big bosses and implied that
sleeping around got you there but that Camilla Stuart was
hardly the type. He quoted Cam saying, "I've been told that
audacity makes the actress. The most audacious thing I've
done since I got here is to sit by the telephone every night
wishing someone would take me out to dinner. No one notices
you here unless you buck the system and break the rules. I've
never learned how to do that." He then suggested that
Camilla would return to England as soon as her small role
was finished and her contract was up. Would she come back?
"I'd come back to California, but it would take a starring role
and six figures to get me to do so."

Russ was gleeful. "If this doesn't do it, nothing will," he
said to Cam. "Jim Jacobs is the most widely read feature
writer in town."

"It's a marvelous story," Cam agreed. "But I'm almost
through with this silly film and then what will I do? Oh, Russ,
I can't stay in that hotel alone forever! I'm afraid I'm home-
sick, and I don't know what I would have done without you."

"Something will break," Russ said. "Give it a little time."

He's always right, Cam thought, but I wish he cared more
about me. Russ had a big apartment on Doheny Drive, and
Cam had quickly learned that she was welcome there on an
overnight basis only. No invitation to move in had been forth-
coming.

The Jacobs story was picked up instantly by the *Daily Mail* in London, and on the day it appeared Russ's prediction came true, although the response came from the opposite direction. Cam had stayed with Russ, and when she called the hotel for messages she found that London had been calling at one-hour intervals all night long. The calls were from David Wolff at J. Arthur Rank. When Cam reached him he spoke to her as if he had known her all her life.

"Well, my dear Camilla, I don't think you have to worry about dying on the vine any longer. How would you like to come home and do some real work?"

"What do you mean?" Cam asked. "As you can see from the story, I'm under contract and I may never work again for having said what I said."

"Now, now, Camilla, we have a first-rate role for you here, one that is a sure-fire starmaker. The picture is called *Death at Delmonico's*. You play an innocent girl who is accused of murder and has no one to protect her. She's the fall guy until a newspaperman falls in love with her and saves her. It's a perfect role to start your career.

"Now, we can't get you out of your California contract, but you can find a way, I'm sure. Can you get back here in two weeks' time? We start shooting at Shepperton on the first. I don't need to test you—I've seen the test you did for Rank—and wardrobe can be taken care of in a few days. Do you have an agent? I can work out your salary with him, and your contract."

"Yes, I have an agent," Cam said. "Myself. I want five hundred pounds a week, my traveling expenses back to England and a one-picture contract. And, yes, I can make it in two weeks."

She heard the silence on the other end of the phone and then she heard David's laugh. "Good girl," he said. "I'm just reading your line about audacity making the actress. You obviously write your own material, too. I'll make your transportation arrangements when you tell me the date you want to travel. We have a representative in Hollywood, Bill Zack; he'll be in touch with you to arrange for advance publicity, although it will be hard to top this story. Look forward to working with you, Camilla."

When he rang off, Cam put down the phone and turned to Russ.

"What in the world have I gotten myself in for?" she asked. "They'll sue me if I leave here."

"You were perfect. For a moment there, you were so good I thought you were me."

Cam laughed. "Birds of a feather we are. But you've taught me a lot."

"One thing I haven't taught you is a California history lesson. I've got a surprise for you. We've been invited to San Simeon for the weekend. Do you know about San Simeon?"

"San Simeon? Vaguely—someone named Hearst, isn't it? He used to come to England. Is it big?"

"Yes," Russ answered. "Fifty-eight thousand acres of it, including the castle, were given to the State of California when Mr. Hearst died. But another two hundred thousand acres or so of what they call the Hearst Ranch still belong to the family, and they have certain perks like using the guest cottages. And a few little ranches are scattered about, including Phoebe Hearst's, W.R.'s mother's, original ranch house. I want you to see that we have some castles here in America, too, so you won't be ashamed of us when you go back to England."

Camilla had no idea what to expect of San Simeon. She had never really heard of it before, and what little Russ told her seemed inconceivable anyhow. A Spanish castle on the California coast, built but never finished by a multimillionaire American publisher named Hearst? He had been dead for five years, but the family still used it even though the castle itself had been given to the state in much the same way the National Trust cared for great estates in England. The whole thing smacked of the eccentricity of the British more than of the Americans.

Russ wanted to be "up the hill," as he put it, in time for lunch, so they left Los Angeles very early in the morning and

drove for miles up the California coast on a strikingly beautiful stretch of road. Rocky foothills on one side tumbled
dramatically down into the bright blue waters of the Pacific
Ocean on the other. They soon ran out of cities and, finally,
even small towns. The farther north they got, the foggier it
became, with low swirls of gray clouds moving swiftly over
the cliffs and shore and slowing them down to a full stop
from time to time. They were in an eerie, beautiful wilder-
ness.

"Almost there," Russ said as they passed a small sign that
said "San Luis Obispo." A few miles from the sign, Camilla
made out some innocuous old wooden buildings, and then the
gates to San Simeon came into view.

The guard asked for Russ's name.

"Yes, sir, Mr. Marshall, Mr. and Mrs. Hearst are expecting
you up top. I believe you've been here before, sir?"

"I have," Russ said, "but not for several years. The last time
I tried to get up this hill a bull elk kept me held up for an
hour sitting right in the middle of the road, halfway up."

The guard smiled. "The signs are still there saying 'Animals
have the right of way,' but I don't think that elk will be there
this time. You might come across a herd of zebra or deer, but
they'll move right on for you. I've marked the turns to the
castle on the map for you, sir, in case you've forgotten. There
will be someone waiting at the top to take care of you."

They were still in deep fog when they started up the five-
mile road from the entrance gates to the top of the winding
hill. Three quarters of the way up they suddenly came out of
the fog into brilliant sunlight, and Camilla got her first
glimpse of the castle.

"Good God," she said, looking at the still-faraway twin
towers of La Casa Grande, the castle itself. "It's the most
fairy-tale place I have ever seen. You were serious."

"That rise the castle is sitting on is called La Cuesta
Encantada—the enchanted hill," Russ said. "That's what the
old man, old W. R. Hearst himself, called it. And that's about
what it is."

"And they call it a *ranch?*" Camilla said. "Some ranch. It's the biggest zoo in history. I've never seen anything like all the animals—the deer and the oryx and those stunning zebra, all roaming free."

"I'm not going to tell you that we have a lot of places like this in America," Russ said. "I'm just glad I could bring you here at all. When Mr. Hearst was alive—and we all called him Mr. Hearst, or 'the Chief'—it was fantasyland. There isn't a big movie star who didn't come here. He had a private train that brought his guests up from Los Angeles every weekend. You weren't allowed to bring a personal maid or a valet—as if everyone had them—but one was assigned to you the minute you got here. No drinking in your room, and we all cheated a little bit on that. You'll see for yourself, but it's the goddamnedest experience in contrasts I've ever seen. The great hall is a hundred feet long; one of the floors is a Pompeiian excavation that was buried under volcanic ash since seventy-nine A.D. The dining room table seats a hundred people, and there are ketchup bottles stretched all the way down it."

"Russ, the flowers! I don't believe them!"

Russ laughed. "I'm glad you're a noticer. There must have been thirty gardeners here when he was alive. I can't imagine what it's going to be like without him; there was never anyone like him. He'd look around at what the gardeners were doing—and he had this squeaky sort of orangeade voice—and he'd say, 'It would be nice to have some rose beds.' They'd all be leaning hard to hear him, and by the next morning the hill would be up to its ears in rose beds."

"There's someone here to meet us," Camilla said.

"Of course. It's our own private butler. Now, don't look to your right, the outdoor pool is there and I want to introduce you to it personally."

Morgan, their butler, led Camilla and Russ to Casa del Sol, one of three guest cottages that nestled at the foot of La Casa Grande. The other two were Casa del Mar and Casa del Monte, and the three of them were reserved for the use of the Hearst family and their guests.

"He called them bungalows," Russ said, as Cam ran through the immense cottage, filled with priceless Renaissance antiques and overshadowed only by La Casa Grande itself.

"Just like he called this place a ranch. My bathroom is bigger than any at Blenheim Palace."

"Plumbing's better too," Russ said, throwing a pillow at her. "Look at the catalogue on the desk. It tells you about the mishmash of treasures up there." He tilted his head toward the castle. Camilla picked up the leather-bound book and looked at the listing of eclectic treasures.

Morgan was back at the door with toweling bathrobes for both of them. "Mr. and Mrs. Hearst are expecting you for drinks before lunch in Casa del Monte, Mr. Marshall. They are at the Neptune Pool now and thought you might like a swim first."

"Right," Russ said. "Put on your bathing suit, Cam, and close your eyes. You haven't seen anything yet."

The Neptune Pool was an acre of aquamarine blue, one hundred and four feet across and holding three hundred and seventy-five thousand gallons of water. It was white marble, striped with black and peopled with pure-white marble ladies both in and out of the water, musing alone or happily arranged in pristine groups. Colonnades bordered the pool, festooned with rambling roses or bougainvillaea, and a small waterfall released a cooling shower of water into the pool. Russ introduced Cam to a dozen or so Hearsts and the few other guests.

The next few days were to remain forever in Camilla's memory. She and Russ roamed every inch of the castle. They rode and picnicked on the "ranch." They walked in the moonlight after dinner. Bill Hearst told family stories and Randy Hearst introduced her to some of the more domesticated animals in the zoo. Camilla had wakened screaming the first night, the sound of a lion's roar in her ears. She had been right: the lion's cage was part of the formal zoo not too far from Casa del Sol. One evening, when they were alone at the

Neptune Pool, she looked at Russ and burst into wild laughter.

"What is it, you silly fool?"

"I was just watching your expression, looking at this simple little swimming pool at this simple little country place. You have a proprietary sort of look about you. You really look as if you own it. And that's exactly the way I feel about it. Russ, we *are* alike. We both want all this."

"You're right. I wish I'd been Hearst."

"You will be someday; you'll have something like this. And so will I."

Camilla felt herself caring more about him, watching him, drawing closer to him in the magic of the atmosphere. The only thing that bothered her was Russ's outward coldness. When they were alone, when they made love, there was nothing cold about him. But in front of the others, she could have been the wallpaper or the maid. It annoyed her, although she laughed at herself for feeling that way. That was the way she usually behaved. It was a British attitude rather than an open, outgoing American one.

The night before they left, having said good-bye to all Hearsts, she fixed him a nightcap from their bar in Casa del Sol, which they had all to themselves.

"Russ, I've never had such a happy time."

"You've never slept in a Pope's bed before, either, have you?" he answered, pulling her toward him.

"I've never made love in a Pope's bed before," she countered, sinking into his lap.

"I'm surprised you haven't had a Pope or two."

"Hold on," Camilla said, a snappish edge to her voice. She couldn't understand why she was reacting so strongly. Obviously, he was teasing. "I've had a few romances before, little ones, but nothing like this. I'm crazy about you. You're the one who's a flagrant flirt and a ladies' man!" Maybe she hadn't told him before how she felt about him. Maybe that's what he needed to hear.

"Come here and shut up," Russ said. "I don't care how

many men you've had. There'll be plenty more. You were made for men, lots of them."

He untied the sash on her robe and pulled it off, throwing it to the floor. She was naked and he ran his hands over her body. She stood clinging to him until he picked her up and deposited her in the Pope's bed. He's better every time, she thought, best of all tonight. And so am I.

"Cam," he said toward dawn.

She heard his voice, soft in her ear, out of her deep sleep. Maybe he's going to say something about next week or next month or the future, she thought, as his hands roamed her again. But instead he began to make love to her brutally, roughly, as if he was trying to prove his domination of her to himself. Or to her. He was as coarse as he had been tender before, forcing her on more and more, demanding, hard, mean, until he hurt her and she began to fight him.

"God damn it," she said. "Stop it. You've hurt me." She got out of bed, pulling on her robe, and went out on the balcony. All was tranquil around her, but she was still shaking from the assault.

She felt his arms around her. The look on his face was the sweet expression that she knew so well.

"Jesus, Cam. I'm sorry. I didn't realize what I was doing." The tender man of times before returned. He carried her back to bed. "Bad dreams," he said, folding her in his arms just before they fell asleep. "Bad dreams, darling. Sorry."

TREBIZOND, TURKEY

October 1953

His Highness Prince Baraket Safwat Osman Abdel-Rahim knew that he couldn't sleep. He didn't have to go to bed to find out; he knew without trying. He'd drunk cup after cup of Turkish coffee at dinner and now he would pay the price. Strange, he thought, I drank coffee to stay awake during the boredom of the afterdinner speeches, and now I couldn't go to sleep if my life depended on it. In reality, coffee had nothing to do with it and Baraket knew it. He never slept for more than five hours a night.

Tarek, his driver, was standing beside the big car with the door open, waiting for instructions. Baraket's dinner companions suggested stopping by the only nightclub in this poor, provincial town of Trebizond, but Baraket was suddenly weary of people. He had been traveling for six weeks already, in as many countries, on his annual business trip. It was the price he paid for a personal income that ran into hundreds of millions: millions of pounds, millions of dollars, liras, marks, francs, Turkish liras. Here in Trebizond, his investments in the shipbuilding facilities of the Black Sea were beginning to take hold. In a few years, income from his Turkish interests could equal those of French or German investments of the same type. Everyone still needed money; the war was not a decade behind them yet. Baraket seemed to be the sole exception. Was he the only man in the world with too much money, a fortune impervious to misfortune? It had been suggested more than once that he might possibly be the richest man in the world. Baraket made no comment to people who had no idea what they were talking about. The fortune was centuries old, almost untraceable, and had increased a hundredfold with the centuries. It was based on vast land and cotton holdings that were family held since the days of the Ottoman Empire, stretching from the far borders of Turkey to the far corners of Egypt. It would have been immense, vast, uncountable, regardless of the number of members of the family, but it had all come down to two people: Princess Tafida, Baraket's mother, and Baraket himself were the sole recipients of it.

Baraket declined the invitation to the nightclub and got into the car. Tarek took his place in the driver's seat and turned to Baraket for instructions.

"Let's drive for a while, Tarek. It's a lovely night. Go down to the sea; I might have a walk." Tarek had been his personal chauffeur since he had started coming to Trebizond on business three years ago, and Baraket enjoyed the man. He was bright and he was an excellent driver, both unusual qualities for the average Turk. Baraket had thought to take him on permanently in the palace near Istanbul, or even in Egypt. Perhaps this time.

"Would you like a girl, sir?" Tarek asked in a soft voice.

"A girl!" Baraket was taken completely by surprise. Tarek

had never suggested anything like that before, another reason
why Baraket liked him. Tarek could not be unaware that a
man of Baraket's stature had the most desirable girls in the
world, the youngest and freshest, brought to him by the best
procurers in London or Paris or Munich. He wanted nothing
to do with street girls or girls from the backwoods of Turkey.

Tarek slowed the car down and turned to face Baraket.

"I have never seen a girl like this one before, sir. She
doesn't belong here." Baraket didn't bother thinking about
what Tarek would know about girls anyway; it was the light
in his eyes and the intensity in his voice that caught his curiosity.

"Where is she, Tarek?"

"In a house a few blocks from here. I have the key. She's
alone; no one else is there."

Tarek's proposal intrigued him. The moon was full and
high on the sea. It was even more difficult to sleep on these
nights of a full moon.

"All right. Let's have a look at her."

The house that Tarek took him to was obviously a private
home belonging to someone who was neither poverty stricken
nor rich. The low white walls were covered with black-green
vines; thousands of white starflowers threw off their jasmine
scent to the night. It was a scent that Baraket loved. Tarek
opened the car door and led the way to the heavy wooden entrance door to the house. He took a key from his pocket and
turned it in the lock.

"Go in, sir. She will be waiting for you in the courtyard. I
will be here."

Baraket stepped across the threshold and Tarek closed the
door quietly behind him. There was no light anywhere, except in the open courtyard which lay washed in moonlight.
As his eyes adjusted to the dark, Baraket gradually made out
a large squarish piece of furniture off to one side, a low sort
of couch. He saw that there was someone lying there, someone lying so quietly that she must be fast asleep. It had to be
the girl; no servant would dare sleep like that. He moved

silently toward her so as not to frighten her. She'd probably been waiting for hours.

The girl was lying on her side and she was sound asleep. The moonlight fell softly on her. She was wearing a thin cotton caftan—white, Baraket supposed, as the moon nullified all color but its own. She had nothing on beneath it and he could see the outline of her body. Long dark hair framed a strong-boned face with fullish lips. Her face was peaceful and eerily beautiful in the pale light. He ran his eyes over her body from the full breasts to the dip of her waist, then to her smallish hips, and he saw that she had fairly long slender legs, unusual for a girl from this part of the world. His eyes came to rest on her small-boned ankles and feet, even more unusual than the length of her legs. Turkish girls never had her delicate quality. He looked at her hands and was not surprised to find that her fingers and wrists were delicate, too. He was fascinated by the tender yet powerful beauty of this sleeping girl. Where could Tarek possibly have found her?

As Baraket watched quietly, drinking in her peaceful beauty, something about her made him feel protective. Perhaps it was her closed eyes that made her seem defenseless, vulnerable to anything that might happen. He sat down beside her and ran his hand softly over her shoulder and one of her breasts. She stirred. He wanted to see her eyes open and the look in them when she opened them. He leaned over her, kissing her throat. Then he felt both of her arms come around him and she moved beneath him, muttering softly in Turkish. He forgot about her eyes as he brought his body down on hers. Instantly wide awake and obviously unafraid, she rolled quickly out from under him and stood up, pulling the caftan over her head, then slamming her naked body gently back against him, reaching for him everywhere, running her hands all over him as he struggled to rid himself of his clothes. He could see her eyes now, dark and demanding, and he could feel her lips move all over his face, tasting him. Her skin was silk in his hands, and the scent her own body exuded mingled with the smell of jasmine. She twined herself around him and they sank down on the low couch. He felt her lips again, all over him, and as she pressed herself insistently against him, the lights went out in his brain.

At dawn he left her, sleeping again, as he had found her. Tarek was waiting for him, his face expressionless. When they arrived at the villa where Baraket was staying, he put his hand on Tarek's shoulder and spoke.

"I want her. Whatever money you need get from my secretary, as you have before. We are leaving here tomorrow for Istanbul, then two days later for Egypt. You are coming, too."

HOLLYWOOD

March 1954

Driving back down the coast from San Simeon, Camilla prattled on to Russ about all she had seen. He was a comfortable companion. After a week together, twenty-four hours a day, she still enjoyed his company.

"I'm going to Texas tomorrow," Russ said casually, cutting her chatter short as they drove along Sunset Boulevard. It sounded as if he were giving a weather report.

"What?" Cam said, caught off guard.

"I have to go to Plainview for a couple of weeks on business. I guess you'll be gone by the time I come back." Again, his tone was as flat as a weather report. Perhaps it was.

"What about me?" Cam asked.

"What about you?" Russ asked. "Aren't you heading back to England?"

"Yes, but not for another five days. I thought—"

"Sorry about what you thought. We've had a good time together; let's leave it that way." He turned the car into the driveway of Chateau Marmont. The bellboy took Cam's bag from the back seat. Cam looked at Russ, puzzled. Was he kidding? She had an odd feeling that his announcement had been carefully timed.

"Maybe I'll take you to Chasen's for a bite to eat tonight. I'll call you later."

Cam felt her face flaming. He was literally dumping her. She would have choked before she let him see that she was angry. What was happening?

"I'm afraid I can't. I have another engagement." Lying, he knows I'm lying.

Russ looked at her. He sat in the driver's seat, half turned toward her. The man facing her now was a stranger, not the man she had been with night and day for more than a month. Even the expression on his face was one she had never seen before. Could he be jealous, or angry, because she had accepted the film offer in London? He couldn't be; it was he who had arranged the whole thing, and with such relish.

"If that's the way you want it, Cam, fine. I'll still call you later."

Cam got out of the car. By the time she got to her room, she was in a towering, helpless rage. What the hell did he mean by "Maybe I'll take you to Chasen's for a bite" and "I'm going to Texas tomorrow"? Who did he think he was and why was he treating her this way?

She ordered a bottle of wine sent up from downstairs. She poured glass after glass of it, pacing the floor of her sitting room, looking at her furious face in the mirror every time she passed. What is the matter with me? she thought; what have I done? She thought back over every moment of the days at San Simeon and she knew that nothing, not one thing, had gone wrong. They had been cocooned in luxury, and Russ had shown himself calm and secure at all times. Alone together at night, they had never been happier.

What had she missed? In the time they had spent together, they never fought. She knew that under the easygoing exterior Russ was a man of deep, sensitive feelings. She was aware of his strength more and more, and she had learned that he wasn't all that easygoing; he was often holding on to a temper that was there somewhere, deeply rooted in him but firmly under control. She admired his strength and she had come to depend on him.

Damn his hide, she thought. I'll show him. She searched through her address book, looking for George Sherril's telephone number at his Long Island house. Dear God, let George be there. She put through the call and was steadied to hear his voice.

"Camilla, darling! Of course I want you to come for the weekend. Fox will meet you. Do you know what flight you're on?"

"Not yet, but I'll call back with the information. Oh, George, I'll be so glad to see you."

Next she called the ticket agent at the Beverly Hills Hotel. Yes, they had her ticket and, yes, they would rewrite it to New York tomorrow but still leave her on the same flight to London on Monday.

Her mood switched around. Why had she gotten so angry with Russ? All he said was that he had to go to Texas. Maybe something was wrong. She picked up the phone once more. When Russ answered she could tell from his voice that he'd been asleep.

"I'm sorry," she said. She had to find out what was wrong.

"Oh, that's all right. I called you but your line was busy."

"Russ, what is all this? Why didn't you tell me you were going to Texas?"

"I didn't think it was necessary." His tone was cool, guarded.

Cam blew up.

"What *did* you think? Why are you acting like this? We've been so happy together all this time, and all of a sudden, boom, you're off to Texas. Don't you think that's a little unusual?"

"Listen, Camilla, you will be in London in less than a week. I'm under no more obligation to you than you are to me. Let's part friends. I don't want to get too involved with anyone at this point. Okay?"

"Too involved!" Cam said, biting her tongue to keep from yelling. "How much more involved can we be? What kind of a bastard are you?"

"Camilla," Russ said, an ugly tone in his voice. "Let's get one thing straight. I don't belong to you or anyone else. I belong to me. As far as I'm concerned, you're a nice girl and just another picture lay. Got it?"

She slammed down the phone. She'd been hurt and humiliated by a gauche madman from Texas who had turned into a monster. No one had ever treated her this way. She liked men and she liked sex but it was she, Camilla, who called the shots. Someday she'd get back at him for this.

She dragged her suitcases out and threw her clothes, shoes, bags, dresses, everything, into them, all in wild disorder. All her life she had been straightforward in her attitude toward herself and others. She had a temper too, and although she still flew off the handle once in a while, she had been disciplined as a child to behave, not indulge herself in useless, ugly tantrums. But when she couldn't understand something, it drove her mad. What had happened to the man she thought she knew? And loved.

Her anger wore off. She was exhausted, and lonelier than she had ever been before. She took a bath and drank the last of the wine. Getting into bed, she knew she would never sleep, but she tried to close her mind to all the jumbled, unchanneled thoughts and, most of all, the hurt. I'll be out of all this tomorrow, she thought. To hell with him. I'm going home, home to a job that could be exciting. She cried for a little while, angry at herself for the tears, and finally fell into an unhappy sleep.

While Camilla was miserable, trying to sleep, Russ was a victim of mixed emotions. Why was he being so nasty to her, what was wrong with him? Dropping her off like that, hurting her, when she had never said an annoying or unkind thing to him. Well, a couple of little things about England had made him feel like an outsider even though she had asked him to come over and visit. By and large, she's one hell of a girl, Russ thought, I can't fault her. She's too strong, was his next thought, and too driving sexually, and something about that was unsettling to him. She must have had hundreds of men. There was nothing she didn't know about sex, nothing she didn't relish doing. He'd learned a lot from her, and what man wants to admit that? No, he took it back, he hadn't learned from her. He had learned that there was one person whose attitude toward sex was as undisguised and strongly motivated as his own. It was a wonderful act, making love, especially to a Camilla whose needs were as great as her desire. But something in Russ wanted a less active recipient of his affections. Camilla didn't need him; she took him. That was a man's role. He winced, thinking about his rudeness to her. How could he explain? He did have to go home tomorrow; another call had come about Sally, this time from her father. She had taken an overdose of pills and was calling for him. Women. They were either too weak or too strong. Camilla was strong enough to take care of herself and Russ decided to let her. He'd make up for it later. For the time being, he wanted to be alone.

EHUKAI FARM, LONG ISLAND

March 1954

"By the way, Camilla Stuart is coming for the weekend," George said, driving carefully on the snowy road, ten minutes from the farm.

"Pretty name," Delphine said. "But who is Camilla Stuart? Am I to be jealous?"

"Would that you were, darling. I love you dearly and resent dearly that my love is brotherly. I'm quite fond of Camilla, too, but you and I are lifelong friends. Friends are everything to me. The three women I fell in love with and married were dogs, greedy dogs, who took everything and gave nothing. I'm masochistic, I'm sure, but at least they cured me of ever marrying again. Three times in ten years is enough. And I do take the greatest pleasure in being able to give you everything in pure friendship."

"George!" Delphine said. "You are waffling. *Who* is Camilla Stuart and why is she coming for the weekend?"

"Oh, right, I am going on. I keep thinking you know everyone that I know. Camilla is an English girl, a beauty. I've known her since she was a child. Her father is Gerald Stuart, the best portrait painter in England. Painted all of my wives."

"George, I know about Gerald Stuart; he is a great portraitist. But if he did such a good job on all your wives, why do you have all three of their portraits hidden away in the attic at Ehukai? I've seen them; you showed them to me."

"Simple, my dear. The only things that triumvirate could not remove from me as each left me were their Stuart portraits. I had him paint all of them early on, when I loved them. They're my skeletons in my closet. The portraits are too good for them. If even one of them had been like her portrait, I'd still be a married man."

"Wait until you see Camilla; she's a stunner. Very English looks, pale blond hair, all that. Quite small, with a body that looks both wild and virginal. Small breasts, very pure. Legs that are possibly the best I've ever seen; when she crosses them, strong men faint. She crosses them often. Green eyes with a greedy look in them. Neat little hands, the hands of a nun. Full of contrasts, Camilla."

"I have a physical picture, but what is she like?"

"Still quite unformed, with a selfish streak somewhere, but she is going to be somebody. She has an iron will and a potentially fine mind. Her education has been country English— the worst. Stuffed full of the classics, which she hates. No economics or history. With the proper training she could be Prime Minister."

"And exactly when is this paragon arriving from England?"

"This evening, but from Hollywood. Fox is at the airport by now." He paused, enjoying Delphine's look of surprise. "She's been out there for several months under contract to one of the studios. It's a rather romantic story. Gerald used to paint her portrait every year for her birthday. A year ago he had one of his rare exhibitions at the Royal Academy. Norman Parkinson, the favorite photographer of the royal family, was poking around the exhibition. Parks never misses a pretty girl. He spotted the portrait called 'Cam at Eighteen.' He jumped on her—sorry, not that at all. He called Gerald—knew him, of course—and went down to the country to see her. That started him off on a quest for British *Vogue* to do a photo essay on the Prettiest Girls in England. Cam turned out to be heads and tail—er, shoulders—above all the rest. He had photographed her in the same position as the portrait, showing both in the article. When it appeared she became an overnight sensation. The press had a field day with her, then Hollywood beckoned, as they say. She's had a role out there in some silly western, but she tells me she's gotten a runaround, and, meanwhile, she's had another film offer from London, so she's on her way home. She was funny on the phone. She said, 'George, they've dyed my hair red and they don't speak a word of English in California. I can't understand one word they say.'"

Delphine laughed. "She sounds marvelous."

"Oh, and something else. Jeremy Kilmuir is mad about her. You don't know about Compton Brooke, do you, or the Brooke press?"

"No, I don't know a thing about it."

"Brooke, Jeremy's grandfather, is getting along now but he's a tiger. An Australian-born tiger. Jeremy's father died when Jeremy was a baby, six, I think, and his mother was a poor little girl who never wanted to leave home. She's still there, somewhere, but Brooke got custody of Jeremy by simply buying her off. Jeremy is his only heir and he was determined to bring him up in England, so when he was a kid, Brooke took him over. Jeremy stands to inherit the title and what is now the largest newspaper empire in England. Brooke, like Beaverbrook in Canada, got the title bestowed on him. Everyone refers to Jeremy as Lord Kilmuir when he's really only an Honorable. I don't think Camilla is all that crazy about him, but she's not stupid. She wouldn't mind being Lady Kilmuir. I have a nice man for you to meet, too."

"Who?"

"Ryan O'Roark."

"*The* Ryan O'Roark? The film director? You haven't mentioned him before."

"Didn't know he could come. Ryan likes doing things the hard way, so he's shooting most of his new film on location in New York in the winter. This snowstorm has closed him down. He called while we were at lunch and said he could make it. You'll like him."

"I'll bet I will. He's got quite a reputation, all very sexy and glamorous."

"Deserves every bit of it. He's one of the most talented men I know and the most brilliant conversationalist."

"I do love his films. How marvelous, I can't wait to meet him." She looked out of the window of the car. The silent snow was falling steadily now, and the weather report on the radio assured them that it was going to get worse, windy and colder, indefinitely.

"Why are you so quiet, what are you thinking about?"

"I'm planning what I'm going to wear tonight; I brought two dresses, both to please you. Now I know which one I'm going to wear, now that Ryan O'Roark is going to be here."

"Which one?"

"The sexy one."

"Good!" George said, turning into the driveway. "Ryan is going to meet his match in someone. It might as well be you, dear girl."

ISTANBUL

October 1953

The bond of friendship between Prince Baraket Safwat Osman Abdel-Rahim, Regulator of the City, Shadow of God and Faithful Ally of the British, and Kenneth Bennett, number three man in the World Development Bank, was based on a bloody fight they had once had on a lacrosse field at Harvard.

"You rotten cheat, you can't do that," Kenneth had said, bashing His Highness Prince Baraket across the nose with his lacrosse stick in a game in which they were not opposing each other but on the same team.

"I shall cheat if I like," was the return, precipitating multiple blows of the sticks from one to the other. Peace was made and from that day forward a close friendship was formed.

Kenneth was not afraid of Baraket, and Baraket had never before met anyone who was not afraid of him. As the years
passed, Kenneth became the only man he trusted, a singular
honor.

There was never any mistaking Baraket's distinctive, raspy
voice on the telephone. Once heard, it was never forgotten.

"Kenneth, I know you have been back in Istanbul for all of
half an hour, but I must see you at once. Does my calling you
this urgently lead you to believe that I have something of importance to see you about?"

Kenneth laughed. "You give me the excuse I need to duck
everything that's piled on my desk after a month in Washington. I'd better come to you. It's been nearly six months since
I've seen you, Baraket. I'll be there within an hour."

"Perfect," the raspy voice said.

Neither man had known that their paths would cross, their
lives intermingle, as they had when their university days were
over. Kenneth Bennett's burgeoning career with the World
Bank had brought him first to Egypt, in the late 1940s, then
Turkey, and some long periods of time in London. All were
home territory to Baraket and had become so to Kenneth. For
a man born in Tennessee, with Deep South attitudes toward
home ties, there was still a lot of nomad in Kenneth Bennett,
and a curiosity that was never satisfied. The growth of the International Monetary Fund and the World Development
Bank after the Second World War suited him perfectly. When
Elsa, his wife, had been alive, she had chosen to live quietly
at their farm on the Eastern Shore of Maryland and had no
objection to his traveling. Kenneth Bennett was a gentleman.
The war had shown him the uglier and more commercial aspects of human nature, and led him into work that would be
rewarding to less fortunate human beings than himself. Elsa
left a considerable fortune and Kenneth intended to use it
more for contribution than for personal use. He had quite
enough money of his own from the family insurance business
in Tennessee. He could never spend lavishly, wantonly, the
way Baraket did under any circumstances. Once in Paris with

Baraket, he had seen him tip the concierge at the Ritz the equivalent of five thousand dollars in francs. When he remarked upon it, Baraket had smiled and said, "You should have known my father. Tafida tells me that every year he tipped the head concierge at the Palace Hotel in St. Moritz twenty thousand dollars. Those men do a lot for you, you know!" As far as Kenneth was concerned, he was satisfied with a good English tailor, a comfortable apartment in whatever city he lived in and ample funds to travel and take a pretty woman out to dine whenever he wanted to. Important money should be used for important purposes.

Kenneth was tall and spare and moved quietly but with authority. His voice was quiet. His sandy hair usually was contrasted by a tanned face. Kenneth had hardly enough time to be considered a sportsman, but he loved horses: riding them, racing them and breeding them. His blue eyes were quiet and merry, and he was one of the best listeners in the western world; one who did not hesitate to zoom in and request huge sums for the bank when the conversation he had listened to leisurely opened up the possibility.

There was nothing shallow about Kenneth Bennett, and nothing unenthusiastic. In the car on the way to Baraket's office, Kenneth was looking forward to a new chapter in their friendship. Intrigue was Baraket's first nature, and Kenneth relished being back in Istanbul. In a month in Washington he had dealt with mundane problems of the bank, plus the final details of settling Elsa's estate, which had taken almost a year to dispose of as she had willed. Now he was back, temporarily, in the fascinating atmosphere of Turkey. London was going to be his main headquarters for the next few years, suiting Kenneth fine, but the years in Turkey had been vital and interesting. Going to Baraket's office—if that incredible old palace could be referred to as an office—was an adventure. The white marble building was set in a garden of sixty acres in the heart of Istanbul. Atatürk, in his brief years, had outlawed palaces, harems, titles—anything to do with the old days—in order to modernize his country, but it had been impossible to change the habits of centuries in a few decades. Palaces still existed, no matter what they were called, and so did harems, and so did titles, albeit they were not referred to as publicly as before. Sultans and pashas were misters now, and the most lavish palace was a house. Ah yes, Kenneth thought to himself, like Baraket's "office."

It was surrounded by a twenty-foot rock wall that contained some formidable gun emplacements. Twenty slate steps, symbolically guarded by two colossal stone lions, led to a colonnade of pink marble columns and to a reception room that was sixty feet long with a ceiling fifty feet high. It was here that Baraket dispensed largesse to those who came to him and dealt with the business and obligations of the family. There were private apartments on either side of the reception room but Baraket used only one small, uncluttered room for private meetings such as the one today with Kenneth. Baraket preferred to live in his great palace of Saadit Sarai—Palace of Happiness—ten miles out of Istanbul on the Bosporus.

Baraket was a tall man, elegant and spare, without an ounce of fat on him. He moved serenely, yet there was a dangerous and strange quality about him, something incalculable. He was like an animal one admired but kept at a respected distance. It showed in his being but particularly in his eyes, which were black and penetrating. No one could read Baraket's eyes. His expression sometimes showed lust, and he was a known womanizer, but most often it was aloof. There was warmth in his eyes but also hate. Kenneth was his exact opposite except for height. Kenneth had the wiry body of a runner and shoulders that led his tailor in London to sniff unappreciatively. "I am supposed to make the shoulders; you are not supposed to have them." They were both extremely elegant men, each in his own way, and they both knew it.

They greeted each other fondly and, once Kenneth had a stiff scotch in his hands, he came to the point. In previous dealings with Baraket, Kenneth had learned that Baraket liked to have someone else open the conversation.

"What is it, Baraket?"

"A girl."

"Aha," Kenneth said, slightly surprised. They had never discussed women. Perhaps he was befriending someone.

"Her name is Alia. She is a special seed. Calm, suspicious, intelligent; she knows everything, forgets nothing that she is told. I want her to have a chance."

"Where is she?"

"At Saadit Sarai. You will meet her tonight. I hope you can dine. I am taking her with me tomorrow to Cairo for one week, then I must send her back. I still have one more intense month of family business."

"Baraket, what can I do?"

"You are much more familiar with certain aspects of the world than I am, and your taste in women is exceptional. Since I must be gone, I would like for you to arrange for the proper people to be brought here to Istanbul to teach her, to train her. She speaks English fairly well, but no French. That must change at once. Then she must have clothes, everything, and learn how to display herself, arrange herself. I want her to have everything. I don't know how to do it." The raspy voice was cuttingly clear.

"Baraket, it would be much easier to take her to the world than to bring the world to her. And far more effective."

Baraket's strong head came up quickly and the black eyes were like live onyxes. That was it! Why hadn't he thought of it?

"Kenneth! I knew you would know. That's the right way, of course. Paris, can you take her to Paris?"

"Baraket, I can take her to Paris for you and make all arrangements as you want them, but I cannot stay with her, nor would it be necessary. We have many friends there to help us, discreet friends who can be trusted. First, we must call Pierre Balmain. He is one of the most tasteful and talented men that I've known. Besides doing clothes and furs for her, he can arrange for the hairdressers and makeup people, all of it.

French lessons there will give her the language and, even though she can't absorb all of Paris in a month's time, she will learn more than she would in a year in Istanbul."

"I am going to marry her."

Kenneth was astonished. He took his breath in quickly. Baraket meant it; he wasn't playing a game this time. But how could he marry a girl from anywhere but his home, Egypt? It was unthinkable. And his mother, Princess Tafida—the powerful old lady who dominated everyone, intimidated everyone but her only son—what would she think of all this?

"I want her to be the most beautiful and envied woman in the world. In order to achieve that, I must begin to create an identity for her."

"What?" Kenneth asked. He was confused. "You can marry anyone you want, from Cinderella to Lucrezia Borgia. Why does this girl have to have an identity created for her?"

"Because she is no one, and I would not marry a no one. So I shall shroud her in mystery and see to it that she is completely protected. Wherever we go in the world, she will have an impeccable, quite obscure but impeccable, background. I've never once considered marrying before and I've made up my mind about this in three days. And I know I am right."

Now it was like being back at Harvard, with Baraket plotting once more, involving everyone in some new intrigue. But this was serious and could be dangerous. Tafida, Baraket's mother, had tried to force him into one marriage after another for years, liaisons that she arranged and Baraket escaped. Now she was about to have some untrained Turkish delight dumped in her lap, and there would be hell to pay. *Marry* her? How could he?

"I am going to make her a princess. Princess Alia. Her mythical family will have kept her hidden away in Trebizond until she is marriageable; then they will present her in Istanbul and she will catch me. It's all very simple. I am giving her a good family, you know, not poor."

"Where are you going to get them?" Kenneth asked. You don't have to lock the barn door now that the horse is out, he

thought. He knew Baraket would already have solved that
problem, too.

"I'm not going to bore you with the arrangement, Kenneth;
that's a story that will unfold. I know that, most of all, I have
to protect Alia from my formidable mother before I marry
her, before it is a *fait accompli.*"

"Then why are you taking her to Cairo, into the nest?"

"Because I cannot do without her."

Again, Kenneth was caught by surprise. He looked quickly
and saw something vulnerable in Baraket's expression, something he had never seen before.

"You've fallen in love. Haven't you ever been in love before?"

"Never," Baraket said. "I have always had an eye open; I
have always searched for this girl, and you will see why almost as quickly as I did. Also, I have a new manservant
named Tarek. He will bring her back to Istanbul in ten days.
I have business all over Africa, and I hope you will be able
to make the Paris arrangements by then. What a brilliant
idea, really, Kenneth."

"I cannot wait to meet the new Princess Alia," Kenneth
said. Verily, verily, he thought.

"Good. You'll find her quite as special as I have told you.
Dinner's at nine at Saadit Sarai. I'll send Tarek for you; you
should get to know him too."

EHUKAI FARM, LONG ISLAND

March 1954

Camilla didn't wait for a formal introduction to Delphine, nor did she knock on the bedroom door. Delphine was lying on her bed reading when the door opened and Camilla Stuart walked in.

"I know you're Delphine and I really couldn't wait to meet you. Forgive me for barging in, but I feel as if I've been on that airplane for a year and I wanted to talk to a woman. Do you know the entire time I've been in California I haven't had a girl friend. Ever since I left England it's all been men, men, men."

"Sit down," Delphine said, laughing. "It's lovely to meet you. Shall I order us some tea or a drink?"

"Mmm," Cam said. "A nice glass of champagne perhaps.

They may have it in California but I didn't have any. I don't drink much, but champagne is so civilized." She had taken off her coat and was inspecting herself in the dressing table mirror.

"God, I'm so glad to be with George again. He's more civilized than champagne, don't you think?"

"Indeed," Delphine replied, laughing again. "And did he tell you that Ryan O'Roark is coming for the weekend, too?"

"No!" Cam exclaimed. "My God, I'd like to be in one of his films. Wouldn't I!"

"Well, here's your chance."

They chatted, very much at ease with each other. Delphine had never had many female friends, and in New York, George more than made up for them. She found herself enjoying Cam's company and her intense femininity.

"Forgive me for babbling on about California, Delphine, but it was a crazy experience in more ways than one. And not being an American, maybe I just don't understand some of the attitudes."

"What do you mean?"

Cam sat down across from Delphine and looked at her seriously.

"Can I ask you something?"

"Of course," Delphine said. That something was obviously bothering her.

"I'm in a state of shock or I wouldn't be talking like this. I met a man in California, a Texan who was working on the film, too. We got involved practically immediately. He was a friend as well as a lover. I've never met anyone like him before. You know how you can tell when somebody really likes you, aside from the sex? Well, I know that Russ likes me; we were like partners. He advised me and helped me in Hollywood." She shook her head.

"What happened?" Delphine was astonished at Camilla's instant candor and frankness.

"I don't know." Cam's tone was hurt and confused. "That's just it. We spent last weekend at San Simeon, where we had a perfect time. Perfect. But when he brought me home he suddenly said he had to go to Texas, just like *that*. I was furious and the whole thing got ugly, and I called George and here I am."

"Wait, wait!" Delphine said. "Too fast for me to absorb. What exactly happened?"

"Delphine, I promise you the man who said he was going to Texas was not the man I have spent the last month with. He was a total stranger to me. Even his look had changed. I've been hours on the airplane today taking stock of myself. What did I do wrong? What was he thinking to make him behave that way? I don't know, I don't know."

"It sounds like a personality quirk," Delphine said. "I've known one or two of those Jekyll-and-Hyde characters. I guess we all have. You're on solid ground one minute and in quicksand the next. But, Camilla, you sound quite serious about it."

"I guess so. I've never been treated this way before. I know Russ is crazy about me, and I can't understand why he's behaving this way."

"Is he jealous? Is there someone else in your life that you've told him about? With you going home to England, could he have gotten suddenly insecure and felt that you were using him?"

"Oh, God, I wish there was someone in England for me to go home to. There's only Jeremy, darling Jeremy Kilmuir, who is mad for me, but I am not even warm about him."

"George mentioned Jeremy to me. Isn't he rather an important man?"

"He's rather an important boy."

"Even so, he certainly treats you better than your Texan friend does, doesn't he?"

"To put it mildly."

"Camilla, Jeremy is known to you at least, is from your own world. Maybe this California experience is a passing fancy that you took too seriously. Does Jeremy want you to marry him?"

"He's panting for me to."

"Then think about it. When an important man wants to marry you, it's never to be taken lightly. He'll grow up, won't he?"

"Of course. One day his grandfather will stop bullying him and one day the whole publishing empire will be his, and then it will all be different." There was a thoughtful look on her face. "Thank you, Delphine."

"Don't be silly. It's time for us to dress."

"I know. And we have darling George and the fabulous O'Roark to look forward to. Things aren't so bad after all. I'll fight you for Ryan at dinner!" With a flashing smile she was gone.

As Delphine dressed she debated about wearing the big diamond necklace and then decided of course she would wear it. It had been Winona's until the night before she left home.

"Take it, darling," Winona had said. "I've hardly had it out of the bank. Diamonds look so out of place in Honolulu anyway and, besides, they stick to your skin in the heat."

"Wear it, darling," Bob Munro followed up. "Spring it on George; he'll love it."

Yes, he will, Delphine thought as she slipped into the dress she had decided to wear. It was navy blue satin with a deeply cut V neckline that was piped in pale green. The full skirt and wide belt made it rather grand and ladylike, but the neckline changed all that. Thank heavens she still had some suntan left, even though it had been three weeks since she'd left home. She snapped the safety clasp on the necklace and took a final look at herself. The necklace was really a stunner, an oval circle of marquise diamonds that zigzagged down her throat to a center point between her breasts where a huge marquise diamond blazed comfortably against her skin. The big sixty-carat marquise was known as the Munro Diamond to the few who knew about it.

Delphine gloried in the excitement she felt. At home everything was so secure, so casual. Here in New York she could wear all the beautiful clothes that she wanted to and even flaunt a few family jewels, such as the necklace. And meet exciting people, creative people, such as Ryan O'Roark. People who were doing things and going places. She thought about knocking on Camilla's door to see if she was ready. No, she'd rather go down alone. There was a long mirror at the top of the stairs. Delphine took a last glance at herself and needed no more assurance. She knew how she looked.

The man standing at the foot of the stairs fixing himself a drink from the butler's-tray bar was silhouetted against the light from the living room. He was tall and gaunt and there was a lock of ash-blond hair loose on his forehead. He had a large brow and gray eyes that varied from dove to granite in tone, depending on his mood. The jacket of his dinner coat was unbuttoned, showing the creamy color of his silk shirt. That's Ryan O'Roark, no one else, Delphine thought as she reached the foot of the stairs. She had seen photographs of him, but she had no idea he would be so tall. He turned as she reached the foot of the stairs and took her in, took all of her in, in one bright second. It was the most comprehensive look Delphine had ever felt from anyone. She smiled.

"I'm Delphine Munro," she said.

Ryan let out a long, soft whistle, his eyes closing in on the necklace.

"Are you legal?" he asked, mocking, yet serious.

She laughed. "Yes, just."

"Good. I hate to break the law, although in your case I'd be compelled to." He handed her a flute of champagne. "What's your ring size? I can't have you going around emptyfingered when you've got that thing around your neck. My contribution will be substantial." He led her into the warmly lit country drawing room and sat her down beside him on the dark red raw silk couch in front of the fireplace. Fox had filled silver bowls with early tulips, bright red ones with jagged yellow edges, harbingers of spring.

"Yes," Ryan said, taking in every detail of background and foreground. Delphine laughed again.

"I have a feeling I am being directed," she said. "What's the film about?" She had never been as attracted to a man as she was to Ryan O'Roark. She couldn't wait to hear what he was going to say next. The intensity of his look fascinated her.

"It's about a famous film director who has never been in love," Ryan said. "He's admired—even adored—hundreds of women, but somehow the *coup de foudre,* the thunderclap, has never hit him. Then one night . . ." He reached inside the green satin edging of the neckline of her dress and ran his forefinger along her shoulder down to the V between her breasts, never taking his eyes off her face.

Delphine felt an electric shock shoot through her. Ryan took his hand away and raised her hand to his lips, his eyes still riveting into hers.

"There's always a first time, isn't there?" he said, the gray eyes warming her skin. "I now feel Camilla and George descending on us. I am going to be very respectful toward you, Miss Munro, through dinner and after dinner, too. But when the others have gone to bed, you and I are not going to. There will be two brandies warming on this table for us." He stood up and held out his hand.

Delphine rose, still feeling the shock of his finger along her breast. George was crossing the room toward them, eyes on her necklace. She looked at the clock on the mantel. Eight-fifteen, it said. In three hours' time her life might begin, right back here where she was standing now.

PARIS

March 1954

Pierre Balmain was sitting in his dove-gray felt-and-satin office on the Rue François Ier, talking to Kenneth Bennett, his most important new client, on the telephone. It was rare conversations like this that gave a couturier the chance to go amok with his talent—to make a complete wardrobe for someone who was young and apparently beautiful, and to know that the bills would be paid promptly with no quibbling over the price. The winter sunshine poured its pale gold over the malachite objets d'art that Pierre had only recently retrieved from the place where they had been hidden away through the war years. What a feast to his eyes they were— the striped-green beauty of two perfect bowls with gold mountings and the perfect small elephant he held in his hands. Just looking at the egg nestled in its golden nest gave him immense pleasure.

"Kenneth, you know everything can, and will be, kept in absolute confidence. I think it would be wise to have her stay in the Bellman Hotel. It's directly across the street from me, owned by the Terrail family, close friends of mine."

"Who own the Tour d'Argent, too?" Kenneth asked. "That's perfect. Book a small suite for her and an adjoining room for her companion. Use the name Princess Fal for both of them. He is the man who will be driving her and taking care of her; he works for Baraket. We will be in Paris sometime over the weekend and, since I will have a number of other things to do for the princess, I would appreciate it if you would make all arrangements for the hairdresser and the makeup people. You know the best ones and you can explain the financial arrangements to them. I want you to oversee the entire venture except for French and English lessons, which I'll take care of. We can come to you on Tuesday morning. How early would be convenient?"

"Eight o'clock. The earlier the better, if we want to keep her under wraps. Fortunately, the workroom is not too busy now; most of the orders from the last collection are finished."

"Good," said Kenneth. "See you then."

When they hung up Balmain sat back, fondling the malachite egg absentmindedly. It wouldn't have been right to ask what she looked like or how old she was. Kenneth Bennett was a gentleman and he knew what he was doing. Balmain was intrigued. A beautiful princess from an exotic world, carte blanche on a wardrobe for her—sky's the limit and all that. His curiosity was killing him. I wonder if gray will become her, he thought, or skin-colored satin, for a perfectly understated dinner dress with a full-length cape of that new honey-colored mink. Yes, that would be nice for a start.

Unbeknown to Alia, Balmain studied her carefully as she walked up the wide stairway toward him with Kenneth. There was something about her—the way she held her head,

some feminine quality that came through the protective coloring of her shapeless black coat and boring shoes. Yes, he
thought, responding instantly, we do have a star. Let's get to
work.

NEW YORK

April 1954

Late winter gave way to early spring. One day it would be cold and rainy; the next would be filled with hard, brilliant sunshine. Delphine watched from her windows for any small sign of spring in the park. She could see the ribbon of yellow taxis winding endlessly through in the early morning and late evening, and the squirrels in the bare trees beneath her were clearly silhouetted as they jumped from branch to branch, teasing the street-smart city dogs on the ground below them. But not a crocus stirred. The musky earth still waited for a sign.

Delphine was in a restless mood. In a few more weeks, the park would be openly budding, and she could imagine how the first pink-and-white blossoms of the fruit trees would look, stealing away the scenes of winter that she had watched for hours. Delphine loved the snow and there had been plenty of it. "Two blizzards and one other big snowstorm since early February. Mother Nature has given you this present," George said one day as they were both watching the white-crystal perfection of the snowclad park. "You and I have been swamped by tree ferns and orchids for most of our lives; that's why nothing stabs the heart like a drift of snow one day . . . and forsythia bursting forth, or a willow tree feathering out, the next.

It was a treacherous time for Delphine. The wild joy of loving Ryan had deepened into something far more serious. One minute she knew that Ryan was going to ask her to marry him; the next, she knew he never would. Her own feelings about marrying him were ambivalent. Her mother and father would not be exactly ecstatic about the liaison. Jay knew. He had come to New York for one visit and was as overwhelmed by Ryan's charm and talent as she had been. Soon she and Ryan would be leaving for Mexico. Ryan was shooting a film with an all-male cast. The locations were primitive beaches or mountain wildernesses. They would have no privacy, a painful situation to Delphine, but Ryan wanted her with him and she couldn't refuse.

They spent long times alone together, rather than going out, in his apartment or hers. Ryan had kept his apartment for years in a huge old converted house on Fifty-sixth Street, a five-minute walk from Delphine. It had two cavernous rooms: one a living room, the other a bedroom overlooking a garden at the back, plus a huge, old-fashioned bathroom and a small kitchen.

Ryan used it primarily as a repository for treasures he'd picked up all over the world. It was his only home. The ample rooms were painted elephant gray, outlined by white woodwork, and in each there was a white marble mantelpiece over a working fireplace. On the living room walls there were two huge Stubbs tiger paintings of such extraordinary quality that Delphine gasped when she first saw them. The furniture ran to the exotic: an elephant howdah sat in one corner covered with dozens of photographs of Ryan's friends, and five black carved Indian chairs with bell tassels on them surrounded a massive glass coffee table. Books in wild disorder were strewn on every table and chest, as well as on shelves from ceiling to floor. Cashmere blankets competed with Scottish mohair throws on every deep-cushioned couch. When Delphine first stayed there, Ryan had dug into a trunk in a closet and brought forth embroidered velvet caftans and Thai silk robes in violent colors for her. Another box held delicate Morocco-leather slippers and sheer silken scarves to tie around her hair. He found a jeweled belt—emeralds and rubies and diamonds embedded in ornate gold—for her. It had been given to him by the King of Jordan. "For my nonexistent wife," Ryan said. "It was unthinkable to him that I would not be married. All this feminine paraphernalia I have here is now yours. No more presents for future hostesses or dear old dowagers who love loot. Take it all, my darling."

As intensely personal as it all was, there was no sign that any one woman had taken precedence at any time of his life. Ryan had told her dozens of stories involving women that he had known, but they were stories typical of him and his style—full of charm and joie de vivre, told to amuse. The women never seemed to be more than longtime friends, married more often than not, or a passing fancy. No love affairs were ever brought out. Delphine began to believe that he had been sincere when he said the thunderclap—the *coup de foudre*—had never struck him. Apparently, he had never been as involved as he was with Delphine.

She couldn't imagine being without him. Had she ever been alone? They stayed, for the most part, in her apartment. Ryan loved watching the constant change of the still-life park scenes as much as she did. At night they would watch as thousands of apartment eyes blinked across at them from the buildings on both sides of the park. Delphine had had her bed built onto a raised platform by the wall of glass windows so she could look out, and she had mirrored the walls so that the room became a romantic cocoon of low lights and myriad reflections.

It was a time of such foolish happiness between them that Delphine bought a journal and wrote fragments of conversation or unforgettable things that Ryan said in it, something she had never done before. She wanted to remember everything. Someday, when it was finished, she would have the journal to help her remember. It was bound to change. Everything changed.

Ryan's work, for the most part, was on the telephone, so Delphine had two lines put in for him. She spent several days a week at the gallery with Rodney, planning out the details of the coming jade exhibitions. They were going to mount a small, important show in Boston in early June. She would be gone for a few days, but even an hour away from him was agony for her now.

At the end of May they drove down to Ehukai for the weekend. The weather was more summer than late spring. George seemed restless. After lunch, when everyone else had gone off to play tennis, he spoke to Delphine.

"What about the summer, dear girl?" he asked. He was more than aware of her romance with Ryan although they had never discussed it.

"I'm going to Mexico with Ryan—the only woman in the wilds of Mexico. I must be crazy."

"I was afraid you'd opt for the primitive rather than the comfortable. I wanted both of you to come on the yacht, you know that, but I know you'd be miserable if you came without Ryan. Next year. Everything is all right, I take it?"

"Oh, yes," Delphine said. "Never better."

PARIS
April 1954

The Bellman Hotel, directly across the street from the House of Balmain, was the perfect place for Alia to live during her secret training period in Paris. It was small—no more than thirty rooms—and had a quiet dining room, rarely used by anyone aside from a few older occupants of the hotel. Alia's small suite was cozy and Tarek was with her every minute, living in the room next to hers. The only favor Alia asked of Baraket had been unnecessary for her to ask: to keep Tarek with her. Tarek was her anchor and Baraket knew it. He was bodyguard, driver, her friend and her servant. Of course Tarek would be with her, driving her to her English lessons, French lessons, or to Guillaume, the best coiffeur in Paris. A little Russian genius named Sergei whisked her off into a pri-

vate room where they would experiment happily together for
hours with dozens of hairstyles for different occasions.

The schedule that Kenneth had arranged for her left no
moment unused. In the first weeks in Paris, she was so
exhausted by the time she returned to the hotel at the end of
the day that she had neither the desire nor the strength to eat.
Tarek had searched out a small Turkish bakery, and each evening he would bring her the one sweet she craved: baklava,
dripping with honey. She would bolt it down and then, having gulped several cups of Turkish coffee, she would fall
sleepily into bed, lapsing into her native Turkish, trying to
forget the English and French that had been forced into her
head during the long hours of the day.

Wherever she went, she was like an anonymous shadow, a
chameleon who saw to it that no one looked at her. When she
was brought to Pierre Balmain by Kenneth, the first thing
that intrigued him about her was her quiet presence. Mystery,
a woman's most powerful weapon, was a natural part of her
makeup. She would be noticed when she desired to be, but
only then. Balmain's second impression had to do with her
coloring. Her dark hair and huge dark eyes were set off by
her skin. She was alabaster, she was cream, she was ivory.
The cold winter light falling on her from the big windows in
the dressing room would have been harsh on the tenderest
beauty; on Alia it was blessed. The mirrored walls of the
dressing room threw back hundreds of reflections of her, each
presenting another astonishing facet of her beauty. In their
first session together, Balmain and Henriette, his best vendeuse, stripped her down, removing the layers of coat and
sweater, blouse and skirt, until she stood completely naked
before them except for her small panties and her shoes. Under
their scrutiny she was totally at ease, holding herself with natural dignity and an excited interest in all that was happening
to her. Alia, as well as Balmain, was seeing herself for the first
time. Balmain saw immediately the value of the treasure
being unearthed. He had been told only a certain amount

about her background by Kenneth, and he was wise enough
to imagine, not question, what it might be.

The big front dressing room had been set aside for Alia
alone and for one solid month it became the scene of such
creative chaos that it was much more of a home to her than
the hotel across the street. A private phone was installed, the
number known only to Kenneth and Baraket. She stood for
endless hours while bolts of chiffons and silks, wools and
satins, were draped on her. Balmain sketched as if he were
driven: coats and dresses and blouses and ball gowns and
dinner dresses, everything. A constant parade of shoes and
belts, bags, scarves and hats were brought to the dressing
room. What didn't satisfy him was sent back, and then the
sketch pad would come out again to show the milliner or the
shoemaker exactly what he wanted. A bond grew quickly between him and Alia. He recognized her intelligence and she
understood his talent. She was warm and uncomplaining
through all the tedious hours of fittings and curious about everything. When he tied a silken thread around her waist, not
tight enough to cut but tight enough to keep her standing
ramrod-straight and breathing carefully, she asked why.
"Good posture is everything in clothes; for the moment this
will remind you to stand tall," he told her, delighted with her
grace. There was no color that didn't suit her, didn't take on a
special Alia quality because of the tones of her skin. All of the
house of Balmain knew about her, although few of them
were allowed to see her. They were admonished to keep their
curiosity in check; she would be introduced to them when the
time came, when the master had finished making her wardrobe.

Something began to bother Balmain, something special that
was missing in her creation. Whatever it was would not come
to the surface of his brain, so he let it be. It would come in
due time.

Strangely, no jewels arrived for approval in the dressing
room. They were a normal part of the couture procedure; one

could hardly go without them. But Kenneth had whispered something in Balmain's ear when they first arrived, something that had to do with the origins and caliber of the jewels that Alia would soon be wearing. The vendeuse had not overheard the conversation, but she did see one of Monsieur Balmain's eyebrows fly up at what was said, a most unusual occurrence.

Alia spent the early mornings working at her English lessons, then stood for fittings. Lunch was sent in to the dressing room, and in the late afternoon Tarek would take her to her French lesson. Twice a week she would go to Sergei at Guillaume for more experimenting with her hair. Makeup people came to the sitting room in her suite and spent hours with her, making her up and teaching her how to do it herself. The tables and chests were piled high with jars and lipsticks and tubes of color for eyes and lips and cheeks. When Balmain came to bring one of the first of the finished dresses, one that she particularly liked, and saw all the paraphernalia of the makeup, it came to him in a flash what had been missing. Perfume! Alia must have a perfume of her own, something to complement her own subtle scent. That was it! It was something he had never done before. With Alia as his inspiration, the time had come. He went to work with a chemist and the next time Kenneth telephoned for the almost daily progress report, Balmain was beside himself.

"There has never been anyone as unusual as Alia in my life," he said. "Now my only dilemma is what to name this exquisite perfume I have made for her."

Kenneth laughed, pleased with the growing crescendo of excitement around Alia. It was all going very well.

"Any candidates? I used to have a tough time naming racehorses every season. I should think perfume would be a cinch."

"No, no, it's not. This one is ephemeral, has a mystery about it, as Alia does. I started with lotus, the flower most like her; then I added a soupçon of both carnation and lily, not too heavy, and finally the lightest *soufflé* of musk. Minimal, as she has her own. She, of course, adores it and it has become hers,

hers alone. But I must have a special name for it and I can't decide between two."

"What are they?"

"The first is 'Ivoire.' Ivory is exactly the color her skin is and is valuable, as she is. Rare ivory has a gleam, as she does. The other is 'Elysée 64-83.'"

"What?" asked Kenneth, not able to follow the abrupt switch. Elysée 64-83?

"It's the telephone number in the dressing room—again, part of the mystery of Alia and this time we are spending together. You and Baraket are the only ones who know it."

Kenneth laughed. "Hold off until I get there next week. You have no problem, Pierre."

"Which do you like best?"

"Both," said Kenneth. "All you have to do is get back with that chemist and more musk. Use both names; just invent one more perfume."

EHUKAI FARM, LONG ISLAND

June 1954

Delphine was lying on one of the blue-padded benches by the pool, almost asleep in the early-morning sun. Since it was Sunday, none of the others would be up before noon. She felt like a sybarite enjoying herself in the cool-warm of the June morning, loving Ryan and Ehukai and all that was happening. They had been together for over three months. When had they not been together? Delphine wondered, eyes closed. Don't think about anything but now.

Eyes still closed, she felt drops of water dripping down on her face, like tiny raindrops falling on her. She opened her eyes to an explosion of color and the mingled scent of sun-warmed flowers filled her nostrils. Purples and reds and pinks of petunias, geraniums and roses burst against the summer blue of the sky. Ryan had dipped the bouquet in the pool and was holding it over her head, shaking drops of water onto her face. Wide awake now, she took the bouquet and threw it aside, flinging her arms around him, covering his face with small kisses. God, he did look marvelous, all six feet four of him, in immaculate tennis whites. Long sharkskin trousers, perfect tennis sneakers and a white cotton shirt with short sleeves, the simplest possible way of dressing, but he looked like millions of dollars in everything he put on.

"Darling, you're so beautiful," she said. "Take off your clothes."

Ryan had been devouring her with his eyes since he'd come out onto the terrace of the house five minutes before. Seeing her lying there at the foot of the long green hill, asleep in the sun, made him want her even more than he had wanted her last night. He crossed over to the riotous beds that lined the hill and picked the flowers. As he moved closer toward her, he was sublimely happy. No woman like this before, and never one like her again.

When she spoke, his eyes changed. Morning was giving them more of what the night had amply provided. Sitting down beside her, he reached for the top of her strapless bathing suit and pulled it down to her waist, then nuzzled his face into her warm breasts. Pacing his passion, he slipped the suit down over her hips, and flung it into the pool. She lay naked and preening beneath him, honey-colored, looking at him with shameless abandon, opening her arms to him.

"Beautiful wanton bitch. Now I'll take off my clothes," he said, tearing his shirt off, pulling at the laces of his tennis shoes and sliding swiftly out of his white slacks.

"Darling, you are beautiful," she said again, looking at all of him before his body closed down on hers. "God," she said, "what about the others?"

"This will teach them not to sleep late, stupid bastards. Shut up."

For both, the next few minutes were filled with pure ecstasy, a kaleidoscope of sun and blue and scent and pulsing
gifts of one to the other. Zenith reached, desire fulfilled, she
lay curled in his arms on the padded bench, the warm sun
kissing their bodies.

NEW YORK
June 1954

Delphine was booked on the last flight to Boston on Monday night. The jades had gone up with Rodney Galliher the day before.

"Darling," Ryan said, "would you like to have an early dinner at 'Twenty-one'? Your flight's at nine, so the car can drop me and then take you on to the airport. I have calls coming in from California, money calls from the boys to finalize everything for the second unit. They are leaving for Mexico this week. God, how the time has flown."

"Damn the jades," Delphine said. "I hate to leave, even for a few days. Use the phone all night while you can. What in the world will you do without a phone in the wilds of Mexico?"

"I'll think of something. I've been training some carrier pigeons: O'Roark Pigeon Services. When in need . . ." He grinned at her, grabbing her by the neck and kissing her on the forehead.

The buzzer rang; the driver was waiting below. When the bellboy arrived to take her suitcase, she took a last look at the park. Boston had better be beautiful to make up for leaving this. Late sunlight wandered lazily through the trees, fading even as she watched.

Harry was on the door at "21." They went into the bar and sat at the first table on the left, Ryan's favorite. They ordered soft-shell crabs, a Bibb lettuce salad and a bottle of Pouilly Fumé. An hour later she kissed Ryan good-bye at the door to his apartment.

"Call me the minute you get to the Ritz, darling," Ryan said.

At the airport there was a delay sign up on the board for her flight. Half an hour. She thought about calling Ryan but decided not to because of his business calls from California. Half an hour later a recorded voice informed the waiting passengers that the flight had been canceled due to a malfunction of equipment. Delphine left her bag checked in and made a reservation for the first flight the next morning. Now she could go back to Ryan!

She let herself into the apartment with her key. The lights were out in the living room, but she could see a crack of light under the bedroom door. He was still on the phone, no doubt. She opened the door quietly.

The woman in the bed with Ryan wasn't young; Delphine saw longish ash-blond hair on the pillow and a round, undistinguished face. The woman's eyes widened, startled when she saw Delphine. She stiffened and Ryan cursed.

"We have a visitor," the woman said.

Ryan rolled off her and turned with the movement of a panther.

"Oh, Jesus, Delphine," he said.

Delphine closed the door in a blind stupor and ran. She let

herself into her own apartment, shaking, knowing what she had just seen could not possibly have been. It was a nightmare; it wasn't true. She poured a neat scotch from the bar and looked out into the night. The bell rang. Ryan was there, pounding on the door.

"Let me in, Delphine; let me in."

She gave no answer. Her body was shaking even more violently and the tears were streaming down her face. It couldn't be true.

"Delphine, for God's sake, let me in. I have the right to explain to you." His voice was desperate.

She went to the door and leaned her head against it.

"Ryan, go away." Her voice was barely audible.

She stood leaning against the door, not capable of moving as Ryan continued to plead with her.

"I'm going to go down and get the man on the desk and a master key and a saw. I am not going to go away. I'll stay here until you open this door if you don't open it for six months. Delphine, open it!"

She took the chain off and unlocked the bolt, then turned toward her bedroom. Ryan moved swiftly toward her and threw his arms around her. He was ghostly white.

Delphine heard a terrible noise and slowly realized that it was coming from her own throat, like a primal scream. She flailed her arms at him, looking for some way to kill him. All she could see was the man she loved, the man she knew loved her, in bed making love to another woman less than an hour ago. She didn't know why and she never would. The betrayal —why?

"Why, why, why?" she screamed at him. "You have your chance now, so tell me—why?" She was in hysterics. Ryan tried to get hold of her, but she ran from him until he grabbed her hard around the waist and shoulders and threw her down on the couch, himself on top of her.

"Stop it, darling, stop."

Delphine lay on the couch, Ryan pinning her down. Her eyes were closed and she felt cold, stony cold, as if she were dead. She didn't speak for a long time and then she released herself from his grip and sat up and looked at him.

"Why?"

"She's a woman who has been in my life for many years. I'm deeply fond of her. I'm not in love with her, nor was I ever, but she's been good to me in the past. There were many times when I needed her help, which she gave me. And she needs love; she's had little enough of it." He got up and lit a cigarette. "We drifted into making love one summer when I was staying in one of her houses. She wanted me and she came into my room one night and it was comfortable and friendly. I don't expect you to understand, but I will not lie to you."

"Are you in love with me?" Delphine said.

"There has never been anyone like you for me and you know it."

Delphine was in limbo, her confidence gone, her dignity destroyed. He's embarrassed me and humiliated me, and he's not even saying that he loves me. We are counterparts, sewn into each other's skin, but he makes love to other ladies. She started to cry again.

"Ryan, please go. You can do as you like. Any woman who would stay with you under these circumstances is either stupid or desperate, and I am neither."

"We have to stay together now; we have to get through this together no matter how it turns out. I can't leave."

"The flight to Boston was canceled. I'm going first thing in the morning."

"No you're not." He pulled her to her feet. "Come to bed."

Delphine screamed at him. "Get out, you animal! You've got a body around the block still warm from yours; take yourself back to her." Her head was splitting and lights were flashing in front of her eyes. Ryan made a lunge at her, but she got away and ran toward her bedroom. She would lock the door and he could stay outside forever if he wanted to, but she was too late. Ryan hurled himself at her and when his body weight hit her it knocked the breath out of her, making her lose her balance, and she fell, tumbling toward the bed. Ryan dragged her onto the bed and, with brutal strength, tore her blouse and skirt off and shoved her back when she tried to rise.

"Let go of me, you bastard," she screamed, using the little strength she had to fight him, but to no avail. He was as furious now, as untamed, as out of control, as she had been when she left him in the door. Flailing an arm, he knocked the lamp off the table, dragging at the cord until it pulled out of the socket, leaving them both panting and groaning, battling in the dark.

"I said come to bed," he said, pinning her arms down and kissing her savagely on the throat. "You'll do as I want you to. You think you know something about love and now you are going to learn some more."

Delphine wept. The damage had been done; she would never feel the same about him again. She should never have let him in; she should have been strong enough to keep the door closed, but she hadn't. No one could fight Ryan when he wanted something.

PARIS

June 1954

Pierre Balmain put through the call to Kenneth in Istanbul. The excitement in his voice was almost contagious.

"Kenneth, come and get her! I can't keep her a secret one minute longer. When I tell you what happened when I took her to Tour d'Argent last night . . . She's already a quiet star in Paris. Everyone wants to know who she is, and Paris has only seen her twice!"

Kenneth interrupted.

"Wait, Pierre, Baraket has to hear every word of this. He arrived back this morning, and he is out of his mind with curiosity to see her and to hear all that's happened. We'll come over to Paris this afternoon."

"She is going to be a sensation. I hate to lose her; we've become such friends. She's not that easy to know, but once she trusts you . . ."

"Pierre, even more important, we're going to cruise out to Istanbul on George Sherril's yacht. I presume you've made her some yachting clothes."

"Of course," Pierre sniffed. "I'd hardly do a complete wardrobe for her without."

"Baraket feels that ten days on the yacht will be a good sort of coming-out party for her, make it easier for her to get used to being with people. He won't be able to come, but I will be with her with a small group of very close friends. Also, it's safer all around. We'll arrive in Istanbul the day before the wedding so we can keep the press at bay, as well as Baraket's mother, at least until then. They won't have any idea where Alia is, or who she is."

"They will if you take her out in Monte Carlo. I tell you, she's unbelievable. She's like a chameleon, but she translates differently; whatever she puts on makes the room look better, rather than the opposite. Yesterday I said, 'We're going out, Alia.' Her face lit up. She's worked beyond belief—sometimes sixteen hours a day—and everyone in the house of Balmain is in love with her. They all protect her. When I send the midinette to wake her in the morning, she makes Turkish coffee for her, and drags her feet while she's doing it so Alia can sleep for ten more minutes."

His voice was at fever pitch. Baraket had picked up an extension; he was elated by what Balmain was saying.

"I made a reservation last night at Tour d'Argent. I gave her a midnight-blue silk suit to wear, one with a pale-pink chiffon blouse and a pink felt hat with a marvelous brim that turns back off her face. When she was ready she walked downstairs into the little lobby of the Bellman and *I* couldn't believe my eyes. I almost fainted. She has elegance, which I did not know when I first saw her, but she also has mystery—which I did know—and which is far more important. The combination is irresistible. When we arrived at the Tour, we hadn't walked two steps from the elevator to our table by the window before Claude was there. You know that Claude Terrail is one of the greatest judges of beautiful women in the world. I had fun teasing him. I said, 'Alia, this is Claude Terrail, the owner of Tour d'Argent,' and she gave him a look that almost felled him."

Baraket stirred, a bit uncomfortably, and Kenneth was amused. Jealousy already? Kenneth had never seen it in Baraket before. Baraket had never felt it before.

Pierre went on.

"She wasn't flirting; it's just the way she looks. I made it clear to Claude that he was not to join us; he was to go away, and he was not happy with me at all. Everyone watched us all through dinner. She has *it*, whatever it is. Claude sent her the biggest bunch of flowers this morning that even I have ever seen, and he's getting very angry because no one can tell him about her except me, and I won't!"

"Pierre, stop!" Kenneth said. "We'll be there late this afternoon."

"All right. I'm going to make a reservation at Grand Vefour for tonight. Alia and I will meet you there at nine-thirty. I want to set this scene properly; I want to present her to you."

"Baraket hasn't seen her for a month, Pierre."

"That's all right, he can take her home," Balmain said. "Right?"

When Pierre came to pick Alia up at the Bellman, he was amazed at her tranquillity. Here was a girl who, a month before, had wondered for days over something as simple as a pair of nylon stockings, a girl who had captured the love of a man more fabulous than any emperor, any king, and who was going to see him again this very night for the first time in a month. She must be excited, he thought, but she certainly isn't showing it. Then it came to him. She is excited, of course, and all her future is involved in this meeting, but she is controlling herself, taking advantage of all she's learned.

Baraket fell in love with a simple, unformed creature who now has another role to play. He wanted to change her, give her everything, and now she has changed. She's not the same and she never will be. She is a new Alia, she is Princess Alia now.

Balmain was right. Alia was longing to see Baraket but even more desirous of his seeing her. She knew her own beauty now. She had been taught it, every hour of the day for thirty days. She knew about her face and her hair, her hands and ankles, her walk and the way she held her head. She had studied herself from every possible angle in every available mirror. She knew exactly how she looked, and all that mattered to her now was how she looked to Baraket.

She chose a blue-gray crepe dinner dress, the simplest one of all the dresses Pierre had made for her, and a perfect dress for dinner in Paris. It had a low, square neckline and a stiff moiré belt tied with a flat bow. It was a new length for Paris, part of the new look that was causing all sorts of rumbles in fashion. Her shoes were suede pumps in a deeper shade of blue-gray. She arranged her dark hair into a shining French knot at the nape of her neck. She wore no jewels, but the blue-gray of her dress brought out the translucent ivory of her skin and she needed none. At the last minute, she wrapped a long, skinny roll of honey-colored sable over one arm.

"Aha!" said Balmain. "If it's possible for you to be more beautiful than last night . . ."

Baraket and Kenneth were waiting at the tiny bar when Alia and Pierre walked in. Baraket's eyes met hers and he looked slowly at her as she walked toward him, taking in every detail. She never looked at Kenneth, and she was not aware of Balmain at her side. She saw only Baraket.

He held out both of his arms, not for her to come into, but in exclamation. Then he took her gloved hand and kissed it, feeling for one second on the inside of her arm the skin above her elbow, never taking his eyes from hers.

"Good evening, Princess Alia," he said.

"Good evening, Your Highness," Alia said, as the maître d'hôtel led them to their table through a labyrinth of eyes that all turned, as if by magic, toward the glorious magnet of Alia.

NEW YORK
June 1954

Delphine was right about Ryan. No one could fight him when he wanted something. He wanted Delphine; he loved her in his way, and he had no intention of giving her up, losing her.

Their lovemaking had taken on a new intensity. After the terrible scene when she'd found out about the women she shared him with, horrible words that they were, it had been more exciting than ever, a fusion that left them exhausted and more desirous of each other at the same time. She closed her mind to the thought of him with someone else when she was away from him, but when they were in bed she did think about it. How could she compare herself with any other woman? How could she compare Ryan to any other man? There never had been any other man. Occasionally she would feel an uncontrollable anger and she would lash out at anything around her, breaking an ashtray or throwing a glass. She'd never behaved like that before and she was ashamed of herself when she did it. But what was love? Was it one man and one woman, or was it one long game that everyone cheated at? Or did anyone really want it, want to be in love, ever? It only hurt, and everyone seemed to get hurt.

Delphine had no idea of what was going on in Ryan's mind. He'd been quiet for days, but she chalked it up to the complicated arrangements being made for the production in Mexico. Then, lying in bed in her apartment, he asked her to marry him.

"Marry you!" Delphine said, sitting up. Everything she wanted was in his line. She wanted to marry him; she wanted to love him for her entire life. There was no other man for her. Now he had asked her.

"Why?" she asked. "Why now?"

"Because I love you. I told you there was no one like you for me. You're the only woman I cannot do without. Just say yes and then we'll go to sleep."

Delphine buried her head in the sanctuary of his shoulder. She stretched her long body out along the length of his, breasts against him, arms around him, thighs entangled with his.

"I can't," she said, surprised at herself.

"You can. And you will. You must. I have never asked anyone to marry me."

"No," she said. "I can't."

What did she mean she couldn't? He couldn't be hearing right; Delphine never said anything that was untrue. The lightest of social platitudes rang with sincerity when she voiced them. He held her close, fondling her hair. She didn't mean it.

It was a still night. The park beneath them was a dark blur. Ryan disentangled himself and got out of bed, pulling on his black silk robe. He lit a cigarette, then crossed back to the bed and turned on the lamp beside her. She was lying on her side, as he had left her.

"Why not?"

She sat up in bed, crossing her legs like a beautiful Buddha, pulling the covers up around her. Her face was clear, the face of an honest child.

"I can only tell you once. I can't fight you, Ryan, and I don't want to go over and over it, negotiating with you. I know how good you are."

"Tell me," he said, not looking at her.

"We're not for each other; you know that better than I do. I've got too much money and you don't need money; you don't even want it. Even if I were poor, I wouldn't marry you. The last thing you need is a wife. It would destroy us."

He lit another cigarette and sat down in one of the armchairs, putting his slippered feet up on the ottoman.

"Are you punishing me?"

"No. I haven't mentioned women, have I? I came back to you, didn't I? At first I hated you and I hated me, but because I do love you I came back. But I've been thinking about us since then."

She paused.

"What is it? Say it."

"Two things. You need yourself and the women that go with you. And all my money complicates it even more. No, not us. You'd hate it even more than I would, cheating on me. I don't want to lose you. You thrill me; you've taught me love. It's not the end of us; it's just the end of now."

"Then you're not coming to Mexico?"

"No."

"There's still more. Say it."

"I can't live on a double standard. You can't live off one. It's not your fault, it's the way you are. I want a man who needs me, only me, and a man who needs and understands all this money. It would drive you to drink and leave me. That's all. We've been perfect together; you made us perfect. Nothing can take that away."

He came back to the bed and held her face in his hands and kissed her softly on the lips.

"You're so smart," he said gently, kissing her once more. "If only you weren't so smart."

He went to the closet and pulled on his trousers, tying his tie over the creamy silk of his shirt. He put on his watch and picked up the soft leather wallet and the money clip with the crisp bills in it. He put his jacket over his shoulders and, without looking at her, he opened the door into the living room and closed it softly behind him. She heard the door to the hall click shut, and she knew he was gone.

She pushed the pillows into a snowy nest of percale and curled up in her bed. His warm scent was still in the room. She thought about him walking down the street, letting himself into his apartment only a few short blocks away from her. I loved him, she thought, and he loved me.

The thought was sitting right there, waiting for her, waiting to be allowed to enter her mind. She refused it, the thought that Ryan would not stay alone tonight or any other night. She faced it. Ryan O'Roark would never spend a night alone.

NEW YORK

June 1954

"Blanquette de veau and a bottle of Puligny-Montrachet?" George asked, wanting to order quickly and get to the business at hand. He had waited for Delphine to come to him, knowing she would when she was ready.

"Lovely," Delphine said. "And some fraises des bois after." They were seated in the first banquette at La Côte Basque under the watchful eye—but never the ear—of Paul, one of New York's finest maîtres d'hôtel. Delphine took a gold mesh compact and a lace-edged handkerchief out of her handbag and put them down on the table.

"What's all that for?" George asked, admiring the perfection of her beige wool Trigère suit. The blouse was quail-printed silk with a soft bow at the neck. Her earrings were jade set in gold and diamonds, and her ring was an exquisite piece of carved jade.

"In case I cry." She looked at him directly and he saw that she had a tight rein on herself. It was not like Delphine to be that way.

"Uh-oh," George said, taking her hand. "Are we in the right place? Would you rather wait until after lunch and we'll walk in the park?"

"No," Delphine said. "This is perfect. I don't want to cry and Paul would never forgive me if I did, so I have a good chance of controlling myself."

"All right, then let's get right to it. It's you and Ryan, right?"

"He's sleeping with three women. I'm one of them."

For once George Sherril was taken completely by surprise. The sommelier poured the obligatory wine in his glass. George tasted it and approved, an absentminded look on his face. When Delphine's glass had been filled, she tipped it to him and he looked at her steadily for a few seconds, saying nothing. She could almost hear the wheels turning in his head. Finally he sighed and there was such a sad look on his face that she reached for her handkerchief.

"Don't," George said. "We'll work this out. I sure can pick 'em, can't I?" The lightness of his tone belied the anger in his eyes.

"And last night he asked me to marry him."

"Well?"

"I am not going to. But I don't know what *is* going to happen. I'm so in love with him; it's so strong for both of us that I know I have to just live through it. I never really wanted anything like this. Too much emotion scares me to death."

"Never mind," George said, an odd expression around his eyes that Delphine hadn't seen before. "Everyone should share it, once in their lives, whether they want it or not. It teaches us all. Wouldn't it be awful if only one of you felt the way you do? Especially if that one was you? You know, and I know, that Ryan cares deeply for you in his way."

"But it's pretty awful right now."

"How did you find out?"

"Accidentally, damn it. One of the ladies, Lisabeth Green, is an old friend of Ryan's. I might have been able to understand that after a while, but the second one, just a few days ago, was a one-night stand and I really came apart on that. He knows I know about Lisabeth but not the other." She shifted uneasily on the banquette. What could she expect George to do? It was so embarrassing. She felt a tiny flash of anger somewhere deep inside. "George, it's boring for you, listening to all this, but I need you so. I don't know what to do."

"It's not boring. This is the only time we are ever going to have to speak about it, sitting right here at this table, and never again. We're going to settle some things this afternoon. You know I wanted you to have everything when you came to New York. I hate the fact that your first lover, the first love affair of your life, is breaking your heart. I thought it would all end up with orange blossoms and ridiculous amounts of useless silver. But I'll say one thing. You may be learning an invaluable lesson."

"What?" Delphine leaned back. The tension she had felt in the beginning of the conversation was lessening.

"It's not all peaches and cream, life. You ostensibly have everything. Girls who have everything, including money such as yours, frequently wind up with lines in their faces at forty and several husbands too many. You're not cut from that cloth, so a little bit of heartbreak may strengthen your resolve. Besides, Ryan's Irish."

"What?" Delphine asked again. What did the fact that Ryan was Irish have to do with anything? She was lost.

"Thank God for the sweetness and friendship that they're capable of giving, and the charm and beauty they possess, because they take everything else. Somewhere in the galaxy of humanity, some peer group must have given the Irish a very hard time. All these eons later they're still trying to get back, to retaliate."

"He spoke softly but Delphine was astonished by the intensity of his tone. She knew that he was furious with Ryan and with himself, all because of her. Why had she bothered him with all this? Anger in George was rare, real anger.

Delphine found the courage, since they were this deep in it, to ask the questions she had been afraid would send her into a pool of self-pity.

"Why couldn't I have had him to myself for just one day, or one week or one whole month? Or why did I ever have to learn that he was cheating on me all along? That's what's making it hell for me. I can't cope with questions I can't answer." The tears were there, unshed but dangerously close to the surface.

George touched her cheek gently. "Oh, darling, we're being too serious about a man we both admire—one that we try to understand only on our own terms, not his. Ryan is a man of constant, intense sexual commitments. He makes them every day; he carries them out, and there is no woman in the world he cares enough about to feel a real passion for—the one next door or across the street twenty minutes later. I thought you both had met your match in each other. Should have known better. Delphine, the women he'll remember are the smart ones, the ladies who catch on to him fast and leave him faster. He'll remember you for infinite reasons because I know he's as much in love with you as he could be with anyone besides himself. And, to his credit, he's not interested in your money. I hope you left him laughing—no weeping or his facing you at the wrong end of a shotgun barrel?"

"The last thing he said to me was, 'You're so smart. If only you weren't so smart.' We weren't laughing; we were very close, but he knows it's over." She felt some spirit coming back, some strength. The lesson was learned; the past was past. There was a gleaming pinpoint of light in her eyes. "Now what do I do?"

"Money is the answer. Your money. You're somewhat of a mystery lady now; the world doesn't know yet that you're the possessor of one of the world's largest fortunes. Wait till the press catches on to you. It's a wonder some bright society columnist hasn't found you out after the lectures on the jades. Right now you're a beautiful unknown girl from a rich family in Honolulu. 'Munro?' they say. 'Who are the Munros?' Nobody knows yet but it won't stay quiet forever, and inevitably you will have a huge responsibility to that money. You and it have to go to work for each other.

"Look how I live my life. All three of my wives found out after they married me how rich I was. Do you think any of them was interested in helping me administer this money power invested in me through inheritance and a certain business skill? Hell no, all they wanted to do was to spend it on themselves."

Delphine found herself smiling. George always referred to his three wives in a lump. They'd never had names. Had one or all of them hurt him, made him feel the way she felt now?

"I don't know anyone who does nothing as well as I do, and I know how deceptively easy it looks. Everybody thinks I'm a sort of social layabout, entertaining at my two houses or on my yacht and doing nothing else. Everybody but the men on the boards I make to administer my money. I don't go on the boards; I make them. And I shoot the moon every day of my life to avoid fools, to find *my* peer group.

"You're walking into that world now. I've known you all your life, and you're not going to be any self-serving Barbara Hutton or Brenda Frazier. Your mind is ticking quietly away, saying over and over, 'What am I going to do with all this money? What am I going to do with all this money?' You'll find the way, and I'll help you. It takes moral stamina, common sense and discipline. You've got 'em all and your salad days are over."

He looked at her carefully. She was calm now.

"Besides, you had a marvelous time with Ryan and you learned a lot about love. An Irishman making love is like a horse breeding. The stallion rarely knows the name of the mare he's covering."

"Hmph," Delphine said. "I don't want to get a social disease from someone I've never met."

George burst out laughing. "Delphine, if you can say that, I'm not worried about your recovery."

"If I can hang on to the thought that my head is more important than my heart—"

"But it's not," George said. "I have the line you need. Sainte-Beuve said it for you. 'Love the man who offers you his entire heart.' That's what you are looking for. Delphine, are you sure that you won't go to Mexico with Ryan, that this is not just a lovers' quarrel that will be made up five minutes from now? You did say you didn't know what might happen."

Delphine looked at him, vulnerable again, eyes filled with tears.

"I'd give anything if we could make it up. George, it's over." He could barely hear her.

The fraises des bois came. "My God," George said, "did we eat the blanquette de veau? We must have. I'd hate to have missed it. Now we'll have a glass of champagne to celebrate."

"Celebrate!"

"Yes. I was the powerful influence who made you come to New York, but not to leave you here with a broken heart. I have a better plan. You know I wanted you both to come on *Ehukai* this summer, but I didn't press it since Ryan couldn't go. Now that's all changed. You are coming, and we are going to have quite a trip. Delphine, I know you know that Camilla and Jeremy were married last week in London, but Jeremy called this morning. They can go with us, so we'll have the honeymooners."

"Oh, George, how marvelous." Ryan's face was there before her. Would it ever fade?

"And now, there are two others coming. You don't know Kenneth Bennett, a lifelong friend of mine and a prince of a man. He's with the World Bank in Istanbul and London. He's bringing a surprise package."

"Who?" Delphine asked, intrigued.

"A Turkish princess. I haven't met her. She's been in Paris for a month, apparently on a shopping spree before her marriage in Istanbul in August. We are going to deliver her by yacht for her own wedding. The man she is marrying is an astonishing figure. I know him slightly, and I'm really doing this for Kenneth. They were classmates at Harvard, a few years before me."

"Who is he?"

"His name is Baraket; otherwise it's a full four paragraphs of Egyptian names and titles that all add up to an international fortune, quiet, and most of the cotton and rice in Egypt and Turkey. Baraket's mother has tried to marry him off a dozen or more times, but she had nothing to do with this alliance and I understand that she is livid about it. In that part of the world, when they are livid they are dangerous. Kenneth feels that the princess—Alia is her name—will be safe with us on the high seas, arriving only two days before her wedding. Nice cast, huh?"

"Fabulous. I'm dazzled."

"So you'll come?"

Delphine nodded, eyes bright again.

"In that case I have a little present for you. One of these is for you." He handed her a thick envelope. She opened it. There were two tickets on the *Île de France*, sailing in five days' time. She was in the Rambouillet Suite, George in the Senlis. She looked at him, a little unnerved.

"Oh, George, did you know all along about Ryan?"

"No," George said firmly. "I did not, I promise. I got the ticket just in case. Wishful thinking."

Delphine sighed, a deep sigh. Ryan, my dearest, we are going in opposite directions.

"What would I do without you?" He took her hand. "Never mind. You were right—what you said a minute ago. Your heart is not as important as your head. A summer in Europe will mend your broken heart. You're a big girl now. You always were."

Delphine left La Côte Basque before George, late for an appointment, her head full of the coming trip. He sat, waiting for the check, musing for a minute. Why did love always have to hurt? He had long ago buried the memories of his three marriages, without regret. Christiane, the French girl in Tahiti with the incestuous stepfather. Six months after he had married her, he found that she and her stepfather knew almost as much about Sherril money as he did and that they had set him up. That hurt. Alicia, his second wife, was a beautiful Navy widow. Again, he'd tried to assuage someone else's hurt with the best of intentions. At least Alicia had helped him build the Ehukai house in Hawaii. When they parted, George had kept it. The property had belonged to George's family for years. Then Dorothy. When he had set about restoring Ehukai Farm on Long Island, Dorothy had been his decorator. This time he didn't feel sorry for his intended. She was as beautiful as the others, and she shared George's taste and love of beautiful things. He had been happy with Dorothy until he had become intensely aware of her inordinate interest in other men. George had resorted to a private detective, hating himself for it, and soon after, to a lawyer. He had been generous with all three of his wives.

The summer of his third divorce, George had a long talk with himself. He was not a sexually driven man. There was more to life than that. No more wives; he wanted friends. He knew how he wanted to live and he could afford to. He had two exquisite houses and a perfect yacht. It was enough.

George and Delphine sailed on the *Île de France* the following Wednesday at midnight. Delphine's suite was filled to overflowing with white peonies. There were only a few words on the card. "Someday," Ryan had written, "you'll come back."

FRANCE

June 1954

On the flight from Paris to Nice the next day, Alia turned to Kenneth.

"How will I know how to behave? I've never met anyone like your friends. I won't know how to talk to them, what to say. I'll be lost without Baraket. I'm always being parted from him . . ."

There were blue circles under her dark eyes. "You haven't been parted from him for long now," Kenneth said gently, taking her hand. Baraket hadn't wanted to let her go, nor had she wanted to leave him.

"Alia," Kenneth said, "listen to me. These are a few very close friends of mine—nice, well-mannered—and they know nothing about you, any more than you know about them. You come from an unknown world to them, so you can't make a mistake. If they ask you about your family, tell them you were born in a small town and that your parents are very simple people. You won't be lying, but they won't believe you since you are a princess; they will imagine that you have a grand palace or two somewhere. If something bothers you, say nothing. Silence is so rarely used; everyone seems to think they have to *say* something. That's what gets us all in a lot of trouble!"

Alia sighed. "You have been so good to me, Kenneth. Pierre was so good to me. Do you know that I have never really known anyone in my whole life? Four men and no women. Tarek, of course. Then Baraket, and now you and Pierre. And I've spent more time with you two than I have with Baraket." When she said Tarek's name, a sad look crossed her face and Kenneth realized that she missed him, too. He was the one who had been her constant protector and companion; now he had returned to Istanbul with Baraket. Kenneth spoke to her in Turkish, for reassurance.

"The man you will learn to love on this trip is your host, George Sherril. He is the owner of the yacht; he adores women and he is a wonderful friend to a woman. And think, Alia, you will be meeting two others, your first girl friends. I haven't met Delphine Munro yet either, but I have heard a great deal about her from George, who is like her older brother. The other is Camilla Stuart, now Kilmuir, a beautiful English girl who has just married Jeremy Kilmuir, who has one of the largest fortunes in England. I find her bright, and nice, too."

"I can't imagine what it will be like to have a woman as my friend."

"It will be fine, as long as you are in the big leagues." Alia looked puzzled at the expression, so Kenneth explained what he meant to her in Turkish. "Women of quality, ladies. And that's another thing that will help. Your English is excellent now, and we will all be speaking in English. If something confuses you, ask me in Turkish. It's forgivable and acceptable between you and me, and it will put you at ease if you need help."

"Oh, Kenneth," she said, linking her arm in his like a little girl. "I don't even know what a yacht looks like. The biggest boats I've ever seen are the small fishing boats in Trebizond. I will make all sorts of mistakes."

"And when you do they will be charming. Alia, look at me and listen. A month ago you had never seen an emerald either, or created a furor by just walking into a restaurant as you did last night! You will be fine, and you must not worry."

Alia smiled. "How lucky I am," she said softly in Turkish.

"Yes," Kenneth said. "You are, and I know how hard you have worked in the last month. It shows. Now, fasten your seat belt; we're landing."

THE MED

June 1954

Reilly, the chief steward of *Ehukai III*, was waiting outside immigration at the Nice Airport when Delphine and George arrived. He was a huge giant of an Irishman who had been in George's employ for almost five years, coming to him when he had been mustered out of the British Navy at the end of the war. Baggage was dispersed in a smaller car. As Reilly chauffeured the big beige-and-white convertible Rolls-Royce along the jagged coast road, he filled George in on conditions aboard *Ehukai III*, what special provisions had been put aboard for their cruise and the latest gossip of the harbor.

"We have the berth at the end of the pool dock, sir, siding up to the palace. John Mill's *Milamba IV* is lying alongside us, and he would like you to bring your guests aboard for cocktails this evening. The long-range weather forecast is good to better. Mr. Bennett arrived earlier today with Princess Alia; he's waiting for you, and I've sent Rob back to the airport to pick up Lord and Lady Kilmuir. Will you be having a late lunch, sir?"

"No, Reilly, but we will have tea. Ah, now look, Delphine." As they drove into the port Delphine could see immediately why Monte Carlo was such a famous harbor. It was an amphitheater, really, a perfect showplace for great yachts. The palace towered above it on one side, and turn-of-the-century villas and the graceful old Hermitage Hotel overlooked it from the other. It was still too early in the season for the Greek yachts to be in, but the English were there in full force. *Shemara*, Lord Docker's pride and joy; *Malahne*, the toy of American film producer Sam Spiegel; *Lady Anne* and her sister ship, *Sarinette*—all lay peacefully in their berths.

At first glance Delphine saw that George had again proved himself a paragon of taste. *Ehukai III* was two hundred feet long with a clipper bow that gave her the look of a long and graceful swordfish. Her coats of white paint were so shiny that she seemed to have been dipped and redipped in white nail lacquer. She cruised at eighteen knots and carried a crew of twenty, most of whom were British. Another of George's pecadilloes, as far as other yachtsmen were concerned, was to have girls in his crew. Mademoiselle, the young French *femme-de-chambre*, was young and immaculately trained as a lady's maid, and two marvelous-looking English girls served as hairdresser and maid. One of them was married to the chief engineer and the other to Reilly. "Nothing's fun without women," George said. "Why should my yacht be an exception?"

Kenneth Bennett was waiting on deck to greet them when they boarded. Delphine saw a tall man, a little over six feet, with sandy hair and the bright blue eyes sometimes referred to as sailor's eyes. He fit the description George had given of him: Kenneth Bennett was a man who could cool off an explosive situation or heat up a cold one. "He should have been an ambassador," George had told her. "But he's too much of a humanitarian to be confined."

"Kenneth!" George said. "What a bad host I am not to be here to greet you. I want you to meet—may I present Delphine Munro. Now, let's catch up. Is everything all right with your Princess Alia?"

"George, this trip will be a lifesaver for her. We flew down from Paris this morning, having had two very tiring nights there. Baraket left us at the airport on his way to Istanbul. Alia has asked to be excused tonight if it's all right with you. She is dead tired and I think it best if we keep her under wraps, don't you?"

Reilly appeared. "Mr. Sherril, Lord and Lady Kilmuir have arrived, coming aboard now, sir."

"Ah, good," George said. "Bring them here, Reilly, and have Mademoiselle unpack for Lady Kilmuir." Camilla burst through the door to the salon and flung her arms around first George and then Delphine.

"What a fabulous trip! Oh, Delphine, I am ecstatic that you're here. You must meet Jeremy. George, you do it."

Delphine was fascinated with Camilla's blond beauty. She's much prettier this way, she thought. She was curious to meet the man she had advised Camilla to marry. Jeremy Kilmuir was tall and dark but not handsome. His features somehow didn't seem to come together; his brow was too broad, indicating early baldness, and his nose was large. He could stand a good haircut, too, Delphine thought. She saw the shyness in his expression, and a nervous quality to the way he fiddled his hands. Delphine was surprised to find him seemingly lacking in sex appeal. Maybe I don't understand English men. Ten days from now, I'm going to know this man much better, she thought.

Ehukai III lay calmly in her berth, the blue-green water of the port slap-slapping against her hull. Reilly was serving tea on the afterdeck.

"Kenneth, you are the only one of us who knows the bride-to-be," George said. "I think you should tell us about her. Everything!"

Kenneth laughed. "Wait until you see her. She looks like a lady who was once rolled out of a rug in order to intrigue a Caesar. Don't be fooled by her looks, though; she is a very gentle girl, and quiet, not used to the sophisticated hullabaloo of yachts and all that."

"Good Lord," Delphine said. "I hope she is as low key as you say. How long has she been in Paris?"

"For almost five weeks," Kenneth said. "With Pierre Balmain, who has made her trousseau. Baraket went off to Istanbul this morning with five other trunks. Alia only has ten suitcases aboard with her, you'll be happy to hear."

"Now I know that I've brought all the wrong clothes!" Camilla said. "I always do."

"I wouldn't be as concerned with the clothes as I would with the jewels," Jeremy remarked. "Kenneth, as I understand it, there is a fantastic collection of emeralds?"

Kenneth looked around, almost furtively.

"If I lower my voice from time to time, even when we're at sea, it's because of those emeralds. Right you are, Jeremy, Baraket's emerald collection is the—well, let's put it this way: they fill an entire room."

"My God," George said. "They're not on my yacht, are they?"

"Only one," Kenneth replied. "That I have seen, that is," teasing George. "The rest are probably locked away in Saadit Sarai, Baraket's palace in Istanbul—one would assume. No, George, you don't have to worry."

"What about the one? Is it on her finger?"

Kenneth savored the moment. They would all enjoy this. "No," he said, "it's not. On the plane Alia asked me if I had seen Baraket's farewell present to her. Naturally, he had to give her a special present. After all, the next time they see each other will be the night before the wedding. I said no. She fished around in her bag—you know, one of those deep bags that the girls carry. 'Look,' she said, and handed me a rock the size of my fist. I have to tell you that I lost my so-called cool. 'It's a paperweight,' she said. It's a paperweight, all right, one that weighs about two hundred carats." Kenneth paused, letting it sink in. "It really isn't fair for me to describe her; tomorrow you'll see for yourselves what a simple, lovely girl she is."

George was called to the telephone, and when he came back, he told them about the plans for the evening.

"Camilla and Jeremy and Kenneth have all been in Monte Carlo before, Delphine, but you and Alia have not. I'm sorry she can't go with us, but there will be other times. And since I've made myself responsible for your European education, I've arranged for us to dine on the terrace of the Hôtel de Paris. I want you and Cam to dress simply, perhaps a white linen dress or a red checked cotton one."

"I can provide the white linen," Camilla said.

"I know," said George. "And Delphine will wear her red checked Norell. I saw both of them in the pressing room after Mademoiselle unpacked for you. Deceptively simple girls in simple dresses."

"George is orchestrating," Kenneth said to Jeremy. "We all know that Friday is Gala Night. All the old girls turn up in the bar at the hotel corseted in sequins and larded with diamonds. So George wants his simple beauties to put them to shame. After a *succès fou* in the bar, he's reserved the corner table on the terrace for dinner where no one can miss us."

"Thank God Princess Alia is staying aboard. One paperweight-sized emerald and we'd never get out of the port alive," Jeremy said.

"I'm still dying to see it," Cam said. "Delphine, you and I should dress. You know, no one comes to Monte Carlo without proceeding as quickly as possible to the bar of the Hôtel de Paris. The old duchesses and countesses, viscounts and dukes, who have lived in Monte Carlo forever, appear each Friday night. Everyone knows that if they don't appear they have died between galas."

"Lots of old people only?" Delphine asked.

"It's still too early in the season for the young to have arrived," Camilla went on. "With the exception of Grand Prix weekend the end of May, the *jeunesse d'or* rarely appear before mid-July."

It was quiet when they arrived in the great high-ceilinged room to the left of the entrance to the hotel. The green walls were a subtle yet insistent reminder of nearby green felt-covered tables where croupiers waited to lure you into breaking the bank, or at least having a shot at it. French doors with etched-glass panes opened to the darkening blue of the Mediterranean and a glimpse of one small sailboat beating it back into port before nightfall. The bar made a perfect backdrop for the tall, elegant American girl and the blond English beauty, as well as their handsome escorts.

Delphine took in the setting with delight.

"The contrasts are wild. That chandelier hanging over our heads must weigh three tons and have cost as much, but these silly bamboo chairs we're sitting on are in every cheap café in the port."

"Wait until you see the human contrasts. That's why I've got us seated dead center here," George said. "In half an hour we'll be fainting from an overdose of Joy or Shalimar, surrounded by overdressed dowagers. I will be demanding *l'addition*, but it's still a sight you must see."

"Old fools," Jeremy said. "They remind me of my father. They only know one way of life. They're archaic; part of a world long gone that will die forever when they do."

The steady Friday-evening parade had begun. Without exception, the women were accompanied either by monocled and titled octogenarians of their own ilk, or by young gigolos.

"It's an old bunch tonight," Kenneth said. "In full season, this bar is filled with the most exciting, the most notorious and some of the most beautiful creatures you will ever see. Even so, I find something refreshing about Monte Carlo. Maybe it's all my years in the simmering exotica of the Middle East; it's so clean here. White sails on the blue sea."

"And a hundred million dollars' worth of yachts in the harbor," George said. "Come now, let's go to our table and discuss the simplicity of the menu."

As she rose, Delphine felt Kenneth's hand on her arm, helping her. He is a terribly attractive man, she thought, with such kind eyes. When he touched her, Ryan's face was suddenly in her mind, and she made a small gesture of withdrawal from Kenneth's light touch on her arm. He felt it, sensed it instantly; years of diplomatic language had taught him touch as well as word. Kenneth simply increased his hold on her arm in a reassuring way and steered her toward their table. His manner was perfectly correct.

As they walked through the lobby toward the terrace, George spied a beautiful young girl coming up the steps. She was with a man who was older than she, but who cut a dapper figure. George, of course, knew them.

"Ceil!" he said, going over to them. "And Guy. What luck to run into you! I haven't seen you since before you were married—last year in Paris. Can you come and join us? We're just going to the terrace for dinner."

The others watched as Ceil threw her arms around George, then Guy Marais repeated her gesture, kissing George on both cheeks in the European style.

"Pretty girl," Delphine said, as George led them toward the group.

"Pretty!" Jeremy said. "She's not pretty, she's a dream. That's Ceil Chambers. I've seen that one film that made her famous—*L'Ange Noir*—and I'm sure that's her husband with her."

George wasted no time making the introductions.

"Happily, Ceil and Guy Marais, dear friends of mine, can join us for dinner. This is Delphine Munro, then Lord and Lady Kilmuir, that's Camilla and Jeremy, and Kenneth Bennett." Before he had finished the introductions, the maître d'hôtel had added two more places to their table.

Ceil was wearing a blue cotton dress, off the shoulders, gathered. Her hair was ash blond and short, and the dress was the same almost Wedgwood blue as her eyes. Her features were exquisite, very pale, and she was very quiet. Guy, on the other hand, was an ebullient man, full of enthusiasm about the film being made, starring Ceil, an original screenplay he had written from one of his own stories. Guy Marais was Bulgarian born, with a French father, long dead, and a great beauty for a mother who had brought him up in Monte Carlo. He was extremely famous in France but practically unheard of in America. His books were too European, full of battles he had fought in various armies he had joined, and the recent themes were all drawn from his love affair with Ceil. He sat beside her at the table, holding her hand whenever possible. Ceil hardly spoke, nor did anyone but Guy and George and Kenneth.

Over coffee Guy apologized to the ladies.

"I can't help it. This flurry of success has made an entrepreneur of me. Here I am, a man with a fine reputation as a writer in France, a country that makes legendary figures of their authors but rarely pays them. Ceil tells me that we should go to America; your writers are more financially secure. We can talk about that another time. George, you have *Ehukai* here, no doubt. I should have looked in the harbor, but it's early for you to be here."

"Alas," George said. "We are leaving tomorrow. I'm taking *Ehukai* out to Istanbul for Baraket's wedding. Ceil, you know Baraket, I believe?"

Ceil's eyes were even more subdued than before.

"Yes," she said. "I know Baraket quite well from the days in Paris, before I met Guy. Guy knows him, too."

"Baraket's admiration for Ceil is how I met her," Guy said, holding her hand once again. "If he hadn't left Paris, I would never have had a chance with her."

Delphine and Camilla exchanged glances, waiting to see if George was going to mention Alia, that she was with them, but he did not.

"Who is he marrying?" Ceil asked.

"As he would," George said, "a beautiful Turkish princess

that he found in Istanbul. Princess Alia is her name. He would marry from his own world, you know."

"Of course," Ceil said. "Baraket is a predictable man in some ways." She turned to Guy. "My call is for six in the morning, Guy; we must go. George, are you coming back to Monte Carlo? We'll be working here for another month at least."

"Even I will have had enough of *Ehukai* after the trip out to Istanbul, Ceil. We will fly back from there, to Paris," George said. "I'm glad we've had a chance to see you." Guy and Ceil rose to say good night, Guy kissing Delphine's and Camilla's hands. When they had gone, Cam and Delphine turned immediately to George.

"Tell," Camilla said. "I smell a romance. It's a good thing Alia didn't come with us."

"It wouldn't really have mattered. Baraket is certainly famous for his liaisons with beautiful women," George said. "And it was well documented that Ceil was one of them. She arrived out of the blue in Paris from nowhere in America and got a job modeling for Dior. In one week, every man in Paris was after her. Then she made that cult film, *L'Ange Noir*, that had such a huge success, and Baraket was seen everywhere with her. She is shy, as you can see; he likes quiet ladies, but I'm glad Ceil has married Guy. He worships her and he can stabilize her. It's a lot of fame, fast. He'll be good for her."

"I'd be good for her. Baraket isn't the only one who loves those quiet beauties," Jeremy said cheerfully.

"Oh, shut up," Camilla said, giving him an affectionate look. "I'm glad she's not coming with us."

"Good God," George said. "With Alia aboard. What a thought."

Delphine looked around her at the low lights on the tables, the dramatic white light on the Winter Casino across the street from them, and changed the subject.

"Is all of the South of France as beautiful as Monte Carlo?"

"Even more so," Cam said. "Too bad we're here for only one night."

"Savor it, my dears," George said. "We'll be out of the harbor by dawn and cruising for some uninterrupted days and nights before we reach Istanbul. Aside from one night in Capri, we'll be moving along at as fast a clip as we can. Having Mr. World Bank with us is both a blessing and a trial."

"Trial?" he said. "Trial? Blessing I understand, but trial?"

"Without him," George said to the others, "we might not have the clout to get through the Corinth Canal without waiting a day or so. The Greeks have been tough about it since the war, but Ken knows how to handle that. And without him, I would not be giving the one and only private party before the wedding of our beautiful princess and guest—and aboard my yacht, at that. Well done, Kenneth, especially since you know the entire world press is in a frenzy about this wedding. Thank God they don't know that I have Princess Alia aboard. When they hear about the party, I'm going to have to issue blowtorches to my crew to cope with the photographers alone."

Kenneth laughed. "My dear George, you are lucky to be giving only a simple, private party where, I assure you, Baraket's legions of guards can and will cope with anything. Baraket is not unaware of your reputation for unexcelled taste and had almost decided to allow you to lend him the yacht for ten days after the wedding so he and Alia could honeymoon on it in privacy. It was then that I suggested that we bring Alia with us. That way, she will be out of sight and safe until the wedding is practically a *fait accompli,* and she also will have enough of the sea. Do you realize you could have been yachtless in Istanbul?"

George looked nervously around him, nodding at the captain to bring him the check.

"By God, I am going back to my yacht. The thought of almost having *Ehukai III* confiscated in the middle of our trip exhausts me! Kenneth, you take everyone somewhere for a nightcap. I want to see that everything's all right aboard, then I'm going to bed."

"Oh no you don't," Camilla said. "Jeremy and I are going to

bed, too, as soon as we've had one little dance at the Sea Club and one little crack at the roulette wheel. Come on, George, you know you love it and you're such a marvelous dancer. Jeremy darling, why don't we all go for a few minutes?"

"Of course," Jeremy said. "Only one night in Monte, we should have a look at the casino." Delphine liked Jeremy's easygoing disposition.

Kenneth turned to Delphine. "This group loves to gamble. Do you?"

"No, not really," Delphine said.

"I have a favorite place that I like to see on the rare occasions when I'm here. It's up the Moyenne Corniche, and I think it should be part of your European education, too. Would you like to have a nightcap there?"

"Yes," said Delphine, "I'd love to."

"I'm not going up that cliff tonight," George said. "Take the car, Kenneth. Jeremy and Cam and I will drop by the roulette wheel for a moment, then walk back to the port. Mind you, we pull up anchor at six in the morning."

"George, we're not going to spend the night up there; just one glass of champagne. Delphine should see it."

Kenneth drove the big beige Rolls skillfully up the winding Corniche road. The top was down and, as they climbed more than a thousand feet above the sea, Delphine watched the coastline take shape beneath them. The night was warm; the pungent spiciness of carnations mingled with the scent of sea air. Yellow lights shone from the roads and gleamed from a few villas, and the higher they climbed, the more the lights looked like fireflies tumbling into the water.

"It's breathtaking."

"Isn't it?" Kenneth said.

"The place is a longtime favorite of mine. It was once a private villa called Château Madrid. Now it's a restaurant, which is even better, because you will see the full beauty of the South of France when you see the view from the terrace."

"Oh, Kenneth, it is kind of you to bring me here."

Getting out of the car, Delphine again caught the scent of

flowers, this time a combination of wild geranium and jasmine. They climbed a flight of smooth steps and went in and
on through a vast old rock house, coming out onto the terrace
on the other side. It seemed as if all of the Mediterranean Sea
lay twelve hundred feet beneath them. The point of Cap Ferrat was a dark hulk in the shining sea and the late full moon
had washed everything in amber and gold. Kenneth led
Delphine to the edge of the terrace. The maître d'hôtel was
delighted to see Kenneth again. A bottle of Louis Roederer
Cristal champagne appeared instantly, unordered: the maître
d'hôtel never forgot his favorite patrons' preferences.

Delphine was quiet. There was nothing to say; one had to
look.

Finally, she turned and looked at Kenneth.

"It's magic."

They sipped the icy goodness of the champagne in slender
flute glasses. A trio was playing lazy Italian love songs from
somewhere inside the old villa. Delphine was mesmerized by
the beauty around her and beneath her.

"You would never have seen it this way from below. In another ten minutes, the moon will settle its golden self down
somewhere between the hills of Africa and the coast of
France. Then we'll go."

Kenneth watched as Delphine leaned her head on her arms,
gazing out on the shimmering color that the sinking moon
gave to the sea. What a beautiful girl, he thought.

"When George said 'red checked dress,' I couldn't imagine
you sewn up in a tablecloth," he said in a light tone. "Once he
informed me that the red checks were Norman Norell's, I understood."

"You know quite a lot about dresses for a banker," Delphine said. He was so relaxed, so easy to be with.

"I've learned quite a lot about dresses lately; I've been in
Paris with Alia."

"Of course, I forgot! I loved your description of her and I
can't wait to meet her."

"Delphine, you and Alia will like each other. Camilla might

be a little unnerving for her at first. Because she is such a private, quiet girl, she will need all the friendship and help you both can give her. And this wedding is apt to be a madhouse."

"I'll do what I can, Kenneth, with pleasure. I find her fascinating."

"I don't know why we are talking about anyone else on this romantic night, and I wish we didn't have to leave. But if we go on like this, we'll miss a yacht."

In the car, Delphine linked her arm through Kenneth's. What a nice man he was, and she enjoyed being alone with him. They drove silently down the darkened road, darker now that the moon was gone, back to the port of Monte Carlo and the calm white beauty of *Ehukai III*.

THE MED

June 1954

Once the others had gone ashore and Alia had *Ehukai III*
more or less to herself, she wanted to see every inch of it.
Kenneth had told her if she needed anything to ring the bell
for either Mademoiselle or Reilly, the chief steward.

She had already inspected every inch of her own quarters.
Her cabin was a cool oasis of pale pink and yellow. The four-
poster bed was hung with striped silk and so were the dressing table and the two porthole windows. The velvety white
carpet was embroidered with wandering tendrils of yellow
and pink tropical flowers that looked so real that Alia ran a
bare foot over them to make sure they were not. Mademoiselle had unpacked for her, hanging away her new dresses in
the long row of closets, shoes lined up directly beneath them.

Her lingerie and scarves and bags—all the accoutrements of
the new princess—had been perfectly arranged in the chests
of drawers. Even her makeup and bottles were placed in perfect order in the pristine-white marble bathroom.

She rang the bell for Reilly. In two minutes he was there.

"What can I do for you, madam?"

"Reilly, would it be possible for me to see the yacht?"

"Certainly, Princess Alia. Would you like to see it now?"

"Yes, please."

Reilly took Alia from stem to stern of *Ehukai III*. By the
time they finished, she knew every nook and cranny of it. The
main salon was like a big library, full of books and good English furniture. The carpeting was emerald green and there
was a working fireplace. Alia liked the beautiful painting
above the mantel; she had no way to know that it was a
Turner landscape. The dining room was silvery blue with a
round table that could seat fourteen. Aside from those two
somewhat formal rooms, the rest of *Ehukai III* was very informal and yachtlike with a few touches of Hawaii in its decor.
The afterdeck had natural wicker furniture with brown-and-
white tapa-cloth canvas covers. Heavy silver ice buckets were
filled with masses of flowers: tall orange plumes of birds of
paradise, tuberoses, and low bowls of coral carnations everywhere. On the top deck, George had put his personal touch
on the design of the bar, which had immediately become the
heartbeat, the gathering place of *Ehukai III*, day and night.
The long, solid old-fashioned bar was presided over by Frank,
Cunard's best bartender until George wooed him away. The
light, airy room was filled with round tables, all white. The
couches and chairs were covered in blue-and-white-checked
palaka cloth. There was a small upright piano in one corner,
lacquered bright red. A wall of glass doors divided the bar
from a spacious outside deck area where there was a swimming pool. The pool was small, and on its side walls sea-blue
and green mosaic mermaids with pearls and seashells in their
hair frolicked. When a button was pushed on the side, jets
of water showered all sides of the pool.

Once Alia had seen everything, Reilly brought her some thin chicken sandwiches and a green salad on a tray in the bar, exactly what she wanted. She sat contentedly, looking at the other yachts in the harbor around them and the lights of Monte Carlo. Just as she was longing for some of her favorite Turkish coffee, Reilly appeared with a potful.

"Does *Ehukai* have everything?" Alia asked, delighted with her supper and especially with the coffee.

"Oh, yes, Princess Alia," Reilly said, with a twinkle in his eye. "All of Mr. Sherril's homes have everything. Is there anything else you would like?"

"No, thank you, Reilly. It's time I went to bed. Thank you so much."

"Pleasure, Princess," Reilly said. "Good night, then."

Unknown to Alia, but known to George and Kenneth, two of Baraket's personal bodyguards were aboard *Ehukai III*, ostensibly as members of the crew.

"There is no necessity for the others to know," Baraket had said to Kenneth in Paris the night before. "Alia has no sense of danger nor any concept of the value of anything, including the emeralds."

"It can't hurt to have them with us," George said. "I'm delighted that they're here."

Ehukai III steamed out of the harbor of Monte Carlo at dawn, all passengers sleeping soundly except Alia. The minute she heard the engines start, she jumped out of bed and pulled on a white cotton skirt with a yellow silk blouse and yellow rope-soled sandals to match. Reilly had introduced her to the captain the night before, so Alia went right to the bridge as she had been invited to do. She sat high on the butter-soft leather couch and watched as the captain maneuvered *Ehukai III* through the intricate motions that were necessary to get them safely out of the harbor with no lines fouled, no sides scraped.

Once they were at sea, Alia returned to her cabin and ordered breakfast. Just before noon, Kenneth knocked on her door.

"I hear that you have been up since dawn and that you have seen every inch of the yacht," he said, admiring the way she looked.

"Yes," Alia said happily.

"You look lovely this morning."

"Thank you. Balmain made a chart for me of my clothes; come and see. It tells me exactly what to wear, what goes with what, all the times, day and evening."

"Clever chap," Kenneth said. Clever chap indeed, he thought. "Now let's go and have some coffee. We'll be there when the others appear and it will be easier all around. Then you and I don't have to make some formal sort of entrance and be introduced, how-do-you-do, how-do-you-do, all that."

"That's good," Alia said. "But I am not the same girl as I was on the airplane yesterday."

Kenneth looked at her. It was true. The lovely girl who sat before him, wearing a yellow blouse and white skirt, with dark hair shining and shining eyes, looked as if she had been on a yacht all of her life.

Ehukai III cruised south to Capri, stopping there overnight, then carried on down through the Straits of Messina and cut across the Ionian Sea, arriving at the entrance to the Corinth Canal a few days later.

"We're going somewhere," George said, "where we have something more important to do than dawdle on a yacht. Next year, we will take this trip again and spend three times as much time; but under the circumstances Istanbul is still one hell of a distance away and if the weather goes off on us, or something unforeseen happens to *Ehukai*, we'll be chartering planes to pick us up. I hate for you to miss Corfu and one or two of the islands owned by some of my Greek friends, but Corinth is a thrill, too. Wait until you see what a feat of extraordinarily modern engineering it is, even though it was dug centuries ago."

At five the next morning they were all on deck to watch as *Ehukai III* entered the narrow passage of the Corinth Canal. The yacht inched slowly through the greenish water with no more than five feet of it on either side of her. She looked as if she were traversing the land: unless you watched ahead or behind at the slender canal itself, the yacht seemed level with the landscape. An hour later, she was freed from the thin confines of the canal and out into the open Aegean Sea. They had saved days, the days it would have taken to cruise south around the Peloponnesus of Greece. Now they were on a course that would take them past some of the Greek islands and up through the Dardanelles, into the Sea of Marmara and, finally, to Istanbul.

As the days full of nothing slipped easily by, Alia was content in the company of Delphine and Camilla. In the beginning, she only wanted to look at them, and listen to them. Delphine's lilting voice contrasted so with Camilla's English accent. They were both so pretty, at least Camilla was pretty. Delphine was the more fascinating, the more elegant, of the two. Alia had learned a little something about elegance from Balmain when he showed her pictures, like teaching a child, of ladies he had dressed, trying to explain to her what it was. Part of it was natural—the way your bones and features hung together—but part of it was cultivated; the way you took care of yourself. "Even your cuticles must be immaculate," he said. Grooming, he kept drumming into her, grooming was all. Alia saw what he meant by observing Delphine. She was perfectly groomed always, and simple, where Camilla was just slightly unkempt. Camilla's charm lay in her vivacity and roguish quality.

Delphine spoke to Alia after lunch one afternoon.

"Would you think it terribly rude of us to ask you to let us see the things that Balmain has made for you? Camilla and I are both great fans of his and everything you wear is so marvelous—well, would you mind?"

"What she means is we're green with envy and dying with curiosity," Camilla said.

"Oh, yes," Alia said, flattered that they wanted to know anything about her. "I've never worn clothes like these in Turkey. . . . I'd love for you to see them. Come, now."

Alia's cabin became the gathering place for the three of them, away from the men, where they could gossip and talk about clothes and get to know each other on a more intimate basis. This was new to each of them. Alia had never had a friend of any sort besides Tarek. Delphine had never needed one—she had grown up basking in the affection and companionship of her brother—and Camilla had always kept to herself, not wanting or needing the intrusion of feminine companionship. It was boys, and then men, who interested Camilla.

Alia's cabin provided the setting for the formation of their friendship. Camilla pawed through the closets, trying on everything, as did Delphine, berating herself for being a good head taller than Alia. They both marveled at the charts Balmain had made, Delphine making a mental note to do the same thing for herself when she got back to New York. They discussed George and the yacht, how attractive Kenneth was, and Delphine and Camilla barraged Alia with questions about Baraket. Alia obeyed Kenneth's instructions to the letter. She answered everything she could to satisfy their curiosity about Baraket and when she didn't know, she said so. When the subject of her family came up she told them that her background was entirely simple, as was normal in Turkey, and that Baraket's falling in love with her had been fate. When they asked where she met him, she retreated into silence and embarrassment.

"None of our darned business," Delphine said to Camilla. "Now stop prying. We do go on, really."

"Oops, sorry," Camilla said.

"No, no," Alia said, not wanting to be secretive or rude, although she could not tell them about her background. "It's just that my English is not good enough to say so many things so soon. Wait until you meet Baraket, he will tell you. It was very romantic."

They had so much to say to each other, and the forming of the close relationship between them all started as they chattered away in Alia's cabin. As different as their personalities and nationalities were, being together on *Ehukai III* gave them the chance to really get to know one another, to blend together, and they did.

"You lock yourselves away for hours and cut yourselves off from us," George said one evening, teasing them. "What goes on behind the locked doors?"

"Everything," Delphine said. "*Verboten* to you. George, it fascinates me. There couldn't be three more different personalities or backgrounds than ours. Do you know, until I talked to both of them, I thought everyone grew up the way I did?"

George laughed. "It's a good trip for all of us but particularly for the three of you. I think you needed each other; heaven knows Alia needed you two as her friends. Being on a yacht is like being on a desert island: we are all isolated from the outside world, practically sealed into our own small space. I know you and Kenneth so well you're both like the inside of my palm, but I'm learning about Camilla and Alia just as you are. This is not the kind of trip one just goes off and forgets."

"He's right," Camilla said when Delphine repeated the conversation to her. "I hate the thought of the trip being over. I'll look around and there will be only Jeremy. I'll miss you and Alia. It's a pretty unusual time, for all of us."

"At least we're aware of it," Delphine said. "I feel like a bridesmaid, which I've been a dozen times, but never in a wedding like this. Alia, are you having bridesmaids?"

"I don't know," Alia said. "Baraket hasn't told me. If I am, I don't know them because I have no friends in Istanbul." Camilla and Delphine looked at her, nonplussed. Again, another of the contrasts showed. Imagine not knowing if you were having bridesmaids at your own wedding. They both burst out laughing, making Alia laugh, too.

"You can have us if you want, Alia," Camilla said. "Under the circumstances, Delphine and I would make better handmaidens, don't you think?"

"I think we should get Delphine married," Alia said. "After all, you are already, I'm about to be, so Delphine has to marry soon. Is there someone, Delphine?"

"No one," Delphine said, not allowing the thought of Ryan into her head. "I'll be the spinster. You two can provide me with hordes of eligible men."

"She has one," Camilla said. "The handsomest Irishman you've ever seen in your life. If I'd known she was going to throw him away, I might not have married Jeremy." Camilla and Delphine had talked briefly about Ryan, only briefly. Camilla threw his name in now to see what Delphine would say.

"Had one," Delphine said. "No, there's no one right now. I'll keep in touch with both of you, and I'll be jealous of your living in London."

"Why don't you think about living there, too?" Camilla asked. "You don't have to live in New York, do you? Think what fun we could have, and there are hordes of attractive men, I promise you."

"Let's think about it," Delphine said, a feeling of excitement coming over her. That might be the answer. She had not faced the thought of returning to New York. Now, in the back of her mind, there was London. She would talk to George about it.

Phone calls came to the yacht daily. Balmain called several times to talk to Alia. He missed her, how was she getting along, and was she wearing the right things? He adored her and he had missed her when she left Paris. Baraket called each evening, talking first to Kenneth and George, then spending more than half an hour talking and laughing with Alia, telling her all the plans. He told her over and over how proud he was of her. "My little caterpillar is now the most beautiful of butterflies," he said to her. But it was then that, after the two nights they had spent together in Paris, when the full impact of her beauty burst upon him, he was crazy to see her, to be with her again.

There were also a thousand details of the wedding for him

to keep them informed about. The small party he had planned to give aboard *Ehukai III* had to be moved to Saadit Sarai. "Even though it's only for family and some of my very dear friends, there would be too many for the yacht." George admitted to himself that he was slightly disappointed. He loved showing off *Ehukai III*. Baraket had scheduled the wedding ceremony down to the fraction of a second. Princess Tafida, his mother, was being as troublesome as possible, but nothing serious. One day she was coming; the next she was not. If her son refused to be married in Cairo, where he belonged, where he had been born, then she could not possibly come to Istanbul, a barbaric city at best, which he obviously preferred. Imagine not receiving a future daughter-in-law she knew nothing about in her own home. Whatever was Baraket thinking about; had he no respect for her? She would not come to Istanbul and she tried to extract a promise from him to bring his bride to Egypt immediately afterward, much to Baraket's relief. Tafida had gone to great lengths, sending dozens of her spies and informers to see what they could find out about Alia, but they had discovered nothing. Tafida knew she was defeated. If her son chose to keep the background of his future wife secret—a dangerous beginning at best—then there was nothing she could do about it. Baraket had won a round. He reported her final decision to Kenneth and George with glee.

"He's plotting again, in top form," Kenneth said after one of the longer telephone conversations. "Enjoying every minute of it, too."

"You can't blame him, can you?" George said. "Baraket couldn't possibly get married without intriguing, scheming, even settling some old scores somewhere, I imagine. He's not a man who is going to have just an ordinary wedding."

"I admire the way he's been able to handle Princess Tafida. I've met her and he is a chip off the old block. It's unusual enough that there are only the two of them, where normally families like this are made up of dozens fighting among themselves. But Tafida produced only one child, and Baraket's father was dead before he was two years old. She kept the reins of their holdings in her hands, ran everything until he was grown and prepared to take on his responsibilities along with her. She's made him her life; she never left him to the care of nannies any more than she ever considered marrying again. He has been everything to her. She even arranged for his training in the art of *imsak*, and that was a break in tradition for a woman. She saw to it that he would be the best lover possible from early on."

"*Imsak*," George said. "The Arabic philosophy and technique of sex, not love?"

"Yes," Kenneth said. "In Arabic, the word literally means 'to hold,' 'to retain'—to control yourself completely in the precise arts of sex, or love, if you want to call it that. It's a normal part of training of the male infant almost from the time he is born. The wet nurse, the mother, the nanny, all the women surrounding the male child stroke him, fondle him, bring him to an awareness of physical sensation even before he begins to think. Baraket is a truly famous lover, known in some special circles for his capacity to pleasure a woman indefinitely, or women, to the extreme."

"Too bad we're not brought up that way," George said. "I might even still have my first wife." Kenneth had to laugh.

"Tafida's reputation is formidable," Kenneth continued. "Though I don't believe she is as dangerous, even murderous, as her reputation would lead one to believe. She simply considers Baraket her personal property, which is why she tries to marry him off to girls of her own choosing. If he had taken Alia to Cairo for the marriage, Tafida would have found a way to destroy it, to get rid of her. Baraket knows that, so his trump card had to be Alia's family. He's probably told her they are too secluded or too ill to make the journey. If Tafida only knew the truth!"

"Actually, I don't know anything either," George said. "Alia has never spoken a word about her family, certainly not to me. She's never talked to me about anyone but Baraket and you."

"There's a good reason for that. Now that Baraket has resolved the situation, a veil of mystery will remain around her family background. The truth is that Alia has no family; she's an orphan. Baraket has invented a family for her and, in this way, he has found a way to marry her in Istanbul. We both know the extent of his holdings in Turkey as well as Egypt; he's probably richer than all of the richest of the Turks put together."

George looked supremely content.

"What a trip! By God, I'll never be able to top this one. Here aboard *Ehukai*, I have the most talked-about newlyweds in the western world. And I have the mystery princess who is about to marry possibly the richest man in the world, whose name is even new to everyone, plus two of his bodyguards in my hold as part of my crew, who are guarding not only a body but one of the largest emeralds ever mined. Where is that thing, by the way? And then I have my favorite American heiress, Miss Delphine Munro, and you, Mr. World Bank. There will never be another trip like this one!"

"Still, we have to remember to be careful with Baraket. He loves fun and tricks and intrigue, and he's seen to it that we are aware of some of the inner workings. But, except in the most private situations, he will permit no familiarity unless he instigates it."

"He's quite right. He's more important than most Europeans even though he's only a prince. I wish I could say what a remarkable resemblance I find between Alia and her mother from this 'family' he has provided and watch his face, but I won't!" Kenneth laughed again. Things were going well.

"You know, George, at first I was concerned about Alia. She's not used to all this. But, as a result of the days we've spent quietly together, Alia has a growing confidence in herself and in her new friends. She has been alone all of her life, and Delphine and Camilla have given her something that she has never had. She's come alive in the security that you've provided her with and in making friends with two girls of her own age. The more I see of her, the more I realize her potential. When Baraket first told me that he was going to marry a girl he had known for three days, I knew that he had either gone daft or else that he had found someone he had sought for a long time. He's no fool, and she is as special as he said. Think what might happen to this orphan from an obscure background. She is not hidebound by family tradition on any side. She is extraordinarily beautiful; she is calm and apparently intelligent and, underneath it all, I think she probably has the killer instinct. I doubt if she will sit placidly by and accept this cornucopia of riches that has befallen her. She will do more than live up to her end of the bargain, develop into her own person as well as be deeply important to Baraket."

George thought about what Kenneth was saying. Cruising with Alia on *Ehukai III* where each day blended into the next, he had found the same qualities in her, and he watched as Delphine and Camilla had taken her in. They were no fools, those two.

"You're right. We have more than one interesting beauty aboard, you know, Kenneth," he said. "I find Delphine as fascinating as Alia, and certainly the opposite side of the coin. No one could have been brought up with a more privileged or conservative background than Delphine, yet she's not stuffy. I thought my interest in her was based on thinking of her as my little sister, and I wanted her exposed to more than just Hawaii. I am very much beholden to her father in a matter that goes way back, but when Delphine came to New York at my instigation, I saw that she could more than hold her own. Her instincts are correct. I wanted to be around her because the one thing that worried me for her was the size of her fortune. She's as rich as I am, and I'm probably worth almost one tenth of Baraket!" George smiled, but his face turned serious. "I don't think anything is as potentially disastrous for a woman, especially an American woman, as to be devastatingly rich. Money so often brings unhappiness, even tragedy. It always makes me happy when I read that a very rich man has married his little brown wren of a secretary, the one that has worked for him for years and knows what he's all about. The wives either die or have divorced them and, as a man gets older, he wants to be assured that if something happens to him, his wife and his money won't go down the drain the minute the first ne'er-do-well fortune hunter or playboy hoves to on the scene."

It was Kenneth's turn to smile.

"True," Kenneth said. "But what about Camilla? She's the beauty from the quite ordinary background. Neither Alia's or Delphine's. What about her?"

"Ah, now here we have the exception to all the rules. Camilla is wild, a wild and untamed girl who is going to have it her way. And she will enrage, outrage, infuriate and drive to drink, or even death, any man close to her. She's a born antagonist, and she uses sex appeal as if it were a light switch; she turns it on and off as she needs it. When she sees a man she wants, she never tries to appeal to his brains; she goes straight for his balls. She looks him right between the eyes and then right between the legs. You've seen her do it with Jeremy on this trip. She's no more in love with Jeremy than she is with you or me. Camilla may very well never be in love with anyone, not even herself. But she is the most intricate of the three and has the highest potential for disaster. She'll never hesitate to hit below the belt because she savors a challenge or a fight; she thrives on them. Winning, which means having it her way all the way and all the time, is what makes her tick. She's Camilla the Conqueror. God help Jeremy. Except, strangely enough, no matter how she drives him, and drive him she will, in the end he will have her to thank for having forced one terribly important thing on him."

"What?" Kenneth asked. George's fervor bordered on passion. He's done a lot of analyzing of the three ladies on his yacht, Kenneth thought. He's truly interested in their characters, what will happen to them, what they will become.

"His backbone," George replied. "She'll give it to him in spades. Come, let's join the others before the radio room catches up with us again."

Baraket called within the hour with an entirely new plan. Since they had changed the party from the yacht to the palace, he'd thought of an even better idea. It must be kept secret from the others, of course. He had arranged for a fast boat to rendezvous with them in the Sea of Marmara the following evening, the night before they were due to arrive in Istanbul. It must be a surprise; Alia and the others were to know nothing about it. He would return to Istanbul later that night in order to be dockside to greet his bride-to-be and his guests when they arrived.

"George," Baraket said over the radio phone, "will you arrange a party for the seven of us? It's the only intimate party we will be able to have, and I have missed being with you. You can set an extra place at the table, and when you go in to dine there I will be, the man who is late to dinner!" He did not disclose a few other small surprises he had planned; they would come later.

"Of course," George said. "What a good idea! Let the captain know exactly the point of rendezvous and I'll take care of the rest."

"By the way, George, you wouldn't want to sell the yacht, would you? Alia loves it; she's told me so much about it that I would like to give it to her as a little present. Maybe at dinner?"

"Good God, no, Baraket!" George said, almost in panic. "*Ehukai* is yours whenever you would like to use her, but she's not for sale; I could never sell her. Christ, you can have one built out here five times her size in about twenty minutes."

"No, no, no," Baraket said. "Forgive me, one never knows when someone wants to sell a yacht. I could have had Farouk's *Mahroussia;* a monstrosity. She was practically forced on me. She's too big and too old and too ugly, three things I have avoided in yachts as well as women. I only want a simple yacht, nothing over two hundred feet."

George put down the phone and repeated the conversation to Kenneth.

"Well, let's get on with it," he said. "Now it's time to change."

At dinner George announced the plans for a farewell party the next night, their last night alone together. A shame Baraket couldn't be with them, he pointed out, but they would have one last sentimental party in the dining salon instead of up on the pool deck, where they had dined most nights.

"Marvelous!" Delphine said. "That poor hairdresser has gone to waste on this entire voyage. She can go all out for tomorrow night, and so can we!"

"Whee . . . !" Camilla said. "What fun we'll have, and it will break us in for the next few days. We haven't even worked out our curtsies to you, Alia, at the receptions. We can practice tomorrow night."

When Kenneth was dressed he went up to the bar. Delphine was already there, alone.

"I'm excited about tonight. I can't wait. I'm always early," she said in staccato sentences, laughing.

"Let me look at you," Kenneth said. "We've been so casual on this voyage. I only know the daytime you."

Delphine was deeply tanned from hours in the sun and pool. She was wearing a dress that was a *soufflé* of chiffon, in shades of yellow that melted into pinks, changed to lavenders and blues and went back to yellow. The skirt was handkerchief points, and silken ties bound her waist. Her hair, usually tied back with ribbons when they were out in the breeze, was loose and full.

"Let me tell you something," Kenneth said, absorbing her. "You're a combination of a rainbow and a willow, and I haven't paid any attention to you at all. That's got to change, starting tonight."

"Why tonight?" Delphine asked, pleased with his compliment.

"Because at the end of the trip, Alia will be a married lady and I will no longer have to tend to her."

"Kenneth, you have been marvelous with her. She adores you. I've watched how she turns to you, looks to you, always finds you there to lean on when she needs you, when she's occasionally a little out of her depth. And you're right, she does look like someone rolled out of a rug to please a Caesar; I loved your saying that. I feel that I've gotten to know her on this trip, too. I had no idea she had been so sheltered, knew so little about the outside world, and yet she is one of the most intelligent girls I've ever met. She's asked me about a thousand people and places, and she never forgets one thing. Where in the world do they school them in Turkey to have anyone turn out like that? Or am I really ignorant?"

"Not at all; very perceptive. I hear Camilla and Jeremy arriving. I'll tell you the whole story someday. Soon. Don't forget my new plan."

"What?" asked Delphine, knowing.

"I concentrate on you, it's called. Frank, pour us another glass, please."

THE AEGEAN

July 1954

When Delphine took her place at the dinner table, she saw immediately that something was wrong with the seating. George never made mistakes, but he had placed her on his right and Alia was seated to his left. Surely tonight, the last night of their voyage, Alia should be placed to the right of her host, as guest of honor. When they dined informally in the bar, George rotated the ladies for the sake of conversation. Not that it mattered, but by protocol alone, Camilla, as Lady Kilmuir, should be on his left tonight and Delphine on the other side of the table.

Once they were seated, she saw an extra place setting at the table on Alia's left, leaving an empty place between Alia and Kenneth. Who else would be with them? The captain?

It wasn't long before she understood. Alia's back was to
the door of the dining salon. Reilly hovered behind her as the
steward brought generous portions of caviar, golden globules
on small gold serving plates. Delphine hadn't had time for the
thought to crystallize that even the caviar was different—an
entirely different color from what they had been having—
when the door behind Alia opened. Delphine caught the look
on Camilla's face and saw that her mouth had dropped open.
Alia was impervious to what was happening.

He came into the dining salon, and even though Delphine
had never laid eyes on him before, she knew it could be no
one but Baraket. She took a quick glance at George and Kenneth. Both of them were smiling as they watched Baraket
enter, but neither of them rose from their seats. Why weren't
they at least standing up?

Baraket was resplendent in black tie with a row of medals
adorning the left side of his dinner jacket. His arms were
raised, and in his hands he held a necklace of green fire and
diamond ice. He took the few steps from the door to where
Alia was seated and reached over her head, holding the necklace suspended in front of her eyes.

Alia came to life. She leaped to her feet and twirled
around, throwing her arms around Baraket's neck, all caution
forgotten. Baraket kissed her, letting go of the necklace, which
dropped from his hands into her plate of caviar. Reilly signaled frantically for the steward to bring something to clean
it off with. George rose and when Alia and Baraket finally
turned back to the table, he seated Alia with Baraket beside
her as it had so obviously been planned. Jeremy and Kenneth
stood, Kenneth helping Camilla to her feet as George offered
his hand to Delphine to rise, too.

George lifted his glass. An aura of excitement, of sophisticated pandemonium permeated the dining salon. They were
drinking champagne and toasting before dinner, it was all
topsy-turvy, and the poor steward was desperately trying to
figure out how to clean globs of caviar off a momentarily forgotten necklace, one that was worth a king's ransom. The con-

sciousness of the moment filled the room; all of them aware
that they were sharing a rare moment.

"I am going to propose one toast, only one, before the
soufflé falls," George said. "To Baraket, the man who is no
longer missing, but the man we have missed on this happy
trip, and to Princess Alia, our Alia. To their happiness."

"Never mind the *soufflé*," Baraket said, rising to his feet and
looking at Reilly, who gave him the necklace. "Even a *soufflé*
waits on a night like this." Baraket's brow was glistening and
his black eyes were full of fun. He put the glistening necklace, now free of any trace of caviar, around Alia's neck and
fastened the clasp. Emeralds and diamonds cascaded down
her throat, blazing in the candlelight, settling on her creamy
skin as if they belonged there.

Delphine was fascinated by Alia's calm control. She knew
Alia well enough now to recognize that she was seething with
excitement and desire under that cool exterior. Although she
showed no sign of outward emotion she turned to Kenneth
when her eyes were not fastened on Baraket, as if his presence
reassured her.

"Now," Baraket announced, king-emperor that he was. "It is
time to give the chef a chance. The rest can wait until later."

"How can I introduce you to Delphine and the Kilmuirs if
you persist in taking over my yacht?" George said.

"I know all about them already. We are friends who need
no introduction," Baraket said, bowing his head to Delphine
and Camilla, saluting Jeremy. He took his seat by Alia, touching her arm lightly, taking in her beauty.

The gaiety of the dinner was unchecked, conversation
flowing about Baraket's surprise appearance, how he had
managed to get aboard without Alia or Delphine or Camilla
knowing, plus more of the endless details of the wedding.
Even the *soufflé*, when it came, was perfect.

Baraket was still not through. He rose once more and
turned to George. "May I have your attention, my dear
friends?" Reilly was waiting with a small tray which he put
down in front of Baraket. Six velvet boxes were stacked on it.

Baraket took them and walked around the table, putting one in front of each of them. "Now," he commanded, dark eyes flashing again with pleasure. "Open them. They are tokens of this night."

In each velvet case lay a golden box, a box that could be used for cigarettes or cigars, as a powder case or just appreciated for the beautiful object it was. Etched into the gold in lacelike tracing was a map of the course *Ehukai III* had taken from Monte Carlo to Istanbul and the dates of the voyage. Monte Carlo was marked with a small diamond and Istanbul with a much larger one. *Ehukai III* was drawn into the gold, too, dressed with her lights that were a string of tiny diamonds. On the reverse side the initials B and A were set in emeralds, the B on top, the A below, with the date of the wedding between.

"You may notice that for the first time B comes before A, but that is how it is," Baraket said, his strong teeth flashing. Delphine and Camilla exchanged glances, both feeling the intensity and fascination of this extraordinary man.

George rose to his feet, waving the others up with him. "Baraket, you have honored us, especially in having had Alia with us."

Baraket roared with laughter. "That was a great concession on my part, my friend, however, I will take her back tomorrow—meanwhile, my beautiful ladies, the bouquet of my favorite roses in the center of the table holds one more small token of my esteem for you. If you will look into the flowers, reach into them, you will find their message.

Three pairs of earrings were dangling on rose stems in the low arrangement on the table. They were only partially hidden behind the curved petals of Baraket's roses. Twenty carat pear-shaped drops, rubies for Delphine, sapphires for Camilla, were set in diamonds and clipped to the ears with a smaller ruby or sapphire. Alia's emeralds were somewhat larger, but the settings were identical.

Camilla let out a gasp. "Baraket," she said, clipping the exquisite stones on her ears, "I've never seen anything like them."

"Good God, Baraket," Jeremy said, "you've wrecked me. I'll never be able to take Camilla on a yacht trip again. She'll think this sort of thing happens every time."

"It doesn't?" Camilla said, eyes aglow. "Come now, Baraket, I'm speechless."

"So am I," Delphine said. "Speechless." Kenneth looked across the table at her as she put on the ruby earrings. Their eyes met and held for an instant. She could hear him thinking that she was beautiful.

George rose and led them to the main salon for coffee and more champagne and endless toasts from everyone until time for Baraket to leave. It was a four-hour trip back to Istanbul. Alia remained her quiet self all evening, although she had rarely looked away from Baraket. Never once had he taken her aside or made any attempt to be alone with her. Only with his eyes did he assure her, over and over, that her behavior was perfect. They would be alone together soon enough.

Delphine and Camilla and Alia were joyously into the spirit of the occasion. They gathered in a corner of the salon, looking at themselves in the mirror, trying on each other's earrings. Kenneth found his attention intensifying on Delphine. For all her subtlety, even to the colors of her dress, there was something deeply exciting about her.

When the time came for Baraket to leave, they all trooped on deck to see him off.

"Tomorrow," he said, waving from the launch. "Wait until you see what I have planned for tomorrow."

"Baraket, even you can't top tonight, for any of us," George said, as they all waved.

When Baraket was aboard his own fast boat, George found Reilly at his side.

"Prince Baraket would like you to stay on deck for a few minutes, sir. He has something else for you." The look on Reilly's face was truly smug; it was the only time he had felt bigger than the boss. Baraket had used him well as major-domo, and Reilly did feel partly responsible for the success and triumph of the evening. Baraket had also given him a thousand-dollar bill.

Suddenly, the night sky was pierced with fireworks; burst after burst sailed into the air, hailing down fountains of light, stars falling everywhere, showers of flower forms, then the American flag, the British flag and, in a final wild burst, the Turkish flag exploded into a million red-and-white particles that wafted gracefully down into the sea. Baraket's voice floated across the water just before the engines on his boat started.

"Good night, again," he shouted across the water. "Wait until tomorrow!"

He was gone.

"Even the wedding will be an anticlimax now," Delphine said. "Alia, you have got your work cut out for you! It's a good thing you've got that great calm quality; you're going to need it."

"I miss Baraket already," Camilla said, fingering her sapphires. "Why didn't you tell us he did things like this?"

Alia laughed. "I'm not feeling too calm right now," she said. "I miss him, too."

"Bedtime, girls," George said. Kenneth looked at Delphine. Maybe she would stay for a nightcap with him.

"Bedtime," Delphine said, not seeing his look. "I can't wait for tomorrow."

Early the next morning they disembarked. Baraket arranged the smooth transition of their move from the yacht into the palace of Saadit Sarai. The wedding was scheduled for five o'clock that afternoon.

"I will be busy until then," he said. As they sat drinking Turkish coffee on one of the flower-hung terraces he asked, "What would you like to do today?"

"I'd like to get my land legs back or I'll be weaving at your wedding," Camilla said. "And I know Del and I would like to be with Alia as much as possible. After all, you are taking her away from us."

Delphine and Alia and Camilla looked at each other, all three of them thinking the same thing.

"It's been a dream," Delphine said. "I didn't realize until this very moment that this time tomorrow we'll be apart. I'm so used to our being together." Alia has Baraket, and Camilla has Jeremy, she thought. She felt very alone. George and Kenneth would take care of her now, but the fairy tale was coming to an end and she dreaded facing reality.

"We have all day, and you and Camilla will be with me while I'm dressing," Alia said.

"Lunch is arranged for the three of you in your quarters, *hayatim*," Baraket said, holding her hand, using the Turkish word for "my life." "Then you belong to me."

"I want to see all of the palace," Delphine said.

"It will take you three days," Kenneth said. "You'd better start now."

"Oh, yes," Alia said. "Let's go and see what we can. I know little more about Saadit Sarai than you do and I should become familiar with my new home. Baraket signaled for Tarek, who appeared instantly at his side, listening intently to instructions of where to take them.

Delphine, Camilla and Alia shared a feeling of nostalgia as Tarek led them through the grandiose rooms. The hour of parting was almost upon them. They walked through salon after salon, the largest one boasting a Baccarat chandelier that weighed two tons. At noon, he brought them to Alia's quarters and left them with time to rest before their lunch. The lunch table was set on the terrace off Alia's huge sitting room. A red and white box, tied with gold ribbon, was at each of their places.

"Baraket is at it again," Camilla said, fingering her package. "One thing is for sure. He can't top himself this time."

"The fairy tale continues," Delphine said, taking the wrapping from her present. Each box held a gold picture frame that bore Baraket's crest. Instead of a photograph, there was a note from Baraket in each. "Before you leave Saadit Sarai," he wrote to Delphine and Camilla, "there will be a photograph for you to put in this small gift, celebrating our marriage and your friendship. Both will be everlasting."

"I think I'm going to cry," Delphine said.

"No you're not," Camilla said. "Alia and I had a chance to talk before we left the yacht, and we both agree that you must come to London. There is all the room in the world for you with Jeremy and me in Eaton Square. You don't even have to go back to New York except to close your apartment, then you must be back by mid-September at the latest. There are dozens of interesting things going on in London in the autumn, and we're friends and we're going to be better friends. So you might as well make up your mind that London is the place for you. Ken will be there, too, you know."

Delphine kissed both of them on the cheek.

"I'll try," she said. "Not only because I know I would love London, but because after what we three have been through together, what we have shared . . . well, it's a beginning for us, isn't it? You know I'll try."

ISTANBUL

July 1954

Baraket's wedding to Alia gave the world a new star to watch, follow and praise. One of the world's richest men, at forty years of age, had taken as his wife an almost unbelievably beautiful young Turkish princess that no one had ever heard of or seen until the television and still cameras zoomed in on her compelling, irresistible face. She was receiving, her husband beside her, at Saadit Sarai, their terraced garden palace on the Bosporus. Who was she? Where had he found her? And why, until now, had so little been written or known about Lieutenant General, His Exalted Highness Sir Baraket Safwat Osman Abdel-Rahim, Regulator of the City, Shadow of God and Faithful Ally of the British, himself?

The wedding could possibly have remained completely private if a local reporter with the Associated Press in Istanbul hadn't also been an early-morning fisherman. During the hot months he lived in a small cabin on the Sea of Marmara, just south of Istanbul, and fished early in the day. He would take his catch to the tiny seaside café near his shack, giving all he caught to the owner in return for being fed whenever he wanted. It was a fair bargain.

Fishing at dawn, he saw the big white yacht lying at anchor just off the shore. He whistled to himself. She was a beauty, a real beauty, close to two hundred feet long. Not *Savarona,* of course—Atatürk's huge yacht that rested now as a Turkish training ship in Istanbul's harbor—but she had the same clipper bow. He wondered whose she was; probably some English millionaire's, but that was only idle thinking. An hour later he took the morning's plentiful catch to the café and found two crew members, obviously from the yacht, there. They were Turkish but when he asked whom the yacht belonged to, they volunteered only that it was American owned. Once they left, the café owner tipped his head to one side and in a loud whisper said "Baraket." Everyone knew Baraket but, all the café owner knew about the yacht was that it had come from Monte Carlo. In Istanbul later that day, the reporter made several phone calls out of simple curiosity and in a few hours he realized he had a story. He knew who the owner of the yacht was; he knew who was aboard, and he knew that the two Turkish crew members worked for Baraket. He sped back down the road taking one of the bureau's photographers with him. The yacht was still there. The long telephoto lenses captured dozens of pictures of everyone aboard—swimming, lunching, sunning. Once back in Istanbul, he stood over the tank until the prints came out, when he knew he had more than just a story; he had a big story.

Baraket had put a clamp on any press coverage of his wedding. As he was the most powerful man in Istanbul, it wasn't difficult for him to do, especially since he owned the news service, and the reporters, therefore, worked for him. All of

Istanbul society knew where and when Baraket was getting married because wedding invitations had been sent out, but no one knew *whom* he was marrying. Princess Alia? Who was Princess Alia, and why was he keeping her so secret? Now, all that was changed. It was quite obvious from his pictures which of the three ladies was the bride-to-be. She was a beauty, to put it mildly.

The reporter knew what to do. He called Baraket's office. He told a secretary that he wanted to speak to His Highness personally; that he had pictures taken this very morning of Princess Alia and he wanted Baraket's permission to publish them. He waited. A few minutes later the secretary's voice came back on the line, asking if he could come to the office immediately with the pictures. His Highness would receive him.

Baraket was in an affable mood as he looked at the pictures. There were head shots of Delphine, Alia and Camilla. Table shots of them eating luncheon on deck. George with Delphine; George with Delphine and Kenneth. Camilla and Jeremy. He laughed.

"Very clever of you."

"Very lucky," the reporter said.

"That you came to me, yes. But the pictures are excellent."

"Thank you, Your Highness. Of a most beautiful girl."

"Yes," Baraket said. "And I see now that she will not remain a private figure. I am glad that you work for me and had sense enough to come to me first. Do you know when the wedding is and where? My secretary will tell you. You may publish these pictures as you choose; that will be your exclusive. But I cannot allow only one of my people to cover the wedding. Therefore, I am giving you the honor of informing the others that Princess Alia and I will receive them for one half hour, immediately after the ceremony, at Saadit Sarai."

It was Baraket's whim that Alia, the star, was born. Princess Alia. Even her name had a glamorous ring to it. And His Highness Prince Baraket no less. Suddenly, like a brush fire, every newspaper and magazine in the world wanted a story of the fabled Baraket and his beautiful princess.

The news came in dribbles. Every day someone seemed to discover, or make up, stories that had to do with Baraket's wealth and Alia's beauty. Over two thousand presents were displayed at the wedding reception. It was whispered that Baraket had a collection of emeralds that filled an entire room, although no one knew the exact dimensions of the room or where it was. How could anyone have a roomful of emeralds? Princess Alia wore a forty-carat stone on her finger, well observed in all her wedding pictures. She was dressed by Pierre Balmain, one of the most revered names in Paris, who, in fact, was beaming beside her in many of the wedding photographs. Her wedding dress was thin white silk, banded with creamy-white satin, falling in ten layers to the ground. Her veil and train were embroidered with seed-pearl roses, tiny at the top but as large as cabbages at the foot of her twelve-foot train. Her family was present at the ceremony, sheltered by her husband's aides; they were quiet figures, protected by Baraket's aides, and did not mingle with anyone.

Baraket, the handsome Egyptian-born, Harvard-educated current-day pharaoh, vanished from Istanbul with his bride after the wedding. It was rumored that he had gone to Cairo, where there would be another wedding ceremony held in the private mosque of Princess Tafida at Al-Hikma, his mother's villa. It had been only a few years since Gamal Abdel Nasser had overthrown King Farouk and seized power in Egypt. In those years, three quarters of a million "foreigners" had left Cairo, the Paris of the Nile—their lands confiscated, their bank accounts frozen, and their very persons subject to bodily harm and death. The royalist elite of former days were no more. How, then, did Baraket still have the run of the country and a mother still living splendidly there?

If the press could have discovered, and they did not, that Baraket played the role of a double Robin Hood, they would have stumbled upon one of the most vital and interesting stories of the time. Baraket was traitor to no one—to his friends or to his country. He had warned his friends of what was to come. He urged them to take the precautions necessary to protect themselves and their money. Few heeded him; most decided to wait and see. Baraket, knowing what was coming, had arranged his affairs so that the worst that could happen to him would be the confiscation of the Abdel-Rahim lands in Egypt, thousands of acres of cotton-growing land that had been in his family for centuries. The new regime of Nasser brought confiscation, but long before that time the Osman fortune had been safely transferred into Swiss, British and American banks and investments, and Baraket's headquarters had shifted to London and Istanbul. Princess Tafida had been given the choice of staying put in Cairo at Villa Al-Hikma, or giving it up and leaving the country. When put to it, she could not leave. Villa Al-Hikma was the house of her birth and of Baraket's. She would die there, regardless of Nasser or whoever else might be in power. Nothing could be worse than the corrupt embarrassment of the Farouk days. That terrible time was behind them. Baraket could run the family business investments from outside of Egypt; in Egypt she would remain.

Baraket had befriended Nasser, not only as the man of the hour, but because he was a man of infinite power and charm, a man that he liked immensely. The compliment was returned. Nasser was the son of a village postman; Baraket's blood line went centuries back to the most powerful days of the Ottoman Empire. They recognized power, one in the other.

Baraket's move from Cairo to Istanbul had been perfectly natural. He was bored with Cairo when all his friends were gone. Istanbul was much gayer, and Saadit Sarai was his favorite palace. His mother remained in Cairo; not in grandeur, but in her same house with her servants and treasures surrounding her.

But where had he found the gorgeous Princess Alia and where were they going to live? Were there answers to these questions? No, there were not. Baraket and his princess were gone, had vanished with all the privacy that money could give them. The press would have to wait.

"It's over," Delphine said. "I can't stand it. I've never had such a time before and I never will again. I have never seen anything as exquisite as Alia, and I never dreamed that I would be given twenty-carat ruby earrings for not being a member of the wedding. What are we going to do now? I can't bear for it to be over."

"It's not," George said, his favorite smug expression on his face. "Camilla and Jeremy are going back to London tomorrow, and I think we've had quite enough of *Ehukai III* for a few months. Kenneth and I have something planned for you: a continuance of your European education."

EUROPE
August 1954

George and Kenneth took Delphine on a whirlwind tour of great cities the following week. They spent three days in London, another three in Paris, and two in Zürich.

The three of them were lunching in the Stübli of the Baur au Lac Hotel in Zürich, watching the boats traveling in orderly Swiss fashion across the lake outside the organdy-curtained windows. Fat red geraniums and purple petunias tumbled from the window boxes. The air was as fresh as the wine. "We're seeing the best cities, Delphine. Rome can wait," George said, tasting his viande de Grisons, the dried-beef specialty of the mountains, along with a bottle of Dole, one of Switzerland's best red wines.

"You and Kenneth have managed to see the inside of a number of banks, too."

"That's our excuse for the trip, bankers' meetings," Kenneth said. "A valid one."

"You managed to do a little dress business in Paris, I noticed," George teased. It was nice to be just the three of them, particularly after all the hullabaloo that had surrounded the wedding.

"Oh yes," Delphine said. "I only had my yachting clothes with me, you know. You two wouldn't take me to the Connaught for dinner in London or Laperouse in Paris wearing a tee shirt that had *Ehukai III* written on it, now would you?" She was having a marvelous time.

"Never," Kenneth said. "Have you told her about the icing on the cake?"

"Not yet. I finished making the arrangements this morning. I hope you bought some racing clothes, Delphine; we're going to Baden-Baden for the Internationale Galopprennen."

"The *what?*"

"Every year at this time, the most attractive people I've ever seen assembled under one roof gather in Baden-Baden for the big international race. You see some of the same group in Deauville and Longchamps and at Ascot. They look even more attractive at Iffezheim, the racecourse. You know, I don't really like horses and racing that much, but I wouldn't miss this. Racing is more Kenneth's field."

"I love it," Kenneth said. "So, since we felt you should see one small place, we chose Baden-Baden. I called Fritz Hartung, an old friend, heir to one of the big American beer fortunes. He's had a villa here since just after the war. He's asked us to stay. Delphine, remember I wanted you to see the view from Château Madrid?"

"Never forget it."

"Wait till you see Fritz's place. And Baden-Baden. No words to tell you."

"When is this dream going to end? Or can we go on educating me forever?"

"It ends for me after this weekend," George said. "I've booked space on the *Liberté*—for both of us. Actually, I booked it before we came over on the *Île de France*. The time has flown, hasn't it?"

Delphine found herself face to face with the reality she had been avoiding. Going home. Going home to New York. Going home to New York and Ryan. He would be back from Mexico before the end of September. As George and Kenneth talked about Baden-Baden, she tried to analyze how she felt. She had spent all the summer in the most escapist of worlds—on a huge white yacht, at a fairy-tale wedding, then flying an Aladdin's carpet with two stunning men showing her around in three of the fabulous cities of the world. And now, Baden-Baden.

She decided to put it out of her mind. It was Rilke who said, "Live with the questions for a while. The answers will come." Still, it was awful not to know how she felt.

LONDON
September 1954

Back in London, Camilla felt terrible. She knew what it was and decided, once and forevermore, that she hated the sea. It would be a long time before she went on anyone's yacht again, even for a cocktail party. She had spent entirely too long a time on *Ehukai III*, plus the excitement of both weddings. She was exhausted. On their arrival back in London she snapped at Jeremy several times, showing him a side to her character that was going to become decidedly familiar to him.

It took several days to open all the mail that had piled up in her absence. The new flat in Eaton Square wouldn't be ready for them for several weeks, but it was already filled with wedding presents that would take forever to sort out, much less put in place and write thank-you notes for. Some of the letters that came amazed her: people she had never heard of, plus some she barely knew, had written as if she were a dear friend of many years. All of them wanted something. When Parks had published her portrait and photograph in *Vogue*, Camilla had gotten quite a lot of fan mail—the flattery of transient fame—but nothing like this.

The film she had made before she married Jeremy had come out and received some nice notices.

"What a shame," David Wolff, the producer, said, "giving up being a star just to be a lady. You could have a great career, Camilla."

"Hmph," Camilla said. "I hate the work, and I'm not an actress anyway. I'm never going to do anything as boring as that again. I would be no one; now I'm going to be someone. Jeremy would back any play I wanted to do—he wants me to do one—but I'm through with all that."

She sniffed; a whole bunch of freeloaders, the lot of them. Now that she was married to a man who was powerful and had money and a title, everyone wanted to know her.

One of the letters was postmarked "Plainview, Texas."

She ripped it open impatiently.

"My dear Camilla," the letter read. Immediately she was annoyed. The way he used to call her "Ma'am" came back. Hadn't he ever been taught that "my dear" was almost an insulting form, or did he perhaps mean it that way? She read on. "Somewhere in your multitudinous wealth of wedding presents you will find a small offering of mine." His handwriting was pinched yet stylish and she was having trouble reading it, but it became clear that he was apologizing for the last terrible conversation they had had on the phone. He was truly sorry; he did not expect her to either understand or to forgive. He went on to say that business was keeping him indefinitely in Texas. His father had died. Camilla read the letter over three times. What a strange man. His apology was sincere. At the end of the letter he wrote, "Dear audacious

Camilla, one of the two of us has succeeded in doing what we set out to do in life. I am happy for you, I think of you and, once in a while when the times are nice, I dream of you."

Days later, at the new flat, she came upon his wedding present. It was a tiny gold clock from Cartier in Paris. The date of her wedding and her new initials were embedded on the top in antique rose diamonds. It was exquisite.

Camilla was in no mood to forgive. She stuffed a few of the many press clippings in an envelope; one was a wedding picture taken with Jeremy on the yacht and another of the two of them on their return to London. "Lord Kilmuir Marries Current Beauty," one of the headlines proclaimed. She scribbled out a short note on her new blue Smythson notepaper. "Dear Russ," she wrote. "Thank you for the clock and your letter. At least you laid a lady-to-be."

Once settled in the flat in Eaton Square, Camilla decided the time had come for a party.

"Actually, Jeremy, a series of parties. But the first ones will be for everyone of any importance at the newspapers. I want to meet all of them and their wives."

"Leave that alone, Camilla. We'll have as many parties as you like, but none involving anyone on the papers. My father would never allow it."

"What do you mean 'allow it'? Compton Brooke may be your father, but the empire is yours—is going to belong to you. It's your birthright so you might as well establish yourself right now. Your father will have to retire some day, reluctant though he will be to do so. So the thing to do is to start letting them know who you are right now. I have the first dinner planned already. We can have thirty in the dining room and twenty in the hall, round tables of ten. You and I will change places at dessert, and I'll take the ladies away when you have your port and cigars. I've ordered extra butlers and told the chef that we're going to start a series of dinners in early September. That's two weeks from now. Everyone will be back from holidays."

Jeremy exploded. "Camilla, I forbid you to do this. You know nothing about my relationship with my father and I'm going to keep clear of him. Why can't you be content with the social life in London and leave my business alone? There are hundreds of important people, the top drawer of society and the peerage, to feed your ego, and that's as far as you are to go. You're not to have anything to do with the papers."

"I shall have both. You've let your father bully you all your life, but he's not going to bully me. I'm going to have every-one of any importance in England in this house within the next three months—everyone in the House of Lords, Com-mons, the music world, the film world, and the publishing world—the heartbeat of it all . . . everyone. Your father buries himself in the country now, removed from the mill-stream, so he can't possibly say we're competing with him. We are going to establish who you are and who I am."

Jeremy's mouth was pinched and he had turned pale.

"I forbid it. You're right, he's bullied me all my life; now you're not going to start the same thing."

"Do you know what he said to me the other day?" Camilla asked. She was wearing a pink and blue silk peignoir and she'd tied two little blue satin bows in her hair. She looks adorable, Jeremy thought. I wish she'd behave the way she looks.

"No, what?" he said wearily. She wasn't going to listen to him.

"He said, 'You should have married me. Jeremy's a weak-ling who will never amount to anything. You never should have married him.' That's what he said. Do you know what I said?"

"No," Jeremy said, sitting down and putting his head in his hands.

"I said, 'Lord Brooke, I didn't marry a man—I married an empire, and your son is that empire. There's nothing weak about either of them.' That's what I said." She came over to him and let her hands drop lightly on his shoulders. Jeremy was a man's man, but he had no sex appeal. Too bad, Camilla thought.

"Did you really say that? How did he take it?" Jeremy put his arms around her waist and kissed her in the deep cleavage between her breasts. She smelled so good. She *was* adorable.

"Yes, I did. And I'll tell you something. He's like all bullies. He backed down when I stood up to him, and I think he respects me for it."

"Darling," Jeremy said, "I'm very touched."

"Right," Camilla said, disengaging herself from his grip. "Now, I am going to be the most famous hostess in London, and you are going to be the most charming and powerful host. Besides, I want to get a lot done before the Christmas season when I'll be showing too much."

"Showing?"

"I'm going to have a baby."

"Camilla!" Jeremy leaped to his feet.

"It's a bore, isn't it? I don't want to be fat and pregnant; that's why I want to start giving the parties right away."

"Camilla! A baby is more important than a party. Darling, I'm so happy . . ."

"And for the first party I'm going to ask all of Fleet Street. It belongs to you. Take it from me."

BADEN-BADEN

September 1954

"Iffezheim is the most beautiful racetrack in the world," George announced, counting the mark notes in his hands. "And I am not saying that because we've just won a packet of money on Baden-Baden's Grand Prix. I've often won this much or more at Deauville or Chantilly or Ascot. It's just that I enjoy it more here."

"You don't have to tell me that," Delphine said. "I can see it in your eyes. Baden-Baden has an elegance that even you can't improve on."

"What I enjoy is that it was Delphine who picked the horse, George," Kenneth said.

"You don't have to tell me that!" said George. "After all, we brought her here. Now, for the next race, Delphine, what are we having?"

"Your turn this time. Why don't we ask Fritz?" she said, turning to their host. "Or do you bet?"

"I did once," Fritz replied. "After the war, when I bought the villa, I also bought my first horse. I didn't know I was going to do either, but I named the colt Pink Villa. He came romping in to win, as they say, and I've never bet again. Owning horses is enough, and I like feeling I'm ahead."

Fritz Hartung was heir to a large American beer fortune in Wisconsin, but his German heritage and background had brought him back to Baden-Baden at the end of the war. He spent most of the year in his large, graceful pink villa, occupying himself with horse breeding and the International Club, where he was one of fewer than one hundred members. He had a passion for anything to do with the club. He had found his milieu and he was perfectly content with it. It gave him a great deal of pleasure to fill the villa in early September, at the time of the Internationale Galopprennen, with his friends. George and Kenneth were there most years and Fritz was delighted to have Delphine with them, not surprised by her beauty and style. George was happy to find that Ceil Chambers was another of Fritz's houseguests, although she had come alone. "Guy has started editing the film in Paris," she told George. "It is still hot and terrible there so I decided to come by myself." Delphine was interested in seeing her again, too. If anything, she was more beautiful than Delphine remembered from dinner in Monte Carlo, but it was not just that. She seems much more vivacious, Delphine thought. She was superbly dressed for the races, wearing what must be her favorite blue again, a silk suit of Dior's, with a pleated skirt and a thin white silk blouse printed with the tiniest of pink rosebuds. Her floppy straw hat was the exact shade of both her suit and her eyes. She greeted Delphine with a quiet smile, but there was a lightness in it. Still, Delphine thought, there is something about her eyes that bothers me, something in the expression. It's not vulnerable, it's as if she were prey to something, or someone. Surely not Guy, he was her shield. Delphine found herself feeling sorry for Ceil, but shook it off quickly. How could you feel sorry for anyone in a setting like Baden-Baden? Everyone blended into the landscape as if they had always been there.

That's what I love about this place, Delphine thought, taking in the graceful scene around her. They were in Fritz's box in the Club Place, the inner sanctum of the International Club. They all belong here. It's like Hawaii to me; there are no strangers. Everyone knows everyone else, and the blue blood flows as freely as the waters of the tiny river Oos. It was a perfect early-September day. The very rich, socially secure group, which they all seemed to be, shared the same interests. They came every year, opening up their villas for the summer or taking over their favorite suites in the Brenner's Park Hotel, meticulously reserved for them year after year on assured dates. They came for the waters, or for racing week, or for the pleasures of the casino, or for all three, but most of all they came because they were cut from the same cloth. Fürstenbergs, Von Hessens, Hohenlohe-Öhringerns, Esterházys, Von Donnersmarcks—all had been known to each other for centuries and frequently intermarried.

"Have you and Ceil had enough racing for one day?" George asked. "There's the Menschikow cocktail party, if you like, but I'd love some tea at Brenner's Park and a bit of time to talk about tomorrow's plans before we have to change for Fritz's party tonight."

"I haven't had enough," Ceil said. "I've got to get my money back, so I'll stay here with Fritz and then we'll stop by the Menschikows' on the way home. I have no one to take care of me tonight, Fritz is busy, who's going to be my date?"

"I am, my beauty," George said. "I will escort you with pleasure."

"Thank you," Ceil said, looking at George. Delphine caught a small, predatory look in her eyes. Maybe that's her natural expression, Delphine thought, and she keeps it camouflaged.

"Fritz," Delphine said, "since you're staying for the last race, would you put a little money on the filly Liebchen for me and bring me our winnings later?"

"Of course," Fritz said, approving. "Good choice." Delphine was another good choice they had brought to him.

Kenneth and George took Delphine by each arm. "Come along now," George said. "Kenneth, we've got to take her away or we'll have a racetrack tout on our hands."

"You don't have to tell me that either," Delphine said, giving Fritz a kiss on the cheek.

The pale-blue haze of early evening crept across the long lawns, erasing the dappled sun shadows that the trees had thrown on the garden and the park beyond. As George and Kenneth sat drinking their tea, Delphine's eyes and mind drifted, watching the long, last light wash the gardens a dusky blue, annulling the pale yellow rays of the sun.

When they noticed her silence, Delphine smiled, returning to them. "I've become a light watcher. I can actually see that this particular day is the last day of summer. It's so strange and wonderful to me because in Honolulu, at Queen's Surf, the sunsets are always spectacular. Our family ritual was to watch them together, but they were always spectacular, same old thing. Gorgeous, every one of them, gorgeous!" She laughed. "I'd like to be here when it snows, or in a blinding rainstorm, or for any change of season, just as we are now while I am seeing the summer end right in front of my eyes." She paused. "Is it just me, or is it maybe a little bit sad?"

"If you think of it as an ending, then it can be sad," Kenneth said, putting his hand on her shoulder lightly to comfort her. "But to me it's the most exciting time of year and always seems like a beginning."

"I guess it's that I hate the idea of leaving and I'll miss our not being together every day. I've gotten so used to it."

"That's another thing, darling," George said. "Tonight is the big farewell—Fritz's gala—and Ken has to leave tomorrow before we do. You and I will drive to Paris, stop off in Avallon for lunch, dinner in Paris, then take the boat train to Le Havre the next morning."

"Ken! Why? I thought we were all going to Paris together

and you were going to take the boat train with us and get off in Southampton."

"I was, Delphine, but I've had to change my plans. A terribly important meeting has come up and I must be there for it, so I'm taking the train at the crack of dawn. But I am going to come down to Southampton to see you off. The ship is there for four or five hours, and I know we can find a way to smuggle me aboard for lunch."

"Oh, I hate all this arrangement of parting. Let's walk a little," Delphine said. They had given her such a wonderful time. Of course it had to end.

The light was softening. George paid for tea and they walked together across one of the small iron bridges that crossed the Oos, the slender silver stream of a river that split Baden-Baden in two. They strolled slowly toward Fritz's pink villa, beyond the casino, which was the setting for his gala tonight. Two hundred guests had been invited for Fritz's annual white-tie dinner dance, a grand gathering to celebrate the end of racing week. The casino, built more than a hundred years before as a summer residence for Fredrika, the Queen of Sweden, was a frothy delicacy, and now that lily was being gilded for tonight's party. Lights were festooned throughout the trees in the flowery garden in front; clusters of balloons were hung everywhere and confetti streamers floated from every tree, blowing lightly in the evening breeze.

"Wait until you see it tonight, lit by thousands of candles," Kenneth said. "It's a true jewel, and you can never tell what century or decade you're in because it's timeless. The candlelight, coaches arriving, champagne, the music—those things never change here."

"I didn't expect to see something like this in Germany," Delphine said. "In France, yes, although I don't know why."

"When the French outlawed gambling in 1838, it didn't take long for them to discover this treasure practically across the street from Alsace-Lorraine, and once discovered, the French all came running as if it were Versailles. Tonight you can gamble some more, this time with gold or silver chips only brought out on special occasions. God knows, Fritz's party is a special occasion."

"Careful, George," Kenneth said, lightening the mood. "Our new gambler will win again."

"Of course she will. We'll let her pick the numbers."

When they reached the villa, George said, "I'm off for a nap. See you downstairs at eight-thirty."

"Perfect," Delphine said. "I'm having a massage."

"And I'm going for a steam," Kenneth said. "Tough life we're leading, isn't it?"

Kenneth left the villa a short time later, but he didn't go to the baths; instead, he drove the car out to a certain entrance to the Black Forest that he knew well. He parked and walked in, looking for and knowing that he would find his favorite viewing bench, even though he hadn't come to the forest for several years. He wanted to think. He was returning to a special place. Many years before, his father had taught him something, right here in Baden-Baden, that he had never forgotten. "Take mental stock of yourself from time to time," his father said. "You don't have to do it like clockwork, every week or every month, but just be sure you're on course, the right course. If you're not, you'll know when you have to sort things out."

Kenneth sat alone looking into the great peaceful trees in the green-black forest, calmed by the eternal silence. He let his thoughts roam back over the happenings of the summer, starting with the day when he had heard Baraket's voice on the telephone summoning him to the palace-office in Istanbul, through it all until this moment alone when they were coming to the end of an unforgettable time in all of their lives. Who would believe—and no one would ever know—the role that he and Pierre Balmain had played at Baraket's bidding in the emergence of Alia, the birth of a princess? Kenneth knew how deeply fond he had become of Alia. All of her attitudes were correct, not by education but from obscure simplicity. In a

way, she had become like a daughter he had never had. He
wanted her to do well on her own, and he knew that she
would. He wanted to be proud of her and he was, but he also
hoped that she would remember to give thought to his role in
what was really her birth. She was still no more than a beautiful young girl, briefly trained, lightly disciplined for her future. She was capable of making her way, of taking her place.
What a fateful opportunity had been given to her, being married to Baraket. She would have to develop, use every shred
of native intelligence that she had, every shrewd instinct she
possessed, in order to survive, let alone win. She would find
aids within herself, without the background and experience
that Delphine and Camilla had, to protect her. Kenneth knew
she had courage, but what endeared her to him most was the
combination of a child's humor and a woman's calm. The
calm was vital, but humor can save all of us, he thought, or at
least it can help along the way.

His mind led him further back. He knew why he had come
here. He had been subconsciously aware for weeks of his necessity to take stock again, to decide upon a course. He had to
search himself out to clean up both his mind and his heart.

Elsa. The years of their marriage, years spent in Washington and at Avatar Farm in Maryland. The house in Washington had been sold years ago, but the farm on the Eastern
Shore of Maryland was home, still home, although he had
seen precious little of it since Elsa had died. After her death,
several friends and a gaggle of real estate brokers had made
serious overtures to him about buying it, but he had never
even considered parting with it.

He still had to go further back. In the early days in Washington, when they were first married, he and Elsa had a small
house in Georgetown. Elsa had immediately become an important hostess. She was a perfectionist and she set scenes
which gave her guests the ultimate in comfort and pleasure,
plus the opportunity to communicate under soft lights in complete privacy. An invitation to the Bennetts' was one of the
most desirable invitations in Washington. She took vicarious

pleasure in planning every detail—the flowers, the food, the music. She broke protocol by not observing it too rigidly with such surety that barriers, impenetrable before, fell. But, with the arrival of the first guest, the smile would fade from her face; the light would leave her eyes, and she would flee, leaving Kenneth alone to greet their guests. She would reappear when it was time to go to dinner, but those sitting on either side of her found the going tough, making light conversation with a hostess who was not really there. It was torture for her. Kenneth discussed it with her over and over, trying to help, but the remote look increased in her eyes, and finally he gave up. A rift grew between them, unspoken. Elsa spent more and more time at the farm, alone for months on end, obsessed with her own interests. When Kenneth was assigned to Egypt, England, Turkey—wherever he was sent—he would try to entreat her, persuade her, even beg her, to join him, but he knew she would quietly, firmly decline. "No, Kenneth, there's too much to be done in the restoration here; you know that. You go; you enjoy all those places." He accepted her absence, and occasionally he felt that she preferred his, as self-sufficient as she was. And then, suddenly, she was gone forever.

Elsa, his cool and perfect wife. Elsa had lived her life on her terms only; no one else had penetrated her privacy or come seriously into her consideration. She hadn't wanted children, so there were none. And yet, in retrospect, on his bench in the Black Forest, it seemed to Kenneth that they had been happy together, in their own way. Certainly they had never fought, and he knew that she must have loved him, but there had been no warmth to her. Even when she learned that she was going to die and faced it, she never once spoke of it, nor would she let him. When he tried, and he had tried, her eyes stopped his words. After her death, he thought that he might find a note or a letter among her things, some message for him somewhere, perhaps even in the voluminous contents of her considerable estate. But there had been nothing, nothing to let him know that she had ever known him, much less been married to him. No, he thought, that's not fair. There had been something. Money.

Elsa's fortune was immense and she had left everything to Kenneth to administer, with not even one special instruction or request in regard to a favorite project. Maybe money had meant love to Elsa.

Kenneth felt the evening's chill. It was getting dark. He knew the time had come to leave the forest. He had done his mental stocktaking, and he was feeling better already for it.

Fritz's villa sprawled around a center tower with bedroom wings that fanned out into the gardens that bordered the woods. Delphine and Ceil had rooms in one wing; Kenneth and George were ensconced across from them. When Delphine returned after her massage, Ceil's door was open.

"Hello, come in," she called as Delphine passed the door. "I'm lonesome here without Guy. I've gotten so used to his being around. Don't you get lonely?" She lit a cigarette and let it droop out of the corner of her mouth. Delphine hadn't noticed her smoking before. Somehow it didn't suit the innocence or purity of her face.

"Not really," Delphine said. "Not lately. We were almost hermetically sealed together on *Ehukai,* and we've been so close all this summer that I don't remember what lonely is." Soon enough, she thought, I'll become reacquainted with it.

"Tell me about the trip and the wedding," Ceil said. "I'd love to have gone; not that I was invited, but Baraket sets quite a scene. It must have been splendid."

"It was," Delphine said. "To put it mildly. You've lived in Europe, so these extravagant gestures must seem normal to you, but the whole thing still takes my breath away."

"What about the girl he married? Alia?"

"Of course, I'd forgotten that you didn't know her. George couldn't tell you that night in Monte Carlo, but we had her with us on the yacht. Baraket was evidently afraid his mother would make some sort of fuss, so Alia cruised out to Istanbul with us. We got to know her quite well." Delphine wasn't going to say anything more, remembering that Ceil had been a girl of Baraket's.

Ceil lit another cigarette, sighed, and sat down on one of the slipper chairs. The smoke curled up around her face and as she brushed it away with her hand, Delphine saw again the pained look in her eyes. Was she carrying a torch for Baraket?

"I wish Baraket had married me," she said. "He was never going to, but I have never met anyone like him and I never will again. We saw quite a lot of each other, even though there were plenty of others in his life at the same time. I don't care about Alia, but I was pretty stuck on Baraket and I think that's why he left me—"

"Ceil!" Delphine said. "I'm sure what George said is true. He would never have married anyone outside of his own world." She was thinking about Ceil's saying they'd seen a lot of each other even though she was not the only one in Baraket's life. Delphine knew what she meant.

"Oh, it's not the marrying; it's that Baraket is so much more exciting than any other man. I couldn't live without Guy, but he's my father and he takes care of me as if I were a baby. That's not exciting."

"It's very securing. Do you come to New York ever?"

"No, not right now, but we hope to when the new film comes out."

"I'd love to see you. Will you let me know when you come?"

"Of course," Ceil said. "And George, too. He's been a good friend to me."

"To all of us," Delphine said. "But he's going to be cross if we aren't ready. What are you wearing?"

Ceil sighed again. "The same old blue," she said. "I'm so bored with it, I'd like to be wearing black tights and a leather jacket with a feather boa. All this blue, blue, blue that Dior goes on about, creating the angel image for me, is depressing me more than I can tell you."

"Angel image?" Delphine said, as Ceil went to the closet

and pulled out a blue ball gown with a strapless satin top and a voluminous skirt made out of yards of blue point d'esprit, looped up like Austrian curtains.

"Yes. 'L'Ange bleu,' he's dubbed me. He hated *L'Ange Noir*, my film, and I hate blue, it's so obvious with my eyes, but he has me drowning in it."

"I think it's divine," Delphine said. "And we'll look marvelous together. I'm wearing yellow. See you later."

George and Kenneth arrived before Ceil was dressed. Delphine gave them each a glass of champagne.

"She's so pretty and she has no pretense about her." Delphine told them about the blue angel. "And she's so funny about Dior and all that blue. Most girls would love to be dressed by him, but I don't think she gives a hoot."

"She's always had a little-girl quality," George said. "That seeming vulnerability is irresistible, and I honestly don't think she cares much about being a success. Thank God Guy married her, because I am sure she needs taking care of, and he is a steadying influence. It will be interesting to see what happens when this second film comes out."

The door opened and Ceil appeared, nothing subdued about her. She had pinned two huge French roses, a real rose pink, to the waistline of the blue dress, and she had taken the pale look off her face with rouge. Her eyes were bright, glistening, expectant.

"I'll liven up this darned blue yet!" she said, linking her arm in George's.

"You still look like an angel no matter what color you wear," George said, teasing her. "Come on, we can't be late for our host."

When dinner was over and the dancing started, the cool September air lured George and Kenneth outside to a table in the garden. They sat contentedly puffing on their Havanas and sipping some of Fritz's finest Armagnac. Through the long french doors, they could see the dancers in the ballroom, and they watched Delphine and Ceil as they danced with one after another of their ardent new beaux. They were the belles of the ball. Delphine's gaiety was irresistible and it was contagious. She was having a great success, and she was enjoying every minute of it.

"Look at her," George said. "She could be engaged to that happy young baron if she flicked her finger at him, and he's one of the best titles in Germany."

"Richest, too," Kenneth said. "Wait until the waltzing starts. You saw her last night; she really staggered them. American girls rarely waltz as well as Delphine."

"You should know. You've been watching her for quite some time now, without being an active participant. I don't understand that, because I do detect that you might be a bit smitten with her yourself."

"I am totally in love with my former charge, our new princess who now belongs to Baraket."

"Oh," George said, surprised. "Really?"

"Just mind your business, George. I don't dare think about Delphine, much less think about being without her. As a matter of fact, I hear a waltz, and I am going to go and cut in. I'm not so bad at it, if I do say so myself."

He straightened his snowy-white piqué tie, gave George a somewhat bewildered look and strode toward the ballroom.

George watched as he cut in. Delphine gave Kenneth a look of delight. I've done one good thing, George thought. Kenneth could more than make up for Ryan.

"Have you had enough already?" George asked when Ceil came back and sank down in the chair next to him after dancing five dances in a row. "It's not even two o'clock."

"Yes, I've had more than enough, it's all so boring. No one has parties like this anymore, they died out with Marie Antoinette. Guy would love it. He should have come instead of me; this is the way he grew up before the family ran out of money and he had to work. Baraket gave me a huge blue sapphire, to match my eyes, and earrings and the whole works, but I had to sell them so we could pay the rent. That's what

I've got left of Baraket. Nothing." There was a bitter look on her face and no cohesion to what she was saying. "Dressing up like a blue monkey just to come to this party, so I can have free clothes. Why does everyone have money but Guy and me?"

"When your film comes out that will change for both of you. You'll be an enormous success, and Guy is even now one of the most respected writers in France. Don't be so impatient."

She lit a Disque Bleu, the flame from the match pointing up the brightness in her eyes. She's had a lot of champagne, George thought, refilling her glass, but she's danced every dance and she's not drunk, she's just tired.

They walked from the casino back to the villa after waving good night to Kenneth and Delphine. George took Ceil to the door and kissed her good night on the forehead. She pulled him by the lapels of his tailcoat, closer to her, kissing him on the lips. George didn't back off, but he made the kiss a friendly rather than a passionate one, taking her arms from around him and kissing both her hands. Ceil looked at him gravely, giving him a little girl's wave as she closed her bedroom door.

George walked to his room across the garden in the moonlight, hearing the faint strains of the music coming from the casino, Ceil on his mind. There was a lot of turbulence beneath the surface. She had such elegance, such a patrician look about her, plus that slumbering sexuality that surfaced occasionally. Like the kiss just now. George was sure she was trying him out, not teasing him, just finding out how he would react. If he had returned the kiss, she would have gone cold and shut the door, he felt sure. Still, something missing, something he couldn't put his finger on, bothered him about her. George remembered when he first met her in Paris. She had been shy but there had been a semblance of delight, a gaiety about her, that now seemed to have disappeared. She couldn't be that upset about Baraket; that was long over and she had been known to have several other lovers, including

Guy. Guy was the answer, if he could just secure her.
Delphine had told George about the star sapphires; having to
sell them to pay the rent. It didn't make sense, Guy made
more money than that. They shouldn't have needed to sell
Ceil's jewelry.

He undressed, thinking about the happier situation of
Delphine and Kenneth. Delphine had been happier, gayer
than ever tonight, especially after her moment of wistfulness
this afternoon. The end of summer was felt by all of them.
Delphine, unlike Ceil, masked her feelings. George had given
some thought to what would happen when Ryan and Delphine were both back in New York, and he knew it was on
Delphine's mind. Even though Kenneth was in the picture
now, he was going to be living in London, an ocean away
from Delphine.

The french windows were open to the cool night air,
moonlight shadows dappling the floor. He could still hear the
music as he lay in bed, eyes closed, waiting for sleep to come.

He had drifted off and was almost asleep when he felt a
movement of the covers. A nude body slipped into bed beside
him. "Ssh . . ." Ceil's voice whispered, putting fingertips
over his lips. "You wouldn't kiss me good night, but now you
can make love to me." She lay stretched against him, her
fingers unbuttoning the top of his pajamas and pulling loose
the string from the pants. She moved against him slowly, vo-
luptuously. Her cigarette was in the ashtray on the bedside
table and she reached for it and took a deep puff; George
knew the smell was not one of her usual Disques Bleus. It
was a joint. She leaned over George, putting her mouth
against his, exhaling into his mouth.

George choked and started to cough. Ceil burst out laughing. The high cackle coming from her throat was so unlike
her that it surprised him more than her presence in his bed.
She was stoned.

"Come on," she said. "Try it once more. You're not much of
a smoker, but, here, I've got something else. Lie back and just
breathe it in." She pushed him back against the pillow and

cracked open a popper, shoving it up his nostril. The amyl ni-
trate stung his nose and made him gasp involuntarily. He
threw the covers off and rolled out of bed, getting on his feet
and switching the bedside light on. Ceil lay naked on the bed,
laughing at him.

"You don't like surprises, George old boy?" she said, the
laugh cackling forth again. "You were my number one target
tonight and I thought I could loosen you up. I can have any
of those boys Delphine and I were dancing with; as a matter
of fact, I think I've had most of them already. You're the one
I want, George, there's something about you that's hard to
get. Tell me, George, you're not a fag, are you?"

There was a thermos of coffee on a tray table, along with
fresh orange juice for the morning. George poured a cup of
the still-hot coffee and took it over to her, sitting down beside
her on the bed, saying nothing. She held the cup in her hands
and began to drink it, looking at him with now somber eyes.

"Who gave you the poppers and the rest of it?" he asked
gently. "You didn't bring them with you from Paris, did you?"

"No, of course not. Guy hates it," she said. "I know this
bunch of men, boys, whatever you call them, here tonight, all
of them. They've always got something. So I took some of it
off them, promising all of them they could come to my room
later. Then I came to yours." She laughed.

"Not very funny, is it?" George said, filling her coffee cup
again. "Have you been taking this stuff for long?"

"Long enough," she said. "Why am I so bored, George? No
one else is bored but me. Men only want one thing from me,
except Guy and you."

"All men want the same thing from all women. You're not
the only one, you just have high exposure right now and that
innocent look that makes them want you more. You ought to
be able to handle that."

"I wish I were innocent. Not after the time with Baraket.
He's the greatest thing that ever happened in bed . . . there's
never been anyone like him . . . and—" George put his
fingers over her lips.

"Ceil, stop it. You're not in love with Baraket, you're just torturing yourself. You liked all the excitement, but you have to settle for having had a big gulp of it, of that kind of life. No one can have it all the time."

He got up and got a silk robe from the closet and helped her put it on, again kissing her on the forehead.

"Come on, little girl, I'm taking you to your own bed, where you belong."

"Can't I stay here with you? I won't do anything. I know there are two of those warm bodies outside of my room right now waiting to be let in. I invited them, I wasn't kidding."

"I'll take care of that," George said. "We wouldn't want them waiting around, or would you?"

"No, no, I don't know why I do things like that . . . how can you get rid of them?"

"Watch me."

George put on another robe and walked out through the french doors, across the garden toward Ceil and Delphine's rooms. Ceil watched him. She heard him speak.

"Good evening," he said, as two figures in white tie and tailcoats came out of the shadows onto the flagstone terrace outside the guest bedroom. "If you are looking for a lady, she asked me to tell you that she won't be available tonight."

A German curse floated through the air.

"Where is she?" one of the voices asked, angrily.

"She's with me," George said. "And I don't think she'll be needing you tonight. Good night, gentlemen."

He turned and walked back across the lawn, watching as the two figures disappeared. When he got back in his room, Ceil was laughing.

"I'd like to have seen their faces," she said. "You were wonderful."

"Now I'm taking you to your bed. If you need any more help, I'm right here."

He walked her across the lawn, saw to it that she was tucked in with the doors closed and locked.

Tough scene, he thought. Disturbed girl, very disturbed girl.

The candles were nub ends. Only a dozen or so couples were left inside, listening to the gypsy music, the violins weeping soft melodies into the night.

"Don't let's go; it's the last night we have together and I know it's late," Kenneth said.

Delphine heard something new in his voice.

"Yes," she said softly. "I know. I still don't want to think about it." She sat down in one of the lacy white wrought-iron chairs on the terrace, spreading the infinite layers of her yellow chiffon skirt around her like the petals of a rose.

"There's some champagne still left in the bottle," she said, smiling up at him. Something was happening.

Kenneth looked down at her. He knew what he wanted to say and he knew how to say it. Now, if he could only get started. He sighed, flipping his coattails behind him, and sat down beside her, making her laugh.

"It's not all that serious, is it?" she asked, as he poured each of them a glass of champagne from the still icy bottle.

Kenneth moved his chair around so that he was face to face with her. He pulled his white tie loose impatiently, as if it would make it easier for him to speak. He didn't touch her, but his face was very close to hers.

They tipped their glasses to each other. "Such a pretty noise," she said.

"I am not an impetuous man," he said.

"I know."

"You haven't been out of my sight for one day or one night since I first saw you—the day George brought you aboard *Ehukai* ten thousand years ago. I have looked at you, watched you without really seeing you, because I was so occupied and preoccupied with Alia. You've been perfection through it all, and I took all of your perfection for granted."

Delphine started to speak, but Kenneth put his forefinger against her lips.

"Don't speak, Del, please. This is not a conversation; it's a thesis. You may be sitting here at dawn still listening to me. Because I don't know how long it's going to take me to say what I have to say. I went out to my go-to-hell rock in the Black Forest this afternoon and did some serious thinking."

She looked puzzled, but she remained silent.

"My father and I used to come here when I was young and full of growing pains. At home in Tennessee he had a favorite place, a big rock that he used to go sit on, way up on one of the hilltops. When he had problems, he'd go and sit there and yell, telling everyone and everything to go to hell until he sorted them, or himself, out. So, when we were here and I was having some difficulties, he told me to go out in the forest and find myself a go-to-hell rock of my own. I did. It's a bench. I went there this afternoon.

"You know that I was married and that Elsa died a little over a year ago." Delphine nodded. "I can't say that we had the happiest of marriages, but I could never say that we were miserable. This may sound strange, but I was as fond of her as I am of the *Mona Lisa*. She was cool and enigmatic, and I'd go visit her, look at her every once in a while. Our farm in Maryland was somewhat like the Louvre in that nearly everyone who came there was interested in art—curators, collectors, art critics—expert appreciators of inanimate objects or paintings. They were the only human beings that Elsa ever had any contact with. None were personal friends; every single one of them called her 'Mrs. Bennett,' never 'Elsa.'

"Over the years, whenever a new post came along, I'd ask Elsa to come along. I needed her and I wanted her to be with me, but it was out of the question. After a while, I knew she was never going to leave the farm; the world would come to her there. A few pretty ladies came through my life, but they were dear thoughtful friends who took good care of me.

"Delphine, I've never been in love. I love beautiful women and I love life, and I'm not through. Remember the first night at Château Madrid?" She nodded, eyes fixed to his, but she did not speak. "I knew then that I had fallen in love with you.

At first sight, at the very first sight of you. But I buried the thought as fast as I could because I was afraid I'd gone crazy and you were sure to find me out. Then once, I felt you retreat when I touched you—just the slightest withdrawal, although I wasn't making a pass at you—and I thought you belonged to someone else. I want you to belong to me. I want to give you everything, and I can. I don't ever want to be parted from you, not for one day or night, ever again. I want you to marry me."

Delphine was at bay. She hadn't been able to keep up with his sentences, much less what he was saying, and his words seemed to be catching up with her a time zone later as she tried to absorb every word that he was saying. When he said, "I thought you belonged to someone else," Ryan's face swam before her eyes for the first time in a long while, she realized. He had been in her dreams and in her thoughts when she couldn't help it, but she had never admitted it, never discussed him with Camilla, even though Camilla had asked her about him one day. He was dead to her, if she could keep him dead, but she was still afraid of going back to New York. Ryan had said it on his card. "You'll be back." She was afraid of the future. Then Kenneth's last words caught up with her. "I want you to marry me," he'd said. Her mind flashed back to the night of Baraket's party on *Ehukai III*, how Kenneth had looked at her. She knew that she had not been unaware of his looking at her, but that night was the first time she had looked at him, looked at the man. Why? Because of Ryan, of course, she thought, answering her own silent question before she asked it. Loving Ryan had hurt her deeply, a hurt still there, one that would never be completely forgotten. She had quite coldly closed her eyes and her heart when it ended. All she needed or wanted was George and his wonderful friendship. Now she had Camilla and Alia, too. She didn't need Ryan or Kenneth or any other man. Men hurt you.

Kenneth touched her face, his finger tracing her cheek.

"Where are you?" he asked, his eyes so tender, his words so sweet, his hand so gentle. George's quote from Sainte-Beuve filled her mind. "Love the man who gives you his entire heart." Here was a man giving her his entire heart and she wasn't even giving him the courtesy of an answer.

Suddenly Delphine felt a strange flash of power, a feeling she had never had before. It was electrifying; she felt gooseflesh run along her arms. Her entire being was suffused with strength and she could see down the long tunnel of life. Kenneth was giving her the life she wanted. Think how they could be, how she could love him, what she might be able to give him, what they could build together!

She took his face in her two hands and looked into the bright blue of his eyes.

"I'm here with you," she said, kissing him. "And I always will be. Where else would I be?"

At dawn George heard the door of his bedroom being opened quietly. Who the devil was coming in at this ungodly hour? Not Ceil again, he hoped. Before he could open his eyes he caught the scent of Delphine's perfume and became aware that she was sitting on the edge of the bed, leaning over him, pummeling him softly with one of the pillows. Eyes opened, he saw she still had on the yellow chiffon ball gown she'd worn the night before, but who the devil was the man in the business suit with her? George shook his head sleepily.

"Wake up, wake up," Delphine said in her lyrical tone, pulling at him.

"Who's the fellow in the pinstripe suit?" he mumbled. "Where's Kenneth? I can't leave you for a minute."

The sound of laughter filled George's ears.

"You fool," Delphine said. "It's Kenneth, and we're getting married and we want you to be best man!"

"In these clothes?" George asked, sitting up and reaching for his robe. "By God, Ken, you were serious when you said you were not bad at waltzing. The last I saw of you, you cut in on Delphine, and here you are in your sincere banker's suit and you've asked Delphine to marry you without my permission."

Kenneth was still laughing. "You have forgotten that I am going to London on the six-thirty train. I'll be in Southampton day after tomorrow to see you off, but I have a lot to take care of in London. I'll be in New York in a week's time. Delphine could come to London with me, but it's too much of a rush."

"You're right about that," George said, sitting up in bed, combing his hair with his fingers. "We've got to get this engagement announced first. Oh, I would like some coffee."

"*A votre service, m'sieu,*" Delphine said, handing him a cup of steaming café au lait.

"You are wonderful, but you don't want to marry Kenneth; you want to marry me."

"I have never wanted to marry anyone in my entire life but Kenneth Bennett, regardless of how much I love you." She sat down beside him on the bed, fresh and beautiful.

"I wish there were a word to describe you," he said, serious now as he took her hand. "There is one—radiant—but it's been used for others and it's not good enough for you." The expression on George's face told Delphine instinctively that for a fragmentary moment, they were both thinking about Ryan.

"I'm taking Kenneth to the train now, then I'm coming right back and we are going to have a huge breakfast on the terrace at Brenner's Park."

"Change your dress, will you? You know how people talk. Kenneth, we'll drink champagne to this on the *Liberté*, eh? I'll take care of her and congratulate you both properly when I'm fully awake."

George's phone rang while he was dressing. It was Ceil. She was frantic.

"George, I can't face you . . . I can't think about last night . . . will you forgive me?"

"Ceil, don't be silly. Come along and have breakfast with Delphine and me, in half an hour. There's nothing to forgive. Chalk it up to a nice wild party and a lot of wine. Don't brood about it."

"I can't come to breakfast; I'm leaving right now to drive to Paris. Guy called and he expects me this evening."

"So are we. Do you want to drive along with us?"

"No, no, I've got to go this minute. Oh, George, what if Fritz hears about this? Those boys. Why do I do the things I do, why is everyone else so strong?"

"There's nothing to hear, nothing happened, and it's time to go on home. Guy will take care of you. Don't worry about it."

"I remember the worst thing, calling you a fag. You know I didn't mean that. I think you're in love with Delphine, from what I've seen, and I don't blame you."

"Well, if I am I've lost her. Kenneth asked her to marry him last night and she accepted. They are both over the moon."

Ceil was silent. It was going all right for everyone, everyone but me, she thought.

"And as to everyone else being stronger than you, that's not true. Think about it, Ceil. You're not putting much value on yourself, and you should. You've got everything within your grasp. If you want it."

"Promise you'll call me in Paris."

"I promise, next time. Delphine and I will be in late tonight and only for a few hours tomorrow before we catch the boat train. But if you want anything, need anything, call me at Ehukai Farm. Much love, darling." He rang off.

Ceil looked at her face in the mirror. The open doors to the garden were reflected in it behind her. She saw the figure of a tall young man standing outside, a yellow sweater thrown over the shoulders of his blue shirt, looking in at her. He was handsome.

"Where were you last night?" he said. "We have some unfinished business."

"So we do," Ceil said, turning and walking toward him, taking off the silk robe that George had given her, the one she had slept in the night before. She'd send it back to him someday. "But I can't remember your name." She stood naked in front of him, reaching for his belt buckle, her eyes holding his.

"Werner," he said, helping her.

"Close the doors behind you, Werner, and draw the curtains. We can pretend it's still last night."

For Delphine, the next few days were a kaleidoscope of movement, conversation, confusion and happiness. Kenneth's immediate leave-taking after his proposal left her dizzy and made the drive across France to Paris with George seem unreal.

"Is all this true?" she asked. "Is it really happening? Who is Kenneth Bennett and where is he now, and why am I in a strange car with a strange man driving through a foreign country, instead of in the arms of my fiancé?" George patted her hand. "Because we have plans to make."

They stopped in Avallon, where George ordered a sumptuous lunch, then talked all the way to Paris. They continued planning and talking while they collected the clothes Delphine had ordered. They dined at Tour d'Argent, and the next day took the boat train to Le Havre. They walked the decks of the *Liberté* as they were crossing the Channel, still talking, except that by then Delphine was so keen to see Kenneth that she couldn't concentrate on what George was saying. She and George hashed over everything; New York and what she would do with her apartment; her family—how they would take the news; where she and Kenneth would be married, and how she had to concentrate on her immediate future, which would certainly be spent in London. George had some suggestions to offer, especially about Winona and her father and Jay. Delphine had written to them often, letters and postcards from each stop, but she'd had no news from them. All was always well at home.

"I can't just spring this on them in a sudden phone call," Delphine said. "Especially without Kenneth. How shall I do it?"

"Ken and you can talk about that today, then when he arrives in New York shortly after we do, you can tell them together."

"I wish they knew him already. I'm not worried about Winona or Dad, but I don't know how Jay's going to take it—my marrying an older man."

"He seemed to like Ryan that weekend he spent with us at Ehukai Farm." There was a wicked glint in George's eyes. "Kenneth and Ryan are about the same age; apparently you were meant for an older man!"

"You are a devil. That's your subtle way of bringing Ryan into this conversation."

"Yes," George said. "What are you going to do about him? You're going to tell him? Or not?"

"Of course," Delphine said. "I have no feeling whatsoever about calling him or telling him or seeing him. Nor introducing him to Kenneth if that moment arrives. You were right; I learned a lot from Ryan O'Roark, and I had a wonderful time before it hurt. If I seemed to get over the hurt quickly, well, emotions are tricky, aren't they, like dynamite. You only know about them when they hit you hard." She stopped, trying to say what she meant.

"Are you in love with Kenneth?"

. There it was. "He's the most . . . he's the finest . . . he's so honorable . . ." She was floundering. She knew what she was trying to say and she couldn't say it. "I'll tell you exactly what it is: the best part of Ken and me is that I didn't go overboard for him the way I did Ryan. I wasn't thinking anything about him at all, and because of that, we had a chance to get to know each other. I had no idea how he felt about me until the other night—you remember how moody I was that afternoon? I was thinking what was going to happen when our trip was over. I'm out of my mind that Ken loves me, is in love with me, and I know what's going to happen with us. There is something absolutely right about us and I know we can only be happier and happier together. I'm so thrilled I'm incapable of speech. George, what more can I say right now?"

"Not much," George said. "If you will just stop talking and take a look at the dock below you, you might even find him there waiting to come aboard."

"George! I had no idea we were so close to Southampton. I've got to fix my hair and face."

"No you don't," George said. "You're perfect. I told you months ago when you were in trouble with Ryan that you were a big girl. Everything you've just said proves it. Kenneth is a lucky man, so let's go find him."

Kenneth came aboard with an armful of English roses for Delphine. George had arranged for lunch to be served in the sitting room of his suite. The air was full of excitement. The three of them talked and planned, laughing together. When the all-ashore whistle blew it startled them. Kenneth got up and pulled Delphine into his arms. She started to weep. "It's too soon. You've just gotten here."

"Darling," Kenneth said, "It's so short—I'll be in New York two days after you arrive. Now, please don't come see me off; stay here with George. I'll call you tonight before you're too far out to sea."

"Two days after New York is two days too long," she said, tears streaming down her cheeks. "You promised me the other night that we'd never be apart, and then you left me. Now you're doing it again."

"Hush," Kenneth said. "This is the last time. I promise I will never leave you again."

After the ship had pulled away from the dock at Southampton, Delphine bathed and put on a simple green silk dress. No one dressed for dinner the first night out, so George suggested that they dine in the *Liberté's* private dining room. When she heard his knock she looked at her watch. George was early. She was ready, but he was fifteen minutes early.

"Ready," she said, opening the door. Kenneth was standing there, leaning against the doorjamb, looking pleased with himself. But the real expression on his face was the one that Delphine would never forget.

"Darling! . . . What have you done?" she said, throwing herself in his arms.

"I told you I would never leave you again." He sat down

and took a small black velvet box out of his pocket. "If it weren't for your family, I'd have the captain marry us tonight. Open this. If you've seen one before, don't tell me."

The most beautiful stone Delphine had ever seen lay in the box, and she had never seen anything like it. It was a forty-five-carat cat's-eye, set in diamonds, domed high and with a flawless yellow eye streaking across its pale-green center. She gasped. Kenneth put it on her finger, knowing it would fit perfectly. He'd seen to that. Delphine held up her hand and watched as the golden eye slit across the green, changing in every light.

"It's the most beautiful thing I have ever seen in my entire life," she said. "I shall never take it off. Baraket is a piker compared to you!"

Delphine and Kenneth were married three weeks later in the garden at Queen's Surf. George was best man. Her father and Winona were delighted with Kenneth. Jay was a little bit miffed that she was no longer his closest companion. "I never should have let George take you away from the Islands," he said, teasing her and kissing her after the brief ceremony.

"You're next," George said. "I have plans to bring you to New York next year. It's your turn now."

Alia knew that there was a hidden part of the palace, a secret place where Baraket's harem lived. She, more than most women, because of her background, was completely aware of the habits formed from the time of birth—that every man of the East found as natural as breathing. Male children, adored because they were male, were revered physically by all of the women surrounding them. Mother, grandmother, aunts, nannies, wet nurses and sisters, touched and kissed them, fondled them from the cradle until they became men and were to be respected when they made their own desires clear. Kissing and fondling all of the young male, rubbing him, holding him close to the breasts, was first to give the great masculine god pleasure, and then to assure that he grew up to be a strong, passionate and assertive lover. Man's word was law. The world was his, and the women who introduced him into the realm of physical pleasures started doing so before he took his first steps.

Baraket was a sensual, passionate man deeply in need of fulfillment. He was insatiable and, if a girl displeased him by lassitude or slovenliness, her skin quickly felt the pinch of cruel fingers in the softest places. He had often been cruel to Alia, hating himself for what, to him, amounted to a weakness. She weakened him because he could never get enough of her. When she simply walked into a room, he felt a desire for her that was beyond his control. If she, the most obedient and passionate of women, so much as looked at him across the dinner table with a certain expression, he started to sweat and was hard pressed to control himself until he could possess her again. He resented the hold she had over him. No one should affect him that way. He had memories of Alia that inflamed his sensual nature. Once, having tea with friends in the subdued atmosphere of Claridge's lounge, she looked at him and moved her legs slightly imperceptibly apart so he, only he, could see halfway up her thigh. Blood rushed to his head and the normal sounds of conversation around him dimmed, leaving him with a pounding in his temple and the inability to drink his tea or concentrate on anything but the taking of her again.

If a man like Baraket could be in love, he was in love with Alia in the early years of their marriage. Alia knew it, and she knew, too, that it was her hold over him and was based on his continuing physical desire for her. She also knew that it was transitory, so she instinctively used her power to please him to a point where, decades later, the memory of her would be supreme. He had taken her out of a miserable life and given her the world. He had defied all rules and conventions to make her a queen, an empress, a goddess—as well as his wife.

She instructed Tarek to find out everything about the harem. How many concubines were there? How young and old? Who was the favorite? When was Baraket there—at what hours—and what did he do? It was a dangerous assignment for Tarek, but he found his way into the confidence of one of the eunuchs and, gradually, he became accepted as a member of the household who had knowledge of the arrangements of the harem. He reported every scrap of information to Alia.

Baraket was there often, almost every evening for several hours. Alia never saw him before midnight, sometimes later, but that was normal. When he finally did come to her, waiting with her ladies, she would belay him, make him wait, and tease and amuse him until they went to bed. He loved to undress her, touching her and running his hands all over her body, but once in bed he would wrap his arms around her tightly and go immediately to sleep, never relaxing his grip on her. In the early morning when he woke he would take her in a strong explosion of passion that left both of them totally exhausted. She matched him all of the way, sometimes demanding even more of him, forcing him to give more than he had to give. No woman had excited him as much as the times when Alia drove him into a fury of desire, beyond even his capacity.

Tarek dutifully reported that one of Baraket's favorite games was played in the lily pond in the harem. Shallow white marble steps led down into the pale aquamarine water which came only thigh high. Baraket, resplendent in his nakedness, with his strong amber-skinned body, would take his place in the center of the pool. The ladies of the harem were all naked except for the flowers in their hair, and each held a candle made into a unique yet practical shape in their hands. They would gather around him, one by one, in the pool. Baraket would watch as they surrounded him, putting out a finger to squeeze or fondle a nipple now and then or to cup a breast in his hand. In the deepening light, a strange dance would begin. First the candles would be inserted in the proper orifice by each girl and lit by one of the eunuchs. At a signal from Baraket, the eunuchs vanished and a slow ritual began. Each girl's objective was to put out the flame of the other candles, while keeping her own alight. The girl with the last candle left burning was the winner and recipient of Baraket's favors for the evening. The new girls practiced the undulating sensuous movements for hours, strengthening inner muscles in working with the candle, hoping to win the game and Baraket's favor. An occasional winner, according to Tarek, was visited often by him afterward—until he tired of her and went back to his never-ending search for variety.

After months of minute planning, Alia and Tarek succeeded in arranging Baraket's ultimate surprise. It took all of Tarek's skill and many gold coins to persuade the chief eunuch that he had discovered a new and especially luscious girl. It wasn't Tarek's business to meddle and the eunuch knew the dangers that could ensue, but when Tarek took him to a certain entrance of the palace and let him see the creamy body and luminous face of the special girl, the eunuch acceded quickly. Tonight this new, ripe girl could appear in the pool; the others would instruct her as to what her duties would be. Since no one in the harem had ever seen Alia, there was no danger of recognition. When Baraket came into the pool, Alia had placed herself at the end, so she would be the last to be seen. When Baraket came down the line, she was waiting for him. She looked him full in the eye and heard the immediate groanlike gasp of shock that came out of him. She knew the risk she was taking. If he so chose, he could put her to death if he felt she had gone too far.

As the candles were lit, Baraket, his eyes flickering dangerously, a challenging look on his face, folded his arms over his chest and watched as the dance began. Alia knew she would have to be the last one or all would fail, and she succeeded. She, too, had practiced for hours and hours the art of keeping the candle flame burning and of extinguishing the others. When she put out the last girl's candle, she turned victorious to her master and handed him the still-lit candle. The hiss of the flame as he dropped it in the water was a tiny noise of triumph to her. He swept her into his naked arms and carried her to the nearby bed, his eyes devouring her beautiful face. Out of the pool, there were no words he could think of to say. He was in ecstasy.

HONOLULU

May 1955

"Fate does take strange turns," George wrote to Delphine in London. "I miss the thought of you being in New York, we had such a short time there together. Now we are poles apart; my three big girls have all settled in London and I am in Honolulu for the greater part of this year, certainly. Your father and I have some new projects that we are fervently working on. I suppose it's because I have lost all of you to other men, and no other women interest me as the three of you do, that I have come back here. Remember, though, that I am always a part of your life, even more than Camilla's or Alia's, and it is vital to me to know what you are all doing. I have made arrangements for the ivory cabinet to be sent to you and Ken in London and I'm sure it will be even more beautiful in your Regent's Park mansion than it was high above Central Park. I'm glad you still wanted it.

"Back to fate. Three marriages within less than six months, and three powerhouse ladies flexing their social muscles in London! God knows the three of you are entirely different. Such a trio of contrasting personalities with such formidable husbands should set London on its ear. It won't be long before Baraket finds a place suitable and acceptable for him and Alia, I'm sure, but meanwhile the penthouse suite at Claridge's can't be too much of a hardship for them. So for the moment, the three of you are equidistant, Cam and Jeremy on Eaton Square, Alia and Baraket at Claridge's and you overlooking the Queen's Rose Garden in Regent's Park. Nice planning.

"I will, of course, make one trip to London before the year is out to see all of you. I've got *Ehukai III* out here with me, so we'll have to postpone a reunion voyage until the summer after next. By then, I suspect there will be several offspring; I would just like to state right off that children under seventeen are not welcome aboard.

"My darling Delphine, I am so happy for you and Ken. You were made for each other, in the deepest, most old-fashioned and most satisfying way. Whatever happens, I know you two will be together forever, Alia and Baraket probably . . . and I would not venture a guess on anything for Jeremy and Camilla, beyond continuous battling that will either destroy or strengthen the marriage. One thing is for sure, you are all big girls now. I send you, all three of you, my dearest love."

Delphine missed George, wished he, too, were in London. She often thought of the role he had played in all of their lives. It was he who had gotten them together, it was he whose interest in them never waned, and he probably understood them better than anyone else except Kenneth. Here it was mid-May in London and she and Kenneth had been married for eight months already. Delphine could not imagine what life would be had she not married Kenneth. They were completely absorbed in each other. Each day of her life she realized a little bit more what an extraordinary man he was. Kenneth Bennett had a special brilliance about him, a quality rarely seen. Looks and breeding were part of it. But somehow, there was more to him—something unique about Kenneth. Delphine was almost ashamed of herself for thinking about her own husband like this, but she knew there was infinitely more to Kenneth than her schoolgirl admiration of him. He was gifted, he was witty and he was sympathetic. The years in Egypt and Turkey had seasoned him. He had the reputation of being a man of reason, capable of being polite under the most agitated of circumstances. He felt deeply the necessity to increase the strength and power of the International Monetary Fund and the World Bank and he was totally dedicated to the job. He was tough, sly and amiable; Delphine marveled as she was exposed to his capacity to shift gears in the most complicated, tense situations and make things turn out as he had planned.

On Kenneth's part he was outrageously devoted to Delphine with all of his heart and all of his mind. He worshiped her, and Delphine was sometimes overwhelmed by the consuming love he felt for her. She had the perfect relationship with the perfect man. Each day she appreciated it more, to the extent that fear crept in. Fear of losing Kenneth, something terrible would happen to him, he'd be run over by a car, an airplane would crash, he would drown, she would lose him . . . something would take him away from her. She struggled with her passions and finally conquered her fears: take one day at a time, and glory in it. Kenneth needed her, she knew how much he needed and depended on her. They were a partnership, and if she was confused for one minute, she cleared her mind by thinking about Kenneth, how he would handle the situation. Their house quickly became one of the most desired meeting places in London. It could not be called a salon, nothing as structured as that, but it was of paramount importance to be a part of the Bennett circle. As Delphine flowered in her role as hostess, Kenneth expanded their horizons more and more.

"You're the power behind the throne, my darling," he said to her as they were dressing for dinner one night. "When I am worried, you soothe me. When I am happy, you make me ecstatic. When I am tired, your touch revives me. And the way you handle some of these people, the important ones who are all dazzled by you and the not so important ones who are stunned."

"You're the diplomat, my love," Delphine said, a trick of hers to take the conversation off herself. "That rude African minister last night . . . I really had no idea how you were going to control him. He was so insulting to you and to the bank and to the United States of America, so deliberately rude . . . darling, how did you settle him down, cool off his filthy temper?"

"Generous helpings of champagne have been known to soothe the most ruffled of feelings. I actually like the chap, and in twenty years he is going to be a formidable world figure. He knows I respect him for that and he also knows that he'd best improve his manners. . . . Delphine, you have done it again, I was telling you how I adore you and you've turned it back to me. You were dipped in diplomacy the day you were born and I would be helpless without you."

LONDON

September 1955

Baraket and Alia were happily ensconced in the penthouse suite at Claridge's but Baraket wanted to get settled into a house permanently, as Delphine and Kenneth were. He didn't fancy Regent's Park; the Nash houses were magnificent, but he preferred Hyde Park to any other part of London. He had his eye on a huge, antiquated house in Piccadilly, one that belonged to a duke whose fortune had been decimated by two world wars. Taxes had finally made it impossible for His Grace to maintain Lindley House, so he sold it to Baraket for a stunning amount of money and retired to his thirty-thousand-acre estate in Somerset.

When Baraket bought Lindley House, he gave a minimum of instruction to the architect in charge of refurbishing it. "It is perfect," he said. "That is why I bought it. I want no visible changes. You must provide me with new kitchens, new baths, and heat, heat, heat. But that is all. I cannot live in this dampness, but remember, I want no visible change."

He watched closely as the modernization work went on. At a certain point, satisfied with what was being done, he called in the architect.

"There is a service hall between the ballroom and the dining room. It measures twelve by thirty feet."

"I know. I plan to seal it up; it is obsolete now with the new kitchens."

"Right," Baraket said. "I thought that might be what you had in mind. However, I have a plan for that space. Come."

The service hall was waste space that in no way disturbed the proportions of either the dining room or the ballroom. Unused for decades, no one was aware that it was even there.

"I want you to make a small, very private sitting room in this space," Baraket instructed him. "A secret place. Find some old paneling, and some small vitrines that can be subtly lit. I have an ivory collection that will be quite pretty displayed in such an intimate room."

It wasn't the ivories Baraket meant to display, but architects didn't have to know everything. Baraket wanted a place where he could openly display the emerald collection. They did indeed fill a room at Saadit Sarai, but a room that was a prison for them; locked, guarded and ominous. What good was it to have the finest collection of emeralds on earth if they were hidden away in the dark? Now, he had a room where he and Alia, and perhaps a few trusted friends, could live with them. He ordered an elaborate lock system installed, electrically triggered by the touch of a knowing finger. Only he would know how to open and close the room. The ivory collection arrived from Istanbul and the decorator would know nothing about his plan to replace the ivories with the emeralds, no more than the architect did. Wall and table vitrines were lined with cream velvet, all softly lit, with no other light in the room. The floors were covered with Persian silk carpets, one overlapping another, and several soft couches and chairs were covered in heavy silk the color of bittersweet. Several ottomans were scattered around the narrow room, covered with tiger-striped French velvet. The hidden room was exactly what Baraket wanted. As soon as it was completed, he brought Alia to see it. He had made it as much for her as for himself.

"But it's exquisite!" she said.

"Aha! Wait until you see what we are going to do with it! Tarek, bring some of the boxes." Tarek was the only person aside from Baraket who knew about the moving of the emeralds; it was he who had made trip after trip to bring them into England. When he set down the first of the many-sized velvet or leather boxes, Alia recognized them.

"Baraket," she said, her eyes shining, "you've made a home for the emeralds." She knew how he loved them. When either of them wore any of them he felt an almost physical satisfaction, and she knew how he even loved to sit holding one or another of them. It wasn't their value, it was their beauty. His favorite was the sloped stone of over two hundred carats that he had given her before they were married. It had once been used as a paperweight, but Alia insisted that he take it back. It was foolish to tempt fate by leaving a stone of that size and incalculable value just sitting around.

Baraket and Alia and Tarek worked for hours replacing the ivories with the emeralds. When they were done, Tarek opened yet another concealed panel that connected with the hallway, disclosing a small sort of butler's pantry. He brought a bottle of champagne. The pantry could be kept stocked without the bodily presence of a servant, and no one would know about the room beyond it.

With the soft lights glowing on the glittering beauty of the collection of boxes, crowns, a scepter, the great paperweight and innumerable loose stones strewn in the creamy background of the vitrines, Baraket tipped his glass to Alia.

"Now we have a roomful of emeralds, my dear. They are almost as beautiful, and almost as valuable to me, as you are."

For Baraket, marriage to Alia simply added one more dimension to his already crowded, busy life. At forty years of age, he was at the peak of his powers and the normal demands made on his time were beyond the grasp of the average man. Effectively administering a fortune the size of his was an undertaking no one man could possibly do, and it was here that Baraket was near genius. He had carefully molded the Osman empire into a smooth running operation; smoothly run by men chosen by Baraket, trained by Baraket, and paid magnanimously by Baraket. His mind worked so quickly, and he delegated authority with such vision, that many people believed he was nothing more than a tycoon whose work was done for him by the men surrounding him. The men who surrounded him knew better. They knew and respected his brilliance and took pride in working for him. No one ever raided Baraket's empire; not one of his top men could be bought away. They had achieved the pinnacle of their success, being part of his vast world.

Goals were achieved, projects were completed as planned, and thus it was with Alia. The project of Alia was successfully completed, one phase of it at least, the day he married her. The next phase had been thought out and made clear to her. First, he wanted no part of his mother meddling in his marriage. Since Princess Tafida could not leave Egypt without endangering or at least unsettling certain integral parts of the empire, any plot she might have in regard to Alia was neutralized. Tafida had a sting, and Baraket felt it prudent to keep her at least at arm's length during the early years of his marriage. Next, Alia's training was to continue so she could contribute eventually to the richly embossed world they lived in. Balmain had done his work well and would continue to, but now there were households to be managed in London and Istanbul, more languages to be learned and the mind to be stretched with books and teachers. As a potential patroness of whatever interested her, Alia was a formidable presence and she had a fine, fair mind.

Thus, Alia, as far as Baraket was concerned, was perfect. He found no flaws in her disposition or in her intelligence. She could only grow. She was a constant delight to him and he never tired of her sexually, but in an almost normal time frame, he began to leave her alone. Alia stayed put in London while the outside world occupied Baraket more and more. She was never without companions; she had her ladies-in-waiting, nannies and maids, and the constant presence of Tarek so no harm could come to her, and she had Delphine and Camilla. But being the man he was, Baraket did want, and have, other women, aside from the harem at Saadit Sarai. Alia knew about them—gossip came to her, but it never ruffled her surface. Of course, he would have other women. She accepted his long absences with good grace, but she missed him, missed his vitality and his companionship. For all her good fortune, she was still a lonely girl.

LONDON
September 1955

"Now that we've been married for almost a year, I would like to discuss something with you," Delphine said.

"Shoot," Kenneth said, putting down the paper.

"A premarital agreement," Delphine said.

"Don't you think it's a little late for that?" Kenneth asked. It was their first night at home alone for months. "I have you in my clutches. Just yesterday, I was thinking about setting up residence in a community-property state and divorcing you, or even killing you off. I could be richer than George." He moved over onto her side of the bed, shifting her up against his shoulder, arms around her. "You must have read my mind."

"We are partners, aren't we? Even in England? And you know that I know more about jade than I do about money?"

"Yes, you do indeed know more about jades than almost anyone. But the Munro Trusts are pretty well handled between your father and George; the Munro-Sherril interests seem to be running smoothly."

"Ken, listen," Delphine said, removing herself from his arms. She sat up in bed, cross-legged, facing him. "This is serious to me. I've been a rich little rich girl all my life. We can go on the same way if you like, I know it's asking a lot of you, to take on any more responsibility. But I think we should. George told me once that I should learn more about money, involve myself with it, beyond just telling the trustees what I need. Don't you think it's right?"

"Yes, darling. What do you want to do?"

"I want another partnership agreement between us. I've spent my life with my father and with George, and now I'm going to spend the rest of my life with you, and I want the two of us working together. You shouldn't be the only one who has to work. I have to do something besides going out to lunch and putting the place cards on the table. Don't I?"

Kenneth reached for her, pulling her back into his arms. "You're darned right you do. We do. Anything particular that you have in mind?"

"Not really. It's just that going through life, lucky enough to have all that I have, and to have you, too . . . As an alliance, think what we could do, with you guiding me, guiding us. I could restore a town, build a hospital, set up scholarships, support the arts—anything. But I don't want to do it without you, none of it. I've never thought about it before, but it's been on my conscience lately. I need you, darling."

"You've got me. We didn't have much of a honeymoon, did we?"

"A week in Honolulu."

"Three days, with your marvelous family. Where would you like to go?"

"When?" Delphine said. She saw the expression on his face, full of fun.

"This weekend. I've been thinking about it. You've never been to Marrakech. I went once, for a bank meeting. Morocco is beautiful now, the almond trees are in bloom, blowing white blossoms all over the countryside. Moroccan snow, they call it. We can go to the Mamounia, the most wonderful old hotel I've ever seen. We can talk about money. The Moroccans love talking about money, too."

"We don't have to talk to them, do we?" She loved the way Kenneth looked.

"Not for a minute. But we'll get something worked out, something simple like one of the most important foundations in the world. Speaking of needs . . ."

"Yes?" She was curious. What did he have in mind for Morocco?

"I need you. Turn off the light."

LONDON
September 1955

The first time Russ came to London he gave no warning to Camilla. Jeremy was on an extended business trip around the world. It did cross Camilla's mind that perhaps Russ had known that fact before he arrived. She recognized his voice instantly on the phone, and she was slightly annoyed with herself for being glad to hear from him. If she hadn't been looking so well, she would never have agreed to see him, but Penelope was seven months old now and Camilla had her figure back. In fact, she was looking better than she'd ever looked in her life. She agreed to meet Russ for tea at the Dorchester.

"No, my chauffeur will bring me," she answered when he asked if he could come for her. Besides, she could get away if she decided she didn't want to spend any time with him. When she walked into the lobby of the Dorchester, she saw him sitting at a table at the end of the room by the big fireplace. He looked quite well himself. A bottle of Dom Pérignon was in a bucket beside him.

"No tea?" Camilla said, brushing his cheek with her lips.

"If you like," Russ said, admiring her. "And I almost didn't recognize you in your natural blond state. You look gorgeous. I was afraid you wouldn't see me, and if you decide to leave now, I can drown my sorrows in something better than tea."

Cam laughed. It seemed as if he could still read her mind.

"Why would you think I wouldn't see you?"

"After your letter, and then your no letters?" Russ answered. "I've written to you at least five times and I've sent enough flowers to support half the florists in London with no word from you. You've got me shivering in my boots."

"Oh, stop it," Camilla said, laughing in spite of herself. "All those vulgar yellow roses. Is that a Texas specialty?"

Russ laughed out loud.

"You do still have it in for me, don't you? Don't give me that 'vulgar' business. I called ten florists here before I found the one you use, and it was Mr. Pulbrook himself who assured me that Her Ladyship's very favorite of all flowers is long-stemmed yellow roses."

"Oh, Russ, I am glad to see you! I have been leading a fairly quiet life lately. Penelope is still young and she's so pretty. And Jeremy has been away more since she was born than he's been at home." As she looked at Russ, she felt the same stirring she remembered from the past and she knew she'd be back in bed with him before the night was over. Damn him anyway. He knew it, too.

Russ took her hand. "Where would you like to go for dinner?" he asked, the sweet, almost forgotten expression in his eyes that she had seen in California.

"To the South of France," she said. "We have a house at Juan-les-Pins that we hardly used all summer, what with Jeremy's trips and too much heat for Penelope and the nanny." She couldn't be seen publicly with Russ around London. "It's lovely there now. There's a flight to Nice at eleven in the morning. How long are you staying?"

"As long as you'll have me. This is my first trip abroad, so I'm in your hands."

"Good," Camilla said. "You haven't met Delphine Bennett or Alia—you know, Princess Alia. My best friends. We're dining together tonight at Alia's. I know she will have you if I ask her." It passed through Cam's mind that Russ was bound to be impressed with Baraket and Alia's Lindley House, if it could be called a house. There wasn't a more stately home anywhere in England. Baraket had restored it to a perfection beyond any it had ever known. Only a man of Baraket's wealth could—or would even want to—maintain a place like Lindley House. And on top of it, he'd added that extraordinary treasure trove, the small room between the drawing room and the ballroom, for the emerald collection. She wondered if Baraket would take to Russ; how Russ would go down in England. California was a different world. If Baraket was cool and polite, Camilla wouldn't even be able to tell Russ about the emeralds. An unspoken code existed in regard to the collection and the room that housed them. They were never mentioned except within the inner circle of close friends who were aware of them. Baraket didn't take to everyone; quite the opposite. It would be interesting to see how he liked Russ.

At dinner, Baraket concentrated on Russ from the beginning, drawing him out on his background, almost to the exclusion of talking to the others, surprising Camilla no end. They got along famously; something about Russ's sense of humor clicked with Baraket. Camilla knew that Russ's big laugh meant that he was at ease, in an easygoing mood. She still remembered the two sides to him, one of them cold and ugly, but no one was as much fun as Russ when he felt secure. The three men talked about nothing but cotton. Baraket wanted to know everything about cotton-growing in Texas and Russ was expert on it. Of course, Camilla thought, when Baraket can learn something that will be turned to a huge profit for the Osman dynasty, he zeroes right in.

Even more to her surprise, Baraket led them to the emerald room after dinner as if he took all his dinner guests there. He made no comment to Russ about the room or its contents, but to Camilla's amusement, Russ almost gulped when he looked around him.

It was just after eleven when they took their leave.

"Jesus Christ!" Russ said, when they were in the car. "There must be twenty million dollars' worth of emeralds in that room. . . ."

"Don't be silly," Camilla said. "They are priceless; no one ever has nor ever could set a value on them. Baraket has never allowed any one jeweler to know the extent of the collection. I must say, it surprises me that he showed you the room. Russ, he never shows it to anyone; it's a real vote of confidence. He obviously liked you."

"And my knowledge of cotton," Russ said. "A roomful of emeralds and I can't even tell anyone. Just as well, no one in Texas has anything even approaching them and it would unsettle them. Cam, where in the world did they all come from?"

"It's a collection that is centuries old, it's been famous and whispered about for years, but Baraket has added to it tremendously. He adores them, and it makes you realize that there are no fortunes like Baraket's. He loves them, too, even though he seems to take them for granted. The first ones came from the Zabarah Mountains in Egypt, as long ago as the mid-seventeenth century, I think. Some are Austrian, and some of the best come from the Russian Urals."

"No Indian emeralds?"

"Indian emeralds were never really any good, according to Baraket. The maharajas bought all the great ones they possessed from outside of India. And sold them, especially at the time of partition. The best ones, of course, went to Baraket, like the huge pigeon egg in the center vitrine."

"That's the one I don't believe."

"It may be the best of the lot. It's Colombian, Baraket has told me a long history of it. They are called Old Mine, and he says they are the finest in the world."

"Well, I may give you a trinket someday, but I can assure you it won't be an emerald."

"That's all right," Camilla said. "You've got plenty of money. Some diamonds will do."

They were close to the Dorchester. "Do you want to go to Annabel's for a nightcap or can I persuade you to come to my room for a bottle of champagne? I managed to secure something called the Messel Suite here. You might find it to your liking."

"It's the most famous hotel suite in London, you nit. Let's go to Annabel's. You must remember that I am married now." Let him wait awhile for her.

"So am I," Russ grinned at her, putting the glass down to give instructions to the chauffeur.

Camilla, to Russ's surprise, burst out laughing. He pushed the button to put the window back up.

"Aren't you the tricky one. Why didn't you tell me? I don't care, you know," she said.

"There are a lot of things I've never told you, and that's part of the reason why I'm here. I wanted to see you again, Camilla. When I left you in California, I went home to a sickly wife—well, ex-wife—and a sicker father. It was a bad time in my life. I didn't mean to take it out on you. My father died; I inherited the ranch. I'm in the land business and the oil business in both California and Texas. I got into the cotton business because it interests me, for the time being, more than cattle or oil or land. Everything I've touched has turned to gold. My personal life is not all that great, partially because I've never gotten you out of my mind. Even though this wife is healthy and a good-looking California girl!"

It was the old Russ talking, the sweet side of him that she remembered. Her feeling for him was stronger than ever. Obviously, his was the same. He was here.

"You know," she said, "I've been to Annabel's three times this week and I haven't seen the Messel Suite for a long time."

They flew to Nice the next morning and spent a week in the villa at Juan-les-Pins. It was on the sea, a big comfortable white house with a red-tiled roof. September was always the best time for weather in the South of France, and the tourists were all gone. The junky places of the summer were closed, but the best of the restaurants remained open, welcoming their serious and more attractive patrons. Russ and Camilla spent the days walking the rocky beaches or swimming off the rocks from the Hôtel du Cap at Cap d'Antibes. In the evenings, wearing pants and cotton shirts, a sweater over their shoulders, they went to the restaurants high in the hills above Cannes and Le Cannet, Nice and Monte Carlo.

It was a new world for Russ, one that he settled into as if he'd been coming there all his life. Camilla reveled in his calm, the steadiness about him that, in turn, made her relax.

"The next time you get a divorce, will you let me know?" she teased, hands full of langoustines, a bottle of the light rosé wine of Provence on the table. They were sitting outdoors at one of the small bistros in the port of Villefranche. *Creole,* Stavros Niarchos's three-masted black schooner, lay calmly in the midst of the harbor. "That gorgeous creature has cost more men more money," Camilla said. "You know, when we drove over here, you looked down and saw her lying there. She represents everything that's glamorous about a yacht, and everyone seems to think all they have to do is buy one and it will be like *Creole.*"

"To answer your question," Russ said, "all I promise is to tell you if I get married again." He dipped his napkin into the finger bow on the table and wiped her fingers with it, bringing them to his lips. "I do love you, you know. Not just today. I have and I will, but I doubt if it's going to have anything to do with marriages or divorces for either of us. We live worlds apart, Camilla. I'm not European, and I can't see you living in America."

"Oh, God, you sound like it's over . . . like you did in California, only nicer."

"We're going back to London tomorrow. I've got to get home. I'll be back."

"Why don't we just make it an annual affair?" Camilla said, picking up her glass of wine, letting out a sigh. She was happy with Russ, happier than with any man. She could feel the sting of tears behind her eyelids, but she would not cry. Let him go, let him go. He always will.

LONDON
May 1958

The corner table in Claridge's dining room had become the equivalent of a strategy room for Delphine and Camilla and Alia. They met each Monday for lunch, never bothering to confirm or cancel their standing reservation unless they knew all three of them would be away. Bruno, the tall maître d'hôtel, took pride in his ladies, and not the grandest of the aristocracy, the richest of the Greeks or the most magnanimous tipper in the land could persuade Bruno to give the table away to anyone else. "It's really our boardroom," Delphine said, when the custom was first established, and it was true. They planned their most ambitious and successful projects from the table. Added to that, they saw everyone who came and went and shared the gossip of the day from their vantage point. Nothing that they said could be overheard; a singular privilege. They were a sight to see—three of the most striking and interesting women in England, holding court. They made a delightfully decorative foreground for an ever-changing, always extraordinary arrangement of English flowers that towered five to six feet behind them on a Regency console table. There was no question about who had the best table in the house.

Camilla had consistently gained weight after her second child was born until she had begun to look like an overstuffed version of herself. At first she had refused to acknowledge it, but now she brought it out into the open with Delphine and Alia.

"Why can't I do something about it?" she said, packing in a large helping of potted shrimps and toast. "I've been to every doctor, on every diet, at all the fat farms I can find, and I have tried. So far, I've managed to give up food and drink for almost two days at a time. There must be something medically wrong with me. If I go on like this, I'm going to burst."

Delphine and Alia exchanged glances.

"You've seen enough doctors to know there's nothing wrong with your metabolism," Delphine said. "It's emotional, don't you think?"

"Maybe no emotions," Camilla said. "What I wouldn't give for a Kenneth or a Baraket."

"We all have our good times and bad times," Alia said. Camilla always thought other people's lives were perfect.

Delphine and Alia had agreed in private conversations, worried about Camilla, that the source of her unhappiness lay in her attitude toward Jeremy. Why couldn't she come to some terms with herself that would give both of them some vestige of peace and order in their lives?

Soon after Andrew, their second baby, had been born, Camilla went after Jeremy like a terrier, yapping at him for a divorce. Jeremy would hear nothing of it; she had no reason to divorce him and he wasn't having one. He buried his personal hurt and stood his ground. His grandfather would never put up with a divorce. Camilla recognized that truth. He would cut Jeremy off if she divorced him, a divorce would give him a reason and she'd be cut off too. Money didn't mean all that much, but it meant something. With ill grace, she agreed to stay on. "But only until he's gone . . ." she told Jeremy. Something or someone always stops me from doing what I want to do, Camilla thought. She wasn't sure if it was a deeply rooted desire to be free that goaded her on, or if, in the back of her mind, she thought Russ would marry her. Beyond that, did she *really* want to marry Russ, or did she just want him to want to?

When she told Delphine and Alia about the divorce discussion, they reacted as Jeremy had, coming to his aid instantly.

"No, no, no, you can't leave him for *no* reason," Delphine said, putting her foot down. "What in the world are you thinking of? Compton is ill and old, Jeremy is just getting his teeth cut at the papers. It's a matter of time before he has to take on the complications of the estate and the title as well as the papers not that I mean to sound a death knell for Compton—but he is eighty-eight and in terrible health. Jeremy needs you and you owe him your loyalty."

Alia put a quiet word in. "Cam, does this have anything to do with Russ?"

Camilla, feeling back against the wall, and surprised by the vehemence of Delphine and Alia's defense of Jeremy, lost control of her temper, not against them, just fed up with herself.

"Certainly not," she said, scathingly. "Jeremy and Russ, Russ and Jeremy, my two paragons of virtue and all that is right. One hangs on to me as if I were his nanny and the other comes into and out of my life, manipulating me as if I were a monkey on a string. I seem to love both of them—Jeremy is my child and Russ my adversary—and yet I hate both of them. Do you know that I have no idea whether Russ is married still, or not? He never bothers to tell me. I'm sick of this shallow life; you two have great men and I don't even have half a man. I wanted a divorce to clean the slate, but since that's off, I want to have some fun."

"That's not all there is to be considered," Delphine said.

"Well, what else is?"

"You tell her, Alia."

Alia, as peaceful as Camilla was turbulent, went right to the point. "Something you'll be interested in. A children's hospital."

Camilla burst out laughing. "That's your idea of fun?"

"Yes, it is," Alia said. "We've never planned anything at this table, or anywhere, of this scope or importance. You may laugh, but up until now, considering what we're capable of doing, we haven't done much."

"You're right there. I'm going crazy with all these silly, time-consuming committees already. And I would work my head off at something a little more important than that silly ribbon-cutting and having my picture in the paper."

"We have great need of you, Lady Kilmuir," Delphine said. "Alia and I are foreigners. If you will be our leader, we could really do this. It will take five years at least and the first thing is the money."

"How much?"

"Ten million pounds."

Camilla whistled. "Now you're talking. You really want me to head it up?"

"Of course, with Alia and me as your cochairmen. We'll have to do it all—first the money, then architects, builders, committees, doctors, specialists, everything. I'm sick of the little things too. If we're going to achieve anything between the three of us, with all we've got, it should be important. Even impossible."

Camilla's mind flew. "It won't solve any personal problems but maybe I'd stop thinking nonstop about myself and all this weight I'm lugging about." She looked at them. "I have an idea. There's someone at the paper I'd like to bring in—in the beginning, at least. He has an innovative mind and more gall than anyone else in London."

"Who is he?"

"Simon Elliott. I'll call him and bring him here, same time tomorrow. All right?"

Delphine and Alia agreed, both thinking the same thing. Camilla had been seen around London recently, in the restaurants and nightclubs, with a series of men who were questionable at best. Was Simon Elliott another of them? When they parted, Delphine and Alia walked through Grosvenor Square, talking.

"If she drags one of those cats or dogs in that she gets involved with, I am going to be—well, shall we say, very angry?"

"She wouldn't," Alia said. "You know she has that terrible drive and she needs something new to conquer every day. We have to give her the benefit of the doubt this time. We can tell when we see him tomorrow."

"Right," Delphine said. "And I shouldn't criticize her."

"We've been together, the three of us, for a long time now. Our lives do seem more stable than Camilla's," Alia said. "I can't keep up with her. Russ is one thing. Once it was clear to all of us, including Jeremy, that he was part of her life . . . well. Even Baraket and Kenneth accepted that situation because they both like Russ. But this new pattern is . . ."

"Pretty tacky," Delphine finished. "If she's started something with Simon . . . it won't do with the hospital project, Alia."

"We'll see tomorrow," Alia said.

Camilla was not pulling any wool over Delphine and Alia's eyes, and she was right about Simon Elliott. He had her qualities of drive and ambition and, more important to Camilla, a wicked sense of humor. Camilla had made few friends in the Brooke newspaper empire although she had entertained them and seen to it that Jeremy began to make friends, form close associations with the men who worked for him. Simon was the only one who did not seem to resent her for being the boss's wife, the arrogant Lady Kilmuir, and for taking an active interest in the paper.

Simon Elliott had risen to become the top feature writer on the *Daily Press*. Politics and finance were his favorite areas. He was English to the core, although his mother was Swiss and he had spent his early years at school in Switzerland, a background that provided him with three languages. "One short of the average waiter," he said.

He was tall and slender, a champion skier and a good all-around athlete. His hair was dark and silky and he had an urgent expression. Ladies were quickly drawn to him. At eighteen, he discovered that he disliked the playboy scene that was part of life in Gstaad, where his school was located. At home in England, he graduated with honors from Oxford, majoring in political science. Between terms, he went to work for the *Daily Press*, contributing items to the gossip page. It was his way into the paper, and after he had apprenticed for a year there was an opening for a full-time reporter. As it turned out, his social contacts were extremely helpful. The first series he wrote on the infiltration of drugs being responsible for the closing of several top Swiss schools won him a prize and brought him to attention in England. He was one of the new guard, more interested in Jeremy than in his grandfather, and he was soon brought over onto the business side of the paper. His practical experience and intelligence earned him Jeremy's trust and he was marked as being a powerful figure in the future of the paper.

Simon recognized the importance of Camilla's interest in the newspaper world and he made no bones about making a friend of her. There was no flirting between them, a fact that first annoyed Camilla, since she found him attractive and possibly useful to have as an escort when Jeremy was away. She invited him to several parties, drawing him into their social set, where he was completely at ease. He was her pet. He made her laugh, he took no orders from her and he advised and helped her on projects she initiated that involved the paper.

"You're good, you know," he said to her, "you catch on fast and you know how to use power. You work both sides of the

street and you get the job done." Camilla had arranged a
benefit for retired employees, much to Jeremy's annoyance,
until Simon pointed out to him that they had raised over four
thousand pounds, an unprecedented amount for that sort of
thing. Simon was a helpful go-between, smoothing over the
continuing irritation that Jeremy felt for Camilla's "meddling"
in the Brooke empire.

"Jeremy should have been doing things like that all along,"
Camilla said, when Simon complimented her. "The system is
antiquated, half the men on the paper don't make a living
wage. I can't do anything about that, but I can raise some
money for them when they're too old to enjoy it."

"Jeremy is in no position to do what you've done. He's
hamstrung by his grandfather, he has to stay upstairs and he
knows it. You're opening the door to the future for him. Don't
knock him; you *should* be doing what you're doing, it's your
duty. That's not why you are doing it. You aren't really chari-
table, you just want everyone to think you're Lady Bountiful."

"Mind your tongue," Camilla said. "And don't forget who I
am."

"How could I?" Simon asked. "You never let anyone forget,
not for a minute."

Camilla liked Simon for not kowtowing to her, and she
liked his standing up for Jeremy. He was a good mate, a
chum, and she had few of them. She fought constantly with
Jeremy, impatient that his mind didn't work as quickly as hers
did, and she complained incessantly about him to Simon.

"Listen," he said. "Why don't you try being as decent to
him as he is to you? I wouldn't put up with you for a minute,
and don't you criticize him to me. He's a good man and, with
any luck, you may have sense enough to see it someday. If
you keep this up, I'm going to ask to be transferred to Paris,
which you have nothing to do with, and I won't help you."
He grinned at her. "I'm a reporter. I'm not a Kilmuir lapdog,
and don't you forget it!"

The thought of not having him at her beck and call

bothered her. She needed him, and he was the only person she needed in life outside of Delphine and Alia.

At lunch the next day, Alia and Delphine saw at once that Simon was all that Camilla had said and more. He was direct, shooting out his sentences as straight as arrows, swiftly reaching the point. He outlined the basic organization needed for them to achieve what they set out to do. Delphine and Alia realized they had been babes in the woods until Camilla had brought Simon into it.

"It takes ambition like yours to even think up anything as important as this," Simon said, returning the compliment they gave him. "You three have all the elements at your beck and call, but before you're through you're going to have to beck and call on every one of them. Raising ten million pounds will be the easy part; the rest is where you can get bogged down. Most people are incapable of thinking on the humanitarian scale that you are, and it's the level *they* operate on that will give us the most trouble."

"Aha!" Camilla said. "'*Us*,' you said. That means you will help us all the way through, doesn't it?"

"The one thing that appeals to me the most is the possibility of success because a combination works. Without being overly familiar, you three are world-beaters. Camilla, Mrs. Bennett and Princess Alia are right: you must head it up, bludgeoning those who might not otherwise be cooperative, by reminding them of the power of the Brooke press."

"Nice word, bludgeon," Camilla said. "You make me sound like a caveman."

"Simon," Delphine said. "Princess Alia and I both have foundations from which to draw. Can we work on a premise of matching funds?"

"And how," Simon said. "Once we get the announcement blazoned all over, the best thing to do is sit back and not ask for anything. It will make all the big money nervous not to know why they haven't been asked on the bandwagon. You three are too well known, too impeccably powerful, for everyone not to want to line up with you."

Over coffee, Delphine and Alia told Camilla and Simon
what their preliminary plans included.

"Why in the world did you want me to advise you, Mrs.
Bennett?" Simon said. "And Princess Alia? You're light-years
ahead of me."

"Not at all," Alia said. "My husband encouraged me."

"And mine," Delphine said. She rose from the table. "I must
go. Another meeting next week?" Alia rose at the same time.
Simon kissed both of their hands, think what quality they
had, what fascinators they were.

"With pleasure," he said. When they had gone, he ordered
a brandy.

"And one for me," Camilla said. "You're right, Simon. The
combination is right. You like them, don't you?"

"*Like* them? I'm crazy about them, just as I am about you.
The three of you are infallible. Now if you'll just behave
yourself and not get bored with this, it will be good for you."

"What are you doing later, Simon? Jeremy has a dinner."

"So do I. With Jeremy." He put his arm around her affec-
tionately. She might be tough, he thought, but she bruises
easily. It was easy to be sweet to her. He knew her, he understood her and he liked her.

"I'll get you yet," she said, laughing, responding to his
sweetness. Simon was the only man she knew who handled
her correctly. Why couldn't Jeremy be like Simon? Or Russ?
To hell with them, she thought suddenly, I'm going to do
something more important than either of them. I'm going to
build a hospital for children, the best in the world, with my
friends. To hell with Jeremy and Russ.

LONDON
December 1958

The project of the Children's Hospital was well under way, and, true to Alia's prediction, Camilla threw herself into it, driving all of them and everyone else she could get her hands on to bring it to the soonest possible completion. Her relationship with Jeremy became less strained, the battles fewer. They bought a second flat in the same house on Eaton Square and enlarged their quarters so they each had floors of their own. There was peace, momentary peace, in the Kilmuir household.

YALI BEYAZ

July 1960

Baraket was traveling constantly, leaving Alia alone for long periods of time. Her time was filled almost entirely with her two children, Karim and Nebila, and the project of the Children's Hospital. Baraket sensed her loneliness without him. They went to Saadit Sarai every year for a month and Alia realized that she missed her native land. She had no desire to go to Trebizond, but her roots were in Turkey and the fairytale world of Saadit Sarai was unreal with all the grandness of their life there.

"Why don't you build a house for yourself?" Baraket asked her, on one of the few nights they spent alone together in London. "You've worked hard on the hospital, you should now do something for yourself."

"Me? Build a house? Where?" she said, astonished. She had said nothing, but Baraket was attuned to her and he understood her feeling about Turkey.

"Why don't you take Tarek and find some land, perhaps on the coast. Explore it with him; we own land all over the country, but that is not a prerogative. Find what you like, go and have a look."

Alia was intrigued. During the summer Camilla and Jeremy were at Juan-les-Pins and Delphine and Kenneth were in America. She took Tarek with her and they combed the Turkish coast from Izmir all the way down to the Syrian border. Near Kusadasi, an ancient and charming town, Alia found what she wanted. It was such a special piece of land that she called Baraket and begged him to come and see what she had found. Several weeks later, at home in London, she found the deed to the property, in her name, under her napkin at the dinner table.

"Baraket! Can I really build a house, a villa, of my own?"

"Of course. It will give you something creative to do. Do it exactly the way you want it; it is for you, no one else. You work enough for others."

"I'd never go without you or the children."

"Then make room for the children, and you will have a place of your own creation, away from the cities, when I am gone. I will not be there as often as you."

Alia built a white villa out on a long point of land, a small peninsula with cliffs that dropped dramatically but not too steeply down into the sea. It was less than two hours from the airport at Izmir. When she finished building, Baraket came to approve and see to it that the security met his requirements. The villa was called Yali Beyaz, which meant "White Villa" in Turkish. It was completely simple. A series of terrace floors were connected by covered outside stairways that seemed to undulate down the cliffs. The entrance through a courtyard garden led to two guest rooms and the children's quarters off to one side. The staircase descended to Alia's floor, which consisted of her bedroom, bath, dressing and sitting rooms, and a garden with a path that led to the children's level. On the lower terrace the living and dining rooms and the kitchens were built out over the beach, which lay a hundred feet below. A small funicular that carried only two people at a time took them to the beach below, a slice of curved golden sand almost a quarter of a mile long. It was patrolled by guards in concealed blockhouses that were built into the walls that edged the property and came right down to the shore-line.

Alia adored Yali Beyaz from the moment she started to build it. Baraket cared little about it; he thought of it as a simple summer cottage to amuse Alia. It was too small in scale for him to consider at all, but he understood Alia's need for a place in her life that belonged only to her.

Toward the end of July, Baraket was off on another long trip. Alia sent the children on ahead to Yali Beyaz and took leave of Baraket in Paris, after ordering her clothes for the coming season from the new Balmain collection. Tarek answered the phone when she called to tell him to meet her at the airport on the late-afternoon flight from Paris. When she arrived, he was not there to greet her. Something had happened to the car, she thought, there is no traffic this time of day. Then she saw him hurrying toward her, a worried look on his face.

"Princess Fal!"

"Where on earth have you been, Tarek?" she asked, concern rather than anger in her voice. Tarek was never late meeting her.

"The police stopped the Rolls halfway between Kusadasi and the airport. There's a film company making a picture in Izmir and now they are moving down to Kusadasi. All of them will be there, the whole company, by next week. Many of them are buying drugs indiscriminately, so the police are after them. They know me and they know I have nothing to do with the film company, but they stopped me anyhow. It was an excuse for them to go all over the Rolls. They would never have stopped me if you had been with me. I am sorry, Your Highness."

"Never mind, Tarek. Let's go. I want to swim before dinner. I've brought some Fauchon things from Paris. The customs men got after me, too. If I weren't Turkish, Tarek, I would hate the Turks. It took three jars of wild strawberry jam and two bottles of perfume to get me through."

"And was your visit to Paris successful, Your Highness?"

"Oh yes, Tarek, but I'm so glad to be back. The weather is lovely, and the moon is full tonight." Alia pulled off her Balmain jacket, letting her hair loose from the bow at the nape of her neck. She climbed into the driver's seat of the Rolls, Tarek beside her.

It took almost half an hour to get through the Izmir traffic, but once they reached the coast Alia enjoyed the winding road that took them by the sea. She loved to drive. It seemed to release some frustration for her, perhaps because it was one of the only things she actually could do. Everything else was done for her, and Baraket scowled if she even suggested driving when he was around.

Small islands dotted the seascape of the long coast road. They were for the most part uninhabited; none of them had any water, and their wild beauty was increased by the absence of houses or villas. An hour and a half later, Alia drove slowly through the narrow streets of Kusadasi, passing the fortress hotel and winding past the port with its busy little boats. Tourists, mostly British, were just beginning to frequent Kusadasi. The hotels were cheap and the boats went to Samos, a favorite tourist island, several times a day.

A mile beyond town, she turned into the driveway of Yali Beyaz. She was home.

After a swim and supper, Alia went to bed early and slept until three-thirty; then she was wide awake, knowing that she would sleep no more before the day came. The moon had drawn a wide white stripe across her room, ending at her bathroom door. She stretched, loving her loneness, luxuriating in the knowledge that she could get up and roam anywhere she chose, or just lie in her simple bed watching the pattern of moonlight on the floor. What a luxury to be here, to have weeks stretching ahead of her when she could do exactly as she liked in her favorite place. Yali Beyaz was the only home that Alia felt was hers; all the rest were places like Saadit Sarai or Lindley House or grand hotel suites that were the fabric of Baraket's life. Yali Beyaz was Alia's—simple, beautiful and on the sea.

Wide awake, she tossed the pale sea-green sheet off her nude body and padded across the moonlit path to her bathroom. The door was ajar to let the breeze flow through. It was held in place by the doorstop, a silken sack filled with pearls. Alia remembered how every door at Saadit Sarai had doorstops made of the sacks of pearls, tied up with golden cords. Here in Kusadasi, they were only in her quarters.

She put on a thin blue cotton caftan with tiny white flowers embroidered on the shoulders and neckline and ran a hairbrush through her long hair. Slipping barefoot out onto the terrace, she tiptoed through the gate and flew down the rock stairs to the beach. The guards would see her immediately; it was almost as light as day, white moonlight in place of the yellow sun. She wanted to feel her feet in the sand and water and walk the beach alone until dawn. Here at Yali Beyaz she could restore herself and show a simple face to the few servants around her, the only ones who would see her. All pretense forgotten—parties, gossip and civilization at bay—a few weeks of sea and sun always gave her back the serenity that was the very fiber of her being. Suddenly, she was aware of someone near her—someone was walking behind her—and she jumped.

"I didn't mean to frighten you, Your Highness."

"What do you mean, 'Your Highness'? You have no idea who I am!" Alia said, still startled. "Who are you?" Who was this pale boy invading her privacy and her property, walking on her beach?

"I call everyone that," he said, further annoying her. "But

I've always looked for someone who looked like a real 'Your Highness,' and you most certainly do. I've been walking on this beach at about this time for two weeks now; I won't anymore. I was told the owner was away, and I slipped a little money to someone to let me walk, just walk, to the far end of the beach and back. There have never been any lights, and I hope I haven't frightened you."

Alia was studying his face. It was obvious that he was homosexual. What a beautiful face it was: dark hair, not too long, curling on the nape of his neck, and eyes that she could now tell were blue, fringed with sweeping lashes that any girl would kill for. She was not afraid of him; there was no reason to be.

"Never mind; come and have your walk," she said. "For my family's safety I will have to report that one of my guards is taking money to allow strangers to have walks, but that is my concern, not yours; you won't get into any trouble. Are you a tourist? You don't live here, do you?"

"Good God, no, Your Highness. I have a small role in the film we're making here in Kusadasi. The whole company is staying in the French Fort Hotel. It's great to look at, that fortress hotel, but the rooms are tiny and hot, and the electrified wailing over the microphones from the mosques keeps sleep from being a friend to me anymore. We start out for location at six in the morning, so when I can't sleep I walk, then take a quick swim and get to work."

As the light came, she saw that along with beauty there was also a cruel quality, something faintly evil in his face. Good for an actor, she thought, but dangerous for a friend. His voice was low and persuasive, too, and as he looked at her in the morning light, she could see that his eyes were slightly hypnotic. He must be hell on wheels when he sees one of his kind that he wants, she thought. But why am I assessing him in my mind at all? He'll be gone in a few minutes.

"Do you do anything besides act?" she asked.

"Only a hobby of astrology," he said. "I don't know how far

I'll get as an actor. I'm working out of London now, and when I'm broke I do charts. I do charts often." He smiled at her, an actor's smile.

"Are you any good?" she asked. Silly little western boys knew nothing about the ancient science of astrology. It amused her to tantalize him a bit.

"Tell me your birthday, Your Highness, and the year, if you will. Let's see."

"Very well." She decided not to lie, knowing if she lied she would hardly be able to tell if he knew anything. As a child Alia had never had her chart done; there was no money for that kind of thing. But since she had married Baraket, she had gone to several astrologists and let them gearshift the stars and planets for her. It was Tarek who told her where she had been born, and remembered the date of her birthday. If he hadn't known, she certainly never would have. Not one of the charts had been accurate. When important things were happening to her, such as her marriage to Baraket, none of them had seen it in the stars. The boy would probably know even less. Still, she did have an innate curiosity about astrology.

"November twelfth, nineteen thirty-six, near Trebizond," she said. "That's in the north of Turkey."

He hung his head for a long time, thinking; then his blue eyes suddenly locked with hers. There was an entirely different look on his face—one of increased interest—and the evil she had seen was there, too.

"But, Your Highness," he said. "You were once a piece of meat."

Alia was so taken aback that she stumbled, catching the hem of her blue caftan on a rock.

"More than that, you still are, but for only one man. You must be married to someone of immensely powerful position. You have been let out of a prison. You are Scorpio, but your moon is in Virgo and that's why you have been in a cage for most of your life." His words came tumbling out compulsively; his head was computing stars even faster than he could speak. Alia was fascinated, and she was also frightened. He was getting to something. How did he know all this? Could he have found out from the servants at the villa? Certainly not; none of them knew anything but Tarek. She wanted him to stop.

"But you have exchanged a poor cage for a rich one, a prison for a palace, so to speak, but still a prison. You were married at sixteen."

"Nineteen," Alia said sharply.

"Sixteen," he said. "I see Venus going directly into your life in your sixteenth year, and it was then that you married. The man you married was foreign to you, from a country in a part of the world that would be profoundly ruled by Leo and which would be part of North Africa. Unquestionably!" The evil eyes lit up again, and he turned triumphantly to her. "Tell me one thing I have told you is not true. You have one of the strongest charts I have ever come across. And I am working only in my mind. Wait until I put it down on paper for you."

Alia was stunned. She stared at him, trying to take his measure.

"What do you mean, 'a piece of meat'?" she asked.

"Probably in a harem." He looked at her almost coldly, challenging her.

"No!" Alia said. "Get out of here! Leave my beach at once and do not ever return." She looked up at the villa, searching for the guards who should be watching over her, the ones this actor boy had paid to invade her security.

"Oh, Your Highness, forgive me," he said, realizing that he was rushing her. "I'm so sorry. I didn't mean to frighten you. I am awful when I come across a chart as strong as yours. Please, please forgive me. Can't we sit somewhere and let me tell you calmly what I see? Please."

He was so contrite, so sincere, that Alia took his hand with an involuntary gesture.

"I don't even know your name," she said softly. "And you are telling me terrible things about my life."

"My name is Anthony Webb. I am psychic, too, but there are some very forceful, wonderful things in your life. I know that."

Alia was fascinated. She had to know more.

"Would you like to come up to the villa for breakfast?" she asked, forgetting that he was working on the film.

"Oh, yes, but I have to be on the set in half an hour." Now his eyes were China blue and the expression in them was little-boyish. All the evil was gone.

"I'm sorry; I should have remembered. Could you come to dinner?"

"Of course!" he said. "It would be a thrill for me. Thank you, Your Highness."

"Come at eight. Tarek, my manservant, can fetch you from the hotel, if you like."

"Oh, Your Highness, that would be so nice. I'm going to take the books and do your chart today, and I will tell you everything tonight." He kissed her hand impulsively, then turned and ran down the beach.

Tarek brought Anthony to Yali Beyaz at eight sharp. Alia had never met anyone like Anthony Webb, and certainly she was a new experience for him. After dinner they sat out on the terrace and talked. She dazzled him; never in his life had he seen anyone quite as beautiful, and on top of it they were almost instantaneous friends. To Anthony, they seemed to have been friends for a long, long time. He was sure it was in the stars, too; he would have to do a comparison chart. He was careful not to speak quickly and to be especially careful of the way he was telling her some of the things he had found in her chart.

"Due to configurations, Your Highness, relating to the star Ceres and Orion, in Hindu astrology, which is the system I use, in one of your past incarnations you had enormous power. You had wealth, fame and dominion. You abused them; thus, in this reincarnation, you were thrust down from the beginning to the most meager lot in life. But the promise in the stars is that you could reach a high position again, especially if you understand that you must work hard this time not to repeat the mistake of before."

"Anthony, I have no memory of anything but the time since my marriage. I have had no choices. When I was a little girl, I always had to accept what was happening to me. If it was bad, I knew somehow the time would pass and the bad would end. And if it was good, I knew that would end, too. Then I married Baraket, and even there I had no choice. Do you know who Baraket is?"

"No, only that he is powerful."

"Well, I cannot describe him or his world. You've said it. He is—to me and many others—all-powerful."

"Yes, but whether you know it or not, until the year you married you were paying back your karmic debt by being abused somehow or other, from the very time you were born. Where is your mother? I see no mother figure in your chart. There is a man, a protector, a father figure, but many men will be drawn to you in your life."

"I don't know," Alia said. "I was so alone as a child; I can't remember much about it. I have no recollection of a mother or any woman. The first thing I remember is that I was in a house with Tarek, who has been like a father to me, and some other girls. Then I was in the harem. I don't like this conversation." She stood up and paced the terrace. "I'm frightened again, frightened of you. No one knows but Tarek that I was in the harem; I'm quite sure that even my husband doesn't know. Now, here I am with you. We meet at my beach, which you invaded at dawn, and you know more about me than I do about myself. I can't trust you."

Anthony jumped to his feet and went to her, taking her hands in a protective gesture.

"You must trust me; you can trust me. I am as singular as you are. I am no one, but I am your friend. It frightens me, too, when I feel that psychic coming in. You must trust me; you have no choice. I will try to live up to your faith in me, Your Highness. I promise you that."

Alia smiled.

"Oh, for heaven's sake, let's sit down and have some raki. You have unnerved me, but I still want to hear what else you have to say. Everything. It's not important; it's probably all silly anyhow. I'm sorry, Anthony; we are friends and we will be even better friends." She clapped her hands for one of the servants.

The milky-white raki was cool and strong. They drank it slowly.

"All right, let me go on," Anthony said. "You made people suffer in your past incarnation. The trick is that in your last life you were a man. And in this incarnation you have again been drawn to the same soul that you were married to in the other life. But this time he has become the husband and you the wife. That is why there has been a change in your attitude toward your husband lately. You find the very act of making love difficult only because he is too masculine and dominating. You had those masculine tendencies within you and they are still there; you prefer to be the dominating influence, and you must be. But you can't be, not even in the subtlest ways with him, or you would lose him."

Anthony paused, hesitant now.

"What is it?" Alia asked.

"You may lose him anyway. I shouldn't say that, but there are two strong love affairs in your life. The present one, as strong as it has been and still is, is going to come to a close. The next—the great love of your life—will bring you a happiness you have never known. Now don't say I only tell you the bad things."

"If Baraket were here, he'd have you put to death," Alia said.

"Baraket is not here nor is he going to be. In the next few days I will work very hard writing out your chart for you. Would you ever consider coming down to the hotel for dinner with me some night? Could you?"

"Yes, of course," Alia said, curling up on the big white cotton couch. "If you promise that you won't tell anyone who I am. 'The princess is coming.' That would only embarrass me."

"You know I swear and I promise. Besides, they're all used to my calling people 'Your Highness.' I call one of the donkeys that."

"Sometimes you go too far, Anthony!" Alia said, laughing.

"I won't; I am teasing. You have been so kind to me. I am already in love with you. And there is someone I want you to meet, someone who's working in the film, too. Would you come tomorrow night? Could you? When you are ready I must go now."

"With pleasure," Alia said. "Tarek is waiting to take you back to the hotel. Good night, Anthony. The beach is yours tomorrow morning. I've arranged right of passage for you."

He kissed her hand.

"Good night, Your Highness." As she looked at him she saw a fragment of the evil look that was there, always somewhere in his face. When he had gone, she walked out to the terrace and stood thinking about him. She gave a little shudder. I can't help what he knows about me, all he knows, she thought. But I wish I had never seen him.

KUSADASI
July 1960

Ian Baldwin was enjoying himself enormously. He had never been persuaded to watch any part of a film being made from one of his books before. He had to admit that he had wanted to; they could do so much visually on film that he struggled to find the words for. Film was the perfect dimension for his sophisticated, fast-paced adventure stories, and Hubbel James was the perfect producer for a film being made from a Baldwin book. The two films already made and released had grossed millions of dollars. Ian's book sales had increased steadily as a result, and if things kept going this way, Ian stood to make a great deal more money himself. Ian had admired and enjoyed both films and that was why he had come to Turkey. When he had seen the second film for the second time, he jotted off a note to Hubbel James, thanking him for the care he took with details that meant a lot to Ian. Immediately Hubbel had called and asked if he would like to come out to Turkey on location with the film unit for a week or ten days. The invitation was an extra bonus for Ian. He had been to the south coast of Turkey once before, as an amateur archaeologist. After he finished watching the scenes they were shooting in Kusadasi, he was going on a "dig" with some Scottish friends he was meeting down the coast at Priane.

"Hello, hello, what's all this about?" he heard Roy Walker, the cinematographer on the film, ask. They were having a tea break while the set was being lit for a night shot. They had started working at two in the afternoon and would go through until nine at least. As always in the hurry-up-and-wait world of filmmaking, only two shots had been made so far today.

"We have a visitor on the set, guv," Roy Walker said. "Look what the astrologist has brought us for tea."

Ian looked. The most beautiful woman he had ever seen was standing across the courtyard from him, watching the activity of carpenters and electricians as they shifted the props for a master shot from another angle. She was a good thirty feet away from Ian, but even at that distance she was exquisite. Peter Rollinson, the director, was being introduced to her by Anthony Webb. A chair was brought so she could sit and watch the proceedings.

"I think I shall leave you now," Ian said. "I'd best get over there, out of the way for the next shot, right, Walker?"

"Right, guv," Walker said. "See if you can get her name for me."

Ian walked across the courtyard, past the center fountain that was being lit as background for the next shot, through all the paraphernalia of props and wiring, never taking his eyes off Alia. It seemed to him that the closer he got, the more beautiful she became. He didn't quite understand her impact; it was not as though he hadn't seen a truly beautiful woman before. But that was the thing; there were, of course, thousands of beautiful women in the world and he had known his share of them, taken them to dinner, made love to one or two and parted from them unreluctantly. As females he admired them immensely, but why was he suddenly so drawn to this one, why was he warm inside as he walked toward her, why, when his feelings in the past had been cool and under control no matter how beautiful the woman was?

"Ah, Ian," Peter Rollinson said. "Do come and meet Princess Alia. Anthony's brought her to watch the shooting and stay for some nosh with us later."

"Princess Alia," Ian said as Peter introduced them, kissing her hand, off balance, and assailed by the faint scent of her perfume. What in the world was the matter with him, why was he so affected by her?

Alia saw before her a giant of a man, not an ounce of fat on him, just a gentle giant of an Englishman, blue-eyed with fine blond hair. He had to be six feet four at least, wearing a pink cotton shirt and beige cotton trousers, pretty much the same sort of thing the crew wore, except for the white silk ascot tied around his neck. She was surprised at his height; Ian Baldwin was a well-known figure in England because of the success of his books and the films, but no photograph she had seen gave any indication of his size.

"Your Highness," Anthony said. "Ian is the writer of the book."

"Yes, I know," Alia said. "I know your books, of course, I live in England. But you also know quite a lot about my country, I believe."

They sat down, the two of them, Anthony having been called on the set, and fell into easy conversation about Turkey and the shooting of the film. Ian explained to Alia what was happening. She was fascinated by the proceedings, and although Ian could not keep his eyes off her, he was so quiet and calm that she was not aware of his obvious staring at her. They moved position several times as the shots were changed, and finally the work was done and dinner was called. Peter Rollinson seated them, Anthony as well, at his regular, large

round table in the courtyard garden. The gypsy-camp atmosphere of the film appealed to Alia. Everyone was at ease,
there seemed to be no formalities and no jockeying for position. They all had their places, they were polite to her and
interested in her, but no one made a fuss over her.

Ian and Peter were amusing conversationalists, brilliant actually, and Alia found herself hoping that she could see more
of them, that they would want her to be with them. Anthony
remained quiet, obviously pleased with himself for having
brought her to the set.

"It's quite clear, Ian, that we might have a new technical
adviser here, one fluent in Turkish at that," Peter said.

"That should require her presence on the set every day,
shouldn't it?" Although Ian didn't show it, he was uncomfortable and baffled to be so. He was stunned by Alia. He had
written about stunning girls in his books, always smart and
beautiful girls, sexy, dangerous girls. They were part of the
Baldwin format. But in Alia's presence, he was reduced to a
bumbling idiot, a naïve, inexperienced hick, a youth. He was
none of those things and his behavior seemed perfectly normal to everyone else, but he felt like the idiot, the hick, the
youth.

"If my presence is not required on Sunday, a day of rest,
would you like to come to Yali Beyaz, my villa, and spend the
day?" Alia asked. "Peter, if you tell me how many of you can
come, I will receive you with great pleasure."

The candles had burned down and Tarek was behind her.

"I must go," Alia said.

As she rose from the table, Anthony caught a glimpse of
Ian's expression. Ian was such a big man and he moved with
care, slowly, in an easygoing way. He was being very careful
about getting up out of his chair now, but what Anthony noticed was that Ian's heart was in his eyes as he looked at Alia.

When Alia had said good night, Anthony escorted her to
the car, along with Tarek.

"Thank you, Anthony," she said. "You will be on the beach
in the morning again?"

"Yes, Your Highness."

"And you'll come Sunday?"

"With pleasure, but I'm jealous already."

"Jealous?"

"Already, I'm not the only one who's in love with you."

"Anthony, are you making predictions again?" Alia was smiling.

"No, just telling the truth. Ian has fallen for you. I know him and I've never seen him behave so carefully before, as if he were going to drop something and break it."

"Anthony, go to bed. You're dreaming already." She got in the driver's seat of the car, Tarek beside her, and drove slowly home to Yali Beyaz. Anthony blithering on like that. Ian was a nice man, big and comfortable, that was all. He had that sort of bigness that reassured you, rather than intimidating you as some men did. He was a very nice man.

Two weeks after her first visit to the set, Alia had become very much a part of the film company life. She had slipped into it as if she were on the payroll, just one more member of the cast who came and went as they worked in a moving museum of filmmaking. She had never felt comfortable in large groups of people, yet the crew made her feel as if she were one of them, and, in her way, she was quite helpful. Half of the cast and the crew were Turkish, and since the British actors spoke English only, she became translator and right hand to Peter Rollinson. The Turks in the crew were well aware of who she was and those who weren't aware that she was Baraket's wife were soon informed. The British members of the crew were fascinated by her and proud to have her working with them. "Our princess," they called her privately, guarding her identity from journalists and photographers who came on the film. Principal shooting was finished; the stars had gone, and Peter Rollinson was now concerned only with second-unit shooting. They moved to a new location almost daily, and Alia marveled at the stunt men's work.

"This is the best part of the film," Peter told her. "The

wrap. To finally have gotten rid of the stars with all their complaints and demands—what a pleasure. Did you know that our hero spent most of his time drugged to his ears? We were shooting at Ephesus a few weeks before you came to us, and one day I looked up and there he was, apart from the scene being shot, in the top row of the theater, smoking like a fool. It wasn't cigarettes: he not only doesn't smoke cigarettes but is the head of an organization in the States called NO SMOKE. Needless to say, an enterprising photographer with a long lens got a shot of him that was in the Izmir paper the next day. I went down and bought the negative. See why I'm glad they've gone? And even gladder that you are here!"

Alia was flattered. She gave an open invitation to Peter, Ian, Anthony and two or three of the stunt men and the script girls to come to Yali Beyaz every night for dinner. Alia knew she would miss them when they left.

Ian stayed in the background after their first meeting. He was content to look at Alia, to watch Alia, to breathe the same air that Alia was breathing. Little by little, his shyness lessened.

"My friends Vicky and George McKenzie will be arriving in a day or so," Ian told Alia. "We will be off to Priane by the end of the week."

"Bring them here for dinner as soon as they arrive," Alia said. "I envy you going down there. I know nothing about digging, but Priane is a part of Turkey that I have wanted to see. We had so many earthquakes in Trebizond, close to where I was born, but that's been true along this whole coast for centuries. Think what's buried beneath it all."

Tarek shuddered, overhearing the conversation. In his mind he saw Dacha's dead body as if it were only yesterday, and could hear the baby crying, the baby who was now Alia.

"Would you like to come with us?" Ian was astonished at himself for asking her to join them. Here he was, afraid to have a conversation with her, and now he'd invited her to go off on a trip with him. She'd make short shrift of him.

Alia was aware of Ian watching her, and of the distance

he'd kept between them. Now he had invited her to Priane. The giant was coming awake. She laughed.

"Of course I would. It's only four hours down the coast. Tarek can bring me for a day or so while you are there, if you would like me to come." She had to smooth over the blurting out of his invitation, seeing his embarrassment in the blush on his face.

"Marvelous. I do expect the McKenzies tomorrow at the latest. They are both experienced archaeologists—come here every year—I have been on several digs with them. I look forward to being with them and to your company if you can come."

Baraket was probably in Paris, Alia thought. He was expecting her back in London by the first of the month and she knew he did not want her to come to Paris. She did not know who the new lady he was seeing was, but it made no difference to her. Baraket was Baraket.

It made a difference to Baraket, however. It suited his purposes perfectly to allow Alia to spend more time at Yali Beyaz and to go to Priane.

"Go, go by all means," he said to her on the phone from Paris. "It's something you should take an interest in. I have been supporting many of the excavations. The more you know about it the better; as a matter of fact, you can be the most attractive archaeology lady in Turkey and be very helpful. We don't need the Swedes or the English or the Americans digging, we can do it better ourselves. Splendid idea. Go, my dear, and report to me."

LONDON
January 1961

Ian had bought a Victorian house on Pont Street in Knightsbridge, three years after the war ended, for practically nothing. Although it had not been bombed, it was in dreadful
shape, but he gradually converted it into a dozen large and
luxurious flats, and got a substantial income from renting
them out. He had kept one, the one he considered best, for
himself. It was a duplex on the ground floor and basement.
The ground floor had a rather grand drawing room with
french windows floor to ceiling, and Ian's library was in the
back, as was the stairway. The walls of the front drawing
room were painted in grayed-off lavender, a perfect background color for several large and small Chinese lacquer
pieces that Ian treasured. Striped Moroccan tent bands, blue

and turquoise medallions embroidered on disintegrating bone-colored silk, were framed, covering half of one wall. It was a formal room; a marvelous atmosphere for the small cocktail parties which Ian gave frequently. "Let the rest of the world hate cocktail parties, they still serve my purposes exactly. Everyone who comes through London comes for a drink at least." Ian worked alone for long stretches of time and never went out to luncheon, so drink time in the evening was something he looked forward to. At least once a week he would have a dozen or so friends in for a drink, depending on who was in town, and he would take five or six of them on to dinner later.

Ian spent most of his time at the typewriter in his library. The four walls had ample bookshelves and some nice paneling. There was a partners' desk with two wing chairs on either side, and two large brass filigree lamps, which gave needed light. It was an oasis of privacy, and he invited no one there.

The downstairs part of the flat was another world, cozy and informal, with a combination sitting room–dining room that had the feeling of a country house. It opened out into a walled garden that was part of Pont Street Mews. There was an entrance from the mews, and Ian often felt as though he were leading a double life. The same was true with Keogh, his manservant. Upstairs, Keogh was proper in his white coat, downstairs he was most often in a canvas apron cooking up something for Ian. As Ian wanted it, there was only one bedroom and bath. They were both large white rooms that contained several excellent pieces of eighteenth-century English furniture. It was a utopian bachelor life that he lived and he had no desire to change it. Every lady in London had set her cap for him at some time or other, especially after his books became famous. He had amiably made close friends of a number of them, and he was a favorite extra man at the best London parties. Ian had never been in love until he had seen Alia standing across the courtyard from him in Kusadasi.

He was a cerebral man and he accepted his feelings for

Alia realistically. His instincts told him that she would like very much to be anonymous in some areas of her life. It was all very well to be as beautiful as she was, but it stopped camaraderie and she was always having to cope with men who were smitten with her, or put her guard up to those whose curiosity held no kindness. The more Ian saw of her, the more he admired her. When she agreed to go on the dig with them he took it as a great compliment. He gloried in her company, and the simplicity that she displayed during the days and nights in Priane only made him fall more in love with her. He held himself on a tight rein, hoping he would get used to her, hoping he would someday be able to take her for granted, but he knew he never would.

When she returned to London months after him, he saw an arrival picture of her in the newspapers and decided to ring her up right away. She was delighted to hear from him, he could tell from her voice, and invited him to dinner a few days later. It was at that first dinner, one being given for the Prime Minister of Laos, that Ian met Baraket. The Laotian government was bestowing one of their top honors on Baraket for financial aid rendered.

"It's hard to believe the name of the order," he said to Alia. "The Order of the Million Elephants and the White Parasol."

"Baraket is very pleased, it has been many years since he started to help the Laotians, and he is proud of this. They are lovely friends, the ambassador and his wife."

"So is your husband. His look is unforgettable, I may have to write him into the next book."

Baraket and Ian were at ease together since Baraket knew a good deal about the restoration at Priane. He saw immediately the attraction this big man felt toward his wife. It was nothing; Ian was one of many drawn to Alia's beauty. He had no objection to Alia's including Ian at parties when the circumstances called for it. He was good company, an intelligent and interesting man. Baraket and Alia went to Ian's flat for drinks once or twice, finding his guests to their liking. When Baraket returned from a trip, Alia told him that she had been to Ian's to lunch or for a party, but he took no notice of it. She was always properly chaperoned and she never went out alone with anyone. Ian posed no threat. No one did.

The rest of London took notice, however. The fabled beauty, the pristine Alia, seemed to enjoy the company of the famous writer. Alia and Ian were observed in deep conversation at parties, and the rumor soon began that Ian was planning to make Alia a heroine in one of his next books. Obviously, he was besotted by her. Soon, it was taken quite for granted that Ian was Alia's property, that she was the one woman who had captured his romantic attention. That didn't sit well with available ladies who fancied Ian for themselves. Ian heard the gossip and took no notice of it, nor did Alia. As long as Baraket had no objection to his interest in her, why should anyone else?

The first person to make trouble was Anthony. He had been in Germany working in another film and when he returned, and found that Ian was usurping his position, he knew how to take care of that situation.

"He's the other man in your chart," he said to Alia one day. "You had better be careful. Baraket will not put up with an Ian for long."

"Anthony," Alia said, annoyed with him, "that is ridiculous, and troublemaking on your part. Ian is a perfect gentleman and I enjoy his company. There is nothing more to it than that. If anything, you should be the one to defend me against this sort of gossip."

"You did go off on that dig with him, and I was not invited. What happened there?"

"Nothing happened there. You were invited but you were working, you may remember. I will not have this, stop it, I do not want to hear anything else from you or anyone else about Ian. He is my friend, and that is all."

Anthony gave her a sarcastic look that showed both disbelief and jealousy. Alia was his princess, she was not to pay attention to anyone but him. He talked to her on the phone and tried to see her every day, but Baraket made it clear that Anthony was not to be invited ever without his permission. Baraket detested him.

When Anthony learned that Ian had been invited to a large important dinner and he had not, he rang up Nigel Clark, one of London's more powerful gossip columnists. They went out for drinks and dinner and Anthony filled him up with the love affair of the famous Ian Baldwin and the above-reproach exotic princess. Anthony got very drunk, and although Nigel Clark was too canny to be taken in by information from a hysterical homosexual astrologist, he went to some pains to check out a few of the things Anthony had told him. As luck would have it, he was at the same ball given the next night at the Dorchester as Ian and Alia. They were at different tables, but Nigel noted that Ian rarely had her out of his sight, and that he watched her inordinately. They danced once, Ian having asked Baraket's permission. The look on Ian's face, dancing with her, was all Nigel needed. This pair would bear watching. There was something to what Anthony said. He did not put anything in the column; that could wait.

NEW YORK
November 1962

Ryan O'Roark put through a call to George Sherril at Ehukai Farm. He had been on location for two years in the South Pacific, and had finished an epic that he knew was going to make him financially secure for the rest of his life.

"I'm due a holiday. I'm sick of everything you ever loved about any island in that vast ocean. If I ever see another palm tree or a crested wave crashing against the beach, I'll be locked up in Bellevue. Where is civilization as I used to know it?" His long legs were stretched out, feet up on an ottoman in the apartment on Fifty-sixth Street.

"Why don't you come out here? I haven't seen you for too long. We've got a lot to catch up on."

"I will, I'll be there tomorrow for the weekend."

"Are you bringing Eloise?"

"No. Eloise is the last of my wives tasteful enough to have recently departed."

"Oh," George said, not surprised. Ryan never changed. He had gotten more attractive and his work more brilliant, but he was the same old Ryan.

The next evening, Ryan stood fixing himself a drink at the butler's tray bar at the foot of the steps.

"Nothing ever disturbs your life," he said cheerfully. "Everything gets better all the time in your houses because it all stays the same. I love knowing where exactly to put my hand for the scotch bottle, and where else would I be assured that Fox will have put one of my favorite Mexican limes on the bar for me? Better skin, you know. I appreciate your consistency. Besides, this is my favorite spot in the house."

"Why?" George asked, sipping his scotch and soda.

"Because it was on this exact spot that I heard the rustle that was to change my life."

George looked at him quizzically.

"Miss Delphine Munro descended those stairs, rustling her satin dress and taffeta petticoat into my life, blazing with first-quality diamonds against her honey-colored skin, and I have never recovered from that moment, or from her."

"My God, you're human," George said. "I didn't think you even remembered her name."

"She's the only woman I remember. The rest of them blend fuzzily and sometimes thornily into each other. But Delphine —she's another story. Where is she?"

"I was afraid you were going to ask me that. She's in London, as you no doubt know. She's lived there since she and Kenneth were married."

"And she's more beautiful than ever?"

"Yes," George said. "And I will not do one thing to help you arrange to see her, which I assume is what you have in mind."

"Yes," Ryan said. "But only, dear boy, because I think I forgot to mention to you that I am going to make a film in Scotland. I'll be going to London right after Christmas, and be on location near Aberdeen for four months. . . . You don't think I should look her up? You won't tell her I'm coming?"

"She reads the papers," George said. "She'll know you're there."

"I am going to find a way to see Miss Munro—er, Mrs. Kenneth Bennett."

"Why, Ryan?" George asked. "She's happy. She wasn't when she last saw you."

"Because I want to make it up to her."

"I suppose you want to meet Kenneth, too?"

"Not on your life. I just want to see Delphine. I may not want to touch her or change her. I just want to know there are women like her. Unforgettable women who play it straight with you, give you everything, and leave you when you don't come up to the mark. I am a shit."

George laughed. "You'll see her," he said. "You won't bother her a bit."

"She'll bother me until the day I die."

"I told you you were human. Come on, dinner's ready."

Ryan checked into Claridge's in early January. He hadn't been there since the war, and the changes were a revelation to him.

"The flower arrangements," he said to Bruno, the tall head-waiter he had known since the war days when Ryan had been in the Air Force. "The flower arrangements alone, Bruno. Quite a difference from nineteen forty-two."

Bruno beamed.

"They are quite glorious, aren't they, sir?" he said, looking at the great arrangement in the corner with pride. It was Sunday night and Ryan was dining alone. There would be dozens of people on the film surrounding him from now on. He relished the thought of one dinner by himself. "Each Monday, the three most attractive women in London lunch here, sir. You should stop by tomorrow if you can."

"I shall," Ryan said. "Who are they?"

"Lady Kilmuir, sir, and Princess Fal, and Mrs. Kenneth Bennett. It's their regular table."

"Really," Ryan said. "How interesting. Keep this table for me at lunchtime tomorrow. I want to see if your taste is as impeccable as ever."

"Of course, sir. I'm surprised you don't know them, sir."

"I do, Bruno, two of them. I'll be here about twelve-thirty."

"They're rarely here before one, sir."

"That's all right, Bruno. I'll want a drink or two before they arrive."

"Of course, sir. I'll look forward to seeing you then."

Delphine and Alia took their places at the table at a few minutes past one. Camilla was always late. Delphine's profile was turned to Ryan, looking out into the lounge. Alia was facing him. Bruno was right, Ryan thought, about these two at least. He knew who Alia was, but her pictures, as exquisite as they were, didn't do her justice. Camilla came bustling in at that moment and started to sit down, looking around to see who was there, and came face to face with Ryan. Our Camilla's gone to fat, he thought, before he realized that he was shaking.

"Ryan!" Camilla said. "Ryan O'Roark. Come over here at once!" She was still standing. "Delphine, didn't you see Ryan?"

Delphine looked at Ryan as he got up and started toward them. He scooped up the small vase of garnet roses on his table and put it down in front of Delphine, not looking at the others, only looking into Delphine's eyes.

"I'm sorry they're not peonies," he said. "They seem to be out of season."

"Ryan!" Delphine said, a smile on her lips and in her eyes as she took the vase of flowers. "Sit down, join us. Why didn't you let us know you were coming? How long have you been here?"

"Last night," Ryan said, fumbling for the thin gold cigarette case in his pocket as he sat down in the empty seat beside her.

"Ryan, this is Alia, Princess Fal," Delphine said. "You don't know each other, do you?"

"No, not until now," Ryan said, taking Alia's hand and kissing it. "I've heard about you, read about you, dreamed of you, and will star you in any film you'll ever agree to be in, but fate has kept us apart all these years." He was still shaking. Delphine, Delphine, where are you, Delphine? Does any small part of you still belong to me? He clung to the martini that Bruno had brought immediately from his table.

Alia laughed. "The famous Ryan O'Roark," she said. "You've made films in both of my countries, Egypt and Turkey, and never come to us. Why not? My husband's admiration for you is immense."

Ryan tapped out a cigarette on the gold box and lit it. His heart was pounding, still. He had thought about Delphine a thousand times, perhaps a million times, since she had left for Europe with George that summer long ago. As the years passed, she had become more important to him, not less. It was her quality, her intelligence, her style, that he missed. There weren't any other women like her, or if there were, he had not found them. In every breakup, with every wife, there had been no regrets on his part, but a growing remembrance of Delphine and a realization that he hadn't known what he had with her. And then, the knowledge that no matter what happened between them, he would have had to let her go. Work was his master, his mistress, his life, and he knew that Delphine understood it. None of the others had. There was no competing with his work, and there was no woman who didn't try, didn't have to try, to blend into the landscape of his work, fruitlessly. Delphine had known better. She was too smart, he had known that and had told her that. She had accepted it and gone her way, and found her way. It was obvious, looking at her now. She was completely at ease and delighted to see him. He was a small part of her past and he had no role in her present or future. Jesus, he thought, I wish my name were Kenneth Bennett.

Over lunch, Delphine and Camilla brought Alia into the memories of the days just before they had met on *Ehukai III*.

"I was working in California," Camilla said. "I had met Russ, and on the way home to England I came to spend a weekend with George at Ehukai Farm. Ryan was there for dinner and I decided that he could change my life, until I saw him look at Delphine at the dinner table. I came home and married Jeremy, and the next thing I knew, Delphine was on the yacht, and you were on the yacht and Kenneth was on the yacht, and Ryan was in Mexico making the first film that won him an Academy Award. And we haven't seen you since then, that was two Oscars ago. Now are we going to see you? I hope so."

"I hope so too, Camilla," Ryan said. "I'll be here for four months, most of the time in the wilds of Scotland. But when I come back to London, I'll call and we will get together. I have three husbands to meet." Suddenly, he was restless. If only I could be alone with her, for five minutes, ten minutes, one more hour of my life, he thought. He could see that nothing like that was going to happen. She was gone, even though she was sitting there beside him, she was gone. His Delphine belonged to someone else. He'd lost her forever.

The four of them parted in the lobby of Claridge's. Ryan was paged to the phone box: a call from California. Delphine decided to walk. She had some errands to do, and then she was going to a meeting at the Hyde Park Hotel. She walked up Brook Street and cut across into Hyde Park, thinking about Ryan. Her reaction to him had surprised her. She had thought many times about what it would be like to see him again. In Baden-Baden, she had been apprehensive about the end of the summer, her return to New York and possibly to Ryan. Kenneth had changed all that.

The park was bare, the sky was gray, it was cold and it was

going to rain. Delphine gathered her amber-colored wool coat around her, loving the damp wind on her face. He looked wonderful, she thought, he is a wonderful-looking man. Am I reacting slowly to having seen him again, she wondered? No, she thought, I'm not. He was a part of my life, a proving ground in my life. He's not a part of my life anymore and he hasn't been for a long time. How strange. When they were together, he had been everything to her, everything. If he called, if he didn't call, when he called, when he couldn't call: her whole life had hung on his presence. Looking at him, making love to him, tasting him, being with him—he had been everything to her. The timbre of his voice when he talked to her, an octave lower when he made love to her. How could she sit at a table with him and feel nothing? I did feel something, she thought. I was glad to see him. I must tell Kenneth he's here.

Kenneth. Kenneth, who had always felt about her the way she had about Ryan. My beloved, she thought, is it possible that I have never told you how much I love you? I know I've told you, but I couldn't possibly have told you enough. She looked at her watch. It was after three-thirty, she was late for her meeting. She turned and walked toward Hyde Park Corner. There was a phone box there, and taxis. Kenneth had said he would be home by four today. She dropped the coin in the red phone box and dialed Kenneth's private number in the library. Maybe he would be home a little early.

"Bennett here," the familiar voice said. She could see his eyes, she knew the chair he was sitting in, looking out across Regent's Park.

"Delphine Bennett here!" she said, hearing the lilt in her own voice. "Darling, I'm at the edge of Hyde Park and missed a meeting and have just hailed a taxi that is stopping for me this very second. Are you going to be there, you don't have to go out again?"

"I'm going to be here, my dearest," Kenneth said. "Get in that taxi quickly. It's cold. Come on home."

PARIS

May 1963

"It's going to be an orgy one way or another," Camilla said to Delphine when the invitations to the De Pavenel party arrived in London. "I wouldn't miss it for the world."

"What do you mean, 'orgy'?" Delphine asked. "You know Kenneth won't go to anything wild, and he hates big parties anyhow. But a lush, opulent, fancy dress ball in high season in Paris, with everyone in the world there—if one believes what one reads in the newspapers—is that an orgy?"

"No, but Graziella will turn it into one, if she has her way. Imagine her giving this party for Halid's twenty-first birthday, her known lover. And Edmond right there on the spot receiving. All the fancy dress part means is that Graziella gets to take off her clothes—you know how she loves to show off—and Halid is worse. That's got the makings of a pretty good orgy."

"Well, at least she's having it at home."

"All the more reason it will get out of control. As I told you, I can't wait. I just wish I could take off some of this weight."

Delphine decided to let that remark go by. "You'll turn up the most glamorous one at the whole party no matter what you wear. But I'm worried about Kenneth, and even about Jeremy. They'll probably take us home by midnight and we'll miss the whole thing."

"You may go home. I'm not. Besides, Russ is coming."

Delphine looked at her in surprise.

"Russ is coming to Paris? Does Jeremy know?"

"Of course not. There may be a strike at the paper, and then he won't be able to go at all. I hope so."

"Cam, you don't mean that."

"I do. I haven't seen Russ for over a year, and I don't need Jeremy around at the same time."

Delphine ducked the second sore subject as deftly as she had Camilla's weight problem.

"Why does Graziella do it? I know she's an exhibitionist, but she doesn't have to prove herself. She did that years ago when she first came to Paris and caught Edmond. With her money and his, she's one of the richest ladies in Paris with one of, if not *the*, most powerful husbands in that whole hierarchy. But a fancy dress ball, and Edmond and Halid under the same roof . . . I think she just likes to shock."

"It takes courage, and she's got it. And she takes chances: she's got to top everyone in everything she does. Marie Pierre will be tearing her hair out. Of course, she hates Graziella and she doesn't have half her guts, but she *is* French and supposedly they are best friends. But I've never seen such a feud. Oh, I can't wait!"

Delphine laughed. "Alia and Baraket will put us all to shame. They'll have at least ten guards, and you know they'll both be wearing some of the emeralds. They have been in

Paris for nearly a month now, and Alia told me that Balmain's making her an emerald-green chiffon dress. Everyone will go bonkers trying to see the emeralds. No color contrast; you'll have to get right next to her to see them, which the guards will prevent anyone from doing. It's clever of her, really. And Baraket will be resplendent, to say the least. He'll have that hundred-carat rock in his turban, and the guards will be going off their heads to protect them. I wonder how much press there will be?"

"Plenty. Graziella will see to it that the photographers and reporters are thoroughly pampered until they have taken every picture she wants taken and written down every word she wants to be quoted as having said. She has four reporters and six photographers covering, but the entire press is going to be thrown out before dinner. After that is when the fun will begin."

"I've got to go home and tell Kenneth every bit of this, except about Russ, and I wouldn't be surprised if he has a World Bank meeting called in Hong Kong. Oh, Cam, I'm just like you. I can't wait."

Camilla did everything she could to discourage Jeremy from going to Paris, to no avail.

"Don't you want me to go?" he asked finally. "You seem to very much want to go by yourself."

"No, not at all," Camilla said. "I know you're worried about the strike, that's all. And you have a habit of going to these things and looking it all over, then dragging me home. Graziella is so crazy and does such wild things that I want to stay through everything this time."

"All right," Jeremy said. "If I decide to go home, I won't make you go with me. Fair enough?"

"Yes," Camilla said. What a bore. Well, maybe she could get him to go home the next day and she and Russ could stay in Paris. Damn Jeremy.

On the morning of Graziella's party, Baraket called Anthony

into the library that he used as an office, on the floor he had taken at the Crillon. His face was dark; his distaste for Anthony showed clearly.

"Several things have come to my attention, Anthony. Your behavior in Paris leaves a great deal to be desired. As you seem to have become part of my entourage, thanks to the favor of Princess Alia, I have overlooked certain reports until now."

"Oh, really, Your Highness? What?" Anthony asked solicitously. He was outwardly calm, but his voice had gone up slightly. He was afraid of Baraket and he hated him. When he was alone with Alia, when Baraket was traveling, they got on perfectly.

"What has come to my attention comes very close to being blackmail. I have been informed that you have bought several dozen shirts here, some suits there, shoes from another place, and, finally, both Cartier and Boucheron have presented bills to my secretary on your behalf. Who gave you permission to acquire these things?"

"Princess Alia told me to go out and pick up a few things." She hadn't exactly, but Anthony had been planning to tell her that if he was going to be part of the entourage in Paris, he had to have some decent clothes.

"Princess Alia knows nothing about your purchases. I'm sure it will come as no surprise to you that I have never been pleased with your presence among us, any more than I have with your obvious influence on the princess. I have reached this conclusion, Anthony. I will arrange payment for the things you have charged, and I will continue to pay your hotel bill until the end of this week. Then you are free to make other arrangements. Do you understand?"

"I don't understand at all. The princess and I are very close, and I promised her that I would stay with you. I've given up jobs to be with you." His voice was still high, but he summoned the courage from somewhere to try to pacify Baraket. He had to stay near Alia. There wasn't a better meal ticket than Alia anywhere.

Baraket rose to his feet.

"Anthony, you may go. If you make any attempt whatsoever to go against my wishes, I'm sure you know that you will regret it. *Au revoir.*" Baraket turned toward the drawing room. The doors opened for him, and Anthony knew that the entire conversation had been heard by one or several of Baraket's aides.

Left alone in the library, Anthony felt anger boiling up in his throat. That bastard. Who did he think he was? Alia . . . where was she? She was the answer. Alia must persuade Baraket to keep him. It was all her fault, and after all he had done for her. Where was she?

Anthony left quickly and went to Alia's rooms, but there was no one there but her maids. He ran down the hall and pushed the button for the elevator frantically. She would still be at Balmain's. He'd find her there.

The elevator door opened and Alia stepped out, with two bodyguards at her side.

"Alia, I must see you at once." He took her arm.

Alia looked at him coldly.

"Take your hand off my arm. I trusted you, although from the very first time I saw you I knew better. Now you've dug your own grave with Baraket. I know what he has said to you. Now, may I pass, please?"

"What about the party tonight?" Anthony was close to tears. "I'm going to the party with you. I've got my costume all ready."

"Anthony, I'm afraid that will be impossible."

One of the guards bumped Anthony as Alia swept past him. Not hard, but a reminder that he was in the way. All Anthony could think about was Graziella's party. He *had* to go; he'd been planning for it ever since the invitations had come. The party was the talk of Paris and everyone was envious of him. None of them had been invited—his late-night friends—but he had; he was going with the fabulous princess. To hell with them all. He would find a way to go to the party. Tomorrow he'd go back to Baraket and offer to take the things back. This would blow over; he'd see to that at Graziella's party tonight.

Graziella Mercati de Pavenel—La Comtesse Edmond de Pavenel—Milanese-born only child of Orlando Mercati of the immensely rich aircraft-building Mercatis, was married to one of the most powerful international bankers in Paris. It was a strange alliance, since Graziella was one of the few Italians born who had absolutely no taste in anything, and Edmond de Pavenel was *raffiné* to a point of antagonism. Edmond was nearly twenty years older than Graziella and was extremely fond of her when he gave her any thought at all. The success of their marriage could very well have been due to her lack of taste. Rather than bothering him, it comforted him. His knowledge was incomparable, and with Graziella there was no competitive spirit to battle. She ran the house—the fabulous Palais Pavenel—wonderfully. If Edmond complained about the chef's choice of menus or the way one of the chauffeurs drove, Graziella good-naturedly replaced the employee instantly. Her clothes and jewels were flamboyant, but somehow they suited her. She exuded sex appeal; she thought constantly about sex, and she had acquired an enviable string of lovers as the years went by. The current one, Halid, was ten years her junior and looked as if he might last. He was Tunisian, with some money; he didn't spoil easily and he never made the mistake of trying to change Graziella.

"How nice," one of Graziella's cattier friends observed when she heard about the huge birthday party being planned for Halid. "Rather sweet of her to celebrate his coming of age. Just think, now he can vote."

Graziella had gone all out with her plans. This party was going to be the most expensive, the most glamorous and talked-about party in Paris for years. Naturally, Graziella was no more inventive than she was tasteful, but the Arabian Nights theme suited her purposes. Her guests could be as ex-

travagant or as subdued as they liked in their choices of cos-
tumes, and she could display herself in an absolute minimum
of clothing, which she loved to do. She also loved giving a
party, and she would see to it that there were a few surprises
as well. Graziella encouraged outrageous behavior in her
friends at all times, but at this party the most outrageous behavior would be her own. They'd see.

The reception rooms, halls, terraces and gardens of the
Palais Pavenel, plus the ballroom, could easily accommodate
six hundred. Florists and decorators took over and worked for
ten days. When they finished, both Palais Pavenel and the
gardens were almost unrecognizable. The Arabian Nights
reigned supreme. Gauzy gold draperies hung throughout, and
from some of the tall trees in the gardens chandeliers lit by
candles festooned across terraces and gardens. In dark corners of the vast gardens, tall torches burned, and thousands
of flowers fought for dramatic priority in tangled profusion.
Anthuriums and proteus, torch gingers and porcelain gingers, lotus and blue lilies of the Nile and copa do oro were
massed against trellises already rampant with bougainvillaea.

It seemed as if all the flowers in Brazil, South Africa, Mexico and Hawaii had found their way to Paris. Graziella saw to
it that there was music playing everywhere. Strolling trouba-
dours wandered in and out. Aimé Barelli held forth in the
ballroom and Raoul, from the Eléphant Blanc in Paris, played
his bossa novas and sambas in an intimate nightclub that had
grown with the help of the decorators and florists from beneath the long colonnade in the far garden. Tables were set
indoors and out; white-gloved butlers served six hundred
guests, as well as providing them with champagne that
poured from innumerable fountains.

Graziella left nothing to chance. Edmond would never consider standing to receive that many people, so she put him in
his favorite small library where he could watch everyone who
entered and decide if he chose to receive them. He had two

friends with him. She would receive with Halid. It was going to be one of the greatest parties ever given in Paris, or anywhere else. Graziella was sure of that.

Baraket felt Alia's nails digging into his arm through the sleeve of his dinner jacket, gripping him hard. He could feel her body trembling; the tension flowing through her culminated in her long nails pressing into him. It wasn't like her.

"What is it?" he asked quietly as they walked up the long marble staircase that led into Graziella's eighteenth-century Palais Pavenel. Cameras were flashing all about them; the staircase was lined with photographers and a pack of them waited at the top. Baraket looked neither to the right nor to the left, nor did Alia, but the pressure increased on his arm.

"Anthony," she said.

"Anthony," Baraket repeated. "Anthony the Uninvited. Where is he?"

"He's at the top of the staircase, just behind the photographers, right across from Graziella. He's got on some foolish ostrich-feather headdress."

Baraket was still looking straight ahead, the official expression he showed to photographers unchanged.

"I wonder how he managed it."

"I don't know," Alia said. "But he will be looking for trouble."

"He'll find it then. But he will not get within twenty feet of either of us; I will see to that."

As they reached the top of the staircase, Alia gave a small token smile to the photographers. Baraket rarely, if ever, went to parties if there was going to be a preponderance of press. Graziella had assured him that, once inside, there would be none. Balmain had managed to camouflage Alia, to some extent at least, until she got past the cameras. Her green dress swirled around her, undulating, cascading as she walked. The color was exactly the shade of the emeralds, subduing them so that only a subtle flash of diamonds glittered through the ruffled chiffon stole as the flashbulbs went off.

At the top of the stairs Graziella waited to greet her guests. Camilla had been right: she was wearing next to nothing. The tiniest of gold lamé bras, encrusted with pearls, topped a draped skirt of thin lamé that dipped far below her navel, wrapping her hips but splitting to reveal her long, beautiful legs. Her head was bound in a gold turban dripping with ropes of tiny pearls that framed her face. A huge canary diamond in the center of the turban, just above her forehead, fastened a shoot of painted gold egret feathers above her head.

"Your Highness Princess Alia," she said. "How nice that you could come."

"Graziella, you look spectacular," Baraket said, choosing his words correctly. He nodded at Halid; that was all that was necessary for a lover. The party was for Halid, but it took guts to receive with your lover and without your husband. Edmond, Graziella's husband, was in his favorite small library, no doubt. Graziella had guts and bore the controversy accompanying her behavior well.

The cameras went off, hundreds of flashbulbs making an aurora borealis around them. Baraket's white turban contained one hundred carats of the world-famous Fal emerald, flawless, one of the most valuable stones in the world of jewels.

A parody of Graziella's voice screeched out from behind them. "Your Highness Princess Alia. How nice you could come." It was Anthony's voice.

Graziella looked toward him. Something was wrong. She had invited Anthony, but through Alia, not by formal invitation. He would be included in Baraket's entourage only if they wanted him to come. Baraket and Alia had moved quickly on into the crowd of guests without acknowledging his presence. Halid, standing beside her, was aware that something out of the ordinary had happened.

"What is it?" he asked.

"Nothing," Graziella said. "It may make for an even better party, if that's possible. Not to worry." She looked at Halid, who was wearing even less than she was. His tanned body was perfect, his deep blue eyes as desirous as ever as she returned his glance. She looked briefly after Anthony—something had obviously gone awry there—but he had vanished into the crowd. Graziella turned her attention back to her arriving guests. She would be receiving for the better part of the next hour. It was all going to go very well. Everyone in Paris, everyone of any importance in the world society, had arrived. She could hear the music playing inside and the growing excitement of the conversation. The party would get going after dinner, not before. Graziella couldn't wait.

A fanfare of trumpets announced Graziella's entrance into her own party after her guests were all assembled. A procession of little Sudanese boys, dressed as blackamoors, led the procession, carrying huge litters overflowing with fruits shaped into huge pyramids on their shoulders. They were moving in from the outside perimeter of the garden to the center. Torches burned high above their heads, adding to the opulence of the scene.

"It's a spectacular beginning," Camilla said. "What next?"

Another fanfare of trumpets sounded.

"Good God, look!" Jeremy said. "I don't believe what she's done this time."

Ten blue-black Nubian slaves, six-and-a-half-foot giants with their bodies oiled to a gleaming perfection, carried a golden litter on their shoulders to the center part of the garden. They were gorgeous specimens and, except for wide armbands and headbands made of huge fake rubies, they were bone-naked. Graziella and Halid were lying on the litter, indolently propped up on their elbows, playfully tossing handfuls of large, gold-sequined confetti into the air.

"Even for Paris and Graziella, that's pretty racy stuff," Kenneth said. "I have heard several audible gasps."

"Envy," Baraket said, his white teeth flashing in a broad smile. "If one must give or go to a big party, this is the way to do it."

The Nubians made their way to the dance floor in the center of the garden and placed the litter on a long table covered with golden cloth. Halid got to his feet and pulled Graziella up beside him, as everyone rose to applaud Graziella for her spectacular entrance. The trumpets were still blowing; the naked Nubians lined up behind Graziella and Halid, waving gigantic torches that stroked lines of flame into the night. Graziella lapped up the "bravos" and the applause like a kitten drinking cream. At her signal, Raoul's samba music filled the garden and Graziella and Halid danced the first dance. In no time, half the party was dancing. The festivities had begun.

Graziella had seated husbands and wives together at tables for eight. Baraket and Alia, Kenneth and Delphine, and Jeremy and Camilla knew already that they were at the same table. Only Camilla, who had discussed the seating with Graziella several days before, knew that Russ would be at their table too.

"Thank heavens we're together," Delphine said. "Who else is with us?"

"Russ Marshall," Camilla said.

So that's it, Jeremy thought. That's why she didn't want me to come, and that's why she wants to stay over. I should have known.

The same exact thoughts went through Russ's head when he arrived a few minutes later. So that's it. Jeremy is here and Camilla thinks she is going to have her cake and eat it, too. We'll see about that. He looked at Camilla across the table from him, her back turned to Jeremy. She's really fat, he thought. Some women were, after a few children. Obviously, she wasn't going to age well.

In the absence of another girl, Baraket and Russ were seated together, to their mutual pleasure. Russ's advice about the methods of cotton-growing in Texas had paid off handsomely for Baraket. Russ was about to ask Alia or Delphine to dance, studiedly ignoring Camilla's signals to ask her, when a half-naked girl, obviously quite drunk, inserted herself between Baraket and himself, draping her arms around Baraket, pressing her breasts against the back of his turban and his shoulders. She had as little on as their hostess but she was far more beautiful. Her face was vaguely familiar to Russ but he couldn't place her. Films? Theater? Before Russ could think about it, she turned on him.

"Don't you know what a gentleman is?" she asked. "A gentleman is someone who gives a lady his chair. Why don't you go dance or do something, I want to talk to His Exalted Highness."

Russ looked at her coolly, neither answering nor rising to his feet.

"I want to meet your exalted princess," Ceil said to Baraket, wedging herself in between the two men. "We have something great in common and I'd like to compare notes. You." She reached for a glass of champagne, anyone's, on the table. She was still standing.

Baraket looked at Russ, not even slightly flustered. That cool cat has been up against stuff like this before, Russ thought, admiring Baraket's posture. Still looking at Russ, Baraket nodded toward Alia and made a slight tap with his fork on the champagne glass in front of him. "Alia, my *canim*," he said, using his favorite endearing Turkish word, the word for "star." "Russ would like to dance with you." She smiled at Baraket and Russ, ignoring Ceil, and Russ rose to go and get her. Ceil sat down, pushing what had now become her chair, closer to Baraket.

"Why don't you call me anymore?" Ceil asked. "I know several other ladies you call when Her Exalted is at home in London with your babies. Why not me?"

"Ceil, my dear, you have never been so beautiful before. What are you doing, and how is Guy?"

"We're divorced. He resented the fact that I liked them young. Except for you. You're the best . . ."

The rest of her sentence was lost in the sudden commotion around them. Anthony was screaming at the top of his lungs, being held off by two of Baraket's bodyguards. "If that cunt can talk to him, so can I," he yelled, trying to get away from them.

Ceil realized what was happening; she had been with Baraket before when others had tried to break the barrier surrounding him. "Shut up, Anthony," she said. "I brought you to this party, that's the only way you could have gotten here, and now you're acting like the oily little fag you are."

Anthony screeched at her: "You brought me so you could get at Baraket and tell him everything I've told you about Alia, you wouldn't know anything except for me . . ."

Ceil threw a glass of wine in his face and turned back to Baraket, knowing her time was limited. "Anthony may not be part of your entourage any longer, your wife's personal adviser, but you should have paid him more or had him shut up permanently. He tells me your princess is, in fact, from a grubby, illegal little harem in a stinking little Turkish town; that she belonged to a dirty little businessman, not even your grand harem. And for that, you gave me up?" The three guards closed in from behind, waiting to lift her out of the chair at the slightest sign from their master. No one was paying attention to the commotion; the party had reached its crescendo. Grapes were being pelted through the air, and pieces of cake flew across tables. A girl at the next table had taken off her top; the man with her had slathered chocolate mousse on her breasts and was licking it off.

Baraket nodded to the guards. At the very moment the guards reached for her, Russ, who had turned Alia over to Kenneth and Delphine on the other side of the dance floor with one word of warning, put his hand on one of the guards' shoulders and said, "I beg your pardon, but I am going to dance with this young lady. Take your hands off her." The guards looked at Baraket, who nodded briefly. They vanished into the crowd as quickly as they had come. It was Baraket's turn to compliment Russ's behavior.

"Now," Russ said, half-dragging Ceil out of the chair, "I'd like another one of your lines about being a gentleman and giving up the chair. Or a lady. Shall we dance?" He had a firm hold on her. "If you want to get out of here, I'll get you out of here," he said. "If you want those gorillas to throw you and your charming companion out, I can arrange that, too." Ceil looked at him, sober for an instant, regardless of the waxy shine in her eyes. This girl is hooked, Russ thought, hooked hard.

"I'd rather dance," she said, eyes boring into him, full attention turned toward him.

Camilla and Jeremy came back to the table just as Russ danced off with Ceil.

"What is Russ doing with Ceil?" Camilla asked Baraket. "I didn't even know he'd met her." Camilla and Ceil had run into each other in Paris, long after their first meeting in Monte Carlo. Camilla had heard all about her love affair with Baraket. No one knew about the nights that Ceil and Camilla had combed Pigalle together with some of the rough-trade characters they picked up in the bars. Camilla kept some things to herself, but Ceil couldn't. She would tell Russ, Camilla knew. Damn her, damn Jeremy for being here, and damn this party, she thought.

"He hadn't," Baraket said, still unruffled. "Not until five minutes ago, but I believe he is going to get to know her." Kenneth appeared with Alia and Delphine and the three of them sat back down.

"Everything all right?" Kenneth asked Baraket.

"What on earth is happening?" Delphine asked. "Russ brought Alia to us and told us to make our way back here slowly. I saw Anthony raising some hell, but what is Ceil doing here with, of all people, Anthony?"

"Nothing of any importance," Alia said. "No one should pay any attention to that poor little girl; she's just drunk and having a good time." Alia had overheard every word Ceil said to Baraket before Russ took her to dance. It was the first time Alia had seen her, but it was not the first time Ceil's name had been spoken in connection with Baraket. Alia chose, as always, to ignore gossip about Baraket, regardless of the source.

Russ and Ceil had vanished from sight.

"Let's go to the powder room," Camilla said, her only desire being to find out where Russ had gone to with Ceil. "We could do with a few cool moments." Alia and Delphine rose, realizing that Baraket and Kenneth would want to know what had happened to Anthony, but Baraket had a different plan. "Alia," he said. "Sit here with me. I think we shall probably leave soon, as soon as Delphine and Camilla return. I want you beside me now."

"Of course, my love." Baraket didn't know where Anthony was at the moment and he was not going to let Alia be accosted by him. Never again.

In Russ's limousine, Ceil began to sob, pawing at her eye makeup, tearing the golden headdress to shreds, trying to get all the pins out of her hair and get it off. The intensity of her sobs increased.

"Why all the hullabaloo?" Russ said. "You could have gotten in trouble. You might thank me for getting you out of there."

"A Turkish harem girl . . . a cheap Turkish harem girl . . . and he married her. When he could have had me . . . when I could have had him . . ." The tears were streaming down her face. Russ reached for her hand.

"Ceil," he said, gently, "it will all seem better tomorrow. Let's go somewhere . . . Calvados maybe . . . and have a drink." She was a pain in the neck, but for some reason, something about her look, Russ felt sorry for her.

"I don't want a drink, take me home with you . . ."

"All right," Russ said. "I just might do that."

When Delphine and Camilla came out of the powder room Anthony was waiting for them in the hall. They hadn't seen him all evening.

"Anthony!" Camilla said, looking at his almost-naked body. "If you were a different color, you could have helped carry the hostess in." She did find him amusing at times, even if he was a little evil. Delphine had never liked him and showed it plainly.

"Good evening, Anthony," she said, as remote as a statue, moving past him.

"I have some gossip for you two intimate friends of the princess, some information that will curl your hair," Anthony said, his eyes glittery.

"Later, Anthony," Camilla said. "How about tomorrow?" Delphine had walked on.

"No." Anthony hissed. "Now is the best time. Your precious princess is a whore. Did you know that? She came from a cheap harem in Trebizond, did you know that? He made her a princess, a phony princess, before he married her; did you know that? Ask him about her background, or ask him if he knows it. I read it all in her chart when I first met her; it scared her to death when I told her. Now you can tell her you know all about her. I've kept her secret for years."

Delphine, having heard him, turned back to Anthony.

"That's quite enough," she said icily. "Camilla, do come along."

"Well, if you're fool enough to doubt it, ask her about a man named Mahmed Maravi. She was owned by Maravi until Baraket bought her. Now she won't be so high and mighty with you anymore, or anyone else—I'll see to it, after the time I've had with her today."

He was gone as swiftly as he had come. Delphine and Camilla looked at each other.

"Bad scene," Camilla said. "He's going to get in a lot of trouble. What shall we do? Shall we tell Baraket?"

"No," Delphine said.

"Do you suppose he's telling the truth?"

"Yes," Delphine said. "I suppose he is telling the truth. It's just the sort of thing people like Anthony do."

"I think it's quite fascinating."

"So do I. If true, it makes Alia even more valuable than before." Delphine was thinking of times when Kenneth had alluded to something concerning Alia and her mysterious background. Kenneth had been trying to tell her something very subtly, something she had paid no attention to. The tip of the iceberg. Kenneth disliked Anthony, too.

"We'd better get back to the table," Delphine said. "You can bet Baraket and Kenneth are going to want to go home. Jeremy, too."

"I told you so when we first talked about this party," Camilla sighed. "And I'm stuck with good old Jeremy, Russ having vanished into the night with Ceil. God damn it."

"Camilla!" Delphine said.

"I mean it," Camilla said, still searching for Russ and Ceil, knowing somehow that they had gone.

Anthony waited, hidden in the shadows near the entrance door. He could see everyone leaving; no one could get out without passing by him. He saw the green of Alia's dress as she walked toward the door with Baraket. Thank God they were by themselves, not with the others. He would just have time to say what he wanted to say to Baraket before the guards would be on him again.

When they were as close as they would get to him, he darted out from the shadows. The guards were on him instantly, but Baraket heard what he had to say. Baraket heard every word.

"I know you are still her husband, Your Highness, but are you also still her lover? She has one, you know. Don't forget that I told you."

Without acknowledging his existence, Baraket and Alia walked on.

Tarek knew from the way Baraket and Alia stepped into the car that something was gravely wrong. He had no idea what it was; no gossip had filtered out from the waiters to the chauffeurs so far.

Alia's face was like stone and she held her head much higher than usual, a sign of tension that Tarek recognized in her. Baraket's body was still and angry, coldly angry.

Baraket ordered Tarek to take them to the Crillon; then he put the glass divider up between them, another sign of trouble. Tarek flipped the switch that opened the two small vents that he had cut beside each window in the back seat. He had cut them as delicately as a surgeon cuts flesh, and he had covered them with painstaking care. He could hear everything said in the back seat when the switch was flipped. It was a good idea for him to know what was being said, no matter who it was. He had made the same arrangement in the cars everywhere that they lived, be it Istanbul, Paris or London. The other drivers, needless to say, were not aware of his private listening device.

Neither Baraket nor Alia spoke for the time it took to drive across Paris to the Crillon. Just as they reached the Place de la Concorde, Tarek heard Baraket's voice.

"Is it true?"

Alia turned to face him.

"That I have a lover?"

"Yes."

"No."

"Don't lie to me. You know I can find out." After the years of trusting her, surely she could not be cuckolding him.

"I have never lied to you."

"Anthony has, to all of us. What did he mean?"

"He is talking about Ian."

"Is Ian your lover?"

"Of course not, he has never touched me." Alia was close to panic. She had seen Baraket's fury turned on others; this was the first time she was the recipient of it. He would never relent until he knew everything about Ian now; what little there was to know was not important, it was how Baraket decided to take it that mattered.

"But he has touched your mind and possibly your heart,

and it is common gossip apparently. The mind is where the greatest infidelity lies, and that I cannot forgive. He has, yes?"

Alia paused. It was a fatal pause.

"Tarek," Baraket commanded, opening the divider. "Keep driving. Go over to the Tour Eiffel. I will tell you when to turn back." He turned to Alia again.

"Now you must tell me everything that has transpired between you and Mr. Baldwin. I gave you my permission to go on the small archaeology expedition with that group when you were last in Kusadasi. Or were you just two?"

"Of course not. Tarek was with me. You know that. And the McKenzies. Anthony had to work, or he would have gone, too."

Baraket cursed. "Anthony this, Anthony that. I indulged you, in all these years, in only one weakness, that of allowing Anthony around you. What a fool I was. He introduced you to the alluring Mr. Baldwin, and now the common gossip of the streets is that you are sleeping with him. Mentally, if no other way."

"No, I have been the fool." It would do no good to defend herself. That she had looked at a man, that she had thought about a man, shared her thoughts with any man but Baraket, that was the mistake. It didn't matter how many women Baraket had, in or out of the harems, or the dozens of Ceils, nor did it matter that he had left her isolated more often than not lately and had been seen and even photographed with other women. Tafida would love hearing all this.

"You are never to see Anthony again, I believe I made that clear this afternoon. I would suggest that you not see Mr. Baldwin either. Do you understand?"

"Yes." There it was. Baraket was even more incensed, she knew, because of Ian's fame. Any man would matter, but the famous Ian Baldwin assaulted Baraket's pride. Camilla's flouting of her succession of waiters, salesmen and meaningless bodies was bad enough, but not as bad as Ian. Why couldn't she lie? But how could she lie to Baraket, who had given her everything? Strangely enough, she had known, even without

Anthony's predictions, that a time would come when Baraket would leave her. Even though he had married her and she was the mother of two children who would inherit the dynasty, she was of no importance now. His pride was involved, his vanity. She had betrayed him.

Baraket was silent. Alia waited. Then he spoke.

"Tarek, take us to the hotel."

Tarek could scarcely control himself and drive the car smoothly. When they reached the Crillon he opened the door, helping Alia out. She looked at him solemnly. Baraket made no move from the back seat.

"Take the princess in and be sure someone escorts her to her rooms. Then come back."

Alia's legs almost gave out under her. It was the first time she had weakened.

"Baraket, please don't leave me alone. Anthony has told Delphine and Camilla about me tonight, too. Did you know that? He's left no stone unturned."

"What Camilla and Delphine think of you is of no concern to me. What I think of you is. Insha' Allah, my dear."

"When will you be back?" She was weeping now.

"Do not wait for me. You may go to London if I should not return." He pulled the car door closed and sat back on the seat. He lit a cigar, not looking at her. Tarek pulled gently on her arm.

"Princess Fal, we must go in. I will be with him. You will hear from me."

Alia took one more look in the window of the car. Baraket was puffing on his cigar, staring straight ahead. She knew he would never look at her. She turned with a sigh and let Tarek escort her into the hotel. She was alone again.

Russ took Ceil to his suite in the Ritz. She was hysterical in the car, but he quieted her down enough to get her through the lobby on the Cambon side, up to his rooms. He ordered some hot milk, to the astonishment of the night waiter, and while Ceil was still in the bathroom, sobbing pitifully now, he dissolved the contents of three sleeping pills in the milk. When she came out of the bathroom, blubbering, he took her clothes off her and wrapped her up in one of the toweling robes from the bathroom door.

"Sit down," he ordered, taking off his shoes and socks. She watched him as he removed his tie and shirt, then trousers and shorts, dropping them all on the floor around him. He picked her up in his arms, cradling her, and carried her into the bathroom, where he had filled the big bathtub with warm water. He forced her to drink the glass of milk down in one gulp; she hardly resisted him, fascinated by what he was doing. Neither of them said a word. He put her in the tub, robe and all, and got in with her, cradling her again in his arms, removing the wet robe and soaping her all over with his hands, rubbing her breasts and the insides of her thighs until she started to moan and respond to what he was doing. He lifted her out of the tub, rubbing her dry with one of the huge towels from the hot rack. She was completely relaxed and trying to keep her eyes open, but the pills had begun to take effect. He laid her down in the bed and put his body down on top of hers, putting himself inside her, making love to her rhythmically, sensuously and swiftly. She was still awake, just barely, when he came. "More . . . more," she begged him, trying to touch him.

"Tomorrow, baby," he said. "Right now we're both going to get a good night's sleep. No one needs it more than we do; we're both rejects." He wrapped his arms around her, holding her body close to him, already asleep himself.

PARIS

May 1963

When Anthony got back to the small hotel on the Rue de Tremoille, he was still very drunk. It was near dawn. Letting himself into his room, he felt a dizzying sense of triumph. Maybe he would order a bottle of champagne and drink to himself. Her Exalted Highness had played it high and mighty with him, had tried to dismiss him from her confidence, and instead it was he who had wreaked havoc with her life. If she thought she could do away with him after all he had done for her, all he had told her, she was a fool. She owed everything to him. It was he who had advised her how to handle Baraket. It was he who had introduced her to her lover, the great Ian. It was he who had instructed her as to her past incarnations and taught her what to reach out for in this one.

And she had betrayed him. She had taken everything from him, bled him of his knowledge and given him nothing. She had used him. The few bills she had paid for him, the pittance that he had had to ask her for—that was nothing. The thin Patek Philippe watch for his birthday was nothing either. She was even stingy with all those emeralds. The little one that he had asked her for, that would have made a wonderful ring for him, had been refused him. He must have misread something in her chart; he would have to go over it again in the morning. Obviously he had missed some nasty side to her character. Originally he had read her as a generous woman, not the stingy bitch she had turned out to be.

Now, thanks to the party tonight, her high-class friends had learned about her. The snobbish Delphine, who had never been polite to him, and that arrogant tramp, Lady Kilmuir, both knew now that their princess was a whore from the cheapest kind of Turkish harem. Nothing was seamier than that kind of background. Her two fancy lady friends wouldn't be fawning around Her Exalted Highness anymore, now that they knew about her real royal background.

And Baraket—His Exalted Highness himself—Anthony had told him off tonight as well, hadn't he? He'd put up with Baraket's animosity for long enough. Now he'd had the wind taken out of his sails, now that he knew about Alia's lover. There must be some scene going on right now. It served her right.

Anthony stood in front of the full-length mirror that took up the corner of his room, preening. Their Exalted Highnesses were bedded down in the grandest suite at the Crillon, and here he was in this miserable, dirty hovel. How dare they have treated him that way? His reflection in the mirror was more beautiful than ever. Thank God it had been a fancy dress party tonight; for once he had been able to display his own beauty. Everyone had noticed him, even more than that drug-crazed Ceil. The tall feather headdress was spectacular, and the loincloth decorated with gold beading and sequins was small enough and shiny enough to draw attention to the perfection of his body. Those black Nubians with their big whangs dangling were nothing compared to Anthony's perfection.

He couldn't get enough of looking at himself in the mirror. The light was low in the room, making his golden trappings look even more mysteriously alluring in the shadowy lamplight. He ran his hands over his honey-colored, glistening body, feeling the insides of his thighs and the long line from his smooth chest down to the edge of the loincloth. He unhooked the loincloth and let it slide to the floor. God, he was beautiful; every part of him was beautiful. He put his hands between his legs and stroked himself, rubbing gently, then fervently, until that particular masterpiece of his stood magnificently erect, pointing at him from the mirror. He swayed back and forth in a sensuous, undulating dance, thrilling himself with his own hands. He stroked his hardness again, then brought his arms up over his head and released the band of the feathered headdress. He wanted to be perfectly nude; he needed no adornment. He looked into his eyes in the mirror, now even more fascinated with his face than he was with his body. The strong set to his jaw, the perfection of his mouth, the great even perfection of his brow and eyebrows. What features, what bone structure he had. And his eyes! He was mesmerized by the hypnotic fascination of his eyes, and they were even the most fabulous shade of blue he had ever seen. Many a lover had tried to tell him, but he knew more about himself than even the most passionate of them ever had. No one could be as familiar with his beauty as he was, and he had every day of his life to enjoy it.

Suddenly there was a small flash of silver metal behind him. Anthony felt one chilling second of terror. There was someone in the room with him. Before the thought crystallized, he felt an iron grip around his neck and saw the flash of steel as the knife slashed like lightning across his throat. He felt nothing; there was no pain, but the expression on Tarek's face was something he would never forget. How could anyone look at him with such hatred? The man must be mad.

Tarek saw to it that no sound was made. For a moment, he examined the heap of flesh and ostrich feathers and blood on the floor at his feet. His face was expressionless as he wiped the knife on a white silk scarf that he found on the top of the dressing table.

He made sure that the double lock and chain were on the door, even though he had seen Anthony fix them. Then he crossed the room to the french doors and pulled the curtains closed. No light would disturb the occupant of the bedroom. He let himself out quietly through the french doors, the same way he had come in. He stole quietly across the slate roof and dropped silently down, like a cat, to the dark alley below.

LONDON
June 1963

Delphine wrote to George.

"You really are amazing. I couldn't believe that you would miss the party, not because Graziella was giving it—I know you care nothing about her or her parties—but because we would be together. It's not often when the seven of us can be together and, if it weren't for you, the six of us wouldn't be in the first place. So, when you told me that you were not coming over until July with *Ehukai III*, I must confess I was disappointed. It never occurred to me that you knew better. It's that instinct of yours; something told you not to come. I would give anything if I had never met Graziella, had never gone to this party, and had been safely on the other side of the world with you. I told you some of it on the phone, but I must put the full picture in words.

"I knew, too, that there would probably be some trouble when Camilla and I first discussed it. She had Russ coming to Paris and was trying to belay Jeremy. Naturally he came, so I started off uncomfortably. I don't like to know about the infidelities of strangers, much less those of my friends. Plus the fact that Camilla has gotten really quite gross—what a terrible word, but I hate seeing her like this. She gorges food and drinks vast amounts. She doesn't get drunk; she's just always got a glass in her hand. You can help in this, far better than I. She'd listen to you, pay attention to you. Remember.

"Anyhow, it started off with the six of us seated together. Graziella knew Russ didn't really know anyone so she put him at our table without a girl, next to Baraket. That, at least, was better than putting him next to Jeremy. Jeremy is bound to know something about what's going on—what's gone on— with Camilla and Russ. Jeremy looks hangdog when they're in each other's company. Russ is just plain uncomfortable. So there he was, talking to Baraket, when along came Ceil like a whirlwind with none other than our favorite in-house astrologist, Anthony. Both of them were very drunk, or something, and very nude; both of them were egging each other on, looking for trouble and they found it. You would not believe what has happened to Ceil. She is as exquisite as ever, and we have seen her fairly often, but, George, she's gone wilder than a March hare. Drugs . . . obviously . . . and it's so sad, and men and erratic behavior. She's totally different from the girl I met in Monte Carlo, saw in Baden-Baden, and have known in Paris. I don't know where Guy is now; they are divorced, but apparently he still takes care of her. She's vain, always drawing attention to herself. I've never seen better material go wrong. Anyhow, Russ was still uncomfortable from Camilla duncing him around by not telling him Jeremy was going to be there, and angry. Jeremy acts like Russ is part of the woodwork, but then Jeremy has looked at a lot of woodwork in his time with Camilla.

"Then Russ got embroiled with Ceil, thanks to Baraket. Actually, Russ was clever to do what he did. Anthony used Ceil to get him invited to the party; she was the only way he could have gotten there. He must have been egging her on about Baraket . . . and Alia. Lately, she's gone on more and more about Alia. It's not that she is jealous of her or dislikes her—you know Ceil—she just wants to be Alia. So Anthony apparently lit the fire: 'Get close to Baraket and maybe you can get him back' sort of thing. Now we have Ceil and Anthony at the table making a commotion. The guards got Anthony at once; Baraket had given those orders, but they left Ceil alone. She slipped right in beside Baraket, plastering herself around him, moving Russ out. The next thing I knew, after Anthony had assaulted Camilla and me with the riveting information about Alia's background, Russ had disappeared with Ceil. That's what I mean about diplomatic, or maybe just nice of him to take a half-crazed girl out of a bad situation, with those gorilla guards standing by. Camilla, may I tell you, was furious. Russ was not dancing to her tune.

"Ken and I knew it was way past time to leave. Baraket and Alia came with us, but we got separated in all that mob and Anthony had gotten loose somehow and he swooped down on Baraket and Alia at the door, telling Baraket that Alia had a lover. Great God, how did you know not to come? Russ is still missing and Camilla is convinced he's somewhere with Ceil.

"Now, of course, the very worst is that Alia's whole world has turned over. Baraket has vanished, and she is *sure* that he killed Anthony. She loves Baraket, you know, and I would swear on all Bibles that Ian's love for her is pure and from afar, and I would also swear that he has never so much as kissed her good night. But he is deeply smitten with her and why Baraket takes exception to him I don't know, but he does. Good old double standard: Baraket's left Alia alone for a great part of the time in the last year and he can have all the women he wants, but a man can't even look at Alia. Was it really ever thus?

"And Anthony is dead. It was even a fluke they found him the day after the party. God knows he could have been dead for a week if the police hadn't gotten some tip to search the room. No one knows who called the police, least of all the police, and none of us has any idea where Baraket is.

"Alia needs you more than Camilla does. Please come soon. I don't *need* you; you have already given me the most valuable thing in my life, forever, and that's Kenneth. I never knew anyone could be as happy as I am, all thanks to you. But your other two girls are having a hard time, and so is Ceil; so come on. Ken and I are planning a dinner for you on the 24th."

George held the letter in his hands, thinking about the girls, his three girls. He had written Ceil off in his mind after Baden-Baden. But the other three had come so far, and now only one of them was all right.

PARIS
June 1963

Anthony's murder was quickly the talk of Paris. Not because he
was homosexual; they always seemed to be up to things like
that, and not because he had many friends. Apparently he
had none, none who came forth or were even under suspicion.
It was because of his association with Baraket and Alia, it was
only through them that he was known at all. That was more
than enough. The French police called first on Baraket at his
quarters in the Crillon only to find that he was gone. They interviewed Princess Alia, his wife. She had returned to the
hotel with her husband just after 3 A.M. Where was her husband now? Princess Alia had bade him good night and gone
to her rooms. Tarek, bodyguard and chauffeur to His
Highness and the princess, was brought in to question. He

had driven Their Highnesses to the hotel, seen that the princess had been escorted to her rooms, where guards vouched for her arrival. She could not have left without their knowing. The hotel manager on duty reported seeing her. Then Tarek had taken his master to Orly, where he had boarded his own aircraft for Cairo. A business trip that had long been planned. They could reach him at his palace in Cairo, surely.

Alia's face changed only slightly when Tarek disclosed Baraket's whereabouts. She knew he would have brought that information to her earlier when he told her about Anthony if it had been true. Where was Baraket? No one could get through to him in Cairo if he didn't want them to.

The police were interested in Tarek's whereabouts at the approximate time of the murder. Tarek had been at Orly with his master, then he had returned to his quarters at the Crillon. The night man had let him in; the garage man had a record of the exact time that the car had returned to its usual parking place. He'd barely had time to get back from Orly.

When the police had gone, Alia turned to Tarek.

"Where is he, Tarek? He's not gone to Cairo, has he?"

"No, Your Highness. He is in Paris. But I cannot tell you where, because I don't know. He made me leave him at a certain apartment on the Avenue Foch and he told me to come right back to you. I couldn't disobey him."

"Oh, Tarek, he's killed Anthony, I know he has . . ."

"No, he has not. You know he wouldn't bother with anyone like that. Princess Fal, it was probably one of those boys that he had around him, it's nothing for you to worry about."

"It's Baraket. If only he would come back."

"I will see if I can find him, Your Highness." Tarek had never seen Alia look the way she did, drawn and anguished. All she could do was wait, and hope that Tarek would return with some news of Baraket.

After Tarek left, Alia gave instructions to the maids that she was not to be disturbed by anyone unless it was her husband or Tarek. She hadn't slept all night, waiting for Baraket to return or Tarek to come and tell her something about him, as he'd said he would. The first thing she'd heard in the morning was from Tarek about Anthony's death. Then the visit from the police. She still didn't know how Anthony had been killed but apparently it hadn't been very pleasant. Where, oh where was Baraket? For the first time in her life she was afraid of him, but overriding her fear was a longing to see him. She lay on her bed, half asleep; dreaming, crying. Why did it all have to change? What a fool she had been to ever let Anthony into her life. She slept for a while and then she was aware that Tarek was in the room with her.

"Princess Fal, I have no news of His Highness, but Lady Kilmuir and Mrs. Bennett are here, they've been waiting to see you for over an hour."

"Waiting to see me, why didn't someone tell me?" Alia said, pulling herself up, remembering that she had left instructions not to be disturbed. But Delphine and Camilla—she hadn't meant them. She went to her bathroom and brushed her hair and freshened her face. What was she going to say to them?

Delphine and Camilla were sitting at the round table by the window, Camilla with a glass of champagne, as always. Delphine was drinking coffee. Alia paused when she came through the door, not knowing what they were thinking. Delphine came to her and kissed her, drawing her over to the table and making her sit down in a chair beside them. Alia didn't know what to say. There were tears in her eyes.

"Well, he certainly made a mess of it, didn't he?" Camilla said, taking one of Alia's hands. "A first-class mess, and he's paid for it. How do you feel about it? That's all that matters to us."

"I don't know," Alia said. "I'm so tired I don't know anything except that Baraket is gone and I'm so afraid that he has killed Anthony." The words tumbled out. "And I'm afraid he will never come back and I don't know what to do." It was a relief to her to see Delphine and Camilla. Her friends. But what must they think of her? "And what do you think of me, now that Anthony's told you all about me?"

"A princess is a princess," Delphine said. "Regardless of where she is from. What Camilla and I want to know is why you didn't tell us long ago? Do you think it would have made any difference to either of us one way or the other? The difference it's made, and we were both talking about it, is how amazing you are. To do what you have done . . ."

Alia realized that her friends, her two friends, were truly concerned about her, cared about her, no matter where she had come from. She should have known.

"I could never have done it without Kenneth. Hasn't he ever told you?"

"Alia, you know Kenneth well enough to know that he wouldn't have told me any more than he would have told the Voice of America."

"Don't you see, if anything, it makes us love you more?" Camilla said. She couldn't bear for Alia to look so forlorn.

"What am I going to do?" Alia asked, tears starting to flow again. She had never cried, why was she crying now? Some of it was fatigue, some of it was relief that Delphine and Camilla were here, but most of it was Baraket. She loved Baraket and she wanted him back. And she had every reason to fear that he would never return.

"You're going to wait, that's all. You will wait. Alia, I told Kenneth that I would call him when we had seen you. Do you want to talk to him?"

"Of course," Alia said. "Would he come over, do you think? He's the only one who could tell me where Baraket might be."

Camilla's fury, when Russ finally called her, knew no bounds. He had spent a week hidden away in the Ritz suite with Ceil, never setting foot out of the place. The vendeuse from Chanel, across the street on the Rue Cambon, had made a visit and come back with beautiful silken at-home robes and pajamas for Ceil, not one of them in blue. Pinks and yellows and corals, white, delicate prints—everything but any shade of blue—were delivered, to her delight. Perfumes and simple jewels, a long pearl necklace and single-pearl earrings were sent. She needed no makeup; her face was exquisite in its simplicity.

They slept and made love and talked for hours. They drank. They ate at any time of the day or night they wanted to. Newspapers, magazines, books and flowers filled the suite.

"Pink roses," Ceil said. "I love them." So pink roses it was, every day a new arrangement would arrive. She never tired of them.

"You are a pink rose," Russ told her. "And you're going to die faster than one if you don't straighten yourself out."

"I can't help it. I'm self-destructive; it's a wave that comes over me, and I can't seem to fight it. I don't care, I don't care, anyway."

"You're not self-destructive, you're self-indulgent," Russ said. "When are you going to start thinking about the rules? They exist, you know, and there are reasons for them."

"You don't understand," Ceil said. "I don't care about anything or anyone."

"Drugs?"

"Pough," Ceil said, snapping her fingers in the air. "They don't mean anything to me either. Everyone says I'm hooked but I'm not. We've been here a week and I've never wanted anything."

"You've had something to substitute for them," Russ said, touching her knees with his, "and besides, a week won't do it. You need help. I'll take you home to California, and I'll pay for you see the best psychiatrist there if you'll come."

"No," Ceil said. "I don't want to."

"All right," Russ said. "But we've only got a few more days. The one thing I can give you that might help is my phone number in case you need me. That's all."

"I'll be all right," she said. As long as he was here, she would. Where was Guy now? Maybe he would take her back.

The day Russ was leaving he called Camilla. Ceil listened, or rather watched, as Russ stood with the phone in his hand, obviously not being able to get a word in. Finally, he spoke into the receiver.

"Camilla," he said. "I've told you where I am and I've told you where I'm going. You have Jeremy. I would never have come to Paris if I'd known he was going to be with you. I don't mind what goes on between you and me, but I'm not going to cuckold Jeremy in his presence ever again. Goodbye."

He gathered up his things and kissed Ceil. "The car is taking me to Orly and coming back for you. The bill is all paid and the chauffeur will take you where you want to go. Be a good little girl."

He was gone.

LONDON

June 1963

Alia waited in Paris for a week and then she knew that Baraket would not be coming back there. He had said she could go to London if he did not return. Delphine and Camilla had left and Alia was alone, waiting, doing nothing else. She wanted desperately to go to Kusadasi, to Yali Beyaz, but Baraket had indicated London and she didn't dare go anywhere else under the circumstances. There was nothing more to be done about Anthony. There were no witnesses, no suspects, and the French police had lost interest in his murder, just as everyone else had. Since Baraket had been paying his bills, the hotel sent his possessions over to the Crillon. Alia had Tarek dispose of them.

At home in London, Alia continued to wait. She called Ian

and told him everything that had happened. He listened quietly, longing to help her. He had known that this day would come, but not like this.

"He's forbidden me to see you and I must obey him. I don't know what he might do to you."

"Is that worrying you?"

"Of course."

"Alia, I understand that we cannot see each other. You are not to worry about me. You wait for Baraket and I shall wait for you."

Alia was desolate about Ian. He was her friend, he loved her so deeply and he had sacrificed himself for her. He was the only man she had ever been allowed to refuse, to say no to. All of her life, she had done what some man wanted her to, when he wanted her to. Ian, who loved her much more than any man ever had, accepted no from her without question or persuasion. It made him mean more to her than ever. Baraket was her master still, and she was his slave. She continued to wait.

Two months to the day after the party, Baraket came home. Alia was in the nursery saying good night to the children when he appeared. The children rushed him, used to his absences and enchanted each time he returned. They clung to him, begging him to play one more game, and promise not to leave them again.

"My dear," he said to Alia. "Could we dine alone? In about an hour?"

"Of course," Alia said. He made no move to touch her and she was afraid to show any emotion, one way or the other. She gave Tarek instructions to set a small table for them in the emerald room. Somehow the opulence of it seemed right for their reunion.

She dressed carefully. Balmain had sent her an ivory silk dinner dress, carefully constructed, as they all were, for the jewels.

At dinner, Baraket never referred to where he had been or anything that had happened in the past two months. He spoke to Alia as if he had seen her that morning and the evening before and the morning before. Over coffee, she decided to speak.

"Baraket, you know what happened to Anthony, don't you?"

"I didn't, my dear, until Tarek told me when he fetched me at the airport this afternoon. Why?"

"Baraket, did you kill him?"

"Hardly. He did his damage well. After his little speech, it was too late to kill him. Come, it's time for bed."

Alia was startled. This was not the Baraket she knew. He was as cold as ice and she could sense that he was testing her, trying to make her respond to something she didn't understand yet. As she undressed, she wondered if being back in bed together would solve anything for them. It would have to.

Baraket appeared in his robe, a bottle of raki on a small silver tray in his hands. Thank God, Alia thought, realizing that for the first time in her life she wanted a drink. It would warm her up, free her from the coldness that had built up between them. She would have to get him back sexually, that was where she had succeeded in the first place, and now that was where she would have to again. He had never been able to resist her. He was a stranger at this moment, but he would soon be the man she knew, her lover, her husband again. She took a long gulp of the raki.

Baraket made love to her without allowing her to make any move to please him. He said things to her that he had never said before, vulgar, twisted things. She could feel hatred flowing out of his body as if he were trying to inject it into her. She couldn't reach him, or touch him or find him. He was all over her, rough and ugly. When he had finished his brutal performance, he slapped her hard across the face. She cried out, more in surprise than pain, and he hit her again, harder this time. He climbed out of bed and went toward the door. Alia followed him, naked.

"Baraket, don't leave me. I begged you not to the night of the party in Paris. I don't care if you hit me, I don't care what you do, just don't leave me alone. I want you back, I want us the way we were . . ."

He grabbed her by the throat and shook her, the pressure of his fingers almost choking her to death. Then he released his hands and knocked her to the floor. Her head hit the side of a chest of drawers, knocking her out. When she came to, however long after it was, she was lying on the floor, her hair soaked in blood from an inch-long cut on the right side of her head. She pulled herself up and went into her bathroom, fighting dizziness and with the room swimming. She turned on the shower, releasing warm water from the hundreds of tiny jet taps, and drenched herself in it. She washed her hair and looked at the lump on the side of her head and the bruises starting to show on her body. He had pinched the insides of her thighs viciously, and bitten her neck and breasts. She felt nothing, neither anger nor pain. So that was how it was going to be, now that he was home. If that was how it was going to be, there was nothing she could do about it. The dream was over.

LONDON
September 1963

The beatings continued. Alia took it, not responding, only crying out when he hurt her so badly that she couldn't help it. They followed a pattern. Whenever Baraket would suggest that they dine alone, she would know what was going to happen. They went out often, and then he would be the same charming, attentive man of the past. She lived for the time when they went to parties together, and she pretended that their life was unchanged. After a party, he would leave her at her door, never coming to sleep with her. It was only when they had dinner alone that she knew he was going to take her to bed and then he was going to beat her.

She began to live in fear. The beatings increased in violence and hatred. She could tell no one, not even Tarek, and

Baraket was very clever after the first time about not bruising her face, only her body, which she could cover with clothes. She stayed at home most of the time, alone always, and her nerves began to go. She could not bring herself to call Ian, but she longed for him. Delphine and Kenneth were in Paris and Camilla and Jeremy had gone on a business trip to Canada. In a way, she was relieved that there was no one around her. What good would it do if she could talk to someone about it? Soon it would end. Baraket would realize that she loved him, and that she was paying her dues for whatever hurt she had dealt out to him.

Then the pattern changed. One evening after dinner, again in the emerald room, Baraket flipped the security locks on all the doors and turned to her. He had a whip in his hands; Alia had no idea where it came from. Baraket never had needed or indulged himself in aberrant tools. He flicked the whip at her, at her breasts, threatening at first and then lashing at her time and again, hurting her terribly. Something in Alia snapped. In her mind, she knew she might not come out of the room alive. If Baraket meant to kill her, all right, but there would be no more beatings, and no whips.

"Stop it, Baraket," she screamed, astonished at the ferocity and volume in her own voice. "No more, no more ever!" She had never defied anyone before, but a point had been reached. And now, screaming at Baraket, she was still under control, still knew exactly what she was doing. She loved Baraket too much to let him behave like a beast. She tore off her clothes, leaving the sea-green embroidered silk dress at her feet, following it with every stitch she had on until she was completely naked, except for the huge pink and canary diamond necklace and earrings that had been Baraket's most recent present to her, a week ago. Ever since the beatings had begun, he had bought her massive, vulgar jewels. She would find a box on her breakfast tray, or on her dressing table when she came from her bath. There was never a card. She wore them immediately but said nothing about them. Every jeweler in London and Paris was benefiting from Baraket's displeasure with Alia, and amazed at the change in his taste. Whenever he bought from them before—diamonds, pearls, rubies—anything but emeralds, his taste had been perfection. Alia understood what he was doing. He had locked the emeralds away, replacing them with the ivories. He did not want her to touch the emeralds; he was replacing them with ugly brutes of jewels. Out of some perverse cruelty, he was saying, "The emeralds are no longer yours, but you will put up with the way I treat you, you will take anything I hand out to you, and I will keep buying you with jewels."

When she started to undress, Baraket stopped flicking the whip. He leaned against the wall, arms folded, and watched her, a bitter smile on his lips. Whatever she was up to, he would wait her out.

She fumbled with the clasp on the new necklace and tore the earrings from her earlobes. She flung them at his feet.

"I am not your piece of meat," she said, not believing her own ears. That was the first thing that Anthony had said to her; Anthony, who had gotten them all into this trouble. "I am now as you found me except that it's London, not Trebizond. I didn't care if you beat me because you were punishing me for what I had done. But you're not punishing me for me, it's for you. I've never had a choice in my life, not one, not about what dress to wear, what street to cross, what party to go to or what man to love. Every decision has been made for me, and I did everything to please you. But I won't go on like this. You will treat me with dignity, if nothing else, or I shall be gone from you forever and nothing—nothing—will stop me. I am not the girl I was. I am Princess Alia, and you, above everyone else, are to remember that."

Baraket dropped the whip and came to her, hearing the truth in her words.

"Alia." He was hoarse. He fumbled, trying to put his arms around her.

"Let me go, Baraket," Alia said. It was a command that she gave. "Open the door, please. I am going to bed."

As if mesmerized, Baraket pushed the switch to release the

lock. Alia looked at him with no expression on her face whatsoever. She walked quietly out of the room, still completely nude, and went down the wide hall to the double staircase that led to the bedroom floors. Baraket stood in the doorway but he did not try to stop her. He watched as she went down the half-lit hall, naked and alone, and it broke his heart to see her go.

KUSADASI, TURKEY

September 1963

Alia went to Yali Beyaz, taking Tarek with her. It was autumn, all the boats were put up and the French fortress hotel was closed. Tarek built the fires and cooked for her. He was the only servant in the house. Alia walked for hours in the hills and on the beach. Her thoughts turned to Anthony when she reached the place on the beach where she had first met him, and to the events after their meeting, events that led to his death. Had she really made such a serious mistake in allowing him to be around her? Remembering the evil in his face, she knew that his hold on her had been her own superstitions, a throwback to her peasant past. His predictions had frightened her, and she had been foolish not to know that he was using her. But wasn't it because of Ian, really, that she had kept Anthony around? She had used Anthony as much as he had used her, giving him things because he had given her something: Ian. At least he had given her Ian.

Alia knew that it wouldn't matter if she swore never to see Ian again, never to think about him, never to mention his name. Baraket could not take Ian from her mind or her heart.

He has formed me and shaped me, Alia thought. Now, if there is to be anything to us, he must learn to accept me.

LONDON
October 1963

———————————

Baraket waited for Alia to return from Yali Beyaz. She had left a note for him and a package. The note said simply where she would be, nothing else. The package held all of the jewels he had given her while the beatings were going on. The message was clear.

Baraket went out every evening with a new, beautiful girl, always to public restaurants. He never saw any of them more than once. He avoided the company of his friends, particularly Camilla and Jeremy, who knew Alia best. When he returned alone to Lindley House, he would sit in the emerald room drinking cognac, thinking about Alia. He could see her naked, vulnerable and beautiful, before she walked out of the room. He missed her.

He was still deeply angry. She had betrayed him. He knew she would come back but he had no idea how he would feel when she did. Why the devil couldn't he get her out of his mind, why was she the only woman who still excited him, the only one he continued to want? And how dare she leave him? It was he, Baraket, who called the shots. She had no right to leave him. His anger deepened, but so did his longing for her.

Three weeks after she left, she was back. When Tarek opened the door, Baraket knew she had returned. Now, now he would see what she had to say for herself. Baraket looked coldly at Tarek. He had left with Alia, without so much as a by-your-leave. Tarek had betrayed him, too.

Suppose Alia had come to a decision that would change their lives, suppose she no longer loved him? He was afraid but he could not admit it. She was only a woman, and he would soon assume control over her again. He would start by leaving her alone, as she had left him. He changed into his evening clothes and called for the car, ordering Tarek to drive him.

"We will fetch a young lady at Forty-four Hill Street, Tarek, and then go to the Café de Paris." His voice still held a warning. Tarek belonged to him, not to Alia.

"Yes, Your Highness," Tarek replied.

After dinner, Baraket decided to stop at the Clermont Club on Berkeley Square and gamble. He rarely gambled; in point of fact, it bored him. A chair was found for him quickly at the table when he indicated that he wanted to take a hand. Chemin de fer at Clermont was the biggest game in London and Baraket could be the biggest player, if they could only intrigue him, finally. . . . He stayed for over an hour, winning steadily. When his *placques* were cashed in for him, he gave the thousands of pounds that he had won to the girl and saw her home, then returned to Lindley House. He had been drinking steadily for hours and in addition to being drunk, he was in a rage. While he was undressing, he knocked back two more large snifters of brandy, then got into his bed and rang the bell for Tarek.

"You may tell the Princess Alia that I am expecting her immediately," he said, folding his arms over his chest.

"Yes, Your Highness," Tarek said, closing the door quietly behind him.

Alia came to him at once, obviously wide awake, although it was past two. She was wearing a delicate white silk caftan and she was very pale. Her huge eyes were suppliant and sad.

"Come to bed, my dear," Baraket said. All he wanted to do was hold her in his arms and make love to her, and block out having ever raised a hand to her.

Alia took off the caftan and got into bed. Baraket saw the obedient expression on her face and suddenly he was murderously angry again. He could see Ian's face before him, not Alia's. Ian had taken her away from him and at this very moment he could actually feel her thinking about Ian.

He made love to her savagely but he might as well have been making love to a stone figure. The moment he touched her, sensing his anger she started to cry, sobbing like a child. When Baraket felt her tears on his body, he stopped and snapped on the light.

"Tell your friend Baldwin to beware, my princess." Baraket spat out the words. "You cannot get him out of your mind, can you? I can feel him in this bed with me. You would rather be in Pont Street alone with him, wouldn't you?"

Alia couldn't stop crying.

"You have Ian in this bed, not I, it is you who cannot get him out of your mind. All the time at Yali Beyaz, I thought about you and hoped that when I came back you would love me as you used to, that we could be as we were. You think all the time about Ian, I do not."

"I am consumed with jealousy of the man who has the taste to worship my wife." It surprised Baraket to hear himself put it into words.

"But you care nothing for the wife who worships you. I am what you made me, Baraket, nothing more. You have made me strong, you have given me dignity. And you cannot take it away. If you don't stop blaming me for Ian or Ian for being Ian, you will destroy us. Is that what you want?"

"Get out of here," Baraket said, throwing the covers off and shoving her roughly out of the bed. "I am leaving in the morning for Cairo and then Istanbul, so you came home in time to say good-bye to me. I leave the field clear for you and I leave you unbruised this time, but I would take care, very good care, if I were you." He turned his back to her.

She was still crying. "As you like," she said. She found Tarek standing silently in the shadowy hall, waiting for her.

"Are you all right?" Tarek saw the paleness and the tears.

"Yes, but he is leaving, and now I'm afraid he will take you with him—"

"No, no, he will not. He's already asked me about everything that happened at Yali Beyaz. He needs me to watch you, so he won't take me away."

Alia looked at Tarek, the saddest expression he had ever seen on her face. Tarek was always there, taking care of her, but this was the first time she had confided in him since he had helped her play the candle game in the harem at Saadit Sarai. Tarek's loyalties had been to both of them. He had no right or reason to choose between them but Baraket would force him to now. Poor Tarek.

"Good night," she said softly, touching his hand for a moment, at the door to her room. "Let me know before he leaves."

On the way to his narrow room, Tarek could feel the knife in his shirt pocket, a cool bit of steel against his chest. No harm would come to her, his princess, he would see to that. He had killed Anthony and he would kill Baraket if he had to. Princess Alia would be safe while he, Tarek, lived.

Baraket spent three days in Cairo. Tafida was her usual acerbic self.

"At first you were afraid for me to meet your wife, in case I would harm her. Now after nine years you must know I care nothing about your legendary beauty of a wife, I want to see my grandchildren. I am isolated here, most of my friends are gone. If you do not arrange for the children to come to Cairo, I shall go to London."

"Go then," Baraket said. "You know the rules we agreed to better than I, and it is you who wants to stay here. If you leave, your grandchildren could prove very costly to you. If it weren't for my long relationship with Nasser, you would not live here as contentedly as you do. A very special trip can be arranged for you, but it would take time. I have given Nasser our promise and I am not going to break it."

Tafida sighed. "I shall always live in Cairo. Have your way. I shall wait."

"You may not have to wait long. The children can come and stay with you if you like. Very soon. Without their mother."

"Strange," Tafida said. "I have now become deadly curious about your wife's staying power as well as her beauty. Now you tell me that the children may come without her. Whatever do you mean? Could there be a tiny bit of trouble somewhere?"

Baraket looked at Tafida. There was no fooling her.

"My relationship with Alia is subject to change. Your grandchildren will come to you, I promise you, and very soon. I will let you know from Saadit Sarai."

So, Tafida thought, what I've heard is true. It is she who has someone else. He will never put up with that. She sat, a tiny piece of steel on the hard horsehair couch. Good, she thought. My grandchildren belong in Egypt.

Baraket's voice on the telephone from Istanbul was cold and impersonal.

"I want to send the children to Cairo to visit Tafida. You will be prepared to let them go when I tell you."

Alia shivered. So that was it. He would take the children away, he would take Tarek away and soon after, she would be moved out of Lindley House. There would be enough money, more than enough money. Large sums had been invested for her in her own name in both Swiss and British banks. She owned land in Turkey, including Yali Beyaz, and large parcels in England and America, but money was not important. Baraket was finished with her, and now he wanted the children. He would take them away from her, as he had the emeralds.

"Very well," Alia said. How could she argue with him? She had nothing to say to him anymore. When she hung up, she sat thinking. It was no longer a matter of keeping Baraket, it was not losing the children. She called for Tarek.

"Tarek, His Highness is arranging for the children to go to Egypt, to . . . I am sure that he will send you with them, but not me. I must go. Can you arrange it?"

"It will be no trouble at all, Princess Alia," Tarek said. "No trouble at all."

Suddenly, Alia knew exactly what she would do. "As soon as you can, Tarek. Baraket must not know we have gone nor anyone know we are coming. How long will it take to make the arrangements?" Tarek was her partner again but each time she involved him she knew she put his life in jeopardy. "Tomorrow, we can leave tomorrow evening."

"Good. We will be ready."

When he had gone, Alia picked up the phone and dialed Ian's number.

"Baldwin here." She hadn't heard his voice in months. She felt his warmth, just hearing his quiet, civilized tone.

"Ian, it's Alia. I am coming to see you."

LONDON
October 1963

Tarek had driven Alia to Harrods, letting her out of the car at the corner entrance on Knightsbridge, two blocks from Pont Street. "I will not be back until tomorrow, early in the morning," she said. He turned a quiet face to her, as if she had told him to pick her up in half an hour. She disappeared into the cavernous department store, moving swiftly through the sea of late-afternoon customers, coming out on the opposite side. She walked the two blocks to Ian's flat, but instead of using the front entrance on Pont Street, she went in through the mews garden at the back.

Neither of them said a word. Ian picked her up in his arms and carried her to the bedroom, never taking his eyes from hers. He undressed her with no sense of urgency, and she could not stop looking at the beauty of his face. She knew that she must have been in his bedroom a thousand times before and made love to him a million times at least. Love. Love, more than all sex. Tenderness, not lust. She wanted him. She had never wanted a man before, she had never been allowed to want. She had been wanted and taken, that was all. Tenderness she had never felt before came to her with Ian. For the first time in her life she was allowed to give, not to be taken, give forever, and the gift was herself. Anthony's words came back to her in a fragment; what was it he had said? "You find the very act of making love difficult only because he is too masculine and dominating." It was true. She loved Baraket but he led, he indicated what he wanted and she obeyed his orders. Being made love to by Baraket was one-sided. She knew what he liked and she gave him what he wanted. What she wanted, even what she wanted to give, was denied. She was a piece of meat.

She had known how it would be with Ian. There was no dominance from either of them. She had turned her thought completely toward making love to him since the moment she had picked up the telephone and called him. When he opened the door to the mews garden entrance to let her in, he had seen on her face what was going to happen. It had always been there, waiting for both of them. Baraket's jealousy had made it possible.

For one time, one time only in her entire life, she was going to do what she wanted to do, what she desired to do. "You will never have to say no to me," Ian had told her in Priane. "I know," Alia had said. "It makes me very sad. You are the only man I have ever been allowed to refuse." And now he was the only man she would ever give herself to completely. She had cast the die. If it was the end with Baraket, so be it. Anthony had told her that she was going to lose him. Damn Anthony. He had also said that another man would bring her the greatest happiness that she would ever know. Alia knew better now than to believe that. She and Ian had this one time, not a lifetime, so her happiness would be for a few hours, never again.

They were insatiable. Through the long night, they shared

each other completely in a world of their own making, in intimacy never known to either of them before.

Now she lay curled in his arms in the big white bed, wide awake, in the dark. Ian slept for the first time, breathing softly into the nape of her neck. She could see his open hand, so big and gentle, relaxed in sleep near her shoulder. The morning light would soon silhouette the willow tree in the garden and the branches would dance against the sheer white curtains. And she would be gone, to Cairo and Tafida and an unknown future. There was another thing, but she was not going to think about it. Even though Tarek knew where she was and she could trust him to death, Baraket might have others watching her, that even Tarek would know nothing about. Baraket could kill, but he would never forgive. He'd never had to before.

She hadn't told Ian about Cairo or the dangers she faced, nor was she going to. She had to take the chance, she had to go her way alone. This was the only time when she and Ian would make love and they both knew it.

Her perfume in his nostrils made him stir. Ivoire, the perfume Balmain had made for her, or had she simply exuded it for him to copy?

She heard his voice, low and warm, and felt his hands and arms again.

"Am I dreaming?" he said.

"Yes, my love." Love, the word love again.

"You are my only dream, I have never dreamt before. I wrote all those beautiful ladies into my books, but I knew them not. My life and I have waited for this one time with you."

"Do not open your eyes. I am going. Remember, dreams can be forgiven."

She slipped out into the early cool of the garden. The chrysanthemums and Michaelmas daisies were yellow and blue blurs in front of her eyes. In ten minutes, she was in Lindley House. Ian was asleep, with no intention of ever awakening from a dream that would not come true.

CAIRO
November 1963

Tarek had made all arrangements for the five of them—Alia, the two children and their nanny—to go to Cairo on the morning flight. Alia knew that he must have used an abundant combination of money and key people to get them there. When Tarek handed their passports over at the Cairo airport, the uniformed man who took them opened the first one and, not believing his eyes, handed all of them back to Tarek and waved them quickly on.

Alia hoped, and she knew the hope was slim, that she wouldn't have trouble arranging to see Princess Tafida. If Baraket knew that she had come to Cairo with the children, defying his orders, his anger would know no bounds. Princess Tafida had been her enemy always, apparently hating her for having captured her only son, for being unworthy of him, and for being Turkish, not Egyptian. All that was changed now. Alia had tried to persuade Baraket to arrange a meeting with his mother after the birth of the children, but he had remained adamant and had given no reason for keeping his wife and mother apart, nor the cruelty of not allowing his mother to know her only grandchildren. Now, with a separation imminent, Alia felt it her responsibility to arrange for a meeting. She knew she had nothing to lose and that, possibly, she had a great deal to gain. Princess Tafida was the key. As her enemy, nothing would change. As her friend, everything would.

Alia had never quite understood why it was that Princess Tafida could not leave Egypt. It was Tarek who explained it to her.

"She can leave, and without special help from Nasser, she would have to leave. But she loves her Villa Al-Hikma better than any place on earth. When you came here the first time, that only time, you did not see it, but it is where the princess keeps her heart." Nasser, grateful for Baraket's help and friendship, had given Princess Tafida the choice. She could stay, safely, or she could go. But she could not go back and forth as if Farouk were still king, as if nothing had changed. She was known as one of the richest of the aristocrats, with centuries of family ties that traced back to the Ottoman Empire. Nasser could see to it that she was left to live in peace only if she stayed put. Three quarters of a million people had left Cairo with Farouk's overthrow, and Nasser had given Tafida sanctuary at no little risk to himself.

Alia was sure that Tafida would receive her, but from then on she had no idea what would happen. She might still want to do away with Alia once and for all, not physically, just remove her from their lives, as if she had never existed, as Baraket apparently wanted to. Alia's only chance was to win Tafida's friendship. Tafida had played games with her son always; who knew, perhaps Alia would be useful to her. It was one sure way for Alia not to lose the children. And Alia also knew that she and Baraket were not through with each other yet; he might think so but she knew better. His jealousy would not last forever but while it did, it stemmed from his continuing passion for her. That had never changed.

Settled into the hotel, Alia put through a call to Villa Al-Hikma and asked for Princess Rifat. That was the proper way to address Tafida.

"Who is calling, please?" a servant's voice inquired.

"Princess Alia. I am in Cairo and I would like to see Princess Rifat this afternoon if possible."

There was a silence, and the sure knowledge that a hand was muffling the receiver at the other end. Soon the voice came back.

"Princess Rifat can receive you at five this evening. Do you know the way to the villa, or shall we send someone for you?"

"My driver will bring me. He knows the way."

Alia presented herself promptly at five. She was curious to see the villa; she had heard so much about it and it was no disappointment. Princess Tafida's Villa Al-Hikma was a personal testimonial to her sense of history combined with her obvious adoration of geography. She had given up a great deal when she had chosen to remain in Cairo: before that she had been an ardent and steady traveler. But the compensation —Al-Hikma—was full of the treasures she had collected on her travels, as well as the treasures of the ages, and it was also the place of Baraket's birth. Al-Hikma—which meant "wisdom"—was more of a palace than a villa and took up an entire block in the old part of the city. "Very new, very new— only seventeenth-century. The old one burned," Baraket had told her.

Princess Tafida was a tiny ramrod of steel waiting for her, her jet-black hair drawn severely back into a knot at the nape of her neck. Her face seemed to have been quarried from some eerie white marble.

"You are either remarkably courageous to have come here like this, or remarkably stupid," she said in a brittle voice, waving Alia toward a carved ivory chair with a tasseled silk cushion on it. "So let us sit down and find out which." Alia knew that Tafida had always been outspoken, but there was no rancor in her voice, only curiosity. A little Abyssinian cat jumped boldly into her lap when she sat down. "This is Mishmish. He has been my only grandchild."

"I am glad to be seeing where you live now rather than nine years ago," Alia said, looking at the delicate tracings of latticework—*mashrabiya*, they were called—that covered the tall stained-glass windows, allowing exotic late-afternoon light to stream into the room. The marble floors, softened with the footprints of the ages, were covered with priceless silk rugs. There was a decayed grandeur to the place that Alia found irresistible. "I would have had no appreciation of it then, and even now I can understand only a small part of what I am seeing."

"Obviously, you are not stupid," Tafida said, a benign little smile on her lips. "And you are as ravishing as I have been told. Tell me, why have you come, and with no warning? I heard nothing from Baraket except that the children might be coming. We could easily have met you and taken care of you at the airport."

Since Tafida chose to be so direct, Alia was the same.

"Tarek arranged everything for us. I am not sure, as you may know, how much longer your son—my husband—and I are going to be together. Since it was never arranged for us to meet in the years we have been married, I could only think that you had refused to receive me. Now that things seem to be changing, I wanted to be the one to bring your grandchildren to you."

"The children! They are here?"

"Yes, of course. As I have no family at all and you and Baraket are quite alone, too, I wanted to be the one to bring them to you." Alia could not put into words that if Baraket was going to try to take the children from her, she wanted at least to know Tafida and how they would be living. Baraket could threaten to take them; at least she would know where they would be. "I envy large families, having been so alone for all of my life. Even my children feel it. In England, they spend weekends in the country with families who number in the dozens. Grandparents, aunts, uncles and cousins. They have often asked me if they didn't have anyone and I have told them about you. Now they will believe me."

"Alia where are they now? You must know how I have longed to see them." Tafida's face had brightened, the cynical expression softened and Alia knew that she had made the right move. Baraket should never have kept the children from his mother. Alia remembered the stories of Tafida's trouble-making, but instinctively she felt that Baraket's mother was essentially a lonely woman who would be grateful for what Alia had done.

"They have been taken by Tarek, whom you know, and their English nanny on one of the feluccas on the Nile for a river trip. When Tarek brought me here to Al-Hikma, he found someone, I believe her name is Omm Niza, to accompany them.

Again, the small smile played on Tafida's face. "Omm Niza was Baraket's nanny," she said. "You have done a very clever thing, whether you know it or not. Omm Niza, even more than I, has suffered from not knowing Baraket's children. Now that you have brought them to us, she will look upon you as the angel who has given them to her. So, Alia, we shall finally get to know each other, after all this time. Where are your things?"

"At Shepheard's Hotel."

"No, that won't do at all. I shall send for everything, you will of course stay here. It won't be long before Baraket will call. We will greet him as a family. Welcome, Alia."

ISTANBUL
November 1963

When Baraket learned that Alia and the children were in Cairo with Tafida, he felt a surge of bitter anger. How dare Alia take the children to Tafida in Cairo without his permission? She had defied his orders, and Tarek was her accomplice. He would have none of it. They would both be punished. Baraket had never been an angry man before and his recent behavior bothered him. He had been proud of himself to some extent for thinking things through, talking things through, before resorting to anger. In his position he could almost say "Off with their heads" a hundred times a day if he so chose and he was well aware of his power and the responsibility that went with it. He had surrounded himself with top brains, allowing the key men in his vast organization to make

important decisions. It was harder to assemble such an operation than it was to do it himself, and venting his wrath was
hardly effective. Why, then, had he been behaving so misera-
bly in his personal life?

He called Tafida from Saadit Sarai, and in their brief conversation his mother offered no more information than the
fact that Alia and the children were staying with her at Villa
Al-Hikma. Very well, if she was going to play her eternal
games, so be it. He never acknowledged to Tafida that Alia
was there without his permission nor did he ask to speak to
her. He made no comment about future plans. Let them
begin to worry about him and the course he would choose to
follow now.

For the next few days, Alia and Tafida were predominant
in his mind. How was he going to handle the defiance of his
wife and a servant, and the behavior of his mother? He was
angry again, and even though he faced the fact that it was he
who had kept them apart through the years, he felt shut out.
Bile rose in his throat when he thought about Ian and Anthony. All the trouble had started with Anthony; he was the
one who had introduced Alia to Ian. It proved Baraket's most
cherished theory in business; not to have anyone around except those of the highest integrity. One small slip, not getting
rid of Anthony in the very beginning, as every instinct had
told him to, had brought all this trouble.

Gradually his anger died and he began to think back over
his marriage to Alia, remembering the happy hours they had
spent together. She was a remarkably pliant woman and she
had spoken to him only once in anger. His thoughts went
back to her, naked in the emerald room, her pride outraged,
her love for him misunderstood, her pliancy nullified by his
brutishness. She had been a warm, sensuous companion,
never groveling, and a grateful child-woman who had assumed her responsibilities with grace and dignity. Baraket
had always been proud of her. Men fell in love with her
wherever they went: Ian was the rule rather than the exception. Why had he taken such umbrage to Ian?

And why had he retaliated by torturing her, hurting her physically? What bad blood, never activated before, had caused him to behave as if a demon had gotten hold of him? He was not by nature a beater of women, but his behavior had not been that of a civilized, educated man, a man who had never indulged in acts of cruelty. He had no reason to suspect Alia of duplicity. He knew better than that.

Suddenly, he was longing for her. He could not apologize, of course, but there would be ways to make up for having behaved like an animal. What in the devil had gotten into him? Ian Baldwin was a successful writer and an intelligent man. He meant Alia no harm, nor Baraket; quite the opposite. Was he going to lose Alia, the woman he loved beyond all others because he was jealous of one of dozens of men who fell in love with her? No, he was not. Nor was he going to pretend any longer that he was not deeply in love with his wife. No other woman excited him as she did and no woman could replace her. Baraket perked up. After all, it was he who found her, he who created her. She was an extremely lucky girl.

He would let them both wait in Cairo for a few more days with no word from him. He knew that no matter what front they put up, both of them were slightly in awe of him and, yes, both were afraid of him. After all, he was their lord and master.

He now admired Alia more than ever for her courage. This was the second time she had defied him and each time she had been right to do so. What would have happened to them if she had let him go on torturing and beating her? A groveling, prideless Alia was unthinkable. And what would he think of her if she let him take the children away? The poor child had had no parents, no friends in her early life, and she adored her children. She had the courage of a lioness.

Baraket felt lighter, as if he had come through a long illness. He picked up the telephone and called through to his secretary.

"Tell the pilots we will leave for London in the morning. And get Tarek on the phone for me at Al-Hikma."

Just as Baraket assumed, the two women waited to hear from him. When two, then three, then four days went by with no word, they began to wonder. What was he doing, what was he going to do?

"He will call, or he will appear," Tafida said. "I know my son; he is too curious to let it go on much longer, but for the moment he is punishing us."

"I wish we would hear something."

"What happened to bring about this trouble?" Tafida asked. She had found no flaws in her daughter-in-law in the time they had spent together, and she had observed a sadness in Alia that was obviously a longing for Baraket. Tafida told her stories of Baraket's childhood in Egypt, old family tales; they talked constantly about him. Tafida, who had been lonely for the years since Baraket had married and cut her off from Alia and her grandchildren, wanted to get to the bottom of the trouble. Suddenly, she pounced.

"I have heard—I have my grapevine, you know, even from the isolation of Cairo—that there is another man in your life. Is it true?"

"There is another man in Baraket's life, not mine," Alia said. "Men often think that they are using me to get to Baraket. But Ian Baldwin, an English writer, is the man in question, and Baraket has taken exception to him. At the mention of Ian's name, he changes completely. I have behaved no differently with Ian than with any other man. It is Baraket who has changed."

"My dear Alia, Baraket is touchy about the smallest things. There was bound to be one man that he would not be able to stomach."

"It may be because of the man who introduced us," Alia said. "An astrologist that I met at Yali Beyaz. He was a catalyst for trouble in our lives and I was very stupid. He seemed to know about me, and he used astrology to influence me. He started off telling me about my past and everything he said was true. I was such a gullible, superstitious girl that I fell under his spell. Baraket never liked him and finally, in Paris, we had to dismiss him from our lives. He was murdered the night we dismissed him from our entourage."

"Who killed him?"

"No one knows. At first, I thought it was Baraket, but it wasn't. It may have been some of Anthony's homosexual friends. No one has ever known."

"Odd," Tafida said.

Tarek came into the room.

"Princess Rifat, Princess Alia."

"What is it, Tarek?" Tafida said.

"Prince Baraket has called. We are leaving for London tomorrow morning."

"Who is leaving, Tarek?" Tafida asked. The old wary look was back on her face.

"All of us, Princess Rifat. His Highness has arranged everything. He is expecting us all at Lindley House tomorrow evening."

There was great excitement at Lindley House with the arrival of Alia, Princess Tafida, the children, the nanny and Omm Niza, who would have died had she not been brought along at the last moment. Tarek saw that everyone was established in his or her proper quarters, helping the butlers and maids as best he could. There had been no sign of Baraket. Tarek took his few things to his room and had no more than gotten inside the door than the special bell rang, summoning him to Baraket's quarters. Tarek knew why he was being called.

Baraket stood, waiting for Tarek, his arms folded across his chest, his dark eyes piercing. Tarek waited. Nothing could excuse his behavior. He had gone against his master's orders. Baraket was going to exile him, Tarek was sure.

"Will you tell Princess Alia that we will be dining alone in the emerald room at eight-thirty?"

"Yes, Your Highness."

"You may go."

Tarek left the room, dazed. Was Baraket going to ignore his behavior? Never. It was a matter of time. Tarek shrugged, baffled. For the time being, he was still Alia's bodyguard. That was all that mattered.

"Good evening, my dear," Baraket said as Alia entered the emerald room.

"Good evening, Baraket," Alia said. She was completely calm. Her white dress was a favorite of Baraket's and she had chosen it deliberately. It was one of the most alluring dresses that Balmain had ever made for her, a column of thin white satin, very low in the neck with small off the shoulder straps, with a narrow belt pulling her waist in tight. Baraket had given her a belt made of twenty different sizes and cuts of emeralds embedded into antique gold, festooned with tassels of emerald beads, but it had vanished when he had taken the emeralds away. Suddenly, Alia noticed the difference in the room. The ivories were gone, the emeralds back. All the vitrines were open again, and the great paperweight that had been his engagement present to her sat on the small table beside her favorite chair. Was this a sign of forgiveness? Alia had no idea what was in Baraket's mind.

Tarek came into the room with a bottle of champagne on a silver tray. "Just leave it, Tarek," Baraket said. "We will dine at once."

"Yes, Your Highness."

When he left, Baraket seated Alia at the table. "I thought it might be a good idea for us to be alone this first evening. Tafida will stay for at least a month and we will be with her often enough."

"Yes, of course," Alia said. "And she loves being with Nebila and Karim. She adores them."

"Well, it's high time she got to know them," Baraket said, as if his mother had never displayed any interest in her grandchildren before he brought them together. He was still standing behind Alia's chair, after seating her. She started to turn to him but he put his hand on her shoulder.

"Wait," he said. Again, the emerald necklace shone in front of her eyes. He held it in front of her for an instant, having put it over her head the exact way he had done on *Ehukai III* nine years ago. He fixed the clasp and leaned down to kiss the nape of her neck.

"There," he said. "It is perfect and you are wearing my favorite dress. Welcome home, my darling. Now for some caviar."

"No," Alia said. "I don't want caviar, the caviar can wait. I want you." She rose, laughing, a great throaty laugh, and flung herself into his arms. He laughed with her, kissing her.

"You are a fine partner," he said, admiring her. "And how you have grown from the girl I first was lucky enough to find."

The war was over and she had won. His family was around him, as he wanted it. The message was clear and had been delivered with infinite finesse. No apologies were necessary. He and Alia were from the same world, they understood the same rules and they had learned how to love each other. He would always desire her, more than all others, but she would not be the only woman in his life, ever. She would be the most important one. He was her husband as well as her master. She was his wife, but no longer his slave.

LONDON
October 1964

"No you're not," Delphine said to Camilla. "If you have to go to Paris today, you can take a later flight. Alia's gone to Saadit Sarai with Baraket and I've wanted to spend some time alone with you. I don't appreciate your calling to break our lunch date at the eleventh hour, the twelfth actually, it's noon already. You come to Claridge's and take the five-o'clock plane to Paris." She hung up.

Bossy today, aren't we, Camilla thought, holding the dead phone in her hand. She was taken aback by Delphine's tone, and annoyed, but underneath she was a little bit afraid. Delphine had never spoken to her that way before, never. She shrugged her shoulders and called Air France to change her reservations. An hour later, when she reached Claridge's,

Delphine had not yet arrived. Odd, Camilla thought, I'm only twenty minutes late and Delphine is always on time. She sat alone at the table, waiting. Delphine walked in on the dot of one-thirty and sat down, Bruno hovering over her.

"You've arrived first, for once," Delphine said, looking sharply at Camilla, a look on her face that Camilla had never seen before. It was more a feeling than a look. The feeling was as new to Delphine as it was to Camilla.

Delphine was in a cold rage for one of the few times in her life, and Camilla was the cause of it. She forced Camilla to pay full attention before she started to speak. Camilla had a nasty little habit of letting her eyes wander all over the room unless she was doing the talking.

"When do you plan to stop indulging yourself in this second-rate behavior?" she asked, the normal lilt in her voice turned to steel. "Second-rate behavior is worse than fifth-rate. Fifth-rate is meaningless, second-rate is a near-miss. Coming from you, it is no longer acceptable."

Camilla was at a loss for words. What had she done to deserve this, especially from Delphine?

"At least you're batting a thousand," Delphine continued, aware that Camilla would have no idea what the expression meant but that she would, nevertheless, get the message. "There isn't one of us that you haven't either let down or betrayed, been rude to or careless with. You've been an embarrassment to Alia and me, and especially to poor Simon, whom you've left stuck with it, about the hospital. You know we've taken over your work, your commitments, all of them, and covered for you. Now you have that charming little bachelor's flat in Eaton Square in your own building and your friend St. John is seen going in and out early and late by your husband, your children and your servants. He's also been very vocal about your easy charms to the boys in the back rooms of the newspapers and the pubs."

"Hang on," Camilla said, an ugly flush spreading across her face. "I don't have to—"

"Just shut up," Delphine said. "We have been friends for

many years now, you and Alia and I, and it has certainly been a one-way street. You've taken everything and given nothing. It's a rapidly ending chapter, Camilla, and this time you have gone too far."

"This time, what's this time?" Camilla asked. She knew now what Delphine meant and the uneasiness that she felt earlier burst into full bloom.

"Your little games in Paris are gutter gossip now and about to break in the English papers. The new gossip is your constant companionship with Ceil Chambers." Delphine looked toward Bruno, who came hurrying. "Bruno, please bring me some coffee and a bottle of champagne for Lady Kilmuir." Her tone to Bruno was Delphine again, not the woman admonishing Camilla.

"You really care nothing about any of us, do you? Now you've taken up with one of Baraket's former mistresses, a half-demented girl who has tried to blackmail Baraket with photographs and forged letters, and has threatened Alia's life. And you plan to be in the cesspools of Paris with some questionable escorts and that pathetic girl tonight. What is wrong with you?"

"What do you mean, 'threatened' Alia's life?"

"That's how far gone on drugs your lovely chum Ceil is. An Algerian pimp, quite known to the Paris police, is going to be with you again tonight, isn't he? He's the one who coerced Ceil into sending anonymous letters to Baraket, threatening to blind Alia. Stupid. Kenneth took care of the matter very quickly, he knows Paris well, as you know. That is how your name came up, Lady Kilmuir, you're caught in the net as a possible accomplice or suspect. What are you trying to do, Camilla?"

Camilla stood up. "I'll do as I like," she said. "And I will see who I like. All this swill about Ceil is a tempest in a teapot. I don't believe what you're saying for one minute, you're all so prissy—"

"Then go your way, Camilla. If you leave this table now, you will be saying good-bye to me, to all of us. Your trouble is that you were never willing to face up to the fact that true pleasure involves strict discipline. Alia and I didn't mind indulging you in your self-deceptions and your increasing selfishness, for years. We've both been used rather than trusted. You've lied to everyone, to Jeremy about Russ, to us, you've lied to Russ, too, little lies for your own purposes. I no longer am willing to bother with you and I wanted to make it clear."

Every word Delphine said was true. Camilla couldn't imagine how she knew so much. Scenes from the past flooded her memory from long ago when they were new friends doing good things, pretty things, in a clean world. Alia, always gentle, always defending her . . . Delphine, subtle, always encouraging . . . her rock of Gibraltar.

Camilla hesitated before speaking. "I guess I am a shit," she said softly. She sat down.

"Yes, you are," Delphine said, knowing that she had gotten through. "Now, if you don't have to rush off to Paris, maybe you'd like to spend some time talking about it."

"Bruno," Camilla said, "bring us the menus."

Delphine and Camilla were both undone by the ferocity of their fight. They talked at Claridge's for hours, then continued for days when Alia returned. They told her what had happened, and gradually they sorted out all of the hurts and misunderstandings that had come between them.

"I don't ever remember being that angry," Delphine said. "Do you know, I had no idea what I was going to say to you, I just knew we were losing you and I had to say something."

"You scared me to death," Camilla said. "Nothing ever seems to frighten me, but you did. I knew that underneath it all, I'd hurt you both."

"What can we do about Ceil?" Alia said. "Poor little thing. I can't mention her name even to Baraket, but I keep thinking that if we tried, we could help her."

"You're dreaming," Camilla said. "I know Ceil better than you two do, and there is nothing to be done about her. She scared me almost as much as Delphine, but that's because she doesn't care. Delphine does."

"There must be something we can do," Delphine said. We *know* what is happening to her. No one else really does, except Guy, and he's tried. Let's invest a little time in it; maybe we can help."

"All right," Camilla said. "I doubt it, but we'll try."

LONDON

March 1965

"George." Delphine's voice crackled through the ship-to-shore telephone. She was in her warm sitting room in London, feet up in front of the fire. George was in his usual suite on the *Île de France*, due in Le Havre the following morning.

"It's happened, Ceil Chambers has killed herself, they just found her body yesterday. Please get off in Le Havre and come up to Paris. Camilla and I will be there tomorrow for the funeral service. I need you."

"I'll be there, the boat train will put me in about ten in the morning. What time do you arrive?"

"Eleven fifty-five at Le Bourget. Alia is already at the Crillon, nothing to do with Ceil, but she'll be with us, of course, and Baraket's plane will bring us back to London to-

morrow night. Baraket will have none of it. Russ is in Geneva
on a business trip, at the Richemond. Call him, or I will, and
see if he can come. Did you know that he knew Ceil . . .
after Graziella's party he tried to help her . . . when Camilla
got so furious, remember? Thank God Ken won't be back
from the Far East until the weekend. George, it's a ghastly
story."

"I'm sure it is," George said. "Del, it isn't a big surprise. I'll
find Russ now that we're within telephone distance, and we
will meet you tomorrow. See you then." George hung up and
put through the call to Geneva.

"This is one funeral I'd like to not even know about," Russ
said to George the next morning. "I hate funerals, especially
suicides. Why are we going?"

"You know damn well why we're going. Delphine needs us,
more than Camilla or Alia, and we were all friends of Ceil's to
a certain extent. As much as anyone could befriend her. And
worse"—he gave Russ a grim look—"we may be the only ones
there. I don't know much about Guy; but I'm sure he is
devastated. He was a good twenty years older than Ceil when
they met, an ill-starred meeting. She fit his romantic image to
a T. Small-town American beauty, considerable, God-given
talent as an actress, and the toast of Paris. Did you ever meet
Guy?"

"No," Russ said. "And Ceil only that once, that week in
Paris." Memories came back. A suite at the Ritz, a warm bathtub and a beautiful confused girl talking incessantly, trailing
around in Chanel robes. Disturbed eyes, pink roses and now
death. "What about him?"

"Very highly thought of as a writer; still a Parisian cult
figure. They met when she had the lead in a small, very
French film that was being made from one of his stories. He
fell head-over-heels for her, including her self-destructive
tendencies. Lots of men fell in love with her but the smart
ones moved on quickly. She wanted everything and nothing;
everything was not enough and nothing wasn't enough, either.
Guy honestly thought he could save her."

"How do you keep up with so many people, George? Like a Ceil Chambers, who hasn't played even a bit part in your life?"

"In a way she did. I was interested in her. There was something about her, something special beyond the touching beauty. I thought she might turn out to be a big girl. But she was lost from the beginning. Guy fancied that he could save her."

"From herself?"

"Yes, and he loved the role at first. She was on wine, hard booze, drugs and men. She tortured him—made him pay for being fool enough to love her, to stick with her, to be there to drag her out of the gutter every two weeks or so. Imagine drying her out, getting her away from the men she picked up in the end? Black ones, yellow ones, dirty old ones, dirty young ones—you name it, she had them."

Russ shuddered, remembering the damaged child he had taken care of for a week. George's mind flashed back to the two Germans outside her bedroom door the night of the party in Baden-Baden.

"When did it get this bad . . . how long ago?"

"Oh, for a long time now. Delphine tried to keep up with her out of the sweetness of her heart. Camilla and Ceil had some wild times together in Paris, driving Jeremy off his head, but she was playing with too much fire even for Camilla. Alia felt sorry for her, but she was in a different position because of Baraket's long-ago affair with her. Alia did what she could out of pity, but I know she did try to help. Then Ceil kept changing addresses; even Guy couldn't find her unless she turned up hungry or half dead from an overdose on his doorstep. He always took her in; I don't know what happened this time."

"The police found her in the Bois de Boulogne?" Russ had read the story in the morning paper.

"Yes. Wrapped in a blanket and nothing else. She'd apparently been dead for several days." He looked at his watch. It's time we went out to meet Delphine and Camilla."

"Would you mind very much if I didn't go with you? I've got to make a tedious phone call back to my office."

"Of course not. We'll pick you up here."

"Fine," Russ said. "I'll be watching for you."

Pink roses in great cascading bouquets filled the small grim room. Tall vases filled with dozens of long-stemmed Queen Elizabeths stood in every corner, their color heightened by the flickering candles. Simple bunches of country blooms from the palest to the deepest shades of pink were banked in tangled profusion at the base of the coffin. Delphine and Camilla and Alia stood together near the coffin and makeshift altar.

A blanket made of thousands of tiny sweetheart roses intermingled with the baby's breath was pulled up over Ceil's thin body like a child's coverlet, tucked just under her chin. The flawless chiseled features were unchanged and she was no paler in death than she had been in life. The one vast difference to the few assembled was that her face in repose, eyes closed, saved them from seeing once again the terrible torture that they had all seen in her eyes. George and Russ stood behind the three girls, listening intently as the priest droned on. From time to time, they glanced at the pale face of the dead girl lying in her narrow coffin. George had been right. There were only four other people in the room. Pascal, Ceil's old concierge, crossed herself again and again, snuffling into her dirty handkerchief. Her husband stood beside her, reeking of garlic and cheap cognac. Jean-Marc, the florist from the corner shop, was trying to count the innumerable roses that seemed to overflow the room, also trying to figure out a way to get his hands on at least some of them later on. When the others left, maybe he could stay behind and take some of them off with him, wrapped in newspapers. He could sell them, and Ceil herself would have wanted it that way. He'd given her enough flowers for nothing in the time she had lived in the apartment next door to his shop. Jean-Marc was fascinated with the roses: every pink rose in Paris must be in this room today, and all of them from the most expensive flower shops. Who had sent them anyway? Jean-Marc had helped arrange them when they started arriving and there wasn't a card in any of the bouquets. He'd seen her with a lot of rich men in the past year, but not with either of the two men standing with the rich-looking ladies. Some of Ceil's fancy friends. Of course, they knew that she had killed herself. It seemed strange to Jean-Marc that there were no other friends there to mourn her. She had been so pretty. Beside him, the gendarme from the Eighth Arrondissment shuffled his feet, praying only for the service to be over so he could go to lunch.

The priest finished, with a final droning prayer. He stared blankly at Ceil's friends for a moment and then turned abruptly and left the room, not saying a word to anyone.

Delphine turned to Pascal, Ceil's concierge, and spoke to her softly in French. "*Et maintenant?* Who takes care of the burial?"

Pascal gestured toward the doors the priest had vanished through. "*Le prêtre. Il n'y a personne d'autre, mais il a reçu de l'argent pour tout ça, le service et les funérailles. C'est triste, madame, elle était si jeune.*"

"*Oui, c'est triste, très triste.*" She turned back to the others.

"Where is Guy?" Camilla asked. "Is he really not coming?"

"He is in Paris," Delphine said. "I called before we left London to see if we could pick him up, but he put me off. I felt sure he would decide to come, but I see now he never was intending to. He must have sent the roses. He knew she adored pink roses. Only Guy could have found so many."

Yes, Russ thought, Guy had sent the pink roses, but only some of them, that filled the ugly room. When George had left for the airport, leaving Russ to make his phone call, Russ had stopped by the concierge's desk. He put a slip of paper with an address on it in the concierge's hand.

"There's an address on the Left Bank on this piece of paper," he said. "I want you to call every florist you know and have every pink rose they have sent to that address. And I want you to send one of the bellboys to the flower market to buy every other pink rose still breathing and have them taken to the same address. They have got to be there within one hour. Do you understand?"

"Of course, m'sieur." His face was granite, with pinpoints of steel light in his eyes.

"Is it possible? I don't know where the place is."

"Of course it is possible, M'sieur Marshall. I understand."

"No," Russ said, "you don't understand. Neither do I." He put a large franc note in the concierge's hands. "Thank you. Put all the charges on my bill."

"Of course, m'sieur. Will there be a card?"

"No," Russ said. "A card will not be necessary."

Now, Russ watched as Camilla and Delphine and Alia went to the side of the coffin to pay their last respects, wrapped in their soufflé-like furs. All three of them looked so vibrant and alive so well cared for. Camilla looked too well cared for, Russ thought. What the hell is she doing to be as fat as she is? Even so, she still had faint vestiges of her bright, gamine appeal. Delphine took a handkerchief from her handbag and wiped a tear from her eye.

"Come on, darling," Camilla said. "It's done. Let's leave her. There wasn't anything we could have changed and there is nothing we could do."

"Poor little girl," Alia said. "She looks about ten years old lying in that coffin." Alia shuddered, thinking back to the De Pavenel party and the beginning of all the trouble with Baraket. Thank God that was long behind them. "I will not go to the funeral," Baraket said. "You go with Camilla and Delphine, you were all good to her. Too bad Ceil learned nothing from any of you."

A small crowd had gathered around the huge black Rolls parked in the street, all of them held at bay by the look on Tarek's face. He leaped to open the door when the five of them came out through the narrow passageway, anxious to get them out of this tough quarter. He tucked light foot rugs around their ankles and fixed the jump seats for Russ and George.

"We'll go to Grand Vefour, please, Tarek."

"Yes, Your Highness," he answered, heaving a sigh of relief as he turned safely into the Boulevard St. Germain.

There were long-branch white lilacs in tall, slender crystal vases on the tables at Grand Vefour, as white as the cold spring sunlight that fell on the snowy tablecloths. George ordered a bottle of champagne and asked the captain to bring menus in half an hour.

"Where did it all begin to go wrong for her?" Delphine asked. "George, Camilla, you remember the night we saw her with Guy at the Hôtel de Paris? I was fascinated by her beauty; that compelling face and those serious eyes, and the vulnerability. She was shy, but she had Guy and the world ahead of her. I thought."

"No," George said. "She didn't. She had it behind her. Two years of Paris, of men falling in love with her, of Dior dresses, of being courted and yessed and flattered, taught her nothing. She did exactly, precisely what she wanted to do. I think there is a moment in life for all of us, when we make a decision to do what we really want to do. Some opt for doing nothing, some are go-getters who go and get, and some don't give a damn. They take, they are users, they may be beautiful, bright, talented, but their heads are on wrong. Ceil's head was never on right. She was talented and beautiful; those two things alone are more than most girls ever have, and she spat on both."

"I agree with you," Russ said.

"How would you know?" Camilla snapped.

"Because she had none of the quality of you or Delphine or Alia. You're all fighters in your way, and you all care about something, someone, you have some sense of responsibility, some values, some honor, and some duties." Russ had ducked answering Camilla's question directly. If I can get Camilla alone, he thought, I'm going to find out why she's beginning to come apart at the seams, too.

"Maybe we're being a little hard on her," Delphine said. "I know that Alia and Camilla and I do have certain strengths—

and we stick together—but that doesn't mean that everyone has them. Ceil was a little girl from a small town in Wisconsin, and it all went to her head, as Paris can."

"You're just a little girl from a small town called Honolulu," George said. "And Camilla from a country village in England and Alia from the wilder parts of Turkey, earthquake land. Why did none of you spoil as effectively, and why have you achieved so much more?" He hoped Camilla was paying attention.

"Oh, George, you *are* prejudiced," Camilla said. "Delphine had the protection of a conservative family, and I had a very strict early background, not that I know what Ceil's was like. I did have some wild times with her, as we all know, but somehow when Ceil and I were being fast and loose, she would go too far for me. She courted trouble, demanded it and got it. I'd creep back to London, having gotten it out of my system, whatever *it* was, but Ceil started going farther down, down, down, with people who were awful—criminals, pimps, the lowest gutter types. Delphine gave me hell about it. Alia put it properly. Poor little girl."

"Everything depends on the man you choose . . . or the man who chooses you," Alia said. "Where would I be if Baraket hadn't wanted me? By the time Guy fell in love with Ceil, it was too late. She flouted everything, it was a sickness of her soul, and no one could change her." Alia remembered Ceil's look, the way she had behaved the night of Graziella's party. Alia had felt pity for her from the moment she first saw her, never jealousy.

"Big girls know better," George said. "They don't make those mistakes. I certainly can't blame Paris for Ceil's tragedy, and I don't, but French society is either so conservative that it bores me to death, or so superfluous that it leaves me wondering what's wrong with me."

"The food is still the best in the world," Russ said. "How about ordering lunch? We'll be in London tonight, thanks to Baraket's plane and Alia's invitation."

George signaled the captain. "And after lunch, since Paris

has the greatest museums, I think we should go to the Jeu de Paume and look at those glorious paintings while the girls are shopping."

"Then we can stop by the Ritz Bar for a martini afterward. Now that I can afford those paintings, the Louvre won't sell. Very frustrating," Russ said.

Russ and George walked in the cold air before going to see the Impressionist collection in the Jeu de Paume. Afterward they settled down in the Ritz Bar to wait for Tarek to pick them up at five-thirty.

"I'm glad that's over," Russ said. "Not the lunch or the pictures, they were both great, but that funeral."

"Unforgettable," George said. "The remains of a flawless beauty and a wasted life."

"How can they be so different?"

"Who?"

"Ceil . . . with all her mistakes, then the difference of a Delphine, a Camilla, an Alia. You keep using the expression 'the big girls.' Is that what you mean?"

"Yes, like the big boys," said George. "They understand power and men and money—but they also know about discipline and sacrifice—pain and patience. It's a job done in a different way. A fine, loving woman is invaluable to a man, and all she stands to gain, with a decent man, is the whole goddamned world. Ceil had none of that. She was a destroyer. The qualities that make a woman interesting to me are all rolled up into Delphine and Alia and Camilla, and they satisfy me. Delphine has been magnificent with Kenneth, and he is her glory. Such happiness, such a true mating is a rare thing. How Alia has grown from a simple girl with nothing, coming from worse than nowhere—into an adored, respected, educated wife and a helpmate to Baraket. Camilla, for all her bravado is still searching, a bit desperately, for the answer. She'll find it."

"I've had a wife or two who think that all you have to have is money and a man." Russ said. "One plus the other puts you on the best-dressed list, makes you the greatest hostess in the

world, and turns you into a linguist overnight. They spend all
their time thinking about themselves."

"The big girls think about others," George said. "The little
girls are only concerned with themselves. They lack the major
elements."

"Which are?"

"The knowledge that they are a little bit different. It's
something of a killer instinct. Camilla is the one who better
make up her mind soon. It's decision time for her."

"Decisions are not all that easy to make. Life gets pretty
confusing sometimes."

"It shouldn't if you have brains, money, power and heart.
And courage."

"Jesus," Russ said. "That's the lot."

"And you have to have the lot. Look at Delphine. I saw her
make a decision once. An emotional one, and I was afraid she
was going to make an irrevocable mistake."

"I can't imagine Delphine ever making a mistake. She has
everything."

"She does. But the winter she came to New York, under my
guardianship, she was involved in the first love affair of her
life, with Ryan O'Roark. He was mad about her. Her emotions ran rampant; she loved him and his brilliance, totally.
But Ryan was Ryan, and even loving Delphine wasn't going to
change him. He had quite a few ladies on a concurrent basis. I
imagine he still does. When Delphine found out about the first
one she came apart at the seams. She ranted and railed, a victim of emotions untapped before. She was devastated but she
grew up. She could not, would not, accept being shared, even
though she tried to work it out. She went back to him once,
or rather her body went back to him; her head never did.
When she told me, I must confess that I was angry. George
Sherril, her mentor and the man who had introduced them
and was patting himself on the back for having done so, had
made a mistake. Ryan was behaving like an Irish alley cat,
sullying my perfect princess, the clay that I was molding, as I
seem to do with all the women I'm drawn to. She didn't take

long to make her decision. We talked about it only once, and then I brought her to Europe. I know she suffered on the ship coming over. I saw the dark circles under those marvelous eyes every day, but somewhere in the mid-Atlantic, she found her true self. It wasn't just carry-on, stiff-upper-lip either, the noble pitch of the head no matter what the bastard had done to her. Her mind worked on her heart. That was the end of Ryan or any man like him. She learned the importance of taste in men, of being discriminating. A week later, she met Ken on my yacht, and I saw that begin. I thought, Oh, Jesus, he's going overboard for her and she's not ready. That killer instinct told her exactly what kind of man he was. Kind, civilized, important, rich and trustworthy. She wasn't in love with him at first, not at all. But when he declared himself, she knew she was *going* to love him and that he was the one man in the world she could commit herself to, heart and soul, as he did to her. That's what a big girl does."

"And Camilla?" Russ said, quietly.

"She has a way to go, but I think Delphine's influence, and Alia's on her, is paramount; they both mean more to her than she knows yet. Camilla is powerful and she should learn how to use it. If she doesn't . . ."

"Then?"

"Then she'll be relegated to the ranks of the little girls whose vanity pulls them down. The little girls forget about the brass ring and you know where they end up? Selling real estate, or doing a little interior decorating, a small boutique maybe, backed by a man they've had an affair with who wants to pay off. Married to or left with the leftover men, or homosexuals, or the drunks, or the weak ones who are looking for a half servant, not a woman. They've had their chance. Like physical beauty, when it's gone, it's gone. You must have noticed how successful women, even if they were never great beauties, have a style, a pride, about them that makes them desirable no matter how old they are? They understand men and the rules and no smart woman wants to live in a world without men. To some, a man is a base or a meal ticket, not much else, and they'll put up with a lot to have one for a husband or a prop. But to the selective woman, the woman who values herself and *is* valuable, man is the zenith. He loves her, makes love to her, defends and protects her, and then she is able to give more than he ever knew he wanted or needed. Delphine's done it, and Alia has, too."

"And Camilla?" Russ asked again.

"Jeremy and Camilla were never suited to each other," George said reluctantly. "They lead very separate lives at this stage. What about you, you've always been in Camilla's landscape, haven't you?"

George's question made Russ uneasy. He was hard put to describe his feelings for Camilla. "I don't want to be with any one woman all the time. I came here, not just to see Camilla, but because of you and Delphine, and Alia and Baraket, too. And a little bit because of Ceil."

"Mostly because of Camilla though."

"Probably. We have a strange relationship. I haven't seen her since that party of De Pavenel. Jeremy was with her, when I thought she was alone. I can't change the fact of a long-term love affair with a woman, but I'm not going to put horns on her husband in his presence. I'm not sure Camilla doesn't get a thrill out of playing us against each other. What is eating her?"

"Jeremy and you. She doesn't want to lose either of you."

"I don't know why I keep coming back; Camilla is the only woman who has never bored me. She's enraged me, she looks like hell now, but we're friends. I care about her; she's my best friend. You know, of the lot of us, Baraket is the brilliant one."

"Why?"

"In the finest tradition of arranged marriages, that's what Baraket has got, an arranged marriage. *He* arranged it. Better than you or I ever have!"

George burst out laughing.

"And you're the fellow from that small town in the Texas Panhandle? Ha! You could probably make some arrangement with Camilla. . . . Did you ever think of marrying her?"

"Of course. I need her, but I can't have her. Neither of us is a finished product yet. I'd bitch it up—just as I have the others—and then I'd lose my best friend."

"Don't be too sure of that. One never knows what will happen, that's the best thing about life, the constant change and renewal. Run some fresh water over your friendship with Camilla. I'm a great believer in validating friendships, deepening them, learning how to give and how to take."

Russ sat back, looking around the pleasant bar.

"I know how to give, but only to a certain extent. I don't want to give too much to any one person. Not right now."

LONDON
November 1965

Baraket's emergence as a world figure had grown steadily and his impact was felt in all corridors of world power. He was truly a modern Arab prince. He had not lost his mischievous sense of intrigue and his delight in scheming, but he had come to grips with the role he intended to play in the future. He had an accurate reputation for brilliance in business, but after years of hard work, he was still labeled as a fabulously rich man surrounded with superfluous, glittering figures. His wife was a great beauty of impeccable behavior and his collection of emeralds was reputed to be the most valuable in the world. Although both delighted him, they were hardly all there was to Baraket. When someone quoted him as having said there were three things that he loved—beautiful women, great jewels and complex business deals—Baraket answered saying, "The first two are really one and the same and the third is rarely the case."

Baraket would no longer allow his reputation to be that of simply a playboy prince. He removed himself from the public eye. He gave no interviews; no pictures appeared of him, with or without Alia, and no mentions of them appeared in the gossip columns or magazines as in the past. To his friends, he was unchanged: gregarious, outgoing and generous, as always. Kenneth and George were intermeshed with him in business. Power and money were beside the point. He ranged the world, finding new interests. At home in London, he was content.

Ian had come back into Alia and Baraket's lives. It was Baraket's apology to Alia—unspoken and two years later, but clearly saying that he had never taken exception to Ian at all. Baraket assumed that Alia would accept Ian's presence among them again as if he had been away from England on a trip and returned. In point of fact he had: he had been in South Africa researching a new book.

"We must have Baldwin to the dinner for Tafida," Baraket announced at breakfast, tossing the newspaper to her. There was a photo of Ian at Heathrow Airport, taken the day before. Tafida was visiting them once again, thanks to an arrangement Baraket had been able to work out with Nasser. Tafida was aging; she was considering giving up living alone at Villa Al-Hikma and looking for a house in London.

"Baldwin?" Alia said. Her calm astonishment was taken by Baraket as a memory lapse.

"Alia!" Baraket said patiently, pleased with her vague response. "Baldwin, the writer you met in Turkey, the one so mesmerized by you I was almost jealous."

"Of course," Alia said. "Yes, I'm sure Tafida would enjoy his company. He's quite knowledgeable in some of her favorite pursuits. Archaeology, for instance."

"We must give a very smart party for her this time, we really never have before. She will object, saying she wants nothing of the kind, but I think she'd like to see us try to outdo the parties she was famous for at Al-Hikma. I think we might consider two hundred for dinner and two hundred afterward for dancing, don't you? Mix up the diplomats with the creators: actors, painters, writers. Like Baldwin."

The party was set, the invitations sent out. Two days before, Alia found a small bouquet of lilies of the valley on her dressing table. Ian had written on the card, "Looking forward to your party. Ian." Alia knew it was a message to her, a message saying that if she did not want him to come, she should let him know.

Tafida was intrigued.

"But he's the one you said was responsible for all the trouble. Ian Baldwin. Why would Baraket have him?"

"Because he finally realizes that there was nothing between us. Tafida, it's his way of apologizing. You look at Ian and tell me what you think."

"I most certainly shall," Tafida said, the tiny narrowing of her eyes visible once more. She knew better than to believe anything anyone said.

As it turned out, Ian dazzled her. From the moment he arrived, she insisted on his staying close to her side. They should have looked somewhat ridiculous together, but instead, the giant of a man and the tiny, imperious lady were by far the outstanding pair at the party. They hit it off perfectly. Alia, seeing to her duties as a hostess, had little time to spend with them, but she was relieved to see things going well between them. When it came time for good nights, she and Baraket stood at the door of Lindley House with Tafida. Tafida promptly invited Ian for lunch the following day. "With or without my son and daughter-in-law," she said, flirtatiously.

"With pleasure," Ian said, kissing her hand. He took Alia's hand and brought it to his lips. "Good night, most beautiful princess," he said. "I am now as devastated by Princess Tafida as I am by her daughter-in-law." He provided just the right touch, delighting Baraket. When everyone had gone, the three of them repaired to the emerald room to talk over the party.

"The man has taste," Baraket said. "I'm delighted he's back."

Tafida gave her thin little smile.

"If there are men like that around who fall in love with your wife and mother, instead of the usual bores and hangers-on, how could you possibly object?" She was looking for at least a soupçon of trouble.

"I have never had any objection to any of your swains—yours or Alia's. I expect that," Baraket said. "Whatever gave you any idea that I did?"

Seeing Ian again threw Alia completely off her guard. Her face was inscrutable and she was thankful when Ian arrived and as she saw him throughout the evening. They never exchanged a personal word. Her look was calm, her expression sincere and her smile lovely, and no trace showed of the excitement, the inner turmoil that seeing him again brought.

As she undressed, she read Ian's card again. It was in his handwriting, not the florist's. "Looking forward to your party." Why had Baraket brought him back into her life?

Alia couldn't sleep. Baraket had her in one of his vise-like grips and she was aching to move, to stretch out. Finally, she disengaged herself gently from his arms and whispered in his ear that she was going to her own bedroom for a while but that she would return. He sleepily agreed. "Too much excitement from the party . . . too much Turkish coffee . . . come back, *canim*, when you like . . ." He was gone, deep asleep again.

Alia got into her bed in her big corner bedroom. From her window, she could see across Knightsbridge, or imagined that she could see right through the walls of Selfridges and Harrods, through the back of the row of red brick Victorian houses that lined Pont Street. Her mind carried her into Ian's flat, into Ian's bedroom, into Ian's bed. She got up and went to the window and looked out at the blue-black night sky, looking toward Pont Street, listening to the late-night silence of the city. Was he awake? Was he thinking about her, did he think about her anymore?

She closed her eyes. She was grateful to Baraket for having forgiven her at last without anger, for having brought them all back together from Cairo as if nothing had ever happened, for being the ever-expanding, powerful dreadnought of a man that he was. She loved Baraket. He had given her everything, but more than that he had encouraged her to learn, to build, to give, to contribute. He made her proud of herself. She was his wife, and the mother of his children, and the trouble they had had was behind them forever.

She fell asleep. Nothing was dark in her dream, everything was pale sun and white, light, lighter. She was back in Pont Street. The sound of the willow beating softly against the window from the mews garden was in her ears and the white sheets on Ian's big bed were silkily crumpled. She was in his arms, his lips were on hers. It was the first time, the only time, the one time, and it would never happen again, but she was living it over, it was happening again. She was giving, not being taken, once more. Half awake, she felt tears on her cheeks. She brushed them away, feeling the sweat on her brow and the dampness at the nape of her neck where her heavy hair was hot on the pillow, and a movement inside her that warmed her and left her trembling, curled up in the bed.

Tafida was leaving at the weekend. Baraket decided to take them to Paris for a few days, then he wanted Tafida to see Saadit Sarai, all that he had done to it since she had last been there. Alia wanted to stay in Paris with Balmain for a few days. "Baraket," she said, "Tafida is getting old. I think she would like to have you to herself. I will go, of course, if you want me to, but she would be so proud to have you to herself."

Baraket agreed. "But I can only stand her for a week," he

said. "She will have everything turned upside down, and as she is brilliant, I will begin to feel like a fool and hate her and send her home to Cairo. But you are right, she is my duty. And I shall carry her out." His white teeth gleamed at his joke and he laughed his big laugh.

LONDON

March 1967

"If we were going to give a fiftieth birthday for George, where would we give it?" Delphine asked. "George will be fifty years old on June third, in the year of our Lord nineteen sixty-seven, and we have to do something special about it."

The three of them were lunching at their regular corner table in the big dining room at Claridge's.

"Why would George or anyone else want a fiftieth birthday party?" Camilla asked, digging into her treacle tart.

"Of course he will," Alia said. "As long as we give it. He loves celebrations, and it's always George who arranges everything for everyone else. I do think we should have it in London, though, don't you? George loves it here, and it's the perfect time of year."

"The most important thing is where," Delphine said. "None of us can give it at home, if it's 'our' party, so that means one of the ballrooms."

"It would be nice to have two hundred of George's most intimate friends, but by the time we make up the list, we're going to have four hundred," Camilla said. "Four hundred is the perfect number for the Savoy ballroom, and we all know it's the prettiest and best ballroom in London." Camilla was right about that.

"It's the only way I'll ever get my parents and Jay to come from Hawaii," Delphine said. "All these years, and I haven't gotten them to budge, but they will now for George's birthday. And Fritz Hartung will come from Baden-Baden."

"Stop!" Camilla said. "We have got to decide on the place before we make the guest list."

"The Savoy, of course," Alia said, with Delphine and Camilla agreeing.

"We'll take all of the river suites and rooms for everyone from out of town. George could fill the entire hotel from *one* of his address books but we'll have to try to hold it to capacity. He was certainly born on the right day for the London season, especially this year. June third is perfect, two days after the Derby, and you know he adores Epsom."

"Righto," Camilla said, as the three of them rose from the table. "Let's call him now. It's nine in the morning in New York, a perfect time to catch him at Ehukai Farm."

George was touched and pleased with the arrangements made for his party. It meant coming to Europe earlier than he would have normally, but that suited him, too. He wanted to spend some time alone with his girls, each of them, and London was the right place for it. Delphine was fine: Delphine was always fine. There was something more remote than ever about Alia, but George knew that some quiet, private conversation would put them back on the intimate basis they had shared. Camilla actively worried him. The gossip had reached a critical peak: the way she looked, who she was being seen with, the way she treated people—all of it bothered George. She was no Ceil, but she was in trouble.

The summer cruises on *Ehukai III* continued, but for the past few years George had not been able to assemble the group as he would have liked to. Once, Alia and Baraket had been at Saadit Sarai when George had brought the yacht into Istanbul and they had taken a long leisurely cruise, the one George had promised them the year of their wedding. They lingered in the Greek islands, went through the Corinth Canal once again, then along the Dalmatian coast of Yugoslavia to Venice. Kenneth and Delphine joined them but only for a few days as they were en route to Washington for a bank meeting. Camilla and Jeremy had not come; they stayed at the villa at Juan-les-Pins preferring the party life of the South of France to being forced into close company with each other on the yacht.

Now George could set himself up in living quarters in one of the graceful river suites for a full two weeks, and see them at leisure, one at a time. He arrived in London the day before Epsom Derby, as planned. Not bad timing, he thought, not bad at all.

The night of George's arrival, Camilla arranged a small dinner for the seven of them in the Eaton Square flat. Jeremy would be in Fleet Street until late for a publisher's meeting, but would be home by the time they finished dinner. Camilla was full of plans for Epsom. "We'll all drive down in tandem, in the two Rollses and the Mercedes. We'll have plenty of room for all the food for the picnic and masses of champagne."

"Never mind the provisions," George said. "Who's going to win the Derby?"

"Moore on H. J. Joel's Royal Palace, I should think," Jeremy said, coming into the dining room. "That's what our sports boys feel anyway, as of half an hour ago."

George rose to greet Jeremy. He looks well, George thought, very well. He's maturing.

"I don't give a fig about the Derby," Camilla said, taking no notice of Jeremy's arrival. The atmosphere in the dining room changed with his entrance. Camilla had been in high spirits before he appeared; now a petulant expression appeared on her face. "There's a filly running in the sixth race. She's a gray, called Ginevra—belongs to a friend of mine. You and I are going to bet a packet on her, and Ken too, George."

"Your good friend St. John's horse, no doubt," Jeremy said, lighting a cigar and blowing the smoke toward her, not looking at her.

"Right as usual, Jeremy," Camilla said, almost viciously, rising from the table.

George was glad to leave the tension of the dining room. He settled down to share a cognac and a cigar with Jeremy. They were easy companions. But how long would he continue to put up with Camilla's behavior? It was very English to ignore it, but Jeremy had once been very much in love with her. Was he still? George wondered. On the way to the Savoy later, Kenneth tried to explain.

"She still drives him and goads him, and because he's good-natured, he takes it. Remember, on *Ehukai,* you once described her to me, and you were right. She's a harridan in her way, but he *has* loved her always. Camilla has taken to other gentlemen's beds with alarming frequency lately. She makes no attempt at discretion; she's a very busy lady."

"George," Delphine said, "I thought she was going to be all right. Remember, I told you about our summit meeting a while ago, when the three of us talked it all out?"

"Of course I remember," George said. "What happened?"

"Since then she's been better about us but worse about herself. Alia and I can't do anything." They had arrived at the Savoy. Delphine kissed him good night.

On the way home, Kenneth reached for her hand. "What is it, darling?"

"It's such a shame. They could be so good together, she and Jeremy. All he's ever done is love her helplessly."

"Ssh," Kenneth said. "You're not to be unhappy about anything. Just don't ever let anyone know how much I love you;
keep it a deep, private secret, so no one will try to take it
away from us."

Camilla came for George at the Savoy at noon the next day.
She drove the car, with George beside her and the chauffeur
stashed away in the back seat.

"Jeremy's not coming, thank heaven," she said. "We'll find
Baraket and Alia and the others in the parking lot. They left
earlier to set up the picnic."

"They left earlier because you drive like a demon. They
know we'll arrive at the same time."

George was right. The three cars arrived together in Epsom's green lawn of a parking lot at a few minutes after one.
In no time, the butlers set up slender tables and popped the
corks from the champagne bottles. Snowy damask cloths covered the tables placed alongside the open trunks of the big
cars, loaded down with platters of smoked salmon and cold
chicken, roast beef and lamb. There were Scotch eggs and a
groaning board of cheese with tins of biscuits and fresh butter
and plates filled with tomato and cucumber tea sandwiches.
Tureens of hot soup gave forth a delicious aroma in the crisp,
brilliant air. The butlers filled and refilled flute glasses with
champagne from silver ice buckets set side by side on the
tables. English trifle, rice pudding, thick chocolate cakes and
a silver samovar of hot coffee were spread on another table,
along with bowls heaped high with the first strawberries of
the season and thick Devonshire cream.

The festive picnic air made Derby Day at Epsom George's
favorite racing day in England, far ahead of Royal Ascot. It
was almost as attractive as Iffezheim, with a flavor unique to
Epsom. The old-fashioned stand was archaic, an eighteenth-
century print come alive. In the center of the racecourse,
gypsy tents with flags flying were filled with fortune-tellers,
bookies, food vendors and a lusty betting and drinking crowd

who cared nothing for either the royals or the "swells" on the "right" side of the fence, in the posh boxes directly across from them.

Alia wore a bright-blue silk dress under a light mohair coat. The emerald clasp on her pearls was almost as large as the one on her finger. Delphine had chosen a pale-coral wool suit. Their matching hats were left in the car until time to primp before going to Jeremy's box in the stands when the racing began. Kenneth, George and Baraket left their gray toppers on the back seat of one of the cars until the racing began, too.

"You all look smashing in your morning coats," Camilla said. She was wearing a printed silk tent dress and a matching silk turban. The dress disguised her weight only slightly.

"I'm so glad you all wear gray," she said to George and Kenneth. "Jeremy insists on wearing one of those funereal black morning coats, as Prince Philip sometimes does. I don't understand it, when gray is so much more attractive on all the men."

"What matters is how much we're going to win today," Kenneth said. Camilla's face brightened.

"Ah, that reminds me. I must go and have a look for Charles St. John and see if his filly is still in top shape. Don't drink all the champagne. I'll meet you in the box."

True to Jeremy's information, H. J. Joel's Royal Palace won the Derby easily, a popular win with everyone.

"Now!" Cam said to George. "We're on; this is the race I care about. Come, let's go down on the rail."

Charles St. John's gray filly, Ginevra, ran in the backstretch in the first quarter, moving easily, not crowded. When the jockey asked her for some speed with the flick of an early whip, she moved to the outside, approaching the uphill run toward Tattenham corner as easily as if she were being shoved from behind. Unfettered by the fourteen other horses in the race, she came around wide but moving strong, and when she reached the downhill point of the corner, she moved out. Her momentum took her easily into the lead, and she raced away to win by two lengths, not lost in a cluster of horseflesh, but all on her own, showing herself to the crowd like the champion she was.

Binoculars in hand, George watched her run from start to finish, letting out a noise when she crossed the finish line that sounded remarkably like a whoop and not at all like George Sherril.

"By God, that filly has run the best race I've ever seen run," he crowed.

"At twelve to one, we haven't done too badly," Camilla said, as excited as George. "I love a winner, especially a filly. How much did we have on her?"

"One hundred quid each, right on her nose."

"We must go and congratulate Charles in the winner's circle," Camilla said.

"Never mind Charles," George said. "I want to congratulate the filly." In the winner's circle, Camilla's face was flushed with a heightened sense of excitement. George heard the conversation exchanged between Charles and Camilla. Charles would be going back to London with them. Camilla signaled up to the others in the box that they would be leaving before the last race, then turned to George.

"We have to wait a few minutes for Charles. Any ideas for the next race?"

"Yes," George said. "There's a horse named for you in this race. We must get up a bet."

"I don't see . . ." Camilla said, running her finger down the racing program.

"The number three horse," George said. "Name is Difficult Dame. Odds are pretty high on her, too."

"All right, George," Camilla said, laughing, "all right."

Camilla drove the big Rolls back into London, the chauffeur beside her in the front seat. George was in the back with Charles St. John. She maneuvered swiftly and skillfully through the traffic, cowing and frightening other drivers with the sheer bulk of the huge car.

"Let me drive, God damn it," Charles St. John demanded.

"You're going to kill someone the way you're bulling your way through."

"Oh, shut up. You breed the horses, I'll drive the car," Camilla replied, good-naturedly. George was looking forward to being dropped at the front door of the Savoy still alive. The chauffeur, obviously used to her driving, snoozed in the front seat. At a roundabout near the Battersea Bridge, Camilla cut in front of a small blue car, causing the man driving it to almost ram into her. At the traffic light half a block away, Camilla brought the car to a stop. Suddenly George saw the angry face of the man from the blue car. He was standing at the window of the Rolls on Camilla's side, screaming. He smashed both of his fists down on the window with all the force he could manage. "You silly bitch!" he screamed, beating on the window. George watched, fascinated. Camilla turned for a brief moment to look at the man, an expression of such insensitive arrogance on her face before she turned away that George could not believe he was seeing the Camilla he had known. This ugly woman driving the car that he was a passenger in was no one he knew, or had ever wanted to know. Time for a talk, George thought. It may even be too late.

LONDON
June 1967

George's party was the success that everyone expected it to be, replete with royalty. Prince Philip was there, and the Queen would have been too, but she had just given birth to her third son, Prince Edward. The dukes of Marlborough, Bedford, Suffolk and Warwick all turned out. A romantic contingent was somewhat dominant, pleasing George, who liked for his friends to be happy. Ian Bedford brought Nicole Milinaire, who everyone knew would soon be the new duchess of Bedford, and "Sonny" Blandford, Marlborough's heir, was with the recently divorced Tina Onassis, both showing great interest in each other. Pamela Mountbatten had already married David Hicks. Margaret Argyll, more beautiful than ever, had recently been through a blatant, scandalous divorce.

The David Ormsby-Gores, old and dear friends of George's, would soon be in Washington, once his appointment as ambassador came through. The yachting group was represented by Norah and Bernard Docker and Loel Guinness, opposite ends of the poles but both ardent yachtsmen. Lord Docker's *Shemara* was a favorite yacht of George's. Paul Getty came, full of plans for his own party two weeks hence, when he was officially opening Sutton Place, the history-riddled Tudor mansion he had bought from the duke of Suffolk.

Before the party started it was Baraket who made it forever memorable to George. Tarek appeared with a huge box as he was dressing; his special present from Baraket. George could tell from Tarek's expression that it was a present of great import, and it was. Baraket had commissioned the family jewelers to make a replica of *Ehukai III*, down to the last minute, exquisite detail. It was carved out of ivory, and in exact scale. Her proportions were perfect, even to being "dressed" with strings of diamonds for the lights which stretched across her deck at night. Her port light was a ruby and there was an emerald on her starboard side. Baraket was bursting with pride. Even he had not been able to hurry the craftsmen along. Two years had gone into the making of his gift, but the ivory *Ehukai III* was a unique present for a special occasion and George's happiness on the evening of his birthday was complete.

One her way to the Savoy the day after the party, Camilla wondered what he wanted to talk to her about. "You three have certainly given me the best party I've ever been to," he had said as they were dancing the night before. "Will you have lunch with me tomorrow?"

"Of course; do you want to spend some of our winnings, or are you having a postparty luncheon?"

"No, it's just the two of us in my suite, where we'll have a chance to talk."

George was on the telephone in his bedroom when Camilla arrived. June was upon them. The river was a hundred million sparkling diamonds. The sitting room looked as if everyone in London had sent welcoming flowers to George. Long branches of forsythia and lilac covered an entire corner, and there were cachepots of fat blue hydrangeas on every table. Lunch had already been ordered, typical of George, and was being fussed over by a pair of tailcoated waiters: omelets Arnold Bennett—creamy finnan haddie folded into fresh English eggs—a red Treviso-lettuce salad and an excellent bottle of white Haut Brion.

As they devoured the omelets, George and Camilla gossiped about the party. When they finished and the table was taken away, with coffee in front of them, George got down to business.

"You know, a man only gets to be fifty years old once."

"I wish a woman never did."

"Some don't," he said. "Camilla, I've never invaded your privacy. I have only encouraged you when you needed it, right?"

"Right," Camilla said. Here it came. She could imagine already what he was going to say, and she wanted to get up out of her chair and flee. Except when Delphine had lectured her and she had paid attention, it was all so boring and she'd heard it all before, from Jeremy, from her father, from Jeremy's grandfather, from her so-called friends . . . Some things—real backbiting gossip—had come back to her. This was going to be more of the same.

"And I'm not going to make a speech now. You are. I want to hear about you from you." George's tone was level; his look impersonal.

There was deep discontent in Camilla's tone. "I don't need to go through this again, especially with you, George."

"Go through what?"

"How fat I am. That my reputation leaves a lot to be desired, that I'm not everybody's favorite"—she sniffed—"not anyone's, for that matter . . . that I'm awful to Jeremy, and so on, ad infinitum . . ."

"Anything more?"

"I'm arrogant, I'm rude."

"What about that ridiculous performance driving back from Epsom?"

Camilla was baffled. What in the world was he talking about?

"Don't you remember the man beating his fists on the car window, screaming at you, when we came to the stoplight?" It was still vivid in George's mind.

"Vaguely," Camilla said. "All that bloody traffic—what difference did it make? I didn't hit the car, did I?"

"No," George said. "You didn't. You frightened him to death, and Charles and me, and half the traffic going back to London. And you didn't even notice?"

"I don't care about such a stupid thing. You're alive, aren't you? George, after all, you're not English. We do things differently here."

"*You* do things differently, and with such a callous arrogance now, that I intend to bring it to your attention."

Camilla had never heard George raise his voice or speak forcefully to anyone before. It reminded her of the scene with Delphine.

"How long are you going to waste yourself, punish yourself and everyone who loves you? I hope this is your nadir and that you still have a zenith to come."

Boring, she thought, boring, but why was she so uneasy? She realized that George's manners and his good nature were only one facet of him, a façade that hid a tough, strong man, one to be respected for more than his taste in women and houses and yachts. She waited for him to speak.

"I know you were never in love with Jeremy, but you have done wonders for him, you know that. Is the problem Jeremy?"

"No," she said, searching for the words to tell the truth. "I have pulled him along and bullied him into doing things he hasn't wanted to do, but I felt I had to. Poor Jeremy . . . left alone he might have been a happy man and a huge success. He's very bright, you know. I may very well have destroyed whatever real strength he has. I believe it's called 'the tyranny of the weak.'"

George looked at her, keenly interested in what she had said. The real Camilla, coming out.

"Are you saying that *you* are the weak one? My Camilla the Conqueror? Weak and tyrannical? Go on."

"Do you know anything about my background, my schooling?"

George remembered what he had told Delphine: "country school, stuffed full of classics when she had a brilliant mind . . ." he'd said. Years ago.

"Tell me, I don't really remember." He did, of course, let her speak.

"My father and the head of the school I went to should both be shot. I had an IQ that went right off the chart, so both of them decided, from the heights of their male chauvinist idiocy, that the best thing for pretty little Camilla would be to quietly bury what potential she had. I should not be sent to the proper school for an unusually bright child. I was to remain cocooned in a lulling country security. They stuffed Shakespeare down my throat when I craved mathematics. The boat of my intelligence was not to be rocked. I think, just think, that perhaps that's why I have been so driven, so restless, so driving of others. I needed discipline, to be taught; my mind needed watering and pruning and fertilizing, and all I got were lessons in how to look pretty in front of a camera and how to catch me a lord."

"You did both."

"Yes, and now I'm a revolting sight and have probably wrecked Jeremy as well."

George was never so glad that he had interfered in anyone's life before. Camilla's fall from grace, in his eyes, was painful to him. How strange to know someone well for years and not to know her at all. He had known that Camilla was special; he had been disturbed seeing her go off, and now it was all coming out. Hope, there is hope, he thought.

"Go on, dig a little more."

"I'm a foolish romantic. I've always thought a man was the answer, a man I could look up to, a man I could help. I thought I'd found him once, a man stronger and smarter than I am, and one who loved me."

"Russ?"

"Of course. But he's been even more erratic in his behavior than I have. He's used me, come into my life time and time again, picked me up and then left me. I would have taken any chance with Russ, but he never would with me."

"Maybe he was right. Then. It can change, you know. You do still see him."

"Yes. When he's been gone for long enough, I get bored with everyone else and I forget what a shit he's been, and then he comes back and it starts all over again. And ends all over again. There must be other men in the world besides Russ and Jeremy. Where's mine—my Kenneth, my Baraket?"

"You seem to have found a few of them," George said. Why not goad her? This conversation was too important to be handled with kid gloves and platitudes.

"Mmm. The St. Johns and a few of the gamblers and a couple of young ones, and some I've forgotten. And there will be others, one hopes. Men have always used me. I might as well use a few of them, as I like. No commitments, just some good sweaty bodies in the dark."

Camilla laid her head on the back of the chair. "George," she said, in a little voice, a vulnerable voice, an un-Camilla voice. "Delphine told me all this, too. What's the point? I can't seem to change."

"Oh yes you can and you will. You're a winner on a losing streak. I think part of the problem is that you would like to be like Alia or Delphine. You seem to feel that you are a failure because they are so successful, so much better than you are in your own mind and eyes. True?"

"Yes, true, but I do love them, you know. They both have supported me, put up with me, been my friends, no matter what I did."

"Camilla, they both work magnificently well with the material at hand. Not everyone can have a Kenneth. He's a saint and, more than that, a saint with a sense of humor. A brilliant man. Delphine and Alia are very lucky women. Baraket is one of the strongest and most powerful men in the world now, and one of the most fascinating. Alia has been incredible in her innate understanding of him. But neither of them has the force of personality or the untapped power that you have. They depend on the man, are at one with the man, live for the man. That's not your role at all."

"What should I do?"

"Get off Jeremy's neck, forget about Russ, and get yourself together. As far as Russ is concerned, if he's the man for you, that's fate. If not, get him out of your life."

Camilla felt a ripple of excitement.

"You mean there might be a decent me somewhere?"

"There is, no doubt about it. A thin one, too."

"Let me out of here. I love you. Thanks for lunch and the lecture. I'll call you."

She was gone.

Camilla called George two weeks later. He was on *Ehukai III*, at Formentor.

"Gorgeous weather, and not a sign of a tourist yet. Majorca is the most beautiful—well, you know, why don't you come for a few days?"

"Too busy," Camilla's voice said, crisply. "I've gotten involved in something."

"What?"

"Something with Ian."

"Ian?" That was a surprise. What was she up to?

"Yes. I didn't have a chance before to talk to you about this, but you know you're not the only one who's been after me about my slovenly character, all this pissing on myself. Ian has too."

"Go on."

"He was talking to me one night at a dinner party about education. Education this, education that, education is the only chance the buggers have is what he was really saying. And all of a sudden he asked me why I let Delphine and Alia down on the hospital. 'If you can't do anything as a partner, you could at least do something on your own—prove yourself,' he said. He struck a nerve, just as you did, but I forgot about it the next day. I called him the day after you and I talked, and he's helped me set up a foundation for special schooling for bright children, children on the genuis level who need out-of-the-ordinary training. It's all my own project, except for Ian's advice on how to do it. He's my adviser."

"I think it sounds marvelous. Ian's the best person I know to help you with it. You are going to work at it, not let yourself down, I take it?"

"Yes, I am. It's exciting, and it makes a difference somehow, that I'm putting my own money into it. I've started off giving enough for three students a year, and in ten years' time we'll have a school that can handle thirty. Ken and Baraket are putting up some money, too, and guess what, old friend? This is a business call. I need some money from you, too. Let's start with ten thousand."

"Dollars?"

"Pounds, you fool. Have it sent to the Bank of England. The account is called Brain."

"I have unleashed a monster!" George was beaming from ear to ear. Maybe she would follow through, get into it, tooth and nail. "I should have known better. I'll never give a woman advice, ever again."

"It's your own fault. Life is looking much brighter. Ian has been a real friend, and Simon Elliott, too, as well as Ken and Baraket and you."

"How does Jeremy like it?"

"He seems quite cheerful, actually."

"Good," George said. "It's all good. Proud of you, love."

"Not yet," Camilla said. "I haven't lost a pound, not one."

"Rome wasn't built in a day," George said. "If you'd been alive then, it might have been."

"George." The voice was the vulnerable one he had heard, only once before, in their conversation at the Savoy.

"Yes?"

"Thank you. You know what I mean."

She didn't say good-bye. The phone simply clicked off.

"You're welcome, Camilla, very welcome." He was talking to himself.

LONDON

February 1970

"We're going to Washington for ten days," Ken said. "How do you feel about that?"

"When? I'll love it. I still haven't seen Avatar Farm."

"You may be seeing it quite a lot. This is just a preliminary meeting, Del, but there's something in the wind. I may have to break in a successor for London."

"Kenneth! That means you'll be the new man, you're going to be head of the World Bank! Oh, how marvelous, darling, and how you do deserve it."

"I've gotten used to Regent's Park."

"You love Washington."

"More than that. It's the culmination of everything I've tried to do. I *should* be in Washington. If you think we've had to entertain here, wait till we move there. In the next five years, I am going to have to persuade friends from more than one hundred nations to triple their volume of support for the bank. In thirty years' time, six hundred million people will be living in absolute poverty—I don't mean just at the poverty level—unless we succeed in getting considerably more support. I can't ask for any more from men like Baraket; there aren't that many Barakets. He's turned up over six million dollars from one Egyptian family alone, plus millions from his own and Tafida's holdings. And George, with the huge sums he's raised from the Japanese interests in Hawaii. Washington is the hub, and it looks like that's where we're going to be."

"It is strange, isn't it? We lavish kilos of caviar and gallons of champagne on hundreds to find the money necessary to feed millions of starving people. We may have to entertain twice a day."

"Avatar will be our hiding place."

"I *will* miss Alia and Camilla. I can't think about that. Times change. We've been lucky to be together as long as we have, this close together in London, that is."

"That won't change, Del. We wouldn't move there before the end of the year, at the earliest. Remember, Baraket and George and I were in school together, and our lives are woven together, just as yours and Camilla's and Alia's are. Your alma mater was actually *Ehukai*. You all grew up and graduated that summer."

Delphine laughed. "George has certainly been a great professor! Let's call him. He'll love our being in Washington."

LONDON

May 1970

"It's your birthday tomorrow," Jeremy said. "I am leaving for Geneva for the beginning of the foreign ministers' conference late tomorrow afternoon. I'd like to take you to Mirabelle for lunch, just the two of us. I have a surprise for you."

"Why Mirabelle? It's such a bore, filled with old people. Why not the Guinea? All the young film crowd go there, and we could ask a few friends. It's *my* birthday," Camilla said, petulantly.

"We're going to Mirabelle, the two of us," Jeremy said firmly, so firmly that she agreed to his choice of place. Not gracefully, but she did agree. She could leave early.

When they arrived, there was a champagne bucket by their table, chilling a bottle of Camilla's favorite Roederer Cristal. A riot of flowers bloomed in the glass-enclosed greenhouse garden behind them. Mirabelle was a dull-looking, conservative restaurant except for the flowers: masses of pink and salmon azaleas, purple and fuschia primroses and daffodils that lit the room with their lavish beauty. A nosegay of Camilla's favorite yellow roses was tucked into a small silver vase on the table—from Jeremy. When the champagne was poured, he lifted his glass to Camilla.

"Happy birthday, darling. You can open your presents after lunch." They ordered asparagus and poached salmon, and Jeremy ordered a raspberry soufflé, knowing that Camilla would hate a birthday cake.

"Now open your presents," he said when they finished lunch, lighting up a cigar and handing her a box from Asprey's and an envelope. Camilla opened the box. In it lay three bracelets, each a band of baguette diamonds set in gold.

"Jeremy!" Camilla said. "You've gone mad. They're magnificent, but what did they cost? I'd say twenty-five thousand pounds."

"Thirty," Jeremy said. "I've never bought you much jewelry —it's all been the family stuff which you don't like. I thought these would suit you. Open the envelope."

Cam was still overwhelmed by the bracelets as she opened the envelope. She pulled out a check and again she gasped. It was for thirty thousand pounds.

"Go buy yourself something," Jeremy said. "And change the bracelets if you want to."

"You've gone daft," Camilla said. "You've never done anything like this before. I love the bracelets and I love the money, but I don't understand what's gotten into you." She looked at her watch and gave him a peck on the cheek. "Thank you, darling, but come on, I have a hair appointment right now. Sorry you have to go to Geneva, but Simon Elliott is taking me to the theater tonight."

"Nice for you, darling," Jeremy said. "What time will you be home?"

"About five, I suppose."

"I'll be gone by then."

"When will you be back?" Not that she cared, but by this time she always ran out of conversation with him.

"I don't know. It depends on a number of things."

Jeremy let Camilla take the car. It was almost five when she got back to Eaton Square.

"Telephone call for you, Lady Kilmuir," the butler said, as she came in the door. "It's a Mr. Arledge. He's called once before, about a quarter of an hour ago."

"Arledge?"

"A solicitor of Lord Kilmuir's. He says it's important."

"All right, Gordon, I'll take it in the library." She sat down on the brown velvet couch and put her feet up on a small tapestry-covered bench, looking up at Gerald's portrait of her above the mantel. Camilla at seventeen, she thought, the portrait that set the course of my life. Would that she still looked like that.

"This is Lady Kilmuir," she said into the telephone.

"Lady Kilmuir, I represent your husband. I believe you had lunch with him today." Jeremy hadn't mentioned any Mr. Arledge.

"Yes, what is it, Mr. Arledge? My husband has gone to Geneva. He didn't tell me that you would be calling."

"I know, Lady Kilmuir. We arranged the final details this morning. I believe he expects to be gone for several months. I was instructed to ask you when it would be convenient for you to come in and sign the papers. I am at your disposal, but under the circumstances, the sooner the better."

"What papers?" Camilla asked. "My husband said nothing to me about papers to be signed." She looked at the three bracelets on her wrist. Lovely, they are really lovely, she thought.

"The divorce papers, Lady Kilmuir. I have them prepared. Your husband asked me to inform you that he has arranged for a more than adequate settlement. He is divorcing you."

"Hmph," Camilla said to Simon an hour later, tossing her head and pacing the floor, still in a state of shock. "He has a nerve."

"A lot of it, I'd say," Simon said. "You knew nothing about this, nothing at all?"

"Not one thing, not even a hint at lunch. What I really don't understand is the thirty. Thirty thousand pounds before a settlement, and another thirty thousand pounds again for the bracelets."

"I understand," Simon said. "You didn't tell me that before. Don't tell me you don't know what thirty means?"

"No," Camilla said, annoyed at the expression on his face.

"In newspaper parlance, thirty means the end. It means the end of the story."

MONTECATINI

June 1970

As planned, Camilla and Simon went to the theater, but the curtain hadn't been up ten minutes before she tugged at his sleeve and whispered, almost fiercely, to him.

"Get me out of here. What in bloody hell am I doing here anyway with all I've got to think about? I can't concentrate on these idiots on the stage."

They left the theater and went to Annabel's, where Camilla devoured a huge dinner, chattering all the while. She finished up with her favorite treacle tart for dessert.

"Do you know how many calories there are in this little dessert?" she asked, answering before Simon could open his mouth.

"Thousands. Thousands more than I am going to consume altogether in the next few weeks."

"Oh," Simon said. "I've heard that song before." Even though he had, there was an intensity about her tonight, and no sign of confusion or self-doubt.

"You may have, but just you wait. Take me home. I have phone calls to make." It was an order she barked to him. She hadn't mentioned Jeremy's name. Or Simon's for that matter. As usual, she was totally absorbed in herself.

"Yes, Your Grace," Simon said, laughing at her. She was impossible, and he didn't know why she was worth it, with all her rudeness and arrogance and treating him like a footman, but she was. He was laughing at her. "I'm not at all sure that you're not enjoying all this."

"You and your double negatives; you keep indulging yourself in them. You'd be a better reporter if you didn't use them."

"At least I knew what thirty meant," he said, easily.

"Fiddle," she said. "As far as I'm concerned, you don't even know that. To me, it means a beginning."

They left Annabel's and when Simon dropped her off at the door of the Eaton Square flat, Camilla called Delphine, then Alia and finally George and told each of them exactly what had happened. Kenneth got on the extension with Delphine and Camilla.

"And furthermore, I admire him for it," Cam said. "I've never been impressed by anything Jeremy has done before, including marrying me. If he's beginning to show his true colors by doing away with me this effectively, then it hasn't all been in vain."

"You're sure you want this?" Ken asked. "You may be overreacting. You know how fond I am, have always been, of Jeremy, but why do you suppose he didn't tell you himself? He's no coward."

"He's too smart for cowardice," Camilla said. "He wasn't sure how I'd react. If I fought him, he'd lose; I could always persuade him to do what I wanted him to do. This way, he was calling the shots, and he read me pretty well. A whole new world will open up for both of us. Now, I've got to call Alia."

"Anything we can do . . ." Delphine said.

"You know I know that," Cam said. "I love you both. Good night."

When Cam told Alia, there was a silence on the other end of the phone.

"Are you there?" Cam asked.

"Yes," Alia said. "I'm thinking about Jeremy. Do you think he felt that for once in his life he was going to be able to do something his own way?" Alia loved Jeremy. Just as she had, Jeremy had done as he was told. It was an easier role for a woman. Now that he'd made his move, she was amazed at Camilla's bravado. Alia felt that Camilla needed Jeremy, needed to dominate him, and that she might not necessarily have been aware of that need. "Are you sure you're not putting up a front?"

Peals of laughter came from Camilla. "Putting up a front? Don't be silly. You know, I know you all are truly fond of Jeremy and feel a little sorry for him because I'm so—well, different than you are with Baraket or Delphine is with Ken. But he's never been the man for me, and maybe this break is what we both need. I think Jeremy is clearing his plate, getting ready for the next course in more ways than one."

"What do you mean?"

"Jeremy is facing a new year with no one to bully him. He'll have the dynasty all to himself, with no family to meddle. It's the best thing on earth for him."

"And you?" Alia asked, worried.

"Wait till you see my dust!" she said, anxious to call George now. "Good-bye, my darling, I'll call you as soon as I can."

She got right through to George on *Ehukai III*.

"You are kidding, Lady Kilmuir," he said. "Now what are you going to do?"

"George," Cam said. "Seriously, I have a feeling that this is the best thing that could possibly happen. I've done a lot of dreadful things to Jeremy and he's suffered them all. Even now, he's being good to me. What do you think?"

"Jeremy's made of strong stuff. He's telling you that he's had enough, he's going his way, and he's taken good care of you. Let well enough alone. What about Russ now, and Simon?"

"Simon's a friend, that's all. Russ is an enemy. I've had my last go-around with Russ. I'll tell you about it sometime."

"You're both loners. Don't close the door all the way, ever."

"To hell with him, he's out of my life forever, especially now."

"Be that as it may. Do you know what you're going to do?"

"Exactly," Camilla said, crisply. "I'll stay in touch."

When she hung up, she locked the doors into her bedroom and sitting room. Now it was Camilla time.

She went to the big three-way mirror in her dressing room and studied herself from head to toe, turning and looking from every angle. She had deceived herself about her appearance for so long that she had almost convinced herself that she was just a little plump, that was all. Slowly and deliberately, she took off every bit of clothing, stripping down to naked flesh with no camouflage, leaving the mirror to tell its story. She looked at her thick shoulders and thighs, the beefy upper arms, the coarse lines of her overstuffed body. She had no waist and a protruding potbelly. She was a repulsive sight, revolting, but she did not flinch from her own image nor turn away.

"Pretty God-awful," she said to her reflection in the mirror. "The only good things left are the eyes and the ankles. I'm a sow."

She put on a voluminous printed silk caftan, and snapped on all the lights in her dressing room and closets. Methodically, she started throwing the clothes in her closet out onto the floor of her bedroom; dresses, coats, suits, evening things, ball gowns, everything—sailed through the air, landing on the floor in silken confusion. When the closets were empty, she gathered up a huge clump of clothes and flung them over the couches and chairs in her sitting room.

"Someone is going to be very lucky," she said out loud to herself. "Mostly, it's going to be me." It amused her to face the fact that half of her extensive wardrobe was made up of dresses that didn't fit, had never fit. As a compulsive buyer, she had often spent thousands of pounds on things that were much too small for her. "I'm taking off all this weight next week so I can wear this . . ." she would say to the salesgirl, who was no more fooled than she was.

When she finished digging out everything in the closets, she salvaged a dark-green loden cape and a pair of black wool trousers and boots. She put them over a chair, the last bare bit of space in her dressing room. She packed a small bag with nightclothes and bottles and creams. Her clock, the one Russ had given her, and a portable radio and a baby pillow with a Porthault pillow slip fit into the bag. When she was finished, she climbed into bed and turned off the light and in two minutes she was sound asleep.

The next morning, she was on the doorstep of Cecil Arledge's office when he arrived. Camilla went over the property settlement with him and after reading through the papers for the second time, without a question, she signed the agreement and bade the solicitor good-bye. Less than an hour had passed.

At noon, she called Delphine from Heathrow.

"Darling, I'm leaving for Italy. I'll need to talk to you and Alia every day at least. I'll call tonight."

Delphine sighed. "I'll miss you, and I don't know where you are going—promise you'll call."

Camilla flew to Milan and from there, took the train to Florence, where she was met by a driver from the Hotel Pace in Montecatini. She climbed into the huge old car belonging to the hotel, impatient to get to her destination.

"*Niente valiggi, signora?*"

"*Niente,*" Camilla said, holding onto her small carrying bag. "*Andiamo, subito, al albergo, per favore.*"

The tall dark manager with the aristocratic face kissed Camilla's hand when she arrived in the flower-laden lobby of the hotel. "Lady Kilmuir," he breathed, looking her in the eyes as he kissed her fingertips. "What an honor you bestow on us again! Come, I must be sure that your suite is satisfactory. It's the same one you had last time, but where is your luggage?"

"I have none this time, and this time I mean business."

Montecatini was a place dedicated to cures—cures for arthritis, liver disorders and the like. But Camilla had stayed in the Pace Hotel before and it had everything she needed to take off weight. She could live comfortably and still discipline herself with the help of the staff. She knew it was the right place for her. The staff of doctors advised her against extremes, but once all her tests were satisfactory, she convinced them that she was going to take off the weight, not go half way and then quit as she had before. She never deviated once: it was as if she had computerized herself into a program that could not fail. She talked on the phone almost daily to Delphine and Alia and George. They sent her the clippings of the mystery surrounding her divorce. Why had both Lord and Lady Kilmuir vanished from England, and where were they? The date set for the divorce hearing was not for six months, so all the press could do was speculate. There was no communication between Camilla and Jeremy.

Four months later to the day, Camilla had taken off sixty-five pounds and exercised her body into a symphony of perfectly tuned muscles. She had gone without makeup, done her own hair, stayed in her suite when she was not on her program of walking, exercising, mud baths and trips to the doctors who oversaw her at the clinic. She had not looked at herself in the mirror once until the day the scales said one hundred and ten pounds.

"That's it," she said, looking down at the numbers on the scale. "Now I'm going home."

Camilla left Montecatini and went to Florence, where she spent a week buying out the shops and boutiques. She had her pale blond hair cut and done in a new, feminine style. Her eyes and skin and body were all so young and alive that she hardly recognized herself in the three-way mirrors when she was trying on dresses, or making up. Looking at herself, finding herself beautiful and—yes, alluring—gave her a confidence she had forgotten. Narcissist, she thought. This is the way you should have looked all along.

After four days, she could no longer sleep. She wasn't drinking, and where at first she was exhausted from shopping and fell into bed, now she was awake at three in the morning, staring into the dark. She was alone, as she chose to be. She found her thoughts turning to Russ. Why Russ? There were plenty of others to think about; why did her mind have to be full of Russ? There was someone else to think of, but not deep in the night: Simon was her friend, always a friend, and she wanted to see him. She called him. "You'll be proud of me," she said. "You've lost *sixty-five* pounds," Simon said. "When you look at yourself in the mirror I'll bet the mirrors whistle back at you." "They do," Camilla said, warm in his friendship. Except for George, Simon was one of the only men friends she had. "When are you coming home?" he asked.

"Soon. I don't know. I'll let you know," she said, realizing that it was not Simon or Delphine or Alia that she wanted to see first. It was Russ.

She had written him a brief note when she arrived at Montecatini telling him that she was out of England, taking a cure, and giving no other explanation. If he knew about the divorce, he had not tried to get in touch with her. That was all right; the divorce wouldn't be final for another two months. Russ became an obsession with her, especially when she couldn't sleep. She thought for a long time before she decided to call him, and late one afternoon she reached for the phone, and got right through to the secretary in his office. The secretary referred her to another number in Southern California, not in Los Angeles. Palm Springs, perhaps? She couldn't tell. She heard his voice, sleepy. It was early in the morning there.

"Russ! Come to Paris and meet me. Wait till you see me. I've got so much to tell you. My whole life has changed. I need to see you."

"I heard you were getting a divorce. Why didn't you tell me?" The voice was not so sleepy now.

"Because I'm not getting a divorce, Jeremy is. I didn't know whether he was going to change his mind or not, but apparently he's going through with it. And I think we should celebrate." She wanted him to see her and be proud of her for what she had done. More than that, hearing his voice, she had never wanted to be with him as much as she did now. Maybe it was she who had created the obstacles between them. Maybe they could start over.

"I am celebrating. I'm at La Quinta. Isn't it odd? You're getting a divorce and I'm on a honeymoon. Maybe the third time is the charm. Aren't you going to congratulate me?" There was a vicious edge to his voice, one that she had heard before.

La Quinta. Where they had first made love, with the fireplace burning as brightly at night as the sun shone during the day. La Quinta. She was back in California, sitting in Russ's car, after the days at San Simeon, in the driveway of Chateau Marmont in Hollywood. Russ was saying, "Maybe I'll call you later and we'll have dinner." It was happening again, all these years later. There was no hope for them, he was dealing the cards from the same old deck. The only difference this time is that I'm not angry, she thought, not a bit. Not yet.

"Good-bye, Russ." She hung up the receiver carefully.

A clean slate. No more Jeremy. No more fat, ugly me. Things to do that were important. And no more Russ. Camilla Stuart, the almost ex-Lady Kilmuir, was on her own.

LONDON
April 1973

As Kenneth was dressing, Delphine saw him suddenly grasp for the dresser top, palms gripping the edge, leaning on it for support.

"What is it, darling, are you all right?" she said, half out of her chair. She flew to his side, fear running through her. Not Kenneth, nothing could be wrong with Kenneth.

"Nothing's wrong, darling, nothing. It's just a dizzy spell." He reached for one of the blue cornflowers that she kept for his buttonhole in a silver vase on the dresser. When they were not in season, she always had the vase filled with the small Harvard-crimson carnations that he loved so. She watched as he put the cornflower in his buttonhole. He turned and looked reassuringly at her. His blue eyes, those bright blue eyes that never failed to link her to him once more in love, were somber.

"Del, I've never been tired before, not like this. I have not been sleeping well. I know you've noticed."

"Of course I have."

Kenneth's color was high.

"Do you remember when Adlai died?" he asked.

"Of course, darling." Neither of them would ever forget that time. Kenneth sat down on the love seat, looking better, pulling Delphine down beside him. He took both of her slender hands in his, touching the great cat's eye.

"Eric wrote it as part of the last interview he did with Adlai. How exactly did it go?"

"Adlai said to Sevareid, 'I just want to sit under the trees with a glass of wine in my hands and watch other people dance.'" Delphine found herself in panic. Clear your mind, she thought, something awful is happening. Don't act or react, just listen and watch him carefully.

"That's it. I thought at first, no matter how touching the words are, that Adlai was in a defeatist mood. Now I understand it. Del, I'm tired, truly tired, for the first time. I can't look away from my responsibilities, but I am just flat beat." There was a slight dampness on his forehead.

Delphine's quick mind took in each word. Now she reacted. He was telling her something, throwing the ball in her court. She spoke quietly, belying the nervousness she felt.

"Darling, can't we retire? Have you finally given enough? Can't we begin to think about having a private life now? We could go home, retire to Avatar forever." Say the right things, Delphine, give him the out that he wants, protect him, help him.

"Tonight we're going to be alone. Pick me up at five, darling, cancel anything else." Kenneth kissed her on the forehead.

Delphine mentally canceled tonight's dinner party. Only six others, she could change it easily. Quickly, Kenneth got up. "I'm still dizzy," he said, "but I feel much better. Some air will do me good." He started for the door. He was being careful about walking.

Delphine didn't like his looks. It was not the old cavalier Ken. Where was the doctor's number?

"Darling, don't go. Stay here. Cancel your day. You can."

In a clear flash of thought, Delphine realized that she had never been afraid of anything in her life before, not one thing. She was in full panic now, and she knew, unwillingly, that it was for good reason. If you feel what I'm feeling now, there's some terrible reason for it, she thought, watching Kenneth as he left the room and started down the hall. Her mind, in light-years rapidity, took her back to a time when she had almost drowned while body-surfing at Makapuu, at home in Hawaii. A huge wave had tumbled her over and over, slamming her against the rocks that lined the shore. They were not jagged, they were smooth from years of Pacific pounding, but they were hard and layers of skin on her body were scraped raw as she was battered onto the beach by the surf. Jay had dragged her out and pumped the water from her lungs. She hadn't been afraid even then because he had been there to take care of her. She'd been pummeled around and helpless but not afraid. Now, she was scared to death.

Something was terribly wrong with Kenneth, something that had been going on for months. She had sensed it before, from his restlessness, the not sleeping. He'd always slept like a baby, but times changed and men changed with age and fatigue. Dr. Atwell had given him a perfectly clean bill of health less than three months ago. Why hadn't she known then that there was something wrong?

She heard an odd noise from down the length of the hall. A thud. A soft noise, but not a normal sound in the house.

Delphine heard herself scream. She knew with an awful clairvoyance that Ken was having a heart attack. The recent dizziness, it had been from pain, and the fringe of sweat on his forehead was his attempt to control himself, to defeat whatever it was that was trying to defeat him. She saw his body lying inert on the oval rug at the top of the stairway. Even as she ran toward him, lying there, she knew it was too late. Again, her mind flashed signals from the past. She saw Ken as he had looked the very first time she set eyes on him, when she and George had boarded *Ehukai III* that summer so long ago. She saw him leaning against her cabin door when he had stayed aboard the ship when he had promised never to leave her again. She saw, in a lightning kaleidoscope, thousands of his faces and along with seeing, she felt him, felt his hands, his kiss, his breath, his body against hers. She heard his laughter again, she was warmed once more by his look, the way he looked at her. So much happiness, so much love.

She knelt down beside him, putting his head in her lap. His eyes were open and she knew he was still alive. Looking at her, he tried to speak but he couldn't. She cradled his head, her tears falling all over his face. She was muttering softly, not knowing what she was saying, only knowing that she was telling him all the ways she loved him, all of them, and that there would never be enough time for that.

She felt him stiffen and then relax. He was dead.

AVATAR FARM

April 1973

The first thing Baraket did when he heard about Kenneth's death was to call his pilot and have his plane, one of the few privately owned Boeing 707s, made ready for the flight to Maryland. Kenneth had stipulated in his will that he wanted to be buried at Avatar Farm, in the family cemetery.

Baraket was the tower of strength who held them all together for the following week. Alia secluded herself with Delphine for the two days before they left London, and Camilla moved into the house for the nights. George made arrangements to come to Washington from Honolulu with Delphine's mother and father and Jay. They would meet at Avatar. George would return to London with them.

Camilla called Jeremy, knowing that he would want to be

there, and he flew from Canada to join them for the short service. He looked well and he was doing well. He was delighted with Camilla's appearance, and told her so. There was no animosity between them; they were old friends. Jeremy's silhouette, waving at them from the private terminal after they had boarded the plane for the return flight to London, was the last thing Camilla saw.

LONDON
April 1973

Back in London, Camilla stayed with Delphine. There was an unreal, unbelievable feeling about the swiftness of Kenneth's death.

"He was here, right here in this room, sitting on this love seat, talking to me about—oh, whatever we were talking about—one week ago today," Delphine said. "Now he's gone." The noon sun was sending yellow messages through the windows overlooking the park, almost as bright as the masses of daffodils blooming in wildest profusion on the lawns. Alia and Camilla and Delphine were talking together. "If we could go to our table at Claridge's, it would be like one of our Monday planning sessions," Delphine said. "That's what it is, a planning session. What in the world am I going to do now without him? I loved him so. Losing him is one thing—I don't quite believe that part yet—but never to have had him would have been worse, I suppose. I don't have to tell you two how I loved him. I just feel like putting it into words. What am I going to do?"

"What are *we* going to do, you mean," Camilla said. "One thing we know we are going to do is have a memorial service for Ken. But after that we'll just stick it out together. I'm glad George is here, and can stay."

"So am I," Delphine said.

Delphine's maid came into the room.

"Lady Kilmuir, there is a Mr. Marshall on the telephone. He would like to speak to you." Camilla looked at her in disbelief.

"Mr. Marshall? Are you sure?"

"Yes, madam."

"Tell him I cannot come to the phone, Trudy," Camilla said, turning to make a face at Delphine. "How dare he call me anywhere, but most of all how dare he call me here at this time?"

Delphine motioned for Trudy to wait.

"Cam," Delphine said, "speak to him. You know you will sooner or later. If you won't, I will."

"That's what he said, Mrs. Bennett," Trudy said. "If Lady Kilmuir would not speak to him, would I ask if you would."

Cam hesitated, undecided.

"I'll take the call, Trudy," Delphine said. "Have it switched in here." She looked at Camilla. "Cam, he does want to know about Ken—"

"Of course he's calling about Ken, but he's also calling about me."

"Camilla, if you're not going to speak to him, give me the phone. You and Russ need each other."

Camilla handed her the telephone. Never again will that bastard set foot in my life, she thought. I've had my last Marshall scene. She looked at herself in the long mirror in Delphine's dressing room; she was even slenderer than when she had left Montecatini. The same vain little thought came to her. Wouldn't I like Russ to see me now, just happen to see me, by accident, without my knowing? She heard Delphine's quiet voice speaking to Russ.

"Russ, it's very kind of you indeed, and terribly thoughtful. You know that Camilla's here, and Alia, too, as well as George. Would you like to come for a drink this evening? Could you come here about six? Fine."

She hung up. Camilla stared at her.

"I do not believe you. I do not believe that I just heard you invite him here. Have you gone mad?"

"Cam, you don't have to be here. But you will. You know that he loves you; you know that you will both always find your way back to each other. You feed on that love-hate relationship, both of you, and having been through the worst now, you might even come into some calm waters. I can only encourage that."

"Camilla," Alia said, "you and I have always thought that Kenneth and Delphine were perfect and that we had all the troubles. That's not true."

"When did you and Baraket ever have any trouble?"

"At one point, not long after Anthony's murder. Baraket was going to leave me and take the children away from me. We got through it."

"What? You're not serious."

"Oh yes she is," Delphine said. "I knew something about it, Alia, only because of Ken. He didn't discuss it with me at all, but I knew he was worried sick about Baraket and you and Ian. It seemed to smooth out after Ian was drawn back into your lives."

"Yes," Alia said. "It was all right after that." Her face was impenetrable.

"Well, well," Camilla said, almost huffily. "There will obviously be a flock of things we'll have to talk about in our old age."

"Camilla," Alia said, "Russ is the only man who is strong enough for you, and you're the only woman who has ever been able to handle him. Why do you think he comes back? And you want him to see how spectacular you look, don't you? You're a fool if you don't." Alia and Delphine were still impressed by what Camilla had done. It hadn't been easy to take off sixty-five pounds. Now she was the piquant, vivacious Camilla of the past.

"You're both devils. And you're both right. I'm dying for him to see me, the new me. But it's a dead romance. I gave up on Russ in Montecatini. The very last hurt was then. Some romances *must* wear out eventually. I don't even know if he's still married."

"Obviously he isn't. I don't think he'd impose on Delphine or call you again unless he was free. He loves you, Cam, in his way. Why shouldn't you let him make amends?"

"I haven't heard a word from him since Montecatini. Remember, I turned over a new leaf there, and there's no point to going back to any of it. George set me on the right path. I've got things to do now, things that mean a lot more to me than Russ Marshall."

"All right, but I'm still glad he's coming. He has warmth and charm and strength, and all of us could use an old friend after the past week."

"Maybe I don't want to see him again; maybe I just want him to see me. Vanity, vanity."

"We'll see, we'll see," Alia said.

Camilla was in the downstairs hall, peeking through the curtains, when Russ got out of his car. She saw immediately that he was looking very well. No bloat, and he was trim. He does get more attractive, damn him, she thought. Here we go again. She opened the door.

"Hello, Red," she heard the familiar voice say. The look in his eyes was tender, beseeching. "You look like a girl I used to know in California."

"Nobody calls me 'Red'!" Cam said, "any more than they call me Blondie." But this time she was laughing. "And you haven't for a long time. Where have you been?"

"Licking my wounds."

"Russ," Cam said, urgently. "I didn't come to the door just to see you alone for the first few minutes. You know what it must be like for her, losing Ken. Listen, Alia and George are in the library, Baraket's coming back today from Istanbul and Delphine is on the phone now, but she'll be down in a minute. I wanted to tell you to be sure and bring him up, talk about him, tell some or all of the old stories. It's the one thing that helps her now, remembering and talking about the past."

"Is she all right?"

"As all right as she'll ever be without Ken. Very fragile now. Come on, let's go in."

As Russ looked around the morning room of the house in Regent's Park, he wondered how it was that some people lived with such taste and some with so little. It wasn't a matter of money. Everyone seemed to think that if you had money, you had taste. Texans spent more money, more often, decorating and redecorating their houses, and sometimes they almost achieved something pretty good, but the best houses in Texas were still the old farms and ranches that no one in his right mind would ever do over. Russ wouldn't touch Z Bar: it was perfect the way it was. It was the real thing. Like Regent's Park, which was perfection, a graceful and tasteful house in every way. Russ was struck by the fact that over the years the prettiest things he had ever seen and the loveliest places he had ever been had all happened to him with Camilla and Delphine and Alia. And George. Baraket's emerald room was unforgettable, the rose garden that would soon be in bloom in Regent's Park, Camilla's house at Juan-les-Pins with the white walls and the red-tiled roofs and the pink oleander trees flanking the wide staircase down to the blue Mediterranean. The only ugly thing, the only blot on the scene, had been Camilla's disintegration, but that was behind her now. He watched and listened quietly as the conversation ebbed and flowed around him. In all the years he had known her, Camilla had never looked better. Her eyes were bright and her skin was glowing. She was taking care of herself, finally, and she was taking care of Delphine, too. Russ had never before seen the protective side of Camilla, if it had ever existed. He was glad he had come. There was such security in this room, and he was grateful to Delphine for asking him. What a magnificent woman she was. Strange, Russ thought, of the three of them, she had had the most and had lost the most.

"Russ," Delphine said, "how long are you going to be here?"

"For a few days, maybe a week. I am at your beck and call; you're why I came."

"Good," Delphine said. "Baraket and George won't be here tonight, and Alia and I are staying in. Why don't you take Camilla to dinner?"

"If she'll have me, I'd like to very much," Russ said.

"I'll have you," Camilla said, an impudent look on her face. "We can go somewhere and talk about old times."

"You're on," Russ said.

"Why did you let me come back?"

They were sitting in the Connaught Grill, dinner over, a brandy in front of Russ.

"Why do you come back? That's a better question, isn't it? After the way I looked and behaved? Not that you're any angel. I guess I'm here with you because there is something between us that is evergreen—there always has been through the years—and because I want to be with you. We started off well and went downhill a thousand times, but you were always there. It's not just all that great sex or those wonderful fights we have; it's much more than that. We've been through too much together. I could never turn away from you forever. I've hated you, but I've loved you, too."

She looked at his hands. Funny how white and delicate they were compared to the rest of him. The big sweet face, the bulk of body, the crisp sandy hair, subdued in color now. His hands never change, she thought, all the sensitivity that exists deep inside him shows in his hands.

"Maybe the storms will pass us by now," he said, "and we won't keep gunning each other down with words. What in the world gets into people like us?"

"There aren't any people like us," she said. An acid tone, a slight sniff of distaste, but more, the real Camilla.

Russ had to laugh at the way she said it. She was proud of the way they were.

He took her hands.

"Camilla, you wrecked a honeymoon for me. After you called from Florence I couldn't get you out of my mind. I was at La Quinta, and you were there, too. But months before that you had left England, left Jeremy and left me wondering what was going on."

"Didn't you get my note from Montecatini?"

"Yes, but all you said was you were 'taking a cure.' You've used that as an excuse before, and I thought you were off with someone else, especially when I heard about the divorce. Montecatini is a very romantic place."

"I didn't notice that once in the four months I spent there," Camilla said, preening. She straightened up, showing off her skinniness for him.

Russ laughed at her.

"You're amazing. All through the years I've known you, you've made a massive effort to destroy yourself. You ignored your mind, brutalized your body, and yet here you are, thin, beautiful and sexy. You've made it. Even your teeth are intact."

"Never mind me. What about your new wife?"

Russ looked uncomfortable.

"You and I have both done some stupid things in the past. I'm not going to try to explain it, let me just say I am not married. We can talk about it later, much later. When I heard about Ken's death, I knew I had to see all of you. Delphine, Baraket and Alia—all of you meant so much to me, more than I knew. I've always felt a little like an outsider—"

"So have I," Camilla said. "We're both too independent."

"Thank God," he said. "And we have each other. We may

both be better off on our own, with our fiercely guarded independence guaranteed. You can be a woman alone, a free spirit, if you want to; you don't need the prop of a man. Neither do I, in reverse. We've both looked for the devotion and trust and loyalty that we consider our divine right, even though neither of us had much of it to offer. We just wanted to take it; neither of us could give much to anyone. We've paid for our selfishness; we've never had what Delphine and Kenneth had, or what Baraket and Alia have. But, having come this far, it is possible that you might end up a complete woman, knowing your role, content with yourself. Or you might even find a man you could love and be secure with, after all."

"Never."

"You might. I might, too. We might."

"What do you mean?" Surely he didn't think she'd fall back into the trap just because he was encouraging her. Oh no, she wasn't going to say it. If he wanted her, if there was any promise to be made, he was going to have to ask for it.

"Together. You could give it some thought. You're a big girl."

"Maybe," she said. "Maybe not. Anyway, you're my best friend."

"There's nothing wrong with that. Think about it."

"All right. I'll think about it."

"You can let me know. Anytime," he said, pulling her to her feet, wanting to hold her. "Come on, it's past your bedtime."

"No it's not," Camilla said. "Something's going on at the house. Come on back with me and let's find out what George and Baraket are up to."

"Can you go? Will you?" George asked.

"Of course I can, and will with great pleasure," Russ said.

"Then it's settled," Baraket said. "I think it's the best thing by far. If it's not, if anything goes wrong with the weather, or the mood, or anything to do with Delphine's happiness, I'll send for the plane. Actually, I think it's a marvelous plan and will be good for all of us."

Camilla and Alia sat together, listening while the men planned. Delphine had gone to bed long before. She wasn't asleep, but she needed to be alone and she wanted to be by herself, knowing that her friends were downstairs if she called. George was staying in the house, as well as Camilla. Baraket and Alia were less than half a mile away in Lindley House, and they were all with her every evening now. Russ was staying at the Dorchester; Baraket would have Tarek drive him home.

"Then it's settled," Baraket said. "Come, my *canim.*" He turned to Alia. "We have a lot to do. Are you ready to go, Russ?"

"Yes," Russ said. "And excited."

"You will tell her tonight?" Baraket said to George.

"Of course," George said. "She's still awake."

"And I'm going to eavesdrop," Camilla said. "I know what her answer will be. I can't wait." She kissed Russ good night, a feather kiss, on the tip of his nose. "See you tomorrow," she said.

LONDON

May 1973

"Delphine," George said. "I have a surprise for you."

"A surprise? What, George?"

"*Ehukai.*"

"*Ehukai?*"

"She's parked, er, moored at the Tower Bridge."

"At the Tower Bridge? Here? On the Thames?"

"Yes."

"Why?" Delphine's mind began to race. Beautiful *Ehukai III.* Where she had first seen Kenneth. "Is she really here?"

"Oh yes, she's really here. And she's ready to go."

"Go? Where?" Delphine's mind was running behind now the way it had in Baden-Baden when Kenneth had asked her to marry him.

"Down the Thames past Greenwich, into the estuary, across the Bay of Biscay. Wherever you want to go. It's May, you know, almost June. It will take two weeks to get to Monte Carlo. We have an anniversary coming up. Almost twenty years. We can go back, even to the Hôtel de Paris. Dinner on the terrace?"

"Without Ken?" Her eyes clouded.

"And without Jeremy . . . without Ceil or Guy. You remember that night. But with Camilla and Alia and Baraket this time; Baraket's never been there with us. And Russ, he hasn't either."

Delphine remembered Kenneth's hand on her arm, taking her from the bar to the terrace, never letting go of her.

"Russ? And Camilla?"

"Yes, darling. They're ready to go. So are Baraket and Alia."

"Ken would want us to," she said, fingering the cat's-eye. He would, Delphine knew he would, and that he'd be there for her again, with her again. The view from Château Madrid came back, soft yellow lights, the fireflies in the water, Cap Ferrat gracing the moonlit sea. Alone with Kenneth. The memories were there to be used again, to be relived, revived. There were no sad ones, they were all beginnings. That year had been the beginning for all of them. *Ehukai III* had set the path, that summer, for all of their futures.

"What's the weather like now there?"

"Cold until we pass Gibraltar. Then it's all mimosa and summer and blue sea. And us."

"Some of us. Not all of us."

"The survivors, darling. The friends. You wouldn't want to do it alone."

"Never. I couldn't. You, Baraket and Alia. Russ. And Camilla. We'd have to be together. Oh, yes, when can we leave?"

A broad grin appeared on George's face.

"Tomorrow, anytime you like."

Delphine kissed him, holding his dear face in her hands.

"Go to bed, George," she said. "I have to pack."

About the Author

Nancy Holmes was born in Washington, D.C., grew up in the Hawaiian Islands and was one of John Powers' "long-stemmed American Beauties" models. She was the first American model in Paris after the Second World War as Pierre Balmain's favorite Yank.

She worked as fashion editor on the New York *Journal American*, then *Look* magazine; married and moved to Texas where she lived in San Antonio for a decade.

She spent ten years in Gstaad, Switzerland, and London, England, which led to her becoming a contributing editor at *Town and Country* magazine and international editor of *Palm Springs Life*. She lives in New York now.

Her first book, *The Dream Boats*, was a non-fiction report on the great power yachts of the world and the lifestyle of their owners.

She is the mother of a son, Peter Thompson, who works in solar energy, and a daughter, Brooke Negley, who works as the mother of three girls to whom the book is dedicated.